Threads of Fate

H.L. WOOD

Copyright © H.L. Wood 2025

The moral right of this author has been asserted.

All rights reserved.

All characters and events in this publication, other than those clearly in the public domain, are fictitious and any resemblance to real persons, living or dead, is purely coincidental.

No part of this publication may be reproduced, stored in a retrieval system, or transmitted, in any form or by any means, without the prior permission in writing of the publisher, nor be otherwise circulated in any form of binding or cover other than that in which it is published and without a similar condition including this condition being imposed on the subsequent purchaser.

Editing, design, typesetting by UK Book Publishing

www.ukbookpublishing.com

ISBN: 978-1-0682429-0-8

THREADS OF FATE

For Sylvie

From the Fells of Cumbria to the Rhône at Vienne.
You were there in every page that breathed,
in every word that seemed written for us,
as if time itself had always known
where our souls would meet.

Author's Disclaimer

This is a work of fiction. While certain historical figures and geographic locations referenced in the novel are based on real individuals and places, all characterisations, dialogue and events involving them are entirely fictional and created for the purposes of the narrative. The story also includes wholly imaginary characters, settings and incidents and in some instances, blends real-world elements with fictional ones. Some historical dates and references have been researched and are believed to be accurate; however, no claim is made to comprehensive historical precision. Any resemblance to actual persons, living or deceased, interacting with real places, events, or institutions is purely coincidental and unintentional.

Prologue

When we dream, we believe it to be our unique existence because there is no line separating reality from illusion. Our senses and emotions follow the dream's story, no matter how strange it may be. Shaped by our subconscious, this other reality becomes a space where our desires, fears and thoughts unfold freely, beyond the limits of time. Here, we can meet the departed, who may appear with a photographic clarity that eludes our conscious state. Upon awakening, a melancholic connection with the past may remain, as though the deceased had been with us in another realm, accessible only when our awareness of the world was dulled during a few hours of sleep.

Lynden Grisdale had never considered himself someone who was interested in solving mysteries. Teaching defined his working day, but fate had other plans: a letter, an unknown relative's death, an inheritance and a vision would unravel a story that had been lived generations before him.

Had he arrived here by chance, or had his destiny been shaped before his birth? As he turned the fragile pages of an ancestral diary, a life he had never known began to rise from history. A man's love would lead to a moment where the past and present collided in ways neither reason nor logic could explain.

Chapter 1

It was two years ago that an unexpected letter arrived from Swann and Cartwright, a firm of solicitors based in the quaint village of Zeal Monachorum. I had just returned home after an exhausting day of lecturing at the local horticultural college in the old county of Westmorland. Feeling tired and exasperated by the incessant chatter of my students, I welcomed the prospect of an evening of peace and quiet.

After collecting three letters from the letterbox, I slumped into my armchair and saw immediately that two were junk advertising destined for the wastepaper bin, but on the front of the third letter it read "To be opened by addressee only". Upon opening it I found an embossed letterhead from Swann and Cartwright Solicitors. Below it was typed, "Dear Mr Grisdale, could you please contact us at your earliest convenience, we believe you to be the relative of a deceased person and to be entitled to inherit part of the estate."

My initial reaction was to discard the letter, suspecting it was a scam. Zeal Monachorum, I asked myself, where the hell was that? However, curiosity got the better of me and a quick internet search confirmed the authenticity of both the village in Devon and the firm of solicitors who were based there.

The following morning between classes I found a moment to ring Swann and Cartwright Solicitors. After an interminable wait, accompanied by a recorded message from a young woman informing me that calls were recorded for training purposes and that I was fourth in the queue, I was finally greeted by a receptionist whose grumpy voice was the complete opposite of the cheerful tone of the recorded message I had just heard.

"Swann and Cartwright Solicitors, how may I help you?" she said.

I introduced myself. "My name is Lynden Grisdale, I received a letter from your office regarding the estate of a deceased relative. Could you connect me to Mr Cartwright, who signed the letter, please?"

"I'm afraid Mr Cartwright is out of the office, may I have him return your call?"

I explained that I would be unavailable until after 6 pm, but if that wasn't too late I would appreciate it if he could ring me back.

"I'll ask him," she replied abruptly before cutting off the communication.

For the rest of the day my thoughts returned to the mysterious letter. It didn't appear to be a scam and the secretary's accent had a south-west twang. In all probability it was a case of mistaken identity, I thought.

At about a quarter past six my mobile phone rang; it was Mr Cartwright. After a brief introduction and an apology for what he was about to ask, he requested that I answer a few security questions to confirm my identity. I reluctantly suppressed my instinct to tell him I knew who I was and listened to what he had to say. I managed to answer three out of four questions correctly, but I was puzzled when he asked me if I knew of any relatives who may have died in Devon in the last two years. My three replies were, however, sufficiently accurate for him to proceed. He had obviously done some homework on my background and appeared to know a lot more about my family history than I did.

Mr Cartwright started, "Our company has carried out some considerable research to find you. We will be happy to proceed further on your behalf if you agree to the terms in a document which we will forward to you in the next few days." Basically, they wanted ten percent of the value of the estate to cover all legal fees and expenses, including the cost of boarding up the property of the deceased which had been done several months before. As I had no idea whose estate I was entitled to inherit and he hadn't revealed any details, it seemed a fair deal and I agreed to it verbally over the phone.

A few days later I received a contract, signed it and returned it by registered post. Shortly thereafter I received another letter with details, naming the deceased as Mrs Alice Farnsworth, an aunt of my late father. I was surprised: who was Alice Farnsworth? My father had once mentioned distant relatives from Devon but he didn't seem to know much about them other than an ancestor had been a copper miner who moved from Devon to work in the Hodbarrow iron mine at Millom in the late 1800s. So, Alice Farnsworth would have been a great-aunt to me and a sister of my paternal grandmother. How was it possible that she could have only recently died when even my father's generation had now all gone? I thought about it for a while and realised that families were larger back in the day, a 25-year generation span could exist between siblings, particularly if more than one wife was involved.

Could it be that a wealthy relative had passed away and left me a fortune? After all, such things happened in novels and on television. Any family contacts with Devon that may have existed had been lost in previous generations.

The letter continued, "We are acting on behalf of the estate of the late Mrs Alice Farnsworth, tracing relatives who may have a claim on her inheritance, she had no direct descendants and left no will. There are three inheritors, yourself and two great-nieces. You are each entitled to an equal share once probate has been passed."

Mr Cartwright did not disclose the precise amount I would receive but mentioned that the estate included a small cottage in need of repairs, some land and a disused private chapel, a few personal belongings and a bank account into which "Aunt Alice's" pension had been deposited over the years. The funeral had been held two weeks after her death and had been attended by only one or two close neighbours as no relatives were known to exist at the time. I was advised against travelling from Cumbria to Devon immediately, being assured that I would be contacted in due course.

Seven weeks later another letter arrived, requesting my availability to attend a meeting at the solicitors' office in Zeal Monachorum. The timing was fortuitous as it coincided with the start of the summer holidays at the horticultural college. I asked my girlfriend Ann, who also worked at the college, if she would like to accompany me. A few days in Devon sounded appealing to her and she readily agreed. So, in anticipation of the mysteries of Great-Aunt Alice's legacy, we prepared our journey to the heart of Devon.

Ann and I embarked on our journey early morning, setting off at 7 am in my trusty old Volvo estate. Heading south, we were fortunate to avoid the flow of holidaymakers making their way north to junction 36 of the M6 towards the Lake District. Most of them would venture no further than Bowness-on-Windermere. The day promised to be a long haul to reach our hotel in Okehampton. The scarcity of suitable accommodations compounded by dubious online reviews and the summer holiday rush left us with few options. The road ahead was riddled with roadworks reducing the three-lane motorway to two lanes and imposing speed limits of 50mph or 40mph on some stretches. Frustratingly for the most part no one could be seen working because, I assumed, the workmen were also all on holiday. The absence of roadwork sections offered little relief, as lorries, often taking two miles or more to overtake one another, competed for slight gains only to lose their position on the next incline.

Ann who was accompanying me, was forty years old and of athletic build. Her shoulder-length black hair framed an attractive face and brown eyes free of makeup, reflecting her preference for authenticity over glamour. Her simple wardrobe consisted of blouses, jeans, small earrings and a Japanese watch; each item was chosen for usefulness rather than display, as if to show she had no need for excess. She organised herself with the confidence of someone who is used to living independently and making her own choices. Whenever she answered a question she always paused, giving the impression that she was used to weighing up situations carefully before giving a direct reply. It was also her way of preventing anyone counter-arguing what she said.

Yet it is Ann's restraint that leaves the deepest impression on anyone she meets. She had and still has, a distrustful nature, being cautious about the depths of involvement with anyone, and with me she is a partner only when it suits her. There are times when she slips away, venturing out alone without a word of where she is going, leaving behind a quiet sense of mystery. It isn't done in defiance or because of mood changes but a core part of who she is, someone who values her autonomy and independence above all else. Despite the connection we shared, there remains a distance, a space she guards carefully, as though to protect herself from the emotional entanglements she never fully trusted.

South of Gloucester after a refreshing break at a service station the traffic eased considerably. We had planned to enjoy a couple of days walking and exploring Dartmoor and its surrounding villages before our meeting in three days' time.

The day of our arranged meeting was started with a full English breakfast at the hotel before we set off to the solicitor's office to uncover the details of Aunt Alice's inheritance. Arriving five minutes before our 9 am appointment we were shown into a meeting room by the same secretary, who I had learned, was called Betty and who had answered my previous calls. Upon entering we found the two ladies already engrossed in conversation. Their chatter filled the solicitor's office, the twangs of a Somerset or Devon accent detectable in their conversation. Mary and Jane Mason, two ladies in their mid-seventies at a guess, spoke in the familiar way that old sisters do. Their words tumbled over one another, recalling fragments of memories, speculating about the mysterious Alice Farnsworth, this great-aunt they, like us, had never known.

"Ninety-seven, did you say? How could we have missed her all these years?" Jane talked loudly, leaning towards her sister's ear who was slightly deaf, while Mary brought up the subject of their youth and of childhood friends who had died.

They chatted about distant cousins, the twist of fate that had brought them here and whispered questions about what Alice might have left behind.

Their chatter ceased as we moved to sit beside them. We introduced ourselves and engaged in small talk for about another ten minutes before Mr Cartwright joined us.

"Good morning, ladies and gentleman," he greeted us. "I trust you've had a moment to get acquainted. As you are now aware, Alice Farnsworth passed away at 97 with no direct descendants. She had been a resident of 'The Oaks' care home in Okehampton for the last three and a half years. You are her only living relatives and we are happy to inform you that you will inherit equal shares of her estate.

"Firstly, let me run through the plan for the day, starting with an explanation of the onerous procedure of probate as it will be several months probably before you receive your part of the inheritance. Before then there will be the sale of her possessions and I have here copies of the inventory of Alice's belongings."

Mr Cartwright handed out an inventory list. "The cottage will be opened at two o'clock this afternoon for you to view. The address is at the top of the first page. It lies on the edge of an old estate mid-distance between the communes of South Tawton, South Zeal and Sticklepath. Let's meet at the main car park in South Zeal. You can either follow me in your cars or I can take anyone who requires a lift. The cottage is only accessible by a private track, it's about two hundred yards from the main road and fifty yards in front of an old chapel. An evaluator has assigned residual values to the items so if you wish to retain anything please let us know. If more than one person is interested in the same item, then you will be invited to make an offer, with the highest offer taking the item. Funds collected will be added to the estate." He continued, "The value of the estate is provisionally valued at £1,448,360. This includes forty-three hectares of land rented out to a local farmer with an estimated value of approximately £900,000; it is composed of grazing meadows and mixed woodland. A cottage is valued at £380,000 and a bank account containing £161,660. Personal items and furnishings are estimated at approximately £6,700. The actual amount you will receive will be adjusted for the sale of the cottage and its contents minus our fees, as stipulated in the contracts you signed."

I asked, "How did Alice Farnsworth come to own such wealth?"

Mr Cartwright replied, "From the information we have been able to gather, the bulk of her wealth is locked up in land that was once part of a larger estate owned by an ancestor of hers, part of which Alice inherited. Unless someone here is interested in any of the land, the farmer who has been renting it for the last fifteen years has made an offer."

"Would it be possible to see which parcels of land are involved and the offer for each?" I asked.

To which Mr Cartwright replied, "I don't have that information at hand but I'd be happy to forward it to you."

The arrangement was well organised, allowing us time to have lunch at a local pub recommended by Mr Cartwright. Betty, his secretary, had kindly booked a table for us all. Browsing the menu filled with healthy salads and vegetarian options I instead opted for a traditional steak and kidney pie with chips, while Ann chose a chicken Caesar salad. Our meal choices reflected our respective body weights and fitness levels. The newly acquainted cousins selected a variety of light pub meals, soup of the day and sandwiches. Our conversation meandered through our family histories with the two sisters knowing a bit about their ancestors but nothing of the Millom connection which I could only vaguely recall. The pub lunch was pleasant and I enjoyed a couple of pints of local beer before Ann took over the driving. We then headed to South Zeal and parked as instructed.

Mr Cartwright met us at the car park. Mary and Jane chose to be driven there with him whilst Ann and I decided to follow in my car. Upon arrival at the cottage, Mr Cartwright asked if we would like to take a torch each as the electricity supply in the cottage had been cut off when it was sealed. Together we all walked towards the cottage where Mr Swann, Mr Cartwright's associate, was waiting with keys to unlock the front door.

As we entered the stone cottage, its history could be felt within its three hundred-plus-year-old walls. The atmosphere had a musty odour, a blend of dust and age, hinting at the months the cottage had remained closed off from fresh air. The entrance hallway was lined with faded floral wallpaper peeling slightly at the edges, and a rug which was worn by years of foot traffic lay on the stone-flagged floor.

Mr Swann invited us to look around the cottage freely and we turned on the LED torches, which, giving a cold white beam of light provided us with a clear enough vision of the house's furnishings and its ambience.

To the left was the living room, reminiscent of a bygone era. A floral-patterned sofa dominated one end, its fabric worn and faded was partially covered with a crocheted blanket draped over the back. Opposite stood an oval oak dinner table, its surface scarred by decades of use. Against a back wall was a display case containing a collection of porcelain figurines and a few journals. A grandfather clock stood solemnly in one corner, its hands frozen in time and an array of sepia-toned family photographs crowded the mantelpiece above a stone fireplace. The fireplace itself was cold and empty with a few charred logs and a scattering of ash suggesting its last use was some time ago. The windows though boarded were hidden behind moth-eaten curtains, contributing to the room's sombre character.

Moving into the kitchen the scent of stale air mingled with the faint lingering aroma of old spices and preserved herbs. The floor was a patchwork of cracked yellowed linoleum and the walls were lined with cabinets painted a faded green. Opening a cupboard door I saw a primrose-decorated tea set where a grimy cracked cup caught my eye. An old-fashioned Aga cooker sat against one wall, its surface speckled with rust. Above it pots and pans hung from a rack, untouched and gathering dust. On the top of a wooden table, stood in the centre of the room were old newspapers, a tarnished teapot, and a vase of dried flowers. Placing the bunch of flowers in the vase was probably one of the last acts that Alice Farnsworth had done before she moved to the care home. Just one wooden chair at the table was a witness to the fact that Alice Farnsworth lived a life of solitude. The white-enamelled sink was chipped and held a few forgotten dishes, now dried and spotted with mildew. The only light came from a small grime-covered window, adding to the room's overall sense of neglect and disuse.

Ascending the narrow staircase, we encountered a narrow corridor leading to two bedrooms and the bathroom. The larger bedroom featured an iron-framed bed with brass knobs. Its mattress sagged and was covered with a handmade quilt. A wooden dresser, its surface cluttered with trinkets, jewellery boxes and a dusty hairbrush, sat against one wall beneath a tarnished oval mirror, its reflective silver backing having deteriorated around the edge. A wardrobe stood in the corner, its door slightly ajar revealing a collection of vintage dresses and hats. On approaching the wardrobe, the smell of mothballs still faintly penetrated the air. The smaller bedroom, more modest, contained a single bed with a faded crochet patchwork bedspread, a small wooden nightstand with a brass lamp and a few shelves filled with old books and knick-knacks.

The bathroom, functional but dated, had white-tiled walls now yellowed with age. An enamel chipped, clawfoot tub stood next to a pedestal sink with a crack running through it. A medicine cabinet hung above; its mirror cloudy with age. The floor covering was tiled with black and white squares in a chessboard pattern.

Every room in the cottage told a story echoing the life of its long-time inhabitant. The furnishings though timeworn spoke of a once cosy and lived-in home now frozen in a state of gentle decay. We could not but feel a profound sense of melancholy as we wandered through the silent rooms, imagining the life of the old lady that once filled the space in solitude.

Outside was a small disused shed housing a rusting push-cylinder mower, a few garden tools, a pile of logs and a few coals.

We all explored though little caught anyone's interest.

"What's in the dome-top wooden travel box in the bedroom?" I asked.

Mr Swann replied, "It's of French style. Inside are old bills, a couple of leather books and a damaged surveyor's theodolite. It was brought down from the loft and we barely got it through the space. It may have been there longer than Mrs Farnsworth's time or else someone put it there for her. She couldn't have done it on her own, I'm sure of that because of its weight."

Mary Mason fancied a pair of King Charles Spaniel pottery bookends and the display case containing the porcelain figurines at £65. Jane Mason the oval oak table in the sitting room priced at £80. To Ann's surprise I expressed interest in the old wooden travel chest, priced at £35 and the push-along mower in the outside shed at a symbolic £5. For the former, it seemed a perfect project to clean up its brass fittings and apply a coat of varnish, making a discreet storage box for my wine bottles. The mower was perhaps just rash thinking; I had no use for it but my professional instincts couldn't let it be thrown away. I asked Mr Swann if we could visit the ruins of the chapel and I asked of its value. "To visit it is no problem. It's just across that field over there; follow the track, it leads straight to it. As for its value, I'm afraid I can't tell you offhand, but it is something we could look into for you."

I replied that I would be grateful if he could do that.

With our selected items packed in the car we parted ways. Ann went to sit in the car while I walked towards the old chapel. A waist-high iron fence stood about thirty to fifty feet from the building and a few gravestones jutted above a tangle of brambles and climbing plants. The little chapel, built of stone and brick, appeared to be in relatively good repair. The roof was intact apart from a few displaced slates and there were no visible holes or structural damage. Its stained-glass windows though mostly intact had one or two broken panes, enough for nesting or roosting songbirds to slip through.

Making my way around to the front door I quickly realised that access was impossible due to the thick undergrowth. Paradoxically, this impassable barrier had likely protected the chapel from vandalism.

I paused near what should have been the path to the front porch, my attention drawn to a gravestone barely visible above the brambles. I stared at it, transfixed, unable to explain why. Who was buried there?

After what I thought had been a few moments, I heard footsteps approaching from behind and a hand was placed on my shoulder.

"Are you alright?" a voice asked.

"I... I think so. Why?" I replied, feeling disoriented.

"I came to check on you. I thought you might've had an accident or something. You've been gone an hour," Ann said. Then, noticing my trembling, she added, "You're shaking... are you cold?"

I couldn't answer. It felt as though I were emerging from somewhere distant and hidden, as if I had been lost in a deep sleep or trance while simply standing there for a few minutes. Ann gently took my arm and guided me back down the track past the cottage towards the car.

As we walked her words began to reach me with greater clarity. "I'm taking you to A&E," she said, her concern growing. "You might have had a stroke or something."

"I don't need a hospital, I'm fine," I insisted, though I wasn't sure I believed it myself. Glancing back, I searched for the gravestone but it had vanished into the thick mass of brambles.

Ann took the wheel, still worried that I wasn't entirely present. As we drove, I tried to explain what had happened. "I must have fallen into a trance," I murmured. "I had... a terrible vision."

"What about?" asked Ann.

"That's the problem. I can't remember," I said, which wasn't at all true for it was still very clear and would be so for a long time to come, but for the moment I dared not share the details.

I was struck by a terrible realisation. I had either killed a woman, caused her death, or witnessed it. The thought came with the force of a lightning bolt splitting through my mind, followed by a crash of thunder that seemed to reverberate inside my head.

Dread gripped me. Fear, disbelief, an overwhelming sense of something beyond my understanding. I stood frozen, trying to grasp what had taken hold of my thoughts. Were these hallucinations? Or fragments of something real, something long buried in my memory? I felt like I'd just woken from a dream, but I was still caught in its grip, it was so real. What had I done? And what was I supposed to do now? Speak of it? Stay silent? And why did the chapel before me feel connected to all of this? Was it a warning or a prophecy of something yet to come?

I recalled that I had found myself in a pine forest, the canopy shielding me from the summer sun. The air was cooler there and on the forest floor grew gorse, heather and bracken in a sandy soil. A shallow stream wound its way through a slight dip in the land, its edges lined with lush ferns. Damsel flies hovered in shafts of sunlight, their delicate wings flashing iridescent blue as they darted above the water. The dappled light painted dark shadows across the forest floor, bringing relief from the heat.

As I walked ahead, I saw a clearing. The ground was soft with waterlogged moss but not boggy underfoot. In the distance I caught sight of the remains of a wooden building, half-consumed by the forest where climbing plants clung to its decaying timbers. The murmur of the stream was the only sound I heard as I moved towards the ruins.

I stepped through what had once been a doorway, now reduced to a gaping empty space. The roof beams had mostly collapsed, some splintered and dangling dangerously overhead.

The wooden floor was dark with moisture and through its gaps I could see stagnant water below. I hesitated, unsure if this was a raised floor over shallow ground or whether there was a deep hidden basement beneath me.

To one side a fallen wooden beam lay smothered in moss and ferns. Moving cautiously across what seemed like a sturdier section of the floor I reached for a hanging plank to steady myself. It crumbled at my touch, releasing a thick, earthy scent of decay and fungi.

Then I saw it.

A glimpse of something white beneath the floorboards. Fabric maybe. I knelt, leaning forward and began to pry at the splintered wood. It came away easily in my hands, rotted and weak, slipping free of the rusted nails that once held it in place. A stronger scent of damp earth and mildew filled the air as I uncovered a narrow gap.

Shifting more of the planks aside, the white material became clearer. My stomach twisted as I reached further, my fingers clawing at the wood, pulling it away piece by piece, and I froze.

A woman.

She lay beneath the boards, her face pale and untouched by time. There was no greyness of death, no decay, just the stillness of someone who might have simply closed her eyes for a moment's rest. The sight of her was at odds with the rotting ruin around her. She had been buried here, hidden away beneath this crumbling place. But her body… it remained untouched.

A delicate ruby necklace adorned her neck, its deep red stone catching what little light filtered through. Her shoulder-length hair softly curled inwards beneath her chin as though it had been arranged with care and her arms lay neatly at her sides, though one hand was clenched tightly holding something, a small metallic object.

It was surreal. Like something from a fairytale, a sleeping beauty preserved in time. But here in the heart of decay it felt more like a cruel paradox. How had her body remained so intact? Had she been placed here just recently? Or had time stopped for her in some unnatural way?

The contradiction unsettled me, no answers, just questions. But that's the nature of dreams, visions and nightmares, they blur the edges of reality, leaving us grasping for something solid even after we wake.

The image in my mind reminded me of Ophelia — Millais' painting of the drowned maiden floating in eerie serenity. It was the closest thing I could compare to the world I had just stepped into.

After a few minutes Ann asked, "Are you feeling better?"

"I'm OK," I said, adding, "Were you really waiting for me for an hour, or did you say that because you were bored and thought we should get moving?"

"No, it's true. You were at that chapel or thereabouts for an hour. Perhaps you were sleepwalking," she said light-heartedly.

I chose not to answer because I didn't have a reasonable reply. What had happened was a mystery to me, but now I was feeling better even though the vision of that woman below the wooden floorboards stayed with me.

"You're not thinking of buying that chapel, are you?" asked Ann.

"Why not?" I replied, opening myself up to criticism.

Ever pragmatic, Ann had already worked out her reply and was waiting for the opportunity to list her reasons.

"You live at the other end of the country, what use is it to you? It will need repairing and maintenance, there's probably no electric supply to it, it might be a listed building and how can you afford it?"

I chose just to answer the last part of the question. "From the inheritance money."

"You've already bought it in your head, haven't you?" said Ann, disappointedly and not expecting an answer. She didn't get one.

"Well, that was rather disheartening," I remarked after we had driven a few more miles. The gloomy mood of our journey stayed with us in the car, not only at what had happened at the chapel but thinking about Alice Farnsworth.

Ann, with a sigh, responded, "The poor old woman. She seemed to live alone, probably unable to clean the place at her age especially if she was infirm."

"We never asked what she died of and where she is buried," I said, a pang of guilt twinging in my chest. "It feels a bit wrong what we've done, helping ourselves to someone else's belongings like that. I'll ring the solicitors tomorrow morning and ask what happened to her remains."

"Don't feel guilty," Ann retorted. "It's just the way of the world; had you known her I know you would have tried to help in some way. And the solicitors are going to take a nice cut."

"I don't begrudge them at all," I admitted. "They did all the work and had they been less conscientious we wouldn't have known a thing about it."

Our journey home was uneventful, filled with small talk, occasional radio tuning for traffic updates, periods of silence and a couple of downloaded albums from Focus and Tangerine Dream.

Upon arriving home, Ann decided to return to her flat for a couple of nights to catch up on work and her independent life. I, left to my own devices, placed the single cylinder lawnmower in my garden shed, not really knowing when I would get it working again. The mechanism was straightforward but the motivation to do it wasn't.

I hauled the wooden travel chest from the car into my living room, cracked open a can of beer and as the weariness of the journey overtook me, thought I'd examine it the following day.

The next morning with a cup of sugarless Earl Grey tea in hand I set it down on the coffee table and edged towards the wooden chest. Kneeling before it I opened the domed lid. Inside the lid in faded stamped letters, it read 'PLM', and I wondered who that was. The musty smell from Devon quickly filled the room as I surveyed its contents.

On one side of the travel chest was a pile of paperwork and on the other a smaller wooden box. Behind the box was what appeared to be a fragment of an old map in a picture frame. The words were faded but I could just make out the word ORX.

I started with the paperwork which consisted of handwritten bills of sale, mainly for fruit, vegetables, eggs and some poultry. The earliest dates I could find went back to the 1850s, predating Alice Farnsworth's time. Under the well-written bills of sale were two leather-bound books. I took them from the bottom of the trunk and opened one, then the other. They were, in fact, handwritten diaries. The pages, written in Victorian-era English, were difficult to read, particularly as the writing was small, sloping forwards in a beautiful script and the paper was seriously yellowing. Some pages would require careful separation if the contents were to be fully appreciated. I decided then that I would scan the pages over a few evenings then I could enlarge the script on the laptop screen which would help me read it better.

I then reached into the chest to take out a beautiful mahogany box. Opening it, I saw an antique brass surveyor's theodolite, slightly damaged and its surfaces tarnished, but it would clean up beautifully.

***

Chapter 2

Leafing through the pages of the two-volume, leather-bound diary over the following days was a reflective and intricate procedure. Various words and phrases caught my eye, each hinting at the life of one Hartley Birkett, a surveyor who traversed the early development of the railways of England and then France between 1844 and 1853. I surmised that the theodolite nestled in the wooden box had once been his trusted companion.

Some of the diary's delicate pages proved too fragile for direct handling, prompting me to photograph and print them for a more thorough examination. I approached this task with the meticulous care of a restorer, ensuring that each page remained in sequence. This painstaking effort felt necessary, becoming a tribute to Hartley Birkett's own dedication and honouring the memories of the life he had decided to chronicle. It seemed as though I was being drawn into his world, spending more and more time immersed in the preservation of the diary, almost to the point of becoming an obsession. This theodolite from the nineteenth century needed preservation rather than any restoration for future use, but that would come later. For now, I gave it a superficial inspection, testing its movements, the alignment of its levels and screws. Evidently it had suffered a heavy fall at some point and an eyepiece was missing. This early, handmade theodolite bore the nameplate William Cary of London, a name I would research later. The dense mahogany box crafted with velvet-lined fittings to cradle the instrument securely spoke of its quality.

How Hartley Birkett connected to Alice Farnsworth still remained an enigma – was he an ancestor of mine? Some preliminary research was going to be necessary.

So, my next quest began. I subscribed to a UK-based ancestry website lured by a free week-long trial. I was to discover that recent records were more difficult to research than older ones. While census data after 1841 was readily available, government restrictions kept the last century's records beyond reach. Births, deaths and marriages were well documented but cross-referencing them to avoid following the wrong lineage was imperative. I then thought of contacting Swann and Cartwright again, the solicitors who had initially contacted me. They should be able to shed some light on my connection to Alice Farnsworth.

Once more, I endured the wait and long-winded automated recorded messages. This time, however, Betty the secretary, greeted me with a bit more warmth. I enquired about any ancestral link to Alice Farnsworth and possibly Hartley Birkett. She requested my email address to forward the information. About an hour later, an email arrived with some of the answers I was looking for.

'Alice Farnsworth was born Alice Grace Birkett in 1922 and married John Farnsworth in 1940 at the age of eighteen. He was four years her senior and tragically he was killed in 1942 in the war, aged twenty-four. They had no children and Alice never remarried. Her father was Henry Birkett, himself the son of Samuel Birkett and Grace, née Walker. Alice had a brother, George, and a sister, Charlotte, who was your grandmother and who married Joseph Grisdale.'

Though the email didn't extend beyond Samuel Birkett, it provided a crucial link to the Birkett lineage. My next step was to bridge the gap between Samuel and Hartley Birkett using online resources. The ancestry website revealed that Hartley Birkett was my third great-grandfather and his son was Samuel Birkett, born in 1847; my lineage being a mix of maternal and paternal ties.

Up to this point I had resisted the temptation of delving into Hartley Birkett's diary. The glimpses I had seen were intriguing and I resolved to devote several uninterrupted hours to it at a time. Interestingly the diary wasn't a daily log; large gaps between entries suggested that some parts were written in hindsight, adding a layer of reflection to Hartley's narrative.

The diary began with a page torn from a later entry that I could not locate and placed at the beginning; its message was confusing, appearing to be at the same time an introduction as well as a final note. Perhaps it reflected the mind of the man who wrote it on that day. Whatever it was, it was a solemn start.

Armed with a cup of tea in hand, I was ready to start reading the journal of Hartley Birkett.

> *"It is with rapidly failing eyesight and lungs that are laden with the dust of the mine from my early years that I finally lay down my quill, having completed a task that I set out to do several months ago. I find solace in the act of recounting the life I once lived, filled with memories of uncharted landscapes in both England and France, where I served as a surveyor in the early days of the railways.*
> *I harboured an unquenchable spirit of adventure. I envisioned great riches as I set forth to map the courses that would eventually knit the towns and cities of our land into a coherent whole. The rugged terrains of England and the picturesque countryside of France became my canvas. It was in the heart of France that I encountered the one who would change the course of my life forever.*

This tale is one of a love unmatched in its depth and the searing pain of its cruel and untimely severance.

In the eyes of many I stand as one who has sinned and shall, one day soon, face judgement before the Almighty. Yet it is here upon this mortal soil that I now bear my earthly punishment, with each waking hour, the bitter remembrance of the loss I have suffered and the pain I have wrought upon a young girl who lost both her mother and her father. Attached herewith is a letter addressed to Sophie Fournier, that she might come to understand.

To whomever may find these pages, I cannot help but feel that the sunset of my life approaches. I find solace in the act of recounting the life I once lived.

If there be any purpose to this account, let it be a caution, perhaps, to those who come after, a reminder of the hazards that beset those who seek to shape their own fate. For now, I find a measure of peace, knowing that my story has been told, though the only ears it may ever reach are those of the silence itself.

Hartley Birkett
17th January 1871

Chapter 3

As I reminisce upon the days of my youth, when my father worked as a sawyer in the local copper mine on the edge of Dartmoor, the world seemed vast and full of marvels. These recollections evoke a sense of wonder and nostalgia that stirs the soul. It would be about the year 1825 that I, a mere child of five years of age, stumbled upon sights and sounds that would forever etch themselves into my memory. My mother took me to gaze upon the site of the mine and with a child's curiosity I ventured further, drawn by the unfamiliar clatter emanating from within the cavernous depths of the mine and the sight of boys only a few years my senior, pushing and tipping wagons of stone and ore freshly dug from the depths of the earth on wooden rails. My father was working nearby cutting timbers to be used in the mine. I remember being attracted by the noise coming from the engine house and escaping my mother's hand; I was drawn with apprehension towards the deep pounding sounds that shook the ground.

Upon entering the engine house, the atmosphere felt oppressive with the smell of hot steam and oil, a pungent mixture that filled my lungs and made me gasp. I was fascinated by the rhythmic movement of the giant steam engine made of iron and brass, the Newcomen, whose sound reverberated through the stone walls with each thump. This engine, a goliath of its time, stood tall, its iron frame glistening with a film of oil upon its surface.

As I approached, the ground beneath my feet seemed to throb in time with the engine's motion. The great beam rose and fell with grace, its pivot point creaking as it transferred its power to the pump below. The sight of this mechanical giant filled me with awe. I stood transfixed, watching the clatter and regularity of connecting rods dancing before my eyes.

The noise was deafening as clanks, hisses and creaks filled the air, yet beneath the surface of this mechanical rhythm there was a certain harmony. The steam, released with a sharp hiss from its cylinder, mingled with the cool winter air, creating swirling clouds.

I can still recall the warmth of the steam as it brushed against my cheek if I got too close. The smell of lubricating oil and grease was pungent and it clung to my clothes and skin, an odour that would forever remind me of that moment of discovery. The workers, young men, their faces etched with lines of fatigue, moved around the engine, tending to its needs with care and precision, greasing and turning wheels that opened and shut valves. Boys had blackened faces through continuously shovelling coal into the furnace, day and night, for the engine could not stop at the risk of water flooding the lower levels of the mine.

I remember also, a short time after that, the old Newcomen was replaced by a beam engine of greater efficiency: the Watt steam engine. James Watt had transformed the steam engine from a basic machine into a marvel of power.

Gone was the laborious clanking of the Newcomen, replaced by the Watt engine, which I observed had a separate condenser and the beam's movements were much quieter with a more refined rhythm. Its balanced flywheel rotated with a grace that spoke of precision engineering and meticulous craftsmanship and the noise had lost its harsh edge, becoming a muffled bellow. The workers had roles that were now more aligned with oversight than permanent manual intervention, as they operated the machinery with a sense of pride and accomplishment.

Years later as a man grown, I reflected upon the passage of time, and I could not help but marvel at the journey from the Newcomen and the Cornish to the Watt. They were not merely machines but embodiments of the spirit of innovation. The wonder of those early days, the awe and excitement of discovering the marvels of steam power remained with me as a cherished memory for the rest of my life.

My curiosity at the workings of the pumping engine had caught the eye of the mine owner and in 1828 when I had reached my eighth year, he then asked my father if he wanted me to start working in the mine. The life of an eight-year-old child employed in the mines was fraught with hardship and peril, so I, but a lad of tender years, was tasked with the duty of greasing the steam-powered pumping equipment. Each day, as dawn's light scarcely rose above the horizon I started my daily task. My small hands, nimble and uncalloused, were fit for the delicate task of applying oil to the myriad moving parts of the grand machinery. The smell of hot steam and acrid oil permeated the air, mingling with the dust and sweat that clung to my skin. The ceaseless clanking and hissing of the engines were my constant companions, their continuous rhythm bore witness to the ceaseless toil that defined my days.

I moved with care and precision, oiling and greasing and cleaning, for fear that a moment's inattention could result in injury or worse. The great beams and pistons in motion demanded respect and vigilance. My role, though humble, was vital for without the lubricant I applied, the mighty machines would seize and falter.

As I reached my teenage years, there was nothing I did not know about the workings of the giant machinery that was used for pumping water out of the mine, which until that day, could only be achieved by tunnelling in adits and letting the excess water drain by gravity alone. My work had now evolved to replacing small worn parts where precision regulation was required. Later, high-pressure boilers gave more power for winding equipment to haul the ore from vertical shafts, and men to be lowered to access the mineral veins with more ease than climbing down dangerous wooden stopes.

Steam power enabled the metal ores of mines to be exploited more efficiently and at greater depths. Following the mineral veins and anticipating where they would lead became a more exacting occupation of the experienced mine manager. The tools of his trade were precision instruments like the circumferentor and later the theodolite, which gave rise to trade surveyors who used the instruments and could calculate the slope of veins, advise on where to best intercept them with shafts and adits, and calculate the volume of material that came to the surface, determining where to tip the spoil so that it wouldn't hinder further mining extensions.

And so, after May Day in the year 1833 at the age of thirteen, I had progressed to working in the rudiments of a machine shop and a young boy we called Danny, of merely nine summers, had assumed my former duties of oiling and greasing the great beam engine. Alas, for the poor boy, after no more than three weeks at his post, tragedy struck. One fateful day as he moved about his duties, he lost his footing.

With a terrible heart-rending swiftness, the merciless flywheel took the boy by his outstretched arm, a jest of trying to balance himself, dragging his small frame into the pit below the floor level. He had but a fleeting moment to emit the briefest of screams, a heartrending cry that was abruptly silenced as the insatiable wheel seized him. His cry, barely a whisper against the roaring engine, was the last sound he made. His body was wrenched apart with a ghastly finality, the sheer force of the mechanical beast rendering him into a bloody state beyond recognition.

In those early days of industrial toil there were no safety rails to shield the unwary from peril.

The tragedy was compounded by the cruel necessities of our work. The engine, vital to the operation of the mine, could not be halted. The continuous pumping of water was imperative to the safety of the men labouring deep within the earth. To stop the machine even in the wake of such a horrific accident would have jeopardised the lives of those below. Thus, the great beam engine continued its ceaseless rhythm, its iron heart indifferent to the boy's fate.

For three interminable days the engine churned on, the memory of the young boy's demise a heavy burden upon our minds and to the horror of his parents who visited the scene. It was only after this period when the danger to the miners had abated that the engine was finally stopped. The grim task of retrieving what remained of the boy's broken form then fell to us. This tragic incident, seared into my memory, served as a sober testament to the brutal conditions of industrial advancement that marked our era, and the sacrifices of those like young Danny, are a distressing reminder of the human cost of death and injury in the pursuit of survival, wealth and social evolution.

Death was a companion in all the workings of the mine. The grim reaper did not care about a man's age, be it at work or at home, neither for his wife or children did the angel of death care. He took all, the tired, the weary and also the fittest men of the parish. Most of all, he knew how to extract the soul of those who did not have their wits about them and for whom the slightest inattention was sufficient. But there were many boys ready to replace poor little Danny.

So, my work had progressed briefly from oiler and greaser to replacing and adjusting worn connecting rods and other moving parts that were made by the smithy. The finest work of all was when I was called upon by the surveyor to set up his instrument for him and to hold the measuring staff whilst he took his readings. Lengths we measured in chains and links, for the surveyor's work was not that of a man alone; an aide was necessary. I soon became his favourite, and I started to learn this new trade. The master surveyor, Joseph Renshaw, was an educated man who took the time to teach me his trade, firstly perfecting reading and writing, then geometry and mathematical calculations.

In the year 1840, passing the age of twenty, I had been learning the surveyor's trade for a full five years. In that time, we had used first the circumferentor, then the theodolite. I had become proficient in the use of both instruments, and when Joseph set me tasks about the mine workings, I was able to narrow my margins of error to within one-thousandth of whatever measurements were made when returning to my original point of departure.

Sunday was a day of rest and with my ailing mother and father, we attended the meeting house of the Society of Friends. Our beliefs centred on simplicity, pacifism and inner spirituality. We emphasised the "Inner Light", believing that God's presence resided within everyone, guiding us towards truth and righteousness without the need for clergy or sacraments. This principle extended to our meetings, characterised by silent worship where anyone moved by the Spirit could speak.

We advocated for social justice, promoting equality across gender, race and social classes and opposed slavery many years before its abolition in 1807. We dressed simply and led lives that rejected showiness, focusing on honest straightforward living. In our meetings we practised consensus decision-making, nurturing a sense of communal discernment and equality. Our yearly meetings helped maintain unity and address issues of doctrine and practice.

Because of historic persecution by the preaching Christian doctrines, the sense of community within the Society of Friends was by no means a disadvantage in business activities where we tended to be sympathetic to like-minded persons.

By now I had progressed from a surveyor's apprentice to a role of greater responsibility within the mine. My skills in measurement and geometry had led me to assist in the anticipation and execution of new tunnels and shafts. We used the theodolite to ensure the precise alignment and slope of our workings, a vital task as we delved deeper into the earth. Our efforts were rewarded with rich veins of copper and tin, and the mine prospered under our meticulous care.

The advancements in steam power continued to revolutionise our operations. The high-pressure boilers enabled us to drive larger pumps and winding engines, making it possible to reach unprecedented depths. The efficiency of these engines reduced the physical strain on the miners and increased the safety of our operations, although the inherent dangers of mining remained ever-present.

The mine owner's investment in technology and skilled labour paid dividends and our mine became renowned for its productivity and safety. The workers, once mere toilers in the dark, now had a sense of pride and accomplishment in their work. We were no longer just extracting minerals from the earth; we were part of a larger enterprise that pushed the boundaries of what was possible with human resourcefulness and industrial power.

Reflecting on these years, I am reminded of the Quaker values that guided my actions. The principles of equality, community and the Inner Light inspired not only my personal conduct but also the way I approached my work. The sense of purpose and fulfilment I derived from my labours was deeply intertwined with these beliefs. They provided a moral compass in a world often dominated by profit and exploitation.

And so, as I look back on my journey from a curious child in the engine house to a skilled surveyor and engineer, the lessons learned in the mine and the determined pursuit of personal improvement shaped the man I have become.

Chapter 4

Parallel to the development of copper and tin mining in Devon and Cornwall in the early decades of the 1800s and aided by the evolution of the steam engine, great innovations were being made in steam locomotion. I learned from Joseph Renshaw, who was old enough to remember the Killingworth engines built by George Stephenson in County Durham that they were conceived as travelling engines, heralding a revolutionary transformation in transportation that would eventually supplant the horse.

In 1825, being but five years of age, I was too young to recollect in detail *Locomotion No. 1* and its inaugural journey from Darlington to Stockton. Yet, within the ensuing decade steam locomotives evolved to become increasingly potent and swift. The tram-road as it was also known was inaugurated in 1830 to facilitate the transport of cotton from the former American colonies via the port of Liverpool to the mills of Manchester, whilst also providing carriages for the conveyance of passengers. Whenever we had access to a newspaper, we were avid readers of the developments from the north of England.

The burgeoning railway industry beckoned with ample opportunities. Rail lines, initially constructed from cast iron and subsequently from wrought iron, required extensive earthworks to maintain their integrity, given that locomotives could only traverse gentle inclines. This necessitated the excavation of cuttings, the creation of embankments, the construction of bridges to span valleys, tunnels and the establishment of railway stations along the route. Lines traversing soft or boggy terrain demanded reinforcement to prevent subsidence and distortion under the weight of fully loaded locomotives and wagons. The North of England led the way, but the South rapidly followed suit, with lines connecting towns such as Bristol and Exeter. I meticulously monitored the progress of the Bristol to Exeter line, which was opened in sections between 1841 and 1844. At the same time, the line from Exeter to Teignmouth was being negotiated with local landowners, presenting an opportune moment to approach the South Devon Railway Company.

In 1843, at twenty-three years of age, I confided my aspirations to Joseph Renshaw to leave the mine and work as a surveyor for the railroads. He informed me that I would need to forsake my current employment, as the mine owner permitted absences solely in cases of severe illness or injury. The notion of feigning an accident crossed my mind, yet it clashed with the moral principles instilled in me. Pondering this dilemma, I resolved to seek counsel from my ageing parents. After an evening meal of rabbit broth and oatcakes, I approached the subject with my father, explaining the promising prospects within the expanding railroad network. Without hesitation he encouraged me to pursue this path if it promised fulfilment, assuring me that he and my mother could manage for another decade or more. As events transpired this assurance proved overly optimistic, but at that time any ailments that my parents may have been suffering were not apparent to me. Nevertheless, such is the optimism of youth that I anticipated earning a considerable income, sufficient to support my parents in their later years.

Within a few days my resolve to leave the mine had been decided upon and before I could tell Joseph of my plan, I had been summoned to the mine manager's office with Joseph beside me. The manager, Edward Winslow, was a small stout man who always walked with the aid of a cane, although many of us doubted whether it was a necessity. He had ruddy features, small staring eyes and a double chin. He was always clean-shaven and, probably in his late forties, had hair surrounding his head but was bald on top. Perhaps because of his advancing baldness he let his greying hair grow over his ears and nearly down to his shoulders. He invited me to sit and related that Joseph had come to him the previous evening. Joseph looked at me and winked. It was a sign that I should not interrupt to speak but listen.

"Hartley," he commenced. "You have been working at this mine for about fifteen years, from the age of eight if I am not mistaken and you are a great aid to Joseph. He tells me you are fully proficient in all the techniques of mine surveying and have developed an innate knowledge of mineral identification and the way mineral veins lie.

"You may be aware that England's railway network is expanding fast and is due to make its way from Exeter to Plymouth. Every town and village will want to link into the main line. It means a lot of exploration. The shareholders of this mine are interested for three reasons: firstly, as an investment in this new form of transport to help even out the years when the mine goes through hard times; secondly, as shareholders we can influence which areas are best served, so taking our copper to new markets in the tram wagons will give us a better standing than horse and cart; and thirdly, earth movements from the cuttings of tramway tracks might reveal some interesting mineral veins worth exploiting and we want to be the first to negotiate with the landowner. Your wages, I believe, are 20s 6d a week?"

I replied, "They are."

"We would like you to take one of the younger boys with you and follow the developing railway network for the next eight weeks. We will pay you 30s a week and cover your boarding at inns along the way. The boy, John, will be paid 5s 6d and board with the stable lads. Tell me, Hartley, are you up for the challenge?"

I told Mr Winslow that I was. Then he said, "Good. I have here a letter of introduction that you must hand to the chief engineer, Mr Isambard Kingdom Brunel. He is expecting you in three days' time at the railway station being built at Exeter."

The following afternoon was spent preparing the instruments for the journey, checking the theodolite for accuracy, training John to hold the staff vertically when I needed to take readings, cleaning, lightly oiling and packing the chains for our measurements. From the east side of Okehampton, with a horse and cart, we made it to Exeter in a day and made our arrival known at the Coachman Inn.

The following day we walked to the railway station under construction, due to be opened the following year and there we saw the renowned Mr Brunel. He was unmistakable with his sideburns wrapping around his cheeks, smoking and wearing his customary top hat. With a little nervousness and hesitation and when he had finished giving orders to the men around him, I approached the great man, offering my letter of introduction. Mr Brunel was quick to understand what my mission was about, and he suggested that whilst the mainly coastal railway from Exeter to Teignmouth was unlikely to show anything in the way of mineral deposits, as we were too far from the granite mass of Dartmoor, I could certainly be useful doing general surveying on both the above-mentioned lines.

And so, I set about general surveying work, which would give indications on the best way the railway line could be routed, covering the need for bridges over rivers, cuttings and embankments, stabilising or avoiding bogs and marshes and wide flat areas for marshalling yards, junctions and stations. Whenever I could, I would either return to see my parents or attend a local Friends' meeting house on Sundays. The return home to the north side of Dartmoor was the long way round, or alternatively I could take the quicker turnpike road through Moreton Hampstead. In either case, a return home had to coincide with reporting back to my employers.

In March of 1845, I was invited to a social event which united landowners and interested partners of the South Devon Railway Company. I was formally introduced to Melinda Lowe. Melinda was the daughter of George Lowe, a tradesman made good, becoming a manufacturer of fine furnishings with an interest in the furnishment of first-class railway passenger carriages. Melinda was of a pale complexion with equally pale blue eyes that could appear grey depending on how the light lit up her face. She had her hair tied in a bun on the top and slightly to the back of her head. Melinda was nineteen years of age and her expression gave nothing away as to what she was thinking. A few freckles adorned the top of her nose and she stood at about 5ft 3ins. The long cream and white dress she wore was tightened at the waist and one could see she was of slight build. First sight of her didn't make any great impression; she seemed as delicate as a glass figurine. Without being particularly beautiful, she was attractive and her facial features were well balanced around a small straight nose. Her eyes looked shaded, but I could not tell if this was through tiredness or powder that had been applied. Her body movement gave the impression of shyness as I bent forward and my lips gently touched the back of her dainty gloved hand that was extended to convey my respectful greeting.

On that occasion there was little opportunity to exchange more than the briefest of formal chatter and I would normally have moved on after a few minutes of polite talk. George, her father, had obviously decided otherwise, keeping the conversation going, telling his daughter of the work I did under the auspices of the great Isambard Kingdom Brunel. The fact that I had met him on no more than the one occasion when I presented my letter of introduction and that no direct working relationship existed between us, did not seem to matter to George. I was then invited to dine at the Lowes' country house, Lowe Manor, the following Sunday.

The Sunday following our initial introduction, I chose to arrive at the Lowes' country manor on horseback rather than in the fashionable hansom cab, the first of which had graced our district but a few years prior. I had no desire to present myself above my true station, steadfast in the simplicity instilled in me since my earliest years.

Upon my arrival, I was greeted by a houseman, a figure emblematic of the respectable household. The Lowes' employ extended to a maid devoted to Melinda, alongside a cook, a butler, a housemaid and a team of workers on the estate. The manor, while by no means extravagantly grand, bore an air of refined taste. It stood in the form of a rectangular edifice devoid of additional wings or ornate carvings, constructed from a harmonious blend of local stone meticulously shaped for the corners and the edgings of windows and doors, with the intervening walls built of brick. Most impressive was the grand open porch, capacious enough to allow a rider to dismount under shelter from any rain. The manor was set within its extensive grounds, encompassing verdant meadows, a tranquil lake nourished by a stream and a copse of woodland. In the corner of a field on the edge of the woodland stood an old disused chapel that had been renovated by George Lowe; his intention was to be buried there when his time arrived. Nearby, a stone cottage was occupied by the head estate overseer.

Upon entering, my gaze was irresistibly drawn upwards to the wooden beams and arches, which revealed the skeletal structure of the abode, features not visible from the exterior. The interior was a masterful yet functional amalgamation of wood, stone and brick, adorned with tapestries that graced the walls.

It was evident that George Lowe possessed a refined taste in the manner these elements were harmonised in the construction of his residence.

My acquaintance with Melinda swiftly blossomed into a more profound connection. There was no longer the presence of Melinda's mother, Victoria, for I learned that she had succumbed to consumption five years previously. Melinda, educated within the confines of her home, revealed herself to be a spirited soul, often challenging her father in a manner I would not have dared to challenge my own father. In the weeks that followed, my visits to the Lowe Manor grew in frequency driven by a genuine desire to spend time in Melinda's company. We would meander by the lakeside or wander through the woods, engaged in conversation, laughter and playful mockery, often walking hand in hand. And when we were sure to be out of sight, tender kisses were exchanged. It dawned upon me that George Lowe might have intended me as a suitor for his daughter from our initial meeting, but within a span of three months, I found myself nervously seeking George Lowe's permission to wed his daughter, to which he gave his hearty approval.

Melinda was an only child and shortly after our betrothal to marriage, my future father-in-law invited me to join his flourishing enterprise. I expressed my intention to consider his offer but only upon the completion of my surveying duties, which had been extended from an initial eight weeks to another two years. Whatever my choice for the years ahead, my career prospects appeared promising at the time of my marriage in the month of May 1846. My parents, though much frailer, graced the ceremony with their presence, as did Edward Winslow, the mine manager, along with several aunts, uncles and cousins of Melinda, whose names now escape my recollection. We had envisioned a modest wedding ceremony restricted to immediate family, yet the guest list rose to over a hundred and fifty. My father-in-law deemed it advantageous for business to invite his clientele, esteemed engineers and local dignitaries.

Among the distinguished guests was Marc Brunel, father of the renowned Isambard Kingdom Brunel. I had already been informed of his stature as a great engineer, a legacy his son had admirably upheld. Marc Brunel, however, had suffered an apoplexy the previous year, leaving him partially speechless and paralysed on his right side. Despite this affliction, our exchange, though brief, proved most enlightening. His French accent occasionally made understanding him a challenge, yet he managed to confide in me intriguing details of the growing opportunities within France's burgeoning railway network. Should I ever consider residing in France, he suggested, such prospects might prove very beneficial to me.

At the time, I scarcely grasped how forthcoming events would unfold.

Chapter 5

I put down Hartley's diary after a couple of hours' reading. I needed to go and get some food supplies from the local supermarket ten miles away. I had the feeling that Hartley Birkett was preparing the way for something dramatic in his life.

Once I returned from shopping, I decided to check out a few dates of historical events in the county of Devon on the internet. For the most part, they checked out. So did my ancestor really cross paths with Isambard Kingdom Brunel and his father? Marc Isambard Brunel apparently did have a stroke in 1845 and died four years later aged eighty, so it's quite possible he could have been present at my third great-grandfather's wedding. I was keen to get back to the diary, but because my eyes were tiring from reading, I decided to go to "The L'al Nook", my local pub, instead for a beer or two, and return to the diaries the following morning after breakfast.

***

From May to August of the year 1846, the skies withheld their mercy and scarcely a drop of rain fell upon our parched lands. July in particular was a month of unrelenting heat, with winds from the south laying a fine red dust on houses and vegetation alike. It was believed locally that the dust came from the Sahara Desert itself. The once bubbling streams had dried to mere trickles, lakes dwindled to puddles of mud and wells, the lifelines of our sustenance became dry. The crops withered under the heat of the sun and many of the watermills ceased their grinding, deprived of the necessary flow. Whispers of a hard winter to come passed from mouth to mouth as the spectre of hunger loomed.

    Amidst these trying times I found myself settling into married life with my dear Melinda at Lowe Manor, a domicile of luxury beyond anything I had ever known. My surveying work, however, pulled me away frequently, oftentimes for stretches of six or more days. The manor was a veritable palace, large enough to house us all with space to spare. A new servant had been employed to ease our burdens and my assistant, John, now accompanied me back to the manor upon my return. His quarters adjacent to the stables, were more than adequate for his needs. George Lowe, ever the generous father-in-law, ensured that I had at my disposal the finest horse and carriage enabling us to return to the manor with all due haste once our work in any given area was concluded. Though I embarked on this new arrangement with some trepidation, Edward Winslow my employer, seemed content so long as our work progressed without delay.

    It was in the oppressive heat of mid-July that a rider approached me while John and I were taking measurements on the railway line between Newton Abbot and Newquay, a section intended to open in 1848. The rider brought grave news from Edward Winslow: my mother had succumbed to cholera. There had been an outbreak in the vicinity of the mine and my father, stricken with the same illness, was not expected to survive more than a few hours. With urgency gripping my heart I made for South Tawton where my parents resided, taking a fresh horse from a nearby coaching inn. Alas, I arrived too late. My parents had already been laid to rest, victims of a disease that claimed many with cruel swiftness. It would be nearly a decade more before a certain John Snow would uncover the true cause: contaminated water. Reflecting on the lack of rainfall I could not help but surmise that the drought had driven people to drink from spoiled wells and dwindling streams. My parents were interred in a Quaker burial ground alongside six neighbours, all of whom lived within a quarter-mile, all had collected water from the same well and all perished from the same terrible affliction.

The loss of my parents bore an added sorrow: Melinda was with child and they would never know their grandchild. Melinda's days grew long and lonesome, her father was occupied with his business and I was frequently away on my travels. Fortunately, Melinda had a friend or two who would call for afternoon tea and her maid was ever-present to attend to her needs. Though my upbringing was simple, I found myself surprisingly at ease in these luxurious surroundings. I attribute this comfort to George Lowe, a self-made man devoid of airs, who was convivial, helpful and easy to be around.

Then came one of the darkest nights of my life, the 12th of September 1847. By the dim light of a flickering candle, I watched in helpless despair as my beloved Melinda, the very light of my life, slipped away. The chill of that night still grips my soul, her cries of anguish echoing through the halls of our home. I clung to the desperate hope that the family doctor might arrive in time to save her, but it was all in vain. Despite the frantic efforts of our faithful maid, Jane, who tended to her with trembling hands, the relentless haemorrhaging would not abate.

Melinda's face, once radiant with the glow of impending motherhood, grew as pale as the life ebbed from her. Her eyes once warm and full of love, dimmed like the flickering flame beside us. She whispered my name, her voice barely a whisper, and I grasped her hand, willing my strength into her failing grasp. But the cruel hand of death was unyielding. Doctor Alistair Jones arrived too late, his face a mask of regret, his words merely confirming the dread that had already taken hold of my heart. Nothing could be done. In an instant, my joy turned to ashes. Melinda, my dearest Melinda, was gone, leaving me with our son, Samuel, the name we had chosen together if the baby was to be a boy.

I held Samuel close, his cries a poignant reminder of life's cruel duality. In his tiny features I saw Melinda's spirit, a fragment of her to cherish amid the ruins of my heart.

Melinda's funeral a few days later drew the whole neighbourhood and beyond. Yet I still remained trapped in disbelief. If there was a God, how could he allow such a thing? The thought filled me with incredulity and anger, a bitter resentment towards a deity who, if he existed, seemed indifferent to my suffering. As people offered their condolences, I caught in their eyes a glimmer of blame as though they thought me responsible, for it was through the birth of our son, for which I was responsible, that had set this terrible chain of events into motion. This suspicion gnawed at my conscience and I could not help but wonder what Melinda's father, George, must think of me also.

The old chapel that George had so lovingly renovated now served a sorrowful purpose. A small burial plot had been hastily prepared, the grass scythed low around the chapel and a modest metal fence erected to mark the boundary. A headstone would be placed at Melinda's grave once the stonemason completed his work. Both George and I agreed that it should be made of polished granite with deeply incised letters to ensure that her memory would endure for centuries. The inscription would read:

In Loving Memory of Melinda Birkett
Beloved Wife and Mother,
Who Gave Her Life So That Another Might Live.
Died 12th September 1847, aged 21.

"Her love endures in the life of her son,
Though she rests in eternal peace,
Her spirit lives on in our hearts."

George recognised the depth of my distress for he shared it also. Melinda was his only child and her loss hurt intensely, yet she had left behind a grandson, a ray of light in his sorrow. It was clear that a practical discussion about Samuel's future would soon be necessary. George surely feared that I might take Samuel and disappear, but I reassured him that this was not my intention. However, I could no longer remain at Lowe Manor; staying there would only prolong my pain and despair. Neither did I wish to involve myself in his successful furnishing business, despite its prosperity.

We reached an amicable agreement concerning Samuel's upbringing though I knew it carried the risk of estrangement. I decided to return to my surveying duties, promising to visit Samuel whenever I could. George would retain Jane, Melinda's maid, as a nanny to care for Samuel, raising him in the manor's safe and stable environment. A week after Melinda's funeral, I resumed my work for the South Devon Railway Company charting any mineral veins as I went. John and I worked from sunrise to sunset, taking measurements in the field whenever the weather permitted. On rainy days I would record our findings onto large-scale plans, often in the rented room of a local inn. John would tend to the equipment though the theodolite remained solely under my care. His learning was slow and I doubted he would ever achieve an independent proficiency on his own. The charting of a railway line was no simple task; we had to consider alternative routes, ensuring the investors could make informed decisions. Every cutting and embankment had to be meticulously calculated, with the geological structure dictating the necessary width and slope to prevent collapse.

The month of March in 1848 was marked by a persistent chill over many days and the earth where Melinda had been laid to rest was still fresh. It was a stark reminder of the cold finality of death. I had been working in the vicinity of a proposed rail line that might one day connect Ashburton with the grander route linking Exeter to Plymouth. The work provided a necessary distraction, though my thoughts often drifted to my departed wife and the son I had left in the care of his grandfather. It was on one such day, as John and I methodically took measurements in a field near Dartmoor's rugged granite outcrops, that I noticed two figures approaching from a distance.

They were well-dressed, their top hats marking them as men of some importance, and one carried a leather briefcase under his arm. As they neared, I noted with amusement that their footwear was poorly suited to the terrain. I had dismissed the notion that they were robbers or highwaymen and instead considered that they might be working for a competitor.

The taller thinner man reached me first, introducing himself as Robert Langley with his companion Jacques Moreau close behind.

"Good morning, sir," he said. "Would I be addressing Hartley Birkett by any chance?"

Before confirming, I inquired, "And what business would you have with him, sir?"

He replied, "I'm afraid I can only reveal that to the gentleman himself."

"Then, sir," I answered, "you have found him, but I am not presently at liberty to discuss any matters. However, you may find me more readily disposed to hear you this evening at the White Hart Inn."

Langley turned to Moreau, who was catching his breath, and spoke something in French. Moreau nodded, indicating agreement. Langley then said, "Monsieur Moreau will be pleased to meet you later. I bid you a good day, sir."

As they shuffled back through the tall grass, I briefly regretted my abruptness but reasoned that if the matter was of any importance they would return in the evening.

As they departed, I watched them struggle once more with the difficult terrain, their figures eventually diminishing into the distance. My curiosity was undeniably aroused, and I wondered what matter of importance could have driven these men to seek me out in such a manner. Now I would have to wait until the evening to discover what business they wished to discuss.

Later that day, as the sun set below the horizon and the air grew cool, I made my way to the White Hart Inn. The warm glow of the hearth greeted me as I entered, and I soon spotted Langley and Moreau seated near the fire, engaged in quiet conversation. Langley sipped from a tankard of ale, while Moreau delicately drank a glass of wine, his refined manner contrasting with the rustic surroundings and habits of the local population. Both men rose as I approached and after the necessary courtesies were exchanged, we took our seats to discuss what matter had brought them to my corner of England.

Moreau, speaking in his native French, began to outline the nature of their visit. His words were measured and precise, each phrase carefully translated by Langley, who maintained an air of professional detachment. It soon became clear that Moreau represented a Monsieur Paulin Talabot a prominent figure in French railway development. Talabot's ambitious project, the Compagnie du chemin de fer de Lyon à Avignon had encountered difficulties due to an economic downturn and the company had been forced into receivership. Now, as the prospects for revival were growing, they sought an experienced surveyor from outside France, someone with a fresh perspective and no prior ties to the previous troubled venture. I enquired by what means I had been sought out, only to learn that the intermediary had been Marc Brunel.

The offer was compelling and the more I listened, the more I found myself interested by the possibilities it presented. The salary was generous, the terms reasonable and the prospect of working in a foreign land under such challenging circumstances stirred within me a sense of adventure that I had long thought buried with Melinda. However, I could not ignore the responsibilities I held in England, most importantly, to my young son Samuel. Thereafter I expressed my concerns, particularly the fact that I was not conversant in French, a considerable obstacle in a land where the language was essential and very little English was spoken.

To this Moreau responded with a proposal that seemed almost too convenient: a translator would be provided for the first year allowing me time to learn the basics of the language. The more I thought it all over, the more I felt drawn to the proposition, yet I knew I should not rush into such a decision without careful consideration.

I promised to give them my answer within four days, time that would allow me to consult with Edward Winslow, my employer, George Lowe and others whose counsel I valued.

Two days later, I returned to Lowe Manor and delicately approached the subject with George. He listened attentively, though I could see the concern etched in his face, particularly regarding Samuel. I reassured him that I intended for Samuel to remain in England under his care, where he would be provided for in a stable and nurturing environment. George understood my reasoning, and relieved ultimately gave his blessing, though not without some reservations. He saw in Samuel a continuation of Melinda's legacy, a bright thread of hope amid the grief that would be forever in our hearts.

The child, only a few months old, cried whenever I attempted to hold him in my arms and as much as I loved him the thought gnawed at my mind that his birth had also brought about the death of his mother. As far as he knew, I was a stranger and his nanny Jane had become his mother in the limited vision of the world he knew so far.

My next visit was to Edward Winslow, to whom I confided my desire to seek new opportunities working abroad. He took the news with a mixture of surprise and understanding for he had always known me to be a man of ambition. We spoke at length, reminiscing about the projects we had completed together and the challenges we had overcome. Finally, I met with my old mentor Joseph Renshaw; time had not been kind to him, and I noted with sadness the signs of age in this once-vigorous man. He now walked with a distinct limp and the aid of a cane, but his mind was as sharp as ever. Our conversation was tinged with melancholy, as we reflected on the losses we had witnessed following the outbreak of cholera nearly two years previously and we spoke of the passage of time that spared no one. It is after such conversations that the mind becomes more determined in the decisions we make, for life is short.

I sent word to Jacques Moreau that I would accept his offer and with a heavy heart I bade farewell to my colleagues and mentors; there was no turning back now. I would leave England behind, carrying with me the memories of those I had loved and lost, and embark on a journey that would take me far from my Devonshire home.

As I prepared for my departure, I could not help but think of Melinda and how different life had become since that fateful night in September. The path ahead was uncertain, fraught with challenges unknown, but I felt a stirring of hope amidst the sorrow. Perhaps, in the rolling hills of France and the vast stretches of uncharted territory, I would find a way to heal the wounds of the past and build a future that honoured the memory of those I had lost.

Chapter 6

I set forth on Wednesday, 25th October in the year of our Lord 1848. It was a departure unlike any I had ever undertaken, for a mere decade earlier my journey would have taken ten days or more. My destination was the city of Lyon, a Roman town built at the confluence of the Rhône and Saône Rivers. The journey itself was a blend of old and new, where the dependable horse still served where the railroad had yet to arrive, for the railroad was being built across the continent, bringing nations together with a steel web, creating a vast, intricate network. As it stretched across Europe, it would link towns and cities, opening new markets and revolutionising trade by drastically reducing transport times.

I had been informed that it was once again safe to traverse the lands of France, for only seven months prior the streets of Paris had borne witness to revolution, leading to the abdication of King Louis Philippe and casting the nation into turmoil. It had led to the creation of the Second Republic, allowing all men over the age of twenty-one to vote, including those who did not own land, a social advancement much in advance of that of England.

The first stage of my venture required that I procure a passport, a task as laborious as it was necessary. I began by writing a formal request to the French Passport Office located at 6 Poland Street, London, and several days after receiving an invitation to present myself, I made my way there. I found myself absorbed in a chaotic and bustling city of contrasts. The air was stifling with smoke from coal fires, mingled with the stench of horse manure and uncollected refuse. The River Thames was little more than a sewer. Narrow winding alleyways were crowded with vendors peddling their wares, street urchins darting between pedestrians and beggars pleading for alms. The clatter of carriage wheels and the cries of barrow boys selling their fruit and vegetables seemed to surround me wherever I turned. As I approached the French Embassy, I found it to be located in an area called Soho, which was alive with a mix of affluent visitors, shopkeepers, ladies trading personal services and working-class residents. Elegant townhouses and fashionable establishments catering to diplomats stood alongside modest lodging houses and busy taverns.

At the passport office I submitted the requisite form, bearing my signature and the essential details of my person. For the sum of four shillings and sixpence, a passport was duly issued. However, forewarned by the experiences of others I insisted that a full and accurate description of my physical appearance be inscribed within the document. It was impressed upon me that any omission or inaccuracy, be it a slur of the pen or a misstatement of height or age, could lead to detainment by the ever-vigilant gendarmes in some remote provincial town. The passport I received, however, was not valid for inland travel, but rather a preliminary document to be exchanged for a *'passe provisoire'* upon my arrival at the port in France.

My adventure commenced with a stagecoach journey to the port city of Plymouth, for the iron rails had yet to extend their reach to that corner of England. From Plymouth I embarked upon a paddle steamer bound for Southampton, where I was to board yet another paddle steamer that would carry me across the English Channel to Le Havre. The Channel, though a narrow stretch of water separating England from the Continent, is often treacherous, and the prospect of crossing its unpredictable waves filled me with a measure of apprehension. Yet, providence was kind and the passage was mercifully uneventful. I arrived in Le Havre after twenty-two hours at sea, a half-hour ahead of schedule, with spirits lifted by the successful completion of the first leg of my journey.

Le Havre is a bustling port and it would be my introduction to the charms and distinctiveness of France. My first task was to acquire French currency, the exchange rate being twenty-five francs to £1 sterling, or one franc equal to about 10d. The term sou, a holdover from the Napoleonic era was still in use, with one franc equal to twenty sous or one hundred centimes, a detail of no small importance when a 'douceur' was required for either exceptional service or as a measure of influencing a decision, a common practice, as I was soon to learn.

I presented my passport to the dockside official, who, for the sum of two francs, issued me a *'passe provisoire'* in exchange. This temporary document authorised my travel to Paris where my passport would be signed by the *'ministre de l'intérieur'* and returned to me. The process of obtaining the *'passe provisoire'* was a tedious affair. The port was teeming with travellers eager to continue their journeys by rail, steam, or diligence, a French stagecoach pulled by four or more horses. Every person was anxious not to miss their appointed departure and a few extra 'sous' discreetly passed to the official ensured that my passport would be dispatched by the mail coach that evening.

The customs officials, or douaniers as they are called, took an excessive interest in my belongings, particularly my theodolite, an instrument of some value. They demanded a tax of five francs for its importation. However, upon presenting a letter of introduction, carefully composed in French and addressed to Monsieur Paulin Talabot, a man of considerable influence in France, the tax was revised to two francs. Whether this reduction was the result of the letter's persuasive power or a simple miscalculation on the part of the douaniers, I cannot say. But I am inclined to suspect that the remaining three francs were destined to find their way into the pockets of the officials themselves.

The scene on the dockside was a bewildering commotion of unintelligible shouts and orders, as men, sweat streaming down their faces, heaved goods onto their shoulders and offloaded a ship that had arrived earlier in the day. This, I was to discover, was one of the many differences that set the Frenchman apart from the Englishman. The volume of speech in France particularly among the labouring classes is considerably greater than that to which I am accustomed. Every word seemed to be amplified as though spoken to everyone else in the port.

And so I embarked upon the next leg of my journey, taking advantage of the French railways which, though less extensive than those in England, had made remarkable progress in recent years. From Le Havre I boarded a train to Rouen, a journey of fifty-nine miles passing through the fertile tablelands of the Pays de Caux. The line had only been completed the previous year, its construction owing largely to the skill and capital of Englishmen. How swiftly the world has changed, I mused, for it was but thirty-three years ago that we were locked in a bitter conflict with France, a conflict that ended with their defeat at the Battle of Waterloo. In my travels I would later observe that while men of my own age bore me no ill will, the older generation of Frenchmen, those who remembered the war, regarded me with a certain coldness, a relic of those not-so-distant days of hostility.

Upon arriving at the Rouen station, located on the rue Verte and built by the English architect William Tite, we had passed through three tunnels and crossed a grand viaduct. From Rouen, I took another train to Paris, a distance of eighty-four miles. This railroad, opened in 1843, terminated at the rue d'Amsterdam in

Paris. I was greatly impressed by the engineering feats along the route: cuttings through white chalk, embankments and wooden-arched bridges set upon stone pillars spanning the River Seine. The journey which took five hours cost me thirteen francs for a second-class ticket. I noted with some satisfaction that the French carriages were more comfortable than their English counterparts, though still far from luxurious. I would make a few notes and drawings and forward them to George Lowe, should they convey to him new ideas. As the fields of Normandy gave way to the more cultivated lands surrounding the capital, I was eagerly anticipating the sights of the great city ahead.

The carriage, one of eight pulled by our locomotive, rattled on through the countryside, its narrow confines pressing six of us together in uncomfortable intimacy. Opposite me, a plump matronly mother in a faded blue dress sat near the door, her large hands busy knitting, the needles clicking softly in the rhythm of the train's motion. Beside her, a tall gaunt man with deep-set eyes glared into the middle distance, his long black coat spilling onto the floor, its hem frayed from wear. His top hat rested awkwardly in his lap, and he seemed annoyed by the constant shifting of the young boy beside him near the window, a restless child of no more than six whose small boots scuffed incessantly against the seat.

To my left, a young woman sat quietly, dressed in a modest gown of grey wool, her bonnet slipping slightly as she gazed absently past her husband through the window. Though her features were soft there was a sadness about her and she scarcely stirred as the countryside sped by. Her husband wore a trim well-cut coat and held a newspaper in his lap, though he made no attempt to read it. Instead, he leaned towards his wife, speaking occasionally in low tones, his gloved hand resting lightly on her arm seeking to offer comfort. She responded with a faint nod but did not lift her gaze from the world outside.

The child on the seat opposite wriggled in his seat, playing with the latch on the window, his impatience growing by the minute. His mother, the stout woman, clucked disapprovingly but made no serious attempt to restrain him while the thin man between them both shifted irritably, his eyes narrowing as the boy's boots grazed his leg. The train's clickety-clack gently rocked us, broken only by the occasional murmur of French I could not understand and the soft click of the needles endlessly knitting as we journeyed south towards Paris.

We arrived in Paris at sunset, the light of which casted the upper parts of the buildings in a golden glow. Paris! The very name conjures images of grandeur and culture, and though I longed to explore its streets my journey was not yet complete. The weariness of the journey began to take hold and I spent the night in a modest inn near the station. I had nearly a full day to explore Paris, awaiting the signature of my passport late the following afternoon, which would thereafter enable me to continue my journey to Lyon. The day was spent on foot not venturing too far from my lodging. I took a walk from the *Jardin des Tuileries* to the *Place de l'Étoile*, a journey that revealed much of the spirit of Paris in those tumultuous times. The *Tuileries* offered a moment of calm with its serene gardens and majestic statues, a brief lull from the city's ever-present unrest.

From there, I walked along the *Rue de Rivoli* lined with arcades and lively shops bustling with activity. Parisians of all classes mingled, and it was here that I was able to procure a post book or *livre de poste*, an indispensable travel aid. The *Place de la Concorde* is a vast square where the grandeur of the past meets the uneasy present. The Luxor obelisk stood as a silent witness to history, both glorious and grim.

The *Champs-Élysées* though incomplete was already becoming the grand avenue of legend. I stepped through the narrow doorway of a perfume shop and a delicate haze of fragrance enveloped me, unlike anything I had ever known. The air carried a blend of many scents and each scent subtly teased the senses as I tried unsuccessfully to identify them: jasmine, rose and strange eastern spices. Glass vials of every shape, colour and size glittered under the soft glow of lamplight, their contents like liquid jewels, some golden, others deep amber and still others a pale, translucent pink. The shelves seemed to offer a glimpse into another world. Each bottle, some sealed with elaborate wax stamps, tempted with the allure of distant lands, unreachable except through the delicate alchemy of scent.

Behind the counter a stately woman in a satin gown moved with the precision of one who had long mastered her art. Her gloved hands hovered over the bottles with reverence. She spoke little yet her motions invited me deeper into the intoxicating labyrinth of essences. I felt the sharp sweetness of citrus mix with the deep smoky warmth of sandalwood as she uncorked a vial, holding it beneath my nose as though revealing a secret meant for my senses alone. The moment hung in the still air suspended between the worlds of Paris and some faraway place I could not name. Alas, a moment of sadness came upon me as I wandered again out of the shop, for here before me was a wondrous selection of perfumes and eau de cologne, yet I now no longer had a wife to bestow it upon.

I continued along the *Champs-Élysées*, lined with trees and elegant houses and it leads directly to the *Place de l'Étoile*, where the *Arc de Triomphe*, still under construction, dominated the scene. The monument, even in its unfinished state, was a powerful symbol of France's storied past and uncertain future. At the end of the day, I made my way to the prefecture of Paris to recover my passport, signed by the ministère de l'intérieur, then returning to my lodgings, I ate well with a generous glass or two of the proprietor's reserve table wine and took to my room, sleeping soundly until daybreak.

With the dawn the following day came the next stage of my journey. The *livre de poste* is published under the authority of the French government and it gives the exact distances travelling from post to post. The postillion who rode and guided the horse-pulled carriage is bound by law to charge at a fixed rate. For the stagecoach I took, there were three other passengers with luggage and a complement of four horses. Although limited by law to charging one franc per myriametre, which is ten kilometres, it was customary to pay double. We advanced at a rate of a myriametre per hour, depending upon the terrain, and it took about thirty minutes to change horses at post houses. I discovered that postillions are not allowed to pass other carriages on the road unless they be drawn by fewer horses or should they be stopped by an accident. A register is held at every post house; it is there where the traveller may make a complaint against the postmaster in that or neighbouring relays.

My choice was to start this first journey from Paris to Lyon by posting. My trunk baggage was secured atop the stagecoach, and I took my place inside, sharing the space with three fellow travellers.

The coach, though sturdy, was a far cry from the smooth comfort of the train. The roads were uneven and the carriage rocked and jostled as it made its way southward. The journey was slow and the hours passed with a monotonous rhythm. The dry weather, at least, spared us from becoming mired in mud when we were required to walk up the steeper slopes, the coaches being so heavily laden that the horses could not bear the strain of passengers and baggage alike. Yet, there was a certain charm in this more rustic mode of travel, a reminder that the old ways had not yet been entirely supplanted by the new.

We stopped for the night at a small inn in the town of Dijon, a place known for its wines and mustard. The innkeeper, a jovial man, entertained us with tales of the region as we dined on a copious meal of beef and bread. Although I understood hardly a word he said, a lady of a certain age, who had sat next to me in the stagecoach, surmised from my silence that I must be English, Dutch, or German, and insisted on translating. She was a person whom time had weathered like an ancient oak. Standing well over five feet eight inches, her once-robust figure had weakened with age. Her skin, pale and creased with the deep furrows of a life long lived, seemed almost translucent in places. Her hair, of whatever colour it may have been, had long since surrendered to a coarse silver-grey, pulled back tightly into a neat bun at the nape of her neck, with a few rebellious strands escaping to frame her angular face. She introduced herself as Thérèse Girard. I had managed to feign sleep for much of the coach journey, though not all was pretence, for the rocking motion of the sprung carriage had lulled most passengers to slumber at some point. Mme Girard now sat next to me at the table and there was little I could do to escape. In broken English she recounted her life story in a thirty-minute monologue, including how she had been widowed twice more than two decades ago. The constant chatter over many years, I thought, had surely hastened her poor husbands to their graves. The food, though simple, was satisfying, and I retired to my room thereafter with a sense of escaped contentment.

 I had been settled in my room for less than an hour when a faint knock disturbed the silence. Before I could decide whether to rise, the door handle turned and Thérèse Girard stepped delicately into the room. Half-opening my eyes, I beheld the woman clad in the lightest of night attire. Deciding that discretion was the better part of valour, I grunted and feigned sleep, letting out a few pretence snores. The sound was sufficient to prompt Mme Girard to turn about and leave the room. My goodness, had she mistaken her room or is this familiarity a characteristic of French women? The following morning, I saw no further sign of Thérèse Girard.

The final day of my journey to Lyon dawned bright and clear. We set out early, winding our way through the rolling hills and vineyards of Burgundy. The landscape was idyllic, a pastoral scene that seemed untouched by the march of time. The floodplain of the River Saône was wide and flat, and much of it was marshland; thankfully, our stony road remained well above the likely level of any floods. As we approached Lyon the signs of civilisation became more evident. The road grew wider and the traffic more frequent, evidence of the growing importance of this city as a hub of commerce and industry.

At last, we arrived in Lyon. The city, nestled between the Rhône and Saône rivers, was a busy city, a far cry from the sleepy villages we had passed along the way. My journey had come to an end, and I felt a sense of accomplishment as I alighted from the carriage and retrieved my luggage. The trials of the road were behind me and I requested through the coach driver that an errand boy be sent to the office of Monsieur Paulin Talabot to inform him of my arrival and to request an audience the following day at his convenience.

Chapter 7

Upon concluding another French breakfast, an affair I was beginning to understand as the most frugal meal of the day in this country, a messenger boy approached my table with a request: Monsieur Talabot would be pleased to receive me in his office at eleven that morning. It was conveyed that a cariole would be dispatched to collect me from the inn where I was lodged, situated on the Presque Île.

I dressed with the utmost care, donning a crisp white shirt and cravat, a finely woven cotton waistcoat and a lightweight grey frock coat. My trousers were of matching colour and I completed the ensemble with a straw hat suitable for the warm autumn weather, light leather boots, a bamboo cane which I carried with a sense of purpose and white cotton gloves.

The meeting took place in a gentleman's club near the hôtel de ville. As I was ushered into the lavishly decorated chamber, I immediately recognised the two gentlemen seated next to Monsieur Talabot. Across from me at the oval wooden table sat Jacques Moreau and Robert Langley, and another young man who now served as translator. After exchanging handshakes with the four gentlemen, I reassured myself that my attire was indeed fitting for the occasion in that I was not overdressed. It was Monsieur Talabot who first broke the silence, and I soon realised that the younger man beside him was to serve as my assistant and interpreter. This young man, I learned, was named Jules Petit.

Inquiries were made regarding the satisfaction of my journey, to which I responded affirmatively. Upon being invited to sit I took my place opposite the four gentlemen.

Paulin Talabot as I observed was a man some twenty years my senior, placing him near his fiftieth year. His presence was as striking as the reputation that preceded him. Of average height, he possessed a sturdy and well-built frame, a testament to a life of steady purpose. His face framed by greying hair and sideburns was marked by well-defined features: a heavy brow, a straight nose and a firm jawline that hinted at an unyielding determination. His sharp contemplative eyes revealed the keen intellect and depth of thought for which he was widely respected.

Talabot carried himself with a composed authority, his movements were deliberate and his presence commanded respect without any need for pomp or show. His attire was ever neat and befitting of his situation, favouring well-fitted garments that reflected his rank as a prominent figure in French industry and commerce. In every regard Paulin Talabot embodied an air both imposing and refined, a man whose labours left an enduring impression upon those who met him.

Before my departure from England, I had inquired through the Society of Friends regarding the character of Monsieur Paulin Talabot. The responses I received spoke highly of his credible reputation. Although fewer in number, the Society of Friends in France maintained close ties with their English counterparts and within three weeks of my humble request a letter arrived containing this valuable information. This intelligence bolstered my confidence in the career choice I had made.

The letter detailed the remarkable achievements of Monsieur Talabot, particularly his work on the railway line from Marseille to Avignon, an engineering marvel. The construction was fraught with technical challenges due to the rugged terrain, including the necessity of tunnelling through the Nerthe massif north-west of Marseille and constructing numerous viaducts and bridges. At the time of my arrival in France, the project was still incomplete, yet it was anticipated to be fully operational by the following year, 1849.

Thus, during this meeting in Lyon, it was announced that I was tasked with continuing the surveying work from Avignon in the south, progressing northward to Lyon. Jules Petit was assigned to me as both an assistant apprentice and a translator. I had suspected that he was nominated to me without any prior approval of his suitability from my perspective in order to report back to his employer on my advancement and to pick up any useful hints he thought might favour him for his career advancement. I was not in a situation to argue the point as my level of French at that point was near non-existent; his level of English was quite good and I learned later this was due to his father being Irish and his mother French.

My theodolite, as in years past, was my most prized possession seldom leaving my sight, certainly never whilst working on site. Jules was, he told me, eighteen years old and keen to become a cartographer. He showed me some rudimentary maps of Lyon he had enthusiastically drawn, but alas, errors of scale were plain to see and his draughtsman's integrity showed much room for improvement. The confluence of the Rhône and the Saône just weren't where they were really positioned. Jules must have been wrapped up in taking many measurements and laying them out on paper without cross-referencing them or using any form of triangulation that I could discern.

Over the following months, I observed that Jules, though possessed of youthful vigour and a passion for learning, was less diligent when it came to details. He often devised clever schemes to circumvent problems that required direct confrontation. Physically, he was marked by a crooked nose and slightly protruding upper front teeth which appeared more prominent due to his receded jawline. Jules had unkempt wavy black hair and held a powerful stride when walking as though every step he took was hurried.

Jules remained in my service for approximately twenty-four months, during which time we assessed the challenges of potential railroad routes between Avignon and Orange, Montpellier and areas north of Valence. The rocky nature of the surrounding hills would be problematic outside the Rhône Valley, yet within the valley itself, an unstable floodplain and the potential for the river Rhône to change its course every few years were the everyday challenges I had to take into consideration. My expertise in geological formations, refined during my work in the Devon mines, proved invaluable.

The work in the Rhône Valley was fragmented and not carried out in the sequence I would have preferred owing to the protracted negotiations conducted by a team seeking land access on our behalf. These discussions with local dignitaries, politicians and landowners dragged on interminably, necessitating frequent travel up and down the valley. Whenever possible we travelled by paddle steamer thereby maximising the efficiency of our time working. The Rhône was a magnificent river and I had the privilege of observing it in all its seasonal grandeur from the torrent of spring meltwater from the Alps to the leisurely flow during the late summer heat.

An Englishman acquainted with Provence only through books and hearsay might envision a land of paradisiacal beauty, adorned with olive groves, vineyards and fields of fragrant lavender. However, save for a few days in early spring and late autumn, nothing could be further from the truth. Nature here takes on an entirely different character under the unrelenting glare of the sun. The atmosphere is thick with dust, stirred by the passage of horses and the wheels of wagons and carriages carrying goods and passengers. The earth is scorched and the blinding reflection from the white limestone hills, stripped of soil by centuries of heavy storms, is near unbearable, causing squinting and tiredness to the eyes. Only on the valley floors, where irrigation channels reach, does any verdure appear.

The summer heat drives the inhabitants to close their shutters, seeking refuge in darkness during the three hours after the sun reaches its zenith. Such is the misery of a hot climate: the sun bleaches all it touches, the hot air shimmers and the atmosphere thick with dust from habitual drought often remains rainless from spring to autumn. The great heat persists from mid-July to September and even in the height of summer scorching heat can give way to piercing cold, driven by the Mistral, a fierce bitter wind from the north that howls down the Rhône Valley, bending tree branches to grow southward. This wind, violent and desiccating, fills the air with a yellow haze and torments the eyes from as far north as Valence to the Mediterranean Sea. In winter, the Mistral's icy wind permeates all clothing, reaching the bones and affecting the movement of the joints. The skin can freeze on the metal parts of machinery and fine instruments, requiring the human breath to ease the fingers away. Canals carrying water for irrigation may freeze and the leaves of olive trees 'burn' with the icy frost.

Another wind, the 'vent d'autan', I had heard, was reputed to drive men to madness. Blowing from the southeast towards Toulouse, it is said to last in multiples of three days.

The farmhouses of Provence are built with local limestone for the most part and are of the same colour as the roads. Men, trees and animals all share the same universal white dust. However miserable this landscape may be, the inns have large coach houses for coolness and shade in the middle of the day for travellers and horses. For in the day, no man works in the fields until the sun is again low in the sky. In Provence there may only be two clement months between the hot and cold seasons.

The temperament of the people, too, seems shaped by the fiery sun, for they know no restraint or moderation. They are fierce in disposition and act on sudden impulses. To the refined English gentleman, they may appear rude if not brutish in manner, with a bluntness of speech to which the English are unaccustomed. Enduring both this climate and its people marked the longest two years of my life up to that point.

As Jules's time with me came to an end, I had acquired enough proficiency in the French language to navigate most interactions without the need for a translator. I could now confidently dispute any discrepancies that appeared on a bill at an inn or debate with the local gendarmes if they questioned the validity of my passport. Mentioning the name of my employer was most often sufficient to allay other enquiries and indeed it sometimes resulted in an offer to partake in a glass of wine at a nearby inn. An invitation I found that often left me with the bill to pay, they believing that I must be earning a salary vastly superior to their own, which, if truth be known, I believe it was. Jules had learned a great deal during his time with me, but by the time he was withdrawn from my service he was still not fully competent to function as an independent land surveyor. I still needed an assistant, but this role was now filled on a casual basis, hiring local labourers from the nearest town to wherever I happened to be working. This method of working presented its own problems, for it was often a local maire who would insist on the placement of a friend of a friend, or to help a simpleton in the village, it being perceived that to hold a leasing staff vertically required no particular skill. Such was the inefficiency of some of these boys or men that we were occasionally required to redo a day's work with someone else. On certain days the person would not turn up and on other days a friend or parent of the boy would pass by and an hour would be lost in idle chatter as arms waved about pointing across the countryside, giving the impression that it was he who was in charge and myself being the assistant.

As the work progressed, I moved further north and in February 1852, nearly four years after beginning my work for Monsieur Paulin Talabot, I relocated to the town of Vienne. This was the final section of the railroad that would eventually link Paris to Avignon and Marseille. It was remarkable to consider that the first significant railroad in France had been built nearby, connecting St. Étienne to Lyon, a distance of just thirty-six miles, only five years after the opening of the Stockton-Darlington railway in England. Yet here in Vienne a generation later, the connection to the south was still incomplete.

I arrived in Vienne by steamer on the Rhône River mid-afternoon. The day was bright and the sun shone, although any detectable warmth from a hazy winter sun was rapidly disappearing. As the vessel docked and the crew secured the ropes to the quay, I took in the view around me. Across the broad river lay the smaller town of Saint-Colombe and to the north beyond the narrow suspension bridge linking the two towns, the Rhône curved towards the industrial centres of Givors and then Lyon, where I had first signed my contract work.

I was searching for an inn of good repute, as I anticipated that I would be stationed here for three months or more. If I had known at that moment what events lay ahead of me, would I have disembarked at Vienne? Or would I have stayed aboard the steamer and continued a little further north to Seyssuel or Givors? Was it a destiny that I could not escape at that very moment? For before me lay the strongest emotions a man can experience: the heights of happiness and ecstasy, and the depths of human suffering.

As I stepped a few paces forward on the quay, an old lady covered in a thick black shawl was sitting a few yards away cowering from the cold air blowing down the Rhône Valley.

She didn't have the appearance of a vagrant; she looked to be wearing clean black clothes not wanting of any stitching nor holes to mend. I noticed she had a begging bowl in front of her and was, I thought, probably a widow without resources. People laden with bags and porters with trolleys looking for business filed past the old woman, completely ignoring her presence. Overlooking the scene of unloading of the boarding plank were two gendarmes, stopping people occasionally to inspect their identification papers. Happily, I was not stopped and after passing them by I walked towards the old lady. She looked up towards me, her face thin and wrinkled and grey hair peeking out from beneath the shawl that covered her head. As she raised her begging bowl I fished in my pockets for a few sous and asked her in my now adequate French if she knew of a reputable hotel or inn in the town. Raising her hand and turning towards the town centre, I heard, through a mouth with a few missing teeth, "Artley à l'Hôtel du Théâtre". The difficulty with which she pronounced the words was, had her situation not been so dire, almost comical. Did she say go "aller" to the Théâtre Hotel, or did I mishear "aller" as "Artley", a pronunciation of my name Hartley without the H, as is common in French? But such thoughts came later, not at that moment. I thanked her, placed a couple of sous in her bowl and began walking towards the town. I had not advanced more than fifteen feet away when a hand touched my left shoulder. I turned around, struggling with my bags, and one of the gendarmes handed me back the coins I had just given the old woman.

"You dropped these, sir," he said. Looking past him, I noticed that the old woman had moved on, or perhaps had been moved on by the authorities. I thanked him, though I was puzzled. While the gendarme had been polite, I found it strange that he would retrieve the coins from the old woman only to return them to me. Perhaps begging was not permitted in that location. Whatever the reason I now had the name of a hotel to seek out. The name "Hôtel du Théâtre" suggested that it was a reputable establishment and so, with my bags in hand, I looked for a carriage that would take me there, pondering the curious interaction with the old woman and the gendarme.

Chapter 8

I had reached the end of Hartley Birkett's first diary which offered a fascinating personal perspective on the customs and transportation of the early nineteenth century. The accounts were not merely informative, they included subtle humour. One detail that particularly struck me was how quickly paddle steamers became a routine means of cross-Channel travel following the invention of the pressure boiler steam engine, something I hadn't fully appreciated before.

I saw Hartley as a kind and thoughtful man with high moral standards originating from his upbringing and beliefs as a Quaker, also known as the Religious Society of Friends. A quick internet search revealed that Quakerism was founded in England in the seventeenth century by George Fox and Quakers were persecuted for their beliefs by the established Protestant cults of the time. It incorporated and presumably still does, the idea that the presence of God exists in every person without the need for clergy or formal rituals. They advocate for simplicity, peace, integrity, community and equality, and their meetings for worship are often silent, allowing space for individual reflection and the possibility of spontaneous ministry. I thought to myself that had I lived in those times perhaps I would probably have turned to Quakerism myself and my reason for not doing so today is that it appears to function in parallel in many aspects to Buddhism, being both a belief and a philosophical system that I hold near to my heart.

Hartley's perspective on working in Provence was particularly striking. My own experiences of that region limited to leisurely holidays had been entirely different. Air conditioning had shielded me from any oppressive summer heat and smooth tarmac roads had softened the journey, sparing me the clouds of dust that must have plagued my ancestor as he toiled in the sun. I tried to imagine myself in the place of my third great-grandfather back in the 1840s and 1850s, working as a surveyor for the railway companies in both Britain and France. As modern passengers hurtle through the countryside on fast comfortable trains, we rarely consider the history beneath us as we travel: the countless navvies that dug the tunnels, or the engineers and surveyors like Hartley who dealt with the geological formations of the landscape and persuaded financiers of the merits of various routes and having to balance technical challenges with the constraints of cost.

Hartley's diary hinted at events yet to unfold, and I was enthusiastic about returning to the second volume of the diary. The brief encounter he described with a beggar woman on the quayside lingered in my mind. It seemed almost cruel, the way she was allowed to beg until the moment Hartley handed her a few coins, only for the gendarmes to swoop in and confiscate the money. His observation that everyone simply walked past her as if she were invisible spoke volumes about the harsh realities of the time, and I was left wondering what had become of her as Hartley continued on his way, her fate being a mere footnote in his travels.

Before immersing myself in the second and final part of the diary my thoughts drifted to the theodolite that had been passed down through the generations. I wondered if it could still function and if its accuracy had withstood the passage of time. But to test it I needed an eyepiece. I resolved to send a few emails to specialists in antique scientific instruments with precise measurements I had taken with callipers and a few photographs of the William Cary theodolite itself. The intricate brass wheel construction suggested it may be one of the first theodolites ever used.

As evening darkness crept in, I drew the curtains of my living room, turned on the table lamp and settled into my armchair with a glass of Lagavulin whisky. The second volume of Hartley's diary lay before me, promising to pick up where the first had left off. It was clear this would be a long night of reading, one that would transport me even deeper into the world of my enigmatic ancestor...

A few metres back from the quayside stood a line of cabriolets with their drivers, each smartly dressed in dark coats and tall hats, patiently awaiting hire. Their horses stood quietly, breathing out billows of steam as it condensed in the cold winter air. I made my way to the front of the line and requested a ride to the Hôtel du Théâtre. A porter dressed in a worn but tidy uniform loaded my personal baggage and the wooden tripod onto the carriage. As for the theodolite, I carried it myself, aware of its delicate nature and the need to avoid any shock or mishandling. By habit I carried it on my knee, nestled securely in its polished wooden box. This curious object often drew stares and murmurs from passers-by. To block any further prying, I would often dismiss it as being of little value, though this was only a half-truth as I feared it could attract the attention of ill-intentioned persons if it was thought to be a chest of gold coins. To the more insistent I would reveal its true nature, explaining it as a precise scientific instrument for surveying the land, an explanation that invariably satisfied their curiosity. On a few occasions when confronted by cheeky boys I would half-jest that the box contained six venomous aspic vipers destined for a local apothecary. This assertion, if followed by a motion to unlatch the box, would invariably send them scattering, allowing me to continue in the peace I desired.

As an Englishman traversing these parts I was often regarded with a mix of curiosity and mild suspicion. Our appearance being fairer and taller than our continental neighbours inevitably drew attention the further south we ventured. My own complexion, however, was darkened by years of exposure to the elements, though it retained a ruddy hue typical of men from northern climes. It was certainly not a trait that classed me as a boiled-lobster or "Rosbif" Englishman typical of many of my countrymen.

As we set off from the nearby quay, I noted that we were heading east, uphill and perpendicular to the Rhône Valley which flowed from north to south and the river Gère flowed down to meet it a few streets away to my left. Some streets were stone-paved, and many bore the unmistakable marks of Roman occupation, with ruts worn by their chariots and wagons. To see a modern European people still using the same streets as their Roman forebears seventeen hundred years later left me with a sense of awe. I wondered how many men, women and children walking on those very stones thought of the men, probably slaves, who toiled for their masters with a feature so permanent that we are still benefiting today. The Hôtel du Théâtre was situated at the Place Jouvenet. Its name, painted in fading letters on the wall, suggested its history had a grander past. Upon arriving I dismounted from the cabriolet and asked the driver to wait a moment while I entered the establishment to inquire about a room.

Inside the air was thick with the smoke of clay pipes, which four men puffed at idly as they sat around a wooden table, drinking wine. The room was dimly lit, the furniture simple and worn but the place appeared clean, if somewhat stale from the constant haze of tobacco smoke. In the corner a log fire was burning in the large fireplace and occasional backdraughts of smoke added to the smell of tobacco. A young girl of about ten years appeared from a back room, which I presumed was the kitchen. She approached me and with a soft barely audible voice offered her assistance. I inquired after a quiet room, mentioning that I intended to stay for several nights. She glanced towards the table where the men sat and called, "Papa".

At the far end of the table, a man looked up briefly, his expression one of indifference. This I was to learn was Benoît Fournier, the proprietor of the establishment and local politician. He was a man of refined appearance, his attire immaculate, wearing a tailored waistcoat over a crisp white shirt and a cravat tied with care. His dark hair was slicked back and his pale cleanshaven face bore the look of a man who had spent his life indoors rather than in the harsh sun. I sensed an unsettling air about him, something in the cold precision of his movements that hinted at a buried force held tightly in check. His eyes, calculating and hard, rested on me for a moment as if weighing my worth, before he returned his attention to his friends, dismissing his daughter's summons with a slight nod.

The girl, evidently accustomed to such rebuffs, excused herself and hurried upstairs to fetch her mother. Eleanor, the proprietress, descended shortly thereafter, her charisma in sharp contrast to that of her husband. She was a petite woman, her movements brisk and efficient and her chestnut hair neatly arranged was cut just below her chin, where it curved inward in a gentle flattering line. Her high cheekbones gave her an air of natural beauty, one that was accentuated by the warmth of her smile, though I noticed a certain guardedness in her manner. She informed me that a room was available albeit at the front of the building, but that a quieter one would be vacant in two days. We agreed on a price for half-board, and I returned outside to settle the fare and retrieve my belongings from the cabriolet.

Eleanor and her daughter assisted with my baggage while Benoît remained seated at his table, issuing abrupt instructions to his wife in a tone that, while outwardly polite, carried an undercurrent of control that tolerated no opposition. His hands, pale and well-manicured, gestured with calculated precision as he spoke, each movement deliberate as if practised to maintain an air of impeccable civility. It struck me that his manner, though courteous, bore the mark of a man accustomed to command, one who could at any moment assert his will with an iron fist. It was this chilling contrast between his outward elegance and the barely veiled threat of violence that made his presence all the more disquieting, a man I thought who I should be wary of and keep at arm's length.

That evening after washing and changing from the day's travel, I descended to the dining room where I was introduced to the other guests, five men in total, who like myself were seated at a communal table. The host family would dine in a back kitchen concealed behind a curtain that separated it from the public area. Eleanor, with her distinctive efficiency, prepared the meal, while Sophie, her daughter, served us with a grace beyond her years. The meal was a modest but well-prepared affair: pâté with fresh homemade bread followed by carp and green beans and concluding with a local St. Marcellin cheese accompanied by preserved figs. A measure of Côte du Rhône wine served in the traditional "pot" flowed freely, though I noted that Benoît, unlike his guests, sipped sparingly, his gaze ever watchful as though he missed nothing of what transpired at our table.

The following morning, I set out to explore the town of Vienne, my curiosity enthused by its Roman legacy. The frost from the previous night was melting wherever the sun's light reached the ground. The amphitheatre and treasury building were impressive as were what remained of the three aqueducts that once supplied the town with water. Though in disrepair, they were a testament to the engineering prowess of the Romans. As I studied the remnants, I marvelled at the precision with which these ancient structures were constructed, reflecting on the methods they might have employed to achieve such feats without the benefit of modern instruments.

Over the next few days, I took charge of surveying a section of the future railway line between Chasse-sur-Rhône and Vienne, including a tunnel that would have to be excavated in the heart of the town. The task was urgent and I calculated that an 800-metre tunnel would be necessary and challenging to build but that it could be completed within a year with the aid of gunpowder and skilled labour.

Upon my return to the Hôtel du Théâtre each evening, I found Benoît seated at his usual place always impeccably dressed, his manner as controlled as ever. He spoke little, his conversations with Eleanor limited to brief commands delivered in that same unsettling tone of practised civility. It was clear that despite his outward charm, he ruled his household with a quiet but unyielding authority, a man who demanded order and obedience without the need for overt displays of temper. It was only in the occasional flicker in his eyes that one glimpsed the true nature of his character, a man who beneath the polished exterior withheld a violent interior, although I doubted he could hold his own if it came to a fist fight. Benoît would never allow his temper to breach the surface of his meticulously crafted façade.

As other guests departed at the end of their stay, I was offered a better room by Eleanor. It was during this transition that I observed her more closely. Despite her petite frame and gentle manner, a calm resolve seemed to define her that intrigued me. Her rapid purposeful movements suggested a life of constant vigilance, of navigating the delicate balance between appeasing her husband and maintaining a semblance of normality for herself and her daughter. I could not help but admire her resilience, though it saddened me to see the contrast between the warmth she displayed when alone and the guarded almost fearful conduct she adopted in Benoît's presence.

If I had entertained thoughts of leaving the hotel due to the oppressive atmosphere created by Benoît's unyielding control, it was Eleanor's kindness and the quiet grace with which she bore her burdens that made me reconsider. For now, I resolved to stay, if only to ensure that she had one less guest to worry about and perhaps to learn more about the enigmatic proprietor who held such a tight rein over his household.

Chapter 9

The days slipped by with an uneventful regularity and I found myself having stayed at the Hôtel du Théâtre for nearly two months. Winter had turned to spring and to see the burst of new leaves on the trees lifted the morale. The smoke from winter fires that enveloped the town on still days was now extinguished and the freshness of clean air that could be inhaled was the bliss of life itself. I estimated that my stay would extend for at least another month, perhaps more. A routine had established itself. Each morning, I set off to my surveying work, often securing the help of a local labourer and travelling by cabriolet to the areas where the railroad would eventually cut its path from Lyon to Vienne. Though my work occasionally took me a few miles south of Vienne, the majority of the surveying focused to the north. Every fortnight I returned to Lyon to report to Paulin Talabot or his associates if he was occupied elsewhere. These meetings were often lengthy lasting several hours, so I would stay overnight in Lyon rather than endure the two-hour journey back to Vienne late at night.

Upon returning to the hotel after my day's work I sometimes found Benoît absent and, on these occasions, Eleanor displayed a freedom in her conduct that was otherwise restrained. I surmised that Benoît, a local councillor, was often occupied with his various business dealings in town. The hotel with its modest number of guests did not seem to require his constant attention. In his absences it was Eleanor who managed the daily affairs, taking on the task of procuring supplies from the market for the restaurant to dealing with hotel reservations and taking payments from arriving or departing guests. With Sophie's help she ensured the cleanliness of the linens and I often observed the two women, baskets in hand, making their way to the lavoir at least twice a week. In the back courtyard a covered area housed a hand-operated mangle and lines for drying the sheets.

One evening as Benoît tended to his affairs elsewhere, Eleanor and I found ourselves alone in the hotel's small restaurant. I was sipping a local wine and our conversation flowed with a newfound ease. The formality that once defined our exchanges had softened, replaced by a closeness that was growing between us. Eleanor with genuine curiosity inquired about my work and my origins. There was a tender sorrow in her eyes when I spoke of the loss of my wife Melinda during the birth of our son Samuel. In turn she confided in me, revealing that although she was born in France, her parents were of Italian origin. They had fled to France illegally 'sans papiers', escaping political unrest. Her parents had found work in one of the Rhône Valley vineyards where no questions were asked, and Eleanor, like many girls of her time, did not attend school as it was not yet a legal requirement.

With a hesitance that spoke to the trust we were beginning to build, Eleanor asked that I keep what she was about to tell me in confidence. She explained that Benoît came from a family of vineyard owners and was ten years her senior. Discovering her parents' illegal status he blackmailed them, threatening to expose them unless they agreed to his demand to marry their daughter. With little choice, Eleanor consented to the arrangement at the tender age of sixteen. Although Benoît was considered a handsome and eligible bachelor by many, once married and after she quickly became pregnant, his controlling nature surfaced, casting a shadow over their union.

As she spoke, a deep sorrow settled in her eyes, and I assured her that her confidences were safe with me and that no one would learn of them through my lips. Just as Eleanor was about to reveal more of her story, the sound of a carriage pulling up outside broke the moment. Startled, Eleanor excused herself disappearing behind the curtain to the private quarters just as Benoît strode in. He passed by me without acknowledgement, obviously angry about something that troubled him. Moments later muffled shouts emanated from their quarters. I sat still, listening, torn between the urge to intervene and the realisation that such a time had not yet come. But one thing was becoming increasingly clear to me, my feelings for Eleanor were deepening and I found myself increasingly troubled by Benoît's treatment of her.

The next two days afforded us little opportunity to talk. The hotel was unusually busy with eight guests occupying all of Eleanor and Sophie's time. On Sunday the household attended mass at St. Maurice's Cathedral overlooking the Rhône River. I suspected that their attendance was more about maintaining Benoît Fournier's appearances than religious devotion. Alone in the hotel when they returned from church, I saw Benoît depart quickly for a business lunch, leaving Eleanor and Sophie to clean the rooms and change the linens.

As I climbed the stairs and Eleanor descended with a basket of bed linen, our eyes met. In that fleeting moment something passed between us, an unspoken understanding, a recognition of the bond that was quietly growing. We held each other's gaze motionless as though time had paused. In her sparkling brown eyes, I saw not just the woman before me, but the depths of her soul and I sensed that she too was looking into mine. The connection was intense, transcending words, a silent communication that only we could understand.

Reality returned with the weight of the sheets in her arms, and I offered to help carry the basket. "Non," she softly replied, her voice gentle yet firm. It was not a refusal born of pride but a recognition of the delicate line we walked. The presence of Sophie and the fear of what she might report to her father dictated the boundaries of our interaction. Yet in that brief encounter on the stairs, I knew that our hearts had begun to speak a language all their own, one that neither Benoît nor the constraints of society could silence.

There comes a point before the foundation of a relationship is truly laid when two people of opposite genders begin to seek each other out with an unspoken urgency. They cross paths whenever fate permits, their hearts in silent accord, yet this behaviour carries its own perils especially in the confined quarters of the Hôtel du Théâtre. For Eleanor and myself, such encounters were fraught with danger. The watchful eyes of others loomed large, particularly those of Sophie, Eleanor's perceptive daughter, and Benoît, her husband, a man consumed by his need to control the wife he had coerced into marriage.

As a guest I navigated the delicate balance of propriety and desire. I dined in the small restaurant, had my room tended to and occasionally spread my plans across a vacant table downstairs, working there when the hotel was quiet. Through these daily routines both Eleanor and I went about our business, always mindful of the lines we dared not cross. Though our hands had never met with intent, though no words of affection had passed between us, I felt the weight of unseen eyes upon me and I was certain Eleanor felt the same. At times she would seem to avoid me unnecessarily, her manner distant and almost aloof. Yet I read this too as a sign of her deepening emotions, a subtle dance of caution and yearning.

My thoughts often returned to my lost wife Melinda, stirring a turmoil within me and the questions that arose were unsettling. Did I ever love Melinda as I now felt myself falling in love with Eleanor? I could not and indeed did not wish to answer. The circumstances of my life were so different now, the two women worlds apart and the very countries that shaped our lives distinct. I told myself not to dwell on comparisons, yet the feeling of guilt gnawed at me, particularly for my son Samuel, whom I had left behind. Living with his maternal grandfather and his nanny, Samuel had lost not only his mother but in many ways his father as well. What did my occasional letters mean to a child of five, nearly six years old? Very little, I feared. I had held him in my arms only a handful of times and I wondered, would he grow up to be like me? Would he inherit my traits, my flaws? I did not know.

As the hotel's guests came and went, none staying more than a few days, Benoît regarded me with growing suspicion. His interest in my work was minimal except for one evening when his role as a local politician compelled him to inquire about the railway's path through the town. To his probing questions I offered only vague answers for it was not my place to provide the details he sought.

A few days after that charged moment on the stairway, I found myself seated at a restaurant table unusually, for a midday meal. I had paperwork to attend to and had not gone out on site that day. Only one other guest was present and I remember the scene with perfect clarity. The sun streamed through the conservatory glass, warming the cooler interior of the restaurant. The heady scent of lemon blossoms from two large potted lemon trees filled the air, a fragrance so potent it was almost narcotic. Eleanor had prepared a meal consisting of boiled potatoes and small pieces of smoked ham covered with hot melted cheese. She brought it to me as I sat with my hands resting on the table. As she turned to return to the kitchen, she glanced back at me with a grace that took my breath away. In that moment as she passed, she allowed her hand to brush lightly across mine as it rested on the table.

It was as if a current of electricity had passed between us, if not physically, then certainly emotionally. The sensation remained long after her hand had left mine, similar to the resonance of a bell long after it has been struck. Eleanor smiled as she continued on her way, her head still turned towards me, a silent acknowledgment of what had just transpired. But beyond her I caught sight of Sophie who had witnessed the fleeting touch; she watched us with an expression I could not fully read. Had she understood the significance of what she had seen? Would she speak to her father about it?

That touch, though brief, echoed within me, a tremor that was both thrilling and unsettling. It was a sign and a confirmation that the bond between Eleanor and I was deepening despite the perils that surrounded us. In that moment I knew we had crossed an invisible line and with the human emotion of desire coming to the fore, I had no inclination of turning back from what may happen thereafter. In the stillness of the mid-afternoon, my room, ordinarily a haven of solitude, had often been left untouched save for the attentions of Eleanor or Sophie. Aware of the weight of their labours, I took to strewing my papers about the room in deliberate disarray, instructing Eleanor to leave it undisturbed two or three times a week even when I ventured out for site work. When first I took residence in the hotel, the care of my quarters fell by chance to either the mother or the daughter, but as the weeks passed it became Eleanor alone who tended to my needs.

In the days following the incident in the restaurant area, I kept to my room, poring over my calculations with a fervour that could not entirely suppress the restless stirrings in my chest. I had resolved to say nothing of my enduring presence within the room, allowing the door to remain unlocked, though it usually would be barred to deter any errant visitor. Two days had passed in such a manner when unexpectedly the door creaked open.

Eleanor, believing the room vacant and the door mistakenly left unbolted, had come to fulfil her chores. Her entrance was tentative and as she stepped inside her eyes widened in startled surprise upon finding me not only present but positioned just to the side of the door, my shirt unbuttoned at the collar.

In that charged moment impulse overtook reason. With a gentleness born of desire and passion I reached for her, my hand closing around her slender arm as I guided her further into the room, my foot shutting the door quietly behind her. She did not resist; instead, she lifted her gaze to mine and as though time itself had slowed down. I looked into her eyes and felt a thumping in my heart. Slowly we moved until our lips met, each of us surely thinking if the other would turn away before our first kiss. The first touch was electric, a spark that ignited within us both a longing that had been smouldering beneath the surface.

We kissed with passion, our bodies entwined and I could feel the delicate arch of her back as my hand slid around her waist, pulling her to me with a possessiveness that was both tender and urgent. My other hand found its way to the nape of her neck, fingers threading through the silken strands of her hair while our kiss deepened, tongues dancing with an eagerness that bespoke the urgency of our passion. Time lost all meaning as we became engulfed in that euphoric embrace, the world beyond the four walls of my room forgotten in the wake of the fire that burned between us.

Eleanor's hands, at first tentative, soon moved with purpose, slipping beneath the fabric of my shirt, the warmth of her touch spreading from my chest to my shoulder and down to my abdomen. Every movement, every breath, was charged with an intensity that threatened to consume us both. But just as swiftly as the moment had ignited it was over. Eleanor pulled away, her cheeks flushed. "I must go," she whispered, the urgency in her voice tinged with emotion. "Benoît is downstairs."

Before I could respond she had slipped from my grasp, the door closing softly behind her. I stood there rooted to the spot, the room now relinquishing the fading gem of her perfume. My mind swirled in confusion and doubt, questioning the boundary I had crossed, yet unable to shake the dreamlike state in which I found myself. The memory of her touch stayed with me as a reminder of the passion that had flared so briefly and intensely, leaving me to wonder if I had ventured too far.

Chapter 10

In the days that followed, my thoughts were entirely consumed by Eleanor. The remaining work on the railway would last no more than a month and I found myself reflecting upon what my next destination might be. Opportunities abounded across France; once a main line was laid, countless towns and villages clamoured for connection. A smaller branch line far from being mundane, often presented the greater challenge, particularly if it cut through the rugged terrain of mountains. Such landscapes required precision and stamina, unlike the gentle sweep of flat plains or the more forgiving valleys. Yet as the time for departure from Vienne drew near, so too did the inevitable separation from Eleanor and it was a depressing thought that gnawed at me. As our relationship stood, there would be no chance that she would follow me if I offered to take her away from the strained relationship with her husband Benoît Fournier. Then of course there would be Sophie who had to be taken into consideration. My thoughts were in turmoil as I projected to the future in what was no other than fantasy.

In every spare moment I spent within the walls of the Hôtel du Théâtre, my eyes sought out Eleanor. She too seemed to hold back wherever I went and we moved about the place with a quiet understanding as though drawn by some invisible thread. If she ventured into the courtyard where the linens swayed gently in the breeze, I would, when certain no one observed, follow. It was on one of these occasions that whilst in the courtyard we looked up towards the Pipet cemetery attracted by the vision of two orbs of light that shone brightly before they slowly moved and disappeared behind the gravestones. "What was that?" asked Eleanor. "No idea" was all I could answer. Our stolen moments, whether a kiss or the warmth of her arms around me, were brief but filled with a sense of eternity. In the solitude of my chamber, I left my door slightly ajar, no longer fully closed and in those silent hours she would pass by, finding some reason to enter. These moments were secret, fleeting but rich with the burgeoning of something neither of us could fully name.

Eleanor's character had started to change with her natural vivacity bubbling to the surface. It was clear we were falling in love with each other, and it was not long before the first signs of suspicion began to stir, for the happiness that is experienced when one is in love could not be concealed for any enduring time by our radiant faces. After an absence, brief but long enough to draw attention, Benoît, her husband, chastised her. "You spend too much time attending to our guest," he remarked, though at first it seemed he suspected nothing beyond mere politeness. Or so we believed. Yet Sophie, their daughter, ever observant and fond of her father, could not help but notice the subtle changes in her mother. Eleanor had grown more light-hearted, more at ease, and while Sophie could sense the shift, she did not question it, content in the belief that her mother's newfound happiness was a thing to be cherished.

It was on a fine Sunday morning that Eleanor, after attending church with Benoît and Sophie, informed her husband that she must tend to her Aunt Jeanne, who had fallen ill. The aunt, a senile woman of over ninety years residing across the Rhône in Saint-Colombe, had been growing increasingly feeble, and Eleanor, dutiful as ever, offered to prepare her a meal and offer general assistance in all homely matters that would concern an ageing relative. Benoît, ever inquisitive and perhaps more concerned for his own health than for Jeanne's, pressed her with questions, wanting to know more about the ailment that afflicted her aunt. It seemed his worry lay not in sympathy but in fear of infection. Eleanor, ever quick-witted, parried his concerns with a sharpness he was unaccustomed to. "I told you of these two days past," she said with a hint of reproach, adding that perhaps his frequent indulgence in drink had dulled his memory. It was not her usual tone, and Benoît, though startled by her firmness accepted the reply without further challenge, albeit with a growing unease. He could not recall the conversation if ever it had taken place but chose to let it pass.

The river Rhône, broad and swift, divides the communes of Vienne and Saint-Colombe in such a way that the two towns, though neighbours, exist with a distinct separateness. The bridge that spanned the river was their only true link, and once across, Eleanor could slip through the narrow streets of Saint-Colombe with little fear of recognition. It was at the Tour de Valois, a derelict relic of the fourteenth century that overlooked the river, that we had arranged to meet. Abandoned and half-forgotten, it had once guarded the crossing of the Rhône but now stood amidst a wild and overgrown garden surrounded by a high wall, its stones worn but resisting the passage of time. I had discovered this secluded spot during one of my solitary rambles and it seemed the perfect place for our secret encounters.

Eleanor first fulfilled her promise to her aunt, entering through the front door to prepare a modest meal and sit with her for a time. She then, in an act of foresight, left through the back door, slipping out into the yard unnoticed. It was fortunate she had done so for Benoît, mistrustful and now driven by suspicion, had followed her at a distance. Upon seeing her enter the aunt's home, his misgivings were briefly assuaged, and he turned back satisfied. As a man of some standing in both Vienne and Saint-

Colombe, it would not have been fitting for him to hide in the shadows spying on his wife. His reputation, ever a source of pride, demanded better.

I, meanwhile, awaited Eleanor at the Tour de Valois. The tower, though abandoned, possessed a certain melancholic grandeur, standing alone amidst the creeping ivy and tall unkempt grass. I had time enough to pace around its perimeter once before I saw Eleanor approaching, her eyes scanning the deserted path to ensure no one was watching. I walked ahead of her by several yards. Our movements were cautious so that any passers-by would see no connection between us. Once we reached the dense thicket that hid the entrance to the garden, we slipped inside, our hearts racing with the exhilaration of our clandestine meeting.

The overgrown path led us to the base of the tower where the grass grew tall and wild, untouched by any human hand for many a year. With foresight I had brought with me a blanket from the hotel, which I spread upon the earth so that we might sit and talk in the solitude of that forgotten place.

We sat upon the blanket laid out upon the grass which was flattened and cushioned beneath us. We absorbed the warmth of the sun, which added to our sense of wellbeing. We were alone in this deserted place, yet it was beautiful. The odour of the grass and fresh herbs crushed beneath us was like freshly scythed hay. Bees buzzed and butterflies settled on new spring flowers, savouring their nectar.

I turned to Eleanor, my eyes filled with a longing. "Eleanor," I whispered. My voice was choked with feeling. "I cannot bear to be apart from you any longer, my heart aches with a yearning that only your presence can soothe."

Her breath caught in her throat, her eyes glistening with unshed tears. "And I, Hartley, feel the same. You are all I want in the world."

With a tenderness that belied the intensity of my feelings, I cupped her face in my hands and leaned in, my lips brushing against her forehead in a gesture of pure adoration. Eleanor closed her eyes, savouring the sensation of my touch and the warmth of my breath on her skin.

My fingers traced the delicate contours of her face. Eleanor's heart raced and her pulse quickened with each caress. The world around us seemed to hold its breath as if it too was captivated by the beauty of our love.

I moved closer, my lips finding hers in a kiss that was both tender and passionate. It was a kiss that spoke of promises and dreams, of a future that we would build together. Eleanor responded with a fervour that matched my own, her arms wrapping around my neck as she surrendered to the depths of her emotions.

Our kiss deepened, our souls meeting in a dance of love and desire. My hands roamed down her back, igniting a fire within her that burned with an intensity she had never known. Eleanor's fingers tangled in my hair, her body pressing against mine as we let ourselves simply be and nature would show us the way.

Time seemed to stand still and the world faded away until only our love remained. Our hearts beat in unison, our breaths mingling as we shared a kiss that was both a declaration and a promise. It was a moment of pure unadulterated passion, a testament to the love that bound us together.

As we pulled apart momentarily, our foreheads rested against each other, our breaths coming in ragged gasps. My eyes bore into hers with intensity, my gaze filled with a love that was unwavering and eternal.

"Eleanor," I murmured, "you are the light of my life, the reason my heart beats. I love you with a depth that words cannot convey."

She smiled, her eyes shining with tears of happiness. "And I, Hartley, love you with every fibre of my being."

We sat there wrapped in each other's arms, our love a beacon of hope and joy. In that moment we knew that no matter what challenges lay ahead, we would face them together, for our hearts were united by a love that was timeless and true. From sitting, muttering a few words and kissing, we slowly laid back. Eleanor lay on her back and I on my side, resting on my left elbow. We were oblivious to the world around us as our lips connected again.

After we had known the fullness of our love, in that sacred union where passion and tenderness entwined, we lay upon the blanket hidden from the world by the soft embrace of the long grass. My arm cradled Eleanor's head and her breath was calm, as though even the air dare not disturb the sanctity of the moment. The distant murmur of town life reached us faintly with the occasional shout or the neighing and whinnying of horses from afar, but nearer still, the songs of birds in the garden and the low hum of insects filled the air. It was spring and the world seemed to vibrate with the same energy that stirred within my heart. Love, in its purest and most unguarded form, seemed to hang in the very air as though each blossom, each fluttering wing, bore witness to the joy of our newfound union.

It was through the worsening condition of Eleanor's aunt Jeanne that we were granted the opportunity to meet as we did with increasing regularity over the course of three weeks, no less than twice a week. Eleanor, ever dutiful, took upon herself the task of carrying her aunt's linens back to the hotel, ostensibly to aid her suffering kinswoman, yet in so doing she afforded Benoît the sight of her frequent comings and goings from Saint-Colombe, thus quieting any suspicion that might otherwise have arisen.

In these moments, Eleanor became an altered being, her manner, once subdued, was now gay, her spirit lifted to such an extent that she could oft be heard humming soft melodies as she went about her daily duties. The savage cruelty of her husband, his harsh words and the foul language that spilled from his lips after drink had mastered him, none of it troubled her anymore. What before had crushed her beneath its weight now seemed light as air and this newfound indifference vexed Benoît greatly. His authority over her, once total, now slipped from his grasp and the frustration of it all burned deep within him.

Eleanor could scarcely conceal her joy though she attempted to do so, for she spoke no word of her newfound happiness, yet her expression betrayed her. The light in her eyes and the flush upon her cheeks were enough to tell anyone who knew her that something within her had changed.

Where once she had borne her husband's amorous advances with a resigned indifference, accepting them as part of the marital contract to which she had been bound, she now recoiled from his touch. The thought of him stirred in her not the dull submission as before but a revulsion so great that she could hardly endure to share the same bed with him. Night after night she contrived excuse after excuse to avoid his embraces and with each refusal Benoît's fury grew, until he had convinced himself that I was the cause of her estrangement.

Indeed, Eleanor and I had already spoken in earnest of leaving together, of how we might accomplish it, when the time would be ripe and to what corner of the earth we might flee. Yet, for all our planning the moment came not by design but by crisis. I had stayed longer in Vienne under the guise of completing my work, seeking to prolong my stay at the Hôtel du Théâtre, though in truth it was only Eleanor's company that held me there. I had even made discreet enquiries about securing more permanent lodging in the area under the belief that I might remain near her unknown and unobserved.

But Benoît Fournier being a man of some standing in local affairs had caught wind of my plans, or so the rumours suggested, and it was known to him that I might stay on for work related to the railway, for Vienne lay advantageously at the heart of the region. Thus, when I departed for Lyon to meet with Paulin Talabot and his associates, celebrating the conclusion of my surveying work, collecting the salary that was due and a generous letter of reference, little did I know that matters at the hotel would take such a turn in my absence.

Upon my return the following midday, the scene that greeted me chilled my blood. Eleanor was nowhere to be found and Benoît was absent as well, whilst Sophie, their poor daughter, stood weeping uncontrollably and the hotel lay abandoned by all its residents. With great urgency I demanded of Sophie to tell me where her mother was and through her sobs she answered, "She is in the bedroom," as tears continued to stream down her face.

I hastened to the private quarters of the Fournier family and knocked firmly upon the door. At first there was no reply, but I persisted until at last I opened the door to find Eleanor lying upon the bed her body racked with sobs. The sight that met my eyes was one of unspeakable horror. Her clothes were torn and strewn upon the floor, her body mostly naked, her face bruised and her arms showing the marks of violence. I scarcely needed to ask what had happened, but the answer came unbidden. Benoît, drunk with wine and mad with jealousy had returned to the hotel the previous night and sought to 'correct' his wife in the only manner he knew, through brute force. Eleanor's cries had echoed through the halls, terrifying Sophie and driving away the remaining guests, who had fled at the break of day.

A great fury welled up within me and I demanded to know where Benoît had gone. Eleanor, through her tears, told me he had taken himself to the family vineyards further down the Rhône valley. She pleaded with me to leave, fearing for my safety should he return and find me there. She assured me that once his temper cooled things would return to their former state, though I knew full well that this was a false hope.

I pressed her. Did Benoît know of our clandestine meetings? She nodded, admitting that he had forced the truth from her and had sworn to kill me should he lay eyes on me again. My mind raced and I asked her what Sophie had seen of the assault. Mercifully, Eleanor told me that the worst of it had been concealed from the child who had not awakened until the screaming began.

Without hesitation I asked Eleanor if she could walk. She affirmed that she could, though her strength was greatly diminished and she walked with pain. "Then pack a few things," I commanded, "and tell Sophie to do the same. We must leave at once."

There is an efficiency to the urgency of flight and within a matter of moments we had thrown together what belongings we could carry. I left behind many of my possessions, bringing only what was necessary. Chief among them was my theodolite, the instrument of my trade. In little more than forty minutes we had departed from the Hôtel du Théâtre, though Sophie hesitated, torn between fear of her father's wrath and the child's love she still had for him.

Eleanor, her voice trembling, asked me where we would go and how we might survive without means. I reassured her that I had thought of where we might hide and had sufficient funds to sustain us for several months, provided we lived modestly.

"But we must be prudent," I warned her. "We cannot stay in expensive lodgings, and we must lay a false trail to confuse Benoît should he attempt to follow."

She nodded and we agreed that she would also take what money she could from the hotel as we departed.

Chapter 11

—

We fled, making a hasty escape from the threats that lurked behind us, taking a private carriage to the east bound for Bourgoin-Jallieu and from there continued by diligence to Lyon. Doubling back on ourselves we then headed southwards to Givors. Our route, though seeming erratic, was carefully chosen to confuse any pursuit. If Benoît Fournier sought to trace our steps I was determined to mislead him at every turn. By first venturing towards Bourgoin-Jallieu it would appear we were making for the Alps or the border with Italy or Switzerland. Then, by turning towards Lyon one might assume a journey north perhaps to Paris or England. Doubling back south to Givors would suggest the intention of vanishing into the heart of France possibly by way of the trains to Saint-Étienne. But my true aim was Bordeaux where I knew work could be found on the expanding railway network in that area and there, we could make a new life for ourselves.

Speed, however, was not our priority. Though it would be possible to traverse the heart of France in as little as five or six days by following the railway to Saint-Étienne and taking post coaches through Thiers, Clermont-Ferrand, Aubusson, Limoges and Périgueux, such haste would expose us greatly. Our primary concern was to escape the watchful eyes of Benoît Fournier without betraying our destination.

Eleanor, with a trembling voice, spoke of her husband's wrath, convinced that no force on earth could restrain his fury once he discovered our flight. Though I was less certain of the extent of his malice, I could not dismiss her fear as mere fancy – she, after all, had been married to him for more than ten years. The man had shown enough cruelty to leave no room for doubt about the darkness within him. I trusted my own strength and I knew that should it come to a contest of arms, I would hold my own, yet prudence whispered that no good could come from such a confrontation. For what man when obsessed by rage remains bound by reason?

He would not come alone of that much I was sure, and he would rally others to his cause, casting us as fugitives deserving no mercy. His mind, already twisted by envy and the need to subjugate, would scarcely be improved by the discovery that Eleanor and his daughter had vanished in his absence. I doubted affection played much part in his pursuit; it was not love that drove him but the desire to reclaim his possessions, to reassert his dominion. His pride, wounded and inflamed, would demand nothing less than to see us punished. Thus, the wisest course was to fade into the shadows, passing unnoticed through the lands where no man would think to search for us, and perhaps he would believe that we had escaped to England where he would know there was no chance of finding us.

The dangers of a direct passage through central France were diverse and grave. The roads were treacherous and the state of the diligences deplorable. Accidents were common, with carriages overturning from the loss of a wheel or the horses spooked on the narrow mountain paths. One could imagine the terror of losing control and being plunged into a ravine. Then there were the storms, the sudden torrential rains that turned the rivers into impassable torrents or bogged down the roads with thick unforgiving mud, leaving passengers to toil, pushing the diligence uphill as wolves lurked in the shadows. And then there was finally the threat of man. In the more isolated regions where industry and commerce had not yet arrived, lawlessness abounded and highwaymen prowled the roads, desperate men who had turned to robbery out of poverty. The dangers both natural and human of traversing the centre of France were too numerous to risk Eleanor and Sophie's safety.

After much deliberation, Eleanor agreed with my plan to take the river. Our course was set for Avignon and we secured passage aboard a paddle steamer at Givors under false names. We took great care in our deception, queuing separately and securing two first-class cabins, one for Eleanor and Sophie, the other for myself. Eleanor kept her face shrouded in a bonnet and her hands hidden beneath a shawl to conceal the bruises that might betray her. We resolved to keep to ourselves for the entire day's journey, avoiding all contact with other passengers as we glided southward towards Valence. It was imperative that we not be recognised, for we knew all too well that Eleanor's sudden flight with her lover had likely scandalised the whole of Vienne. The Hotel du Théâtre where she had lived as the innkeeper's wife must now have been alive with gossip; and under the Napoleonic Code, her defiance was no longer a scandal but a crime, adultery being punishable by up to two years in prison. It was not only her freedom at stake but mine as well, for aiding her escape would also cast me in a criminal light.

Though we had spent two days cleverly crossing eastward the départements of Isère and Rhône, north to Lyon and then south again it was still possible that someone in Vienne might recognise us when the steamer briefly docked there. We kept the porthole window curtains tightly drawn, maintaining vigilance as we passed by the town. I was somewhat alarmed when I overheard a conversation between a gendarme who had come aboard and the captain just above my cabin. The gendarme inquired about a man, woman and child travelling together and the captain pointed towards a family at the bow and the gendarme, satisfied it was not the people he was looking for, turned away. Just as the steamer pulled out of port, I risked a glance through the porthole and to my great unease, I spotted the old woman from Vienne at the same place on the quayside, the same who had observed me the day I first alighted there. She stood gazing directly at me with a smile upon her lips. She raised her hand in what might have been a farewell gesture, and a shiver ran down my spine. Who was she, how could she know? Was it mere coincidence, was she waving at someone she knew on the steamer or perhaps it was just the stress of the situation that had begun to unravel my senses?

Upon reaching Valence, I quietly approached Eleanor's cabin and advised her to remain within until we reached Avignon where we would disembark separately. During the half-hour stop and seeing no gendarme on the quayside, I ventured ashore to purchase some provisions, bread, pâté and fresh fruit for our onward journey. Sophie, for her part, had grown silent and subdued, likely confused by the secrecy surrounding our evasion. Her mother's bruises, still visible, were a painful reminder of the violence she had witnessed at the hands of her father. Keeping my distance from her, I believe, helped. She still looked at me with the wide-eyed shock of a child grappling with the ruin of her once-stable world.

At Avignon we took a series of stagecoaches bound for Toulouse, passing through Nîmes, Montpellier, Narbonne and Carcassonne. The journey though gruelling took us only four days, a considerable saving over the alternative of travelling by barge along the Canal du Midi, where numerous locks would have slowed our passage by nearly a week. We continued the pretence of separate rooms until Narbonne where we at last presented ourselves as a family. Eleanor and Sophie were instructed to remain quiet at the inns, feigning ignorance of the French language to avoid suspicion, whilst I spoke with my inevitable English accent. We were careful in every step, purchasing our diligence tickets separately, Eleanor and Sophie under assumed names, while I, as a gentleman, carried a passport signed by the Interior Minister. We believed and perhaps hoped that our elopement had not stirred enough attention to warrant a nationwide manhunt, albeit Benoît Fournier being a politician and from a well-known wine-making family would have long arms that could reach out widely. Though we had fled under duress, the eyes of the world, we prayed, remained fixed elsewhere.

At last we reached Toulouse and there we secured passage for the final leg of our journey, a steamer bound for Bordeaux along the River Garonne. The two-day voyage promised a welcome reprieve, offering both comfort and swift passage. With the dangers behind us now seeming distant, we judged it safe to travel openly as a family, reserving a single cabin for all three of us.

The boat itself, with its great paddle wheels churning the water, delighted Sophie, who, after hours of confinement in diligence and paddle steamer cabins was eager for freedom. She begged to leave and explore the deck above, her bright eyes filled with excitement at the prospect of walking under the open sky. Eleanor with a gentle nod permitted her to go, but reminded her to return before we reached Moissac, the next stop along the river and where the River Tarn met the Garonne. With eagerness Sophie disappeared through the door, leaving us alone.

As the door closed gently behind her, Eleanor turned the key in the lock, our eyes met and I reached for Eleanor's hand. My fingers found hers; there was no hesitation, only a mutual feeling that our connection had grown stronger.

She moved towards me, her body felt light as she settled across my lap and for a fleeting moment we laughed, a soft, nervous sound which was more a release from the anxiety we were experiencing than amusement. For though closeness eased the fatigue of our journey, the enormity of our actions remained as an ever-present reminder that the path we had chosen was fraught with peril yet bound by love.

When her lips first touched mine, it was as though time itself ceased to exist. The world beyond our cabin, the boat, the river, even Sophie's distant singing faded into oblivion, leaving only us suspended in a perfect stillness. Her lips were warm, soft, pressing against mine with the lightest of touches. The kiss was at first innocent, merely a brush of mouths, tentative and sweet. Yet beneath that initial gentleness lay something deeper, a quiet current that swelled with each passing second.

I felt her lips part slightly and with that small motion, a deeper desire unfurled between us. My own lips responded, parting in kind, and our tongues met, not with haste but with a slow deliberate tenderness. Her tongue, tentative and warm, moved against mine in a way that made my breath catch. It was an offering, a wordless invitation that I accepted with equal care, letting our movements flow with the same quiet grace that had defined our short time together.

As our tongues intertwined the kiss deepened but without urgency. There was no rush, no desperate need to consume one another, only the slow deliberate exchange of feeling of longing. The warmth of her mouth, the softness of her touch created a connection so profound that words would have been an intrusion. We were communicating through the kiss, each movement a quiet conversation, each gentle stroke of her tongue against mine a promise of something deeper than mere passion. It was as though in that intimate moment our very souls were meeting, exchanging vows in the silent language of touch.

Her hand soft and trembling slightly came to rest on my cheek. Her fingers traced the line of my jaw and in that simple gesture I felt her give herself to me completely and without reservation. It was a gift, one that stirred something deep within me and as her lips remained on mine, I let my hand drift downward, moving with the lightest touch to her skirt. Slowly almost imperceptibly I allowed my fingers to find her leg, caressing her skin with a gentle circular motion just above the knee.

At that Eleanor pulled back slightly, her lips parting from mine, her breath shallow. Her eyes, wide and filled with something unspeakable, searched mine for a moment. Then with a sudden urgency she took my hand in hers and guided it higher, her fingers pressing over mine with a growing intensity. There was no need for words. The quickened pace of her breath, the way her body tensed beneath my touch, spoke louder than anything she could have said. Her need, her longing had built to a crescendo, and with a soft almost inaudible sigh she showed me how that tension might be released with her body softening as she let go.

When the moment passed, Eleanor leaned forward and kissed me once more, this time with a tenderness that seemed to thank me for understanding without needing explanation. Her hand now resting in my lap moved lightly exploring me as though seeking to know the effect she had wrought. Her fingers lingered, teasing, until she smiled with a mischievous glint in her eyes. "You will have to wait," she whispered, her voice low and playful, "keep it ready for me."

From the cabin we could feel the slight pleasant vibration of the giant wheels of the steamer as it churned through the water, the engine also providing a background hum that did not cause us to raise our voices to be heard. I suggested to Eleanor that we ought to find Sophie, whose absence though brief now felt too long. Eleanor, ever capable of swiftly turning from passion to practicality, regarded me with that familiar expression of hers, a slight affectionate movement at the corner of her lips as though she had already distanced herself from the intensity of what had just passed. She had a remarkable way of moving fluidly from one emotion to the next, not out of coldness but out of a practised grace that I was only beginning to understand.

With an alertness that belied the moment we had shared, she stood and smoothed her dress, her movements swift and decisive. "Let's go," she said simply, her voice steady as though the brief spell of intimacy had been folded away, carefully preserved for another time.

We stepped out of the cabin together and the cool breeze from the river greeted us as we ascended to the deck where Sophie no doubt awaited lost in her own innocent excitement, unaware of the world that had shifted so profoundly in the cabin below.

We arrived in Bordeaux on the 12th of June 1852. My time in Vienne had lasted but four months and yet those months seemed to span a lifetime. So much had transpired, not least of which was the affair with Eleanor and the very thought of her gave me a sense of mellowed happiness. But other duties now beckoned and among my foremost tasks was the writing of a letter to my son Samuel in England. Though too young to read at the tender age of five, I trusted his grandfather George Lowe would gladly undertake the task of reading it to him. Samuel in three months' time would reach his sixth year, and though distance separated us, my thoughts were ever with him.

As we disembarked from the paddle steamer at the bustling quay, our first concern was to secure lodging, a hotel perhaps or a modest guest house. We needed time and space, particularly for me as I intended to explore opportunities for work in the city. Rumours had spread far and wide that the government was soon to grant a concession for the railway line extending southward to Irun on the Spanish border. With such prospects in mind, I resolved to call upon the offices of the British Chamber of Commerce at the earliest opportunity.

The port of Bordeaux was busy with activity, with the cries of merchants and the clatter of carts on the cobbled streets. It reminded me of my first arrival in France at Le Havre. Then, some three and a half years ago, I had been overwhelmed by the noise and confusion, by the unfamiliarity of everything. But now having become fluent in the language and well-adjusted to the customs of French life, I felt at ease with the country, with its people and most of all with Eleanor. The thought of returning to England held no allure; I could live here forever if fate allowed.

With my theodolite by my side my skills as a land surveyor were much sought after and I had earned a reputation for accuracy and precision. Such qualities commanded a fair price, and I hoped they would serve me well here in Bordeaux. By the next morning, we had secured furnished rooms a kilometre from the city's bustling centre found through the local newspaper *L'écho des locations*. It was cheaper than a hotel and afforded us a welcome degree of privacy, free from the comings and goings of strangers. The rooms were rented by a widow whose husband had perished at sea more than a decade previously. Eleanor with a mixture of truth and discretion had confided in her that she had fled from her husband in Lyon due to the violence he had inflicted upon her. The widow, a sympathetic soul, asked no further questions, especially after noticing the faint bruises that still marred Eleanor's face.

The following day I took to the streets of Bordeaux, walking along the riverbanks where the commerce of the city was in ceaseless motion. The river, the lifeblood of the port, brought ships from all corners of the world and it was plain to see that trade sustained every aspect of the city's thriving economy. My steps led me to 2 Place de la Bourse, a grand square overlooking the Garonne, where I sought the British Chamber of Commerce. I had in mind to gather information on the railway developments in the southwest, and at eleven o'clock the next morning I found myself seated before Mr William Bennett, a man of considerable administrative experience though perhaps somewhat lacking in spirit.

Mr Bennett, a white-haired gentleman with a stiff collar that seemed to pinch at his neck, greeted me with the resolve of a man who had long been accustomed to the intricacies of paperwork. His office was a labyrinth of documents piled high on his desk with rows of dusty books lining the shelves behind him, some seemingly untouched for years as evidenced by the cobwebs that clung to the highest corners. Though his voice was a monotone and the heat of the day pressed in through the windows making concentration a struggle, the information he imparted to me was of great value.

I briefly recounted my work in England and since October 1848 my work in France, including my recent departure from Vienne and I expressed my intent to continue as a land surveyor in the southwest. Mr Bennett, after offering a few general remarks on the region, directed my attention to the Pereire brothers Émile and Isaac, prominent financiers and industrialists of Jewish descent, locked in a fierce commercial rivalry with the Rothschild family. The brothers, he informed me, were poised to establish the 'Compagnie du Chemin de Fer du Midi', which would oversee the construction and operation of railway lines throughout southwestern France.

Intrigued by this information I made my way to 13 Place de la Comédie, a short walk from the chamber, where the offices of the Pereire brothers were located. Upon my arrival, however, I found the building deserted, this being the customary hour for 'déjeuner', the French midday meal. Not to be deterred, I returned shortly after two o'clock and enquired at the reception. A small officious man greeted me with an air of irritation and after some difficulty in understanding my accent, he informed me that I could not simply walk in and expect an audience with either Émile or Isaac Pereire. I was advised to write a formal letter of request and wait for a reply, a process which as he pointed out could take a month or more as the brothers were often away on business in Paris or Toulouse, but they would receive the letter upon their return to Bordeaux.

Unwilling to leave matters to chance and remaining unconvinced by this attitude, I purchased writing materials from a nearby shop and composed a letter of introduction at a café across the street. I was resolved to wait and observe who might come and go from the building, hoping to catch sight of one of the brothers. Not long after, my patience was rewarded. A gentleman of unmistakable distinction appeared, making his way towards the offices; his tall dignified bearing and carefully groomed appearance marked him as a man of importance.

It gave me the opportunity to return to the offices a few yards ahead of the gentleman but not so close as to appear rude by cutting ahead of him. A doorman opened the door and I proceeded again to the reception desk holding in front of me the letter I had just written. In a thoughtful manner as the door was being opened once again behind me, and wanting to be overheard, I addressed the same man at the reception desk, asking if he would be good enough to give the letter to Messieurs Pereire upon their return from Paris. Advancing the letter slowly in my hand but also keeping a firm grip on it. The effect was instantaneous. From behind me a voice said, "Antoine to whom have you said that I am away in Paris?"

Antoine muttered and blushed, but by not speaking clearly it allowed me the time to turn and introduce myself, briefly explaining the purpose of my visit and to hold out the letter I had written less than two hours previously.

The gentleman then introduced himself as Isaac Pereire and was intrigued enough to invite me into his office. There I met his brother Émile and the two listened as I detailed my work on the Lyon to Avignon railway under Monsieur Talabot. I spoke of how I had reduced construction costs through careful surveying, and though their faces betrayed little, I sensed their interest.

The conversation took a curious turn when Isaac Pereire asked about my religious background, to which I replied that I was a Quaker. This seemed to strike a chord with him as he shared the experience of marginalisation due to his Jewish heritage. After a brief pause, he revealed that the surveying work south of Bordeaux had already begun, extending as far as Labouheyre and beyond, but the section from Dax to the Spanish frontier at Irun remained to be done.

Although I carried a letter of recommendation from M. Talabot, Isaac Pereire was cautious. He proposed that I spend a week with their chief surveyor in Pessac before they made any final decision. I readily agreed, hopeful that this would mark the beginning of a fruitful collaboration.

The arrangement with the Pereire brothers filled me with a renewed sense of purpose. I took my leave of their office, heartened by the prospect of securing the employment I had sought which would afford me the means to provide for Eleanor and Sophie with a modest though not extravagant degree of comfort. The task ahead was significant. I was to prove myself in the coming days for the week in Pessac would be my test and I was determined to rise to the occasion.

Returning to our rooms that afternoon, I found Eleanor resting by the window, the late light of the day casting a warm glow across her face. She looked up at me, a faint smile playing upon her lips, though her eyes remained thoughtful.

"How did it go?" she asked, folding her hands neatly in her lap, her voice as steady as ever. It was a tone I had grown accustomed to, composed, always searching for a hint of what lay beneath my outward confidence.

"It went as well as could be hoped," I replied, settling myself in the chair opposite her. "I am to spend a week with their chief surveyor in and around Pessac. A test of sorts before they make any final decisions."

Her smile widened though it was tinged with that familiar mix of relief and concern. "Then you will be leaving soon?"

"Yes, tomorrow at first light," adding, "if I am accepted, we will need to travel a little further south, probably to Dax and Bayonne."

She said nothing further, but her gaze drifted out towards the street below. There was a silence between us, one I could not fully read. Eleanor had grown quieter since our arrival in Bordeaux, and though I had assured her that our future was being set in motion, I knew that there remained a degree of uncertainty. Her past, the wounds of her life before we met still cast a shadow upon our present. Though we had fled from her oppressive husband, I feared that his hold over her might never fully cease. I crossed the room and stood beside her, placing a hand gently on her shoulder. "Do not worry, Eleanor. Once this work is secured, we shall make a life here, one free from the past." She looked up at me, her eyes softening. "I know," she said quietly, though her tone betrayed a deeper hesitation. "I only hope that here it holds the promise you believe it does."

The following morning, I left for Pessac. The journey was short and I arrived at the small office where the chief surveyor, Monsieur Gaspard Delacroix, awaited me. He was a man of middle age, stout and serious, his grizzled beard betraying years spent in the field. He wasted little time with pleasantries, preferring instead to lay out the work ahead. We would begin by inspecting the ongoing survey lines south of Bordeaux, ensuring the accuracy of the measurements taken to date. The Pereires, he informed me, expected nothing less than perfection.

The week passed in a flurry of activity. From dawn until dusk I worked alongside Gaspard Delacroix and his small team, trudging through the thick woodland and marshy lands that stretched southwards. The work was gruelling but invigorating. Each measurement taken, each marker placed, felt like a step towards solidifying my place in this new venture. Delacroix, though reserved, eventually warmed to me, acknowledging my skill and precision in the field. By the end of the week, he confided that he would send a favourable report to the Pereires, recommending my hire for the remaining stretch of the line from Dax to Irun.

At the end of the week, weary but satisfied, I was greeted by Eleanor with a mixture of relief and pride. There was a serenity in her expression that had not been present before as though the time apart had given her space to reflect on our new path. She asked few questions about the work itself, content with the knowledge that I had succeeded in proving my worth.

It was only a matter of days before I received official word from the Pereire brothers. A letter arrived at our lodgings delivered by hand bearing the unmistakable seal of the Compagnie du chemin de fer du Midi. My heart quickened as I broke the seal and read the contents. I was to be employed as their principal surveyor for the Dax to Irun line, with work beginning in earnest within two weeks, giving us time to find a place to live.

That evening as I sat with Eleanor, the letter resting on the table between us, I felt for the first time in months a true sense of peace. The uncertainty that had weighed upon us since our departure from Lyon began to lift. I had brought with me a box too large to fit in a pocket and I offered it to Sophie, who looked at it with a broad smile stretching from ear to ear. What a sweet satisfaction it is to bring a little happiness into the life of a child, especially one already aware that the trials of life begin long before adulthood. Without further delay, Sophie tore away the outer wrapping with some haste, revealing a box of handcrafted chocolates made by local artisans. Turning her sparkling eyes towards me, I told her to enjoy them in moderation so as not to fall ill. Her first gesture of generosity was to offer one to her mother and then another to me.

I then took from my pocket a small package which I handed to Eleanor. She looked at me with curiosity, her head slightly tilted to one side. Sophie came over and watched as her mother held the small box in her delicate hands. I encouraged her to open it and when she did so carefully, she discovered a ruby stone resting on a silver necklace. Eleanor leaned towards me and gave me a passionate kiss of thanks. Sophie helped her clasp the necklace around her neck, as Eleanor declared that she would always wear it and never take it off as a token of the love that bound us together.

In the days that followed I busied myself with preparations for the task ahead. The line from Dax to Irun would be a challenging one, cutting through varied terrain, from the marshland known as the 'Barthes', the floodplain of the river Adour, across the bogs of the 'Marie d'Orx', crossing the river Adour at Bayonne to the rugged foothills of the Pyrenees, finishing on the French side of the border at Hendaye. I felt ready, bolstered by the success of my work in Pessac and the confidence placed in me by the Pereire brothers.

As for Eleanor, she seemed to find solace in the quiet rhythms of our few days in Bordeaux. And Sophie was starting to accept me, freely asking me questions of the life I had left behind in England, although surely, she was torn at being separated from her father, for however Benoît Fournier had mistreated his wife, he had never lifted a finger against his daughter.

Chapter 12

We embarked upon our journey southward, venturing deep into the département of Landes, a region whose very name in French conjures the image of expansive moors. Unlike the elevated and rugged terrain of England's Pennine chain or the dome-shaped Dartmoor moors, these stretched for a hundred miles close to sea level, vast and flat, their sandy soil lying in wait to trap the unprepared travelling on wheels. It was ill-advised to make the passage by diligence for the narrow wheels of the coach often sank into the soft sand, meaning progress would be laborious and slow.

In readiness for what we hoped would be the final stage of our journey, the matter of appropriate clothing and provisions pressed upon us. With the heat of summer nearly upon us and winter to follow, which though milder than the harsh cold of the north, winter near the Atlantic coast would surely bring much wind and rain, much like the moors of my native Devon. I imagined it to be damp and blustery, though perhaps spared the biting chill I had long grown accustomed to. With mules and horses now to bear our burdens, it became clear that the cumbersome trunk and holdalls which once rode atop the diligences would prove ill-suited to such a mode of travel. Thus, before leaving Bordeaux, the trunks and holdalls were sold off to merchants who no doubt saw in them a promise of journeys yet to come. In their stead we procured sturdy oiled canvas saddlebags well-suited to endure the elements and to hang easily upon the backs of our mules. We retained, however, our beloved carpet bags, those faithful carriers of smaller necessities which could be lashed securely to our mounts. So it was that, with two mules burdened with provisions and another reserved for Sophie, Eleanor and I each took to horseback, the open road ahead and the promise of an uncertain but hopeful future calling us onward.

The journey to Dax would take us four days, though it could be made more swiftly. Yet I wished to take my time, meeting along the way the other surveyors in the employ of the Pereire brothers. Moreover, by travelling at a leisurely pace we spared our animals from undue strain, avoiding the need for frequent changes and in the stifling humid heat we wisely refrained from pressing on during the fiercest hours between noon and three o'clock in the afternoon.

The département of Landes has a reputation as being the most desolate in all of France, not only in the scarcity of its inhabitants but also in the harshness of its landscape. The sandy expanses, particularly the coastal dunes, are reminiscent of the distant Sahara and much of the rest of the land is dominated by swamps and moors. Where the land rises slightly there are small groves of pine, but agriculture is nearly non-existent, the ground being too marshy and flat with no natural means for the water to drain away. Sheep-rearing is the principal occupation of the few hardy souls who make their lives here and the sight of the shepherds moving across the land on their tall stilts clad in sheepskins provided Sophie with endless amusement. She expressed an eager desire to try walking on stilts herself, but we assured her that such an adventure could wait for another day.

Each evening, we took our rest in the simplest of lodgings, post houses and rustic inns. Monsieur Isaac Pereire, anticipating our arrival, had sent word ahead ensuring our welcome at these modest establishments. At Labouheyre, about midway between Bordeaux and Dax, we were met by one of my French colleagues, Gustave Leroy, a man of genial disposition and a few years my senior. Gustave was kind enough to explain the challenges we would face in our work. First and foremost, he explained the issue was one of drainage. Without proper measures the waterlogged land would render the railway bed unstable. Secondly, there were no stones to be found until Dax some sixty kilometres away, which made reinforcing the track a laborious affair. Finally, the mosquitoes, those incessant summer pests, would surely be the bane of our existence for they descended in swarms, relentless and voracious.

As we rode on, the rustic charm of the local houses caught our eyes. These timber-framed dwellings, their vertical supports filled between with clay and straw, spoke of a simple yet enduring way of life. Eleanor, ever curious, asked Gustave why, with the sea so near, there was so much standing water. His answer was enlightening. The coastal dunes, driven by the ceaseless winds from the ocean continually shift and move, blocking the rivers and forcing them to carve new paths to the sea. Thus, great lakes such as Biscarrosse, Léon and Soustons now lie inland, their waters trapped behind the towering dunes, remnants of riverbeds long forgotten.

Gustave graciously invited us to dine with him that evening at his home where his wife Celeste and their four children, ranging from two to eight years, welcomed us with open arms. Celeste was a busy woman, tending not only to her brood but also to an assortment of ducks, geese, rabbits and hens, and cultivating a bountiful kitchen garden. It was there in their warm and lively household that I tasted foie gras for the first time, a delicacy I found exquisite. Eleanor, more accustomed to such fare from her time in Vienne, smiled knowingly as I savoured each bite.

That night Eleanor and I were given a room of our own, a rare and cherished privilege. The day had been oppressively hot and the evening had not yet brought a welcome coolness for the air was humid with the promise of a storm. We left the shutters open, draping the mosquito netting over our bed for protection. As we settled in, the distant rumble of thunder reached our ears, growing louder with each passing moment. The sky, which had glowed bright orange and red before the sun's setting, was now swallowed by thick clouds and a warm wind began to stir, sweeping through the house and rattling buckets in the yard. A sudden flash of lightning startled Eleanor and she clung to me, burying her head against my chest. In the brief illumination her form was revealed, silhouetted beneath the thin fabric of her nightdress. The heavens opened wide, releasing a deluge of rain in an incessant downpour, drumming fiercely upon the roof and drowning out all other sounds from the yard below. I rose from the bed, moved by the sudden chill in the air to pull the shutters closed but left the window slightly ajar, allowing the cool breeze and the fresh scent of rain to circulate around the room. The night felt alive, charged with the energy of the storm and as I turned back the flicker of the candlelight caught my eye.

There in the dim glow Eleanor stood revealed. Her nightdress lay discarded over the chair, forgotten in the warmth of the room and the heat of our shared moment. She beckoned me with only a subtle movement of her body, an invitation, lifting the edge of the sheet with a grace that stirred my heart. I slipped beneath it, the cool linen in sharp contrast to the warmth of her skin. Her body pressed close to mine confirming the desire that existed between us. The rainfall outside continued to fall steadily, a perfect contrast to the rhythm of our quiet, urgent movements.

In the cool darkness we became lost in each other and the storm outside was forgotten as we found our own. Every touch, every breath, seemed amplified in the quiet stillness beneath the sheets, leaving only the two of us entwined, our hearts beating in time with the distant thunder. As the storm's rage slowly ebbed, we had each found our peace, falling into sleep with our limbs still wrapped around each other, the remnants of the rain a soothing lullaby to our night's passion.

When morning dawned, the freshness and scent of damp earth prevailed and a fine mist clung to the land, veiling the trunks of trees while their crowns stood clearly visible above the fog. As we descended the stairs, Celeste greeted us with a hearty breakfast of toasted bread, homemade jam, eggs and strong coffee. Sophie, ever the sound sleeper, had been entirely unaware of the storm and she chattered excitedly with the other children over their meal. An hour later after a brief conversation with Gustave about work in the following days, we took our leave, feeling that in this remote corner of France we had made friends of true worth.

Our journey southward resumed and though the road was long and straight, cutting through monotonous stretches of moorland dotted with the occasional group of pine trees and cork oaks, the quietude of the landscape afforded me time to think. As I swayed in rhythm to my horse's pace, my thoughts turned to practical matters. Where should we settle while I conducted my surveying work? It was clear that I would need to move frequently but Eleanor and Sophie could not be expected to uproot themselves the whole length of the railway line. I also thought about the idea of enrolling Sophie in school, though it was unlikely that any classes for girls would be found in such a remote region. Perhaps private lessons in reading and writing could be arranged and I could take it upon myself to teach both Eleanor and Sophie English, should our future take us to England. Yet whenever I raised the subject, Eleanor would dismiss it with a wave of her hand, insisting that the language was far too complicated and that her fluency in Italian, learnt from her parents, sufficed for all her needs.

By late afternoon we crossed the river Adour on a bridge of unique design and the imposing Château d'Ax came into view, a fortress that once housed the powerful Dukes of Aquitaine and boasted a history reaching back to Richard the Lionheart. Massive walls surrounded and protected the town of Dax. We had been directed to lodgings near the Fontaine Chaude, a natural hot spring renowned for its hot mineral waters, and Sophie, with her persistent youthful energy despite the day's journey, eagerly led the way to the bubbling basin. Though the water could scald one if it was held there for too long, the sight of it, gushing forth from the earth through brass lion heads, fascinated her.

We resided in Dax for over four weeks, during which time I began my survey of the land, seeking the best route for the railway. My exploratory work took me as far as the foothills of the Pyrenees where I crossed many rivers and streams flowing north to meet the river Adour. So, the railway station it seemed would be best situated on the north side of the river at Dax and continue on the north side where the terrain was easier to traverse and a bridge could be built nearer to Bayonne before eventually continuing south to meet the border town of Irun.

During this time Eleanor and Sophie found work at one of the thermal establishments in town for Dax had been known since Roman times for the healing properties of its hot springs. I heard the tale of the Roman soldier who, in despair, had thrown his lame dog into the river to drown, only for the animal to emerge miraculously cured by the warm mud on its banks. Such were the legends that drew rheumatic sufferers from far and wide to this quiet town, seeking relief in the mineral-rich hot waters.

Our stay in Dax gave me ample time to reflect on our future. Eleanor and Sophie were content here and it seemed wise for them to remain while I travelled to complete my work. There was talk of grand projects to drain the entire département of

Landes, transforming it into a vast man-made forest to become the largest in Europe they said. If such an undertaking were to come to fruition, it would provide work for surveyors like myself for a lifetime. The timber from this future forest would be transported by rail to Bayonne and Bordeaux, fuelling the growth of the region. Yet as my work progressed and travel to and from our lodgings in Dax took longer, it became clear that we would need to move nearer to Bayonne.

Chapter 13

An integral part of my duties was to meet with the *maires* of the communes through which the proposed railway line would eventually pass. This task was preceded by correspondence initiated by the associates of the Pereire brothers, ensuring that my arrival would not take the local officials by surprise. Etiquette required that I introduce myself to the landowners and explain the nature of my work, which was often with a certain measure of suspicion. I would indicate with perhaps a slight embellishment of the truth that several routes were under consideration. The reactions I encountered varied widely from those who eagerly sought to profit from the railway's intrusion into their lands, to others who opposed it with fervour, and lastly to the few who appeared uncertain or indifferent, struggling to comprehend the implications of such an undertaking.

It was during this period after I had discreetly made it known that my family sought more permanent lodgings, that I was approached by Monsieur Pierre Garnier, a local *maire*. He informed me that a miller had passed away some months prior, leaving vacant a modest mill on the banks of the Boudigau, a stream which drained the marshes of Orx. The estate's owner, a certain Madame Marguerite Dufour, had as yet found no successor to the mill, nor anyone to inhabit the adjoining house, and Monsieur Garnier suggested that perhaps she might be persuaded to let the property to us.

Upon visiting the premises, I found the house to be a humble one-storey wooden structure, its simplicity offset by the air of quiet repose that surrounded it. The dwelling comprised a single spacious room at its heart, dominated by a vast stone hearth, large enough to accommodate a small adult within its embrace. This fireplace not only served as a place of warmth but also as a stove for cooking, and the table positioned before it bespoke of evenings spent in quiet companionship. On either side of the main room were two bedrooms, one on each side, with the addition of a modest pantry and a small storage area. A broad strip of fabric hung around the fireplace, a rustic solution meant to protect the room from gusts of wind that might send smoke billowing back down the chimney. After a brief inspection I informed Madame Dufour that the house seemed agreeable to me, though I wisely reserved final judgement until Eleanor could see it as well and partake in the decision.

Madame Dufour, a woman of considerable refinement in at least her sixtieth year, carried herself with the unassuming grace of one who has long presided over both family and estate with measured authority. Her silvered hair neatly gathered beneath a lace cap framed a face of pale delicate complexion, softened yet dignified by the passage of time. Her attire, a sober dress of fine material, bespoke her position without ostentatious display. She wore a simple yet elegant dress made of fine fabric which reflected her status without arrogance. Her speech indicated a thoughtful intelligence, revealing a dedication to the land she had cared for over the years and the sense of responsibility that came with it. At the mention of Eleanor's inclusion in the decision I observed a softening in her manner; it was evident that she appreciated the gesture, perhaps finding in it a reflection of her own values as I made clear that Eleanor's counsel was not to be excluded.

A few days later I returned with Eleanor and "our daughter" Sophie to inspect the house more thoroughly. Though the residence had accumulated a fine layer of dust since the miller's demise, it was in all respects suitable for our needs. We agreed upon the terms of the rental and Madame Dufour, true to her station, insisted that a formal contract be drawn up. During the course of our negotiations, it was further agreed that Sophie would assist with the household tasks while Eleanor would offer her help as circumstances required.

The contract, beyond settling the matter of monies, also granted us the use of the surrounding land for the keeping of small farmyard animals and the millpond, abundant with fish was likewise available for our benefit. However, it was stipulated that the mill itself was to remain untouched should a future miller wish to restore it to working order. Given that Sophie would likely spend a good deal of time in Madame Dufour's company, we deemed it best to be forthright regarding our family situation, preferring to reveal the truth ourselves rather than leave it to the conjectures of a sharp-witted girl soon to turn eleven. Madame Dufour, however, proved to be both discerning and discreet. She quietly confided to Eleanor in tones touched with amusement that our secret was evident to anyone with eyes to see. "It is plain," she whispered, "in the manner with which you and your gentleman regard one another that you are not a married couple, neither is he the father of your ten-year-old child."

Thus, in Madame Dufour we had found not only a landlady but perhaps a sympathetic ally, one who would hold our confidence with dignity.

And so, we settled into our first home which was modest in size but with it held the sense of new beginnings for us both. For those furnishings we lacked, Madame Dufour in her generosity, provided us with from the ample stores of her grand country house. The task of unpacking our meagre possessions was quickly accomplished and I set up my theodolite on its tripod near the entrance doorway, mindful to place it where it would stand far from the clumsy reach of a passing arm and in a position to be easily cleaned and prepared for its next day's use.

It was only a few days until Christmas and I made haste to light the first fire in the hearth using the dry wood neatly stacked beneath the overhanging eaves on the leeward side of the house. The wood had likely been cut by the late miller and though more would soon be needed, it sufficed to warm us through those first days in our new abode.

That evening we sat around the sturdy oak table, Eleanor, Sophie and I, our first meal prepared over the roaring fire, a meal made more substantial by the gift of a plump duck from Madame Dufour. The crackling of the fire mingled with the soft clink of cutlery and as the shadows of evening deepened, we found ourselves in that comfortable silence which follows a well-savoured meal, filling the belly. The fire, though still strong began to settle into a smouldering glow and the room, now lit by only two candles, took on an air of intimacy. The flickering light danced across Eleanor's face, casting a soft luminescence that reflected in her eyes, bright and warm.

As the hour grew late, Sophie, her eyes sleepy with the day's exertions, excused herself to bed. Eleanor and I exchanged a glance, one of those wordless communications known only to those who have shared much. Her head dipped in a small nod as I winked and we too rose to retire, each carrying a candlestick to light our way. As was our custom I undressed first and slipped into the bed, choosing to lie on Eleanor's side to warm the sheets for her. When she joined me, she surprised me with a soft whisper, "Close your eyes."

When I was finally allowed to open them there, she stood before me, her figure framed by the candlelight, clothed in a delicate knee-length nightdress of the finest translucent silk. She had purchased it in Dax, no doubt as a secret indulgence and now she wore it with a playful elegance that made my heart quicken. The soft glow of the candles carefully placed behind her amplified the effect, casting her in a shimmering light. She stepped onto the bed, standing above me with a grace that made the moment feel almost sacred.

"Shall I blow out the candles?" I asked, my voice low.

"No," she replied with a smile that sent a thrill through me. "Let them burn out on their own, tonight they will keep us company."

Madame Marguerite Dufour called upon us two days after our arrival to see how we had settled into our new house. During the course of her visit, she extended a kind invitation to join her for a Christmas evening dinner on Friday the 24th of December, an event she confessed she was accustomed to spending alone most years past. Unsure at first how best to respond, I accepted with gratitude, sensing that to decline might be thought of as a rebuff. As for a suitable token of appreciation, Eleanor suggested we bring chocolates and Sophie, eager to contribute, decided to make a drawing of Madame Dufour's house. To procure chocolates involved a ride to Bayonne, a journey of some three hours on horseback, but the ride back to Dax would have taken an hour longer.

The evening of Christmas Eve was cold as we walked the short distance to Marguerite Dufour's house, and we were welcomed warmly. As we were led into a large room, I noticed a branch from a pine tree with ribbons and dried orange slices lay across the mantel. The table at which we would sit was draped in white linen and was set with rustic ceramic plates and pewter cutlery. In its centre an oil lamp gently flickered over a bowl of walnuts, and from the kitchen came the savoury scent of roasting meat and herbs. We sat and talked for a while before being served with garbure, a robust cabbage and bean soup with pieces of duck. It was accompanied by thick slices of warm country bread, and we shared a pungent sheep's cheese wrapped in chestnut leaves.

Madame Dufour had roasted a fine goose for the occasion, its skin browned and crisp, served alongside potatoes roasted in duck fat and a stew of wild mushrooms, ceps from the forest she told us. A dish of cardoons baked in a creamy sauce accompanied the meal; it was new to me, but delicious. We raised our glasses of wine, a deep red from Madiran, in a modest toast to the season.

Dessert came in the form of a golden tourtière made of dried apple slices rehydrated in Armagnac until tender and fragrant, and a local almond tart, its pastry paper-thin, scented with lemon and vanilla. Sophie was served a second helping of almond tart by Marguerite Dufour, having refused the Armagnac-soaked tourtière.

We ended the meal with dark coffee in small cups and a glass of walnut liqueur beside the fire. Outside the wind sighed against the shutters, but inside there was warmth, laughter and the subtle wordless ease of good company.

It was a humble gathering, unadorned and without ceremony, yet it moved me more deeply than many grander occasions I have known. Here in this quiet corner of France on a winter's night we were made to feel not like strangers but friends.

It was the following week we had occasion to meet Monsieur Marcel Dufour. He was estranged from Madame Dufour, a separation marked not by formal decree but by his preference for living differently. He passed by the house occasionally though few had laid eyes on him, and he had retreated into the woods some years ago, preferring the company of animals and nature to the social duties and comforts of domestic life. He lived by his wits and the fruits of the land, hunting, fishing and foraging in the forests, rather than returning to the refined world into which he had once married.

Monsieur Dufour was a thin, weathered man in his late fifties, clearly shaped by a rough lonely life in the forest. His clothes were old and patched, his once-dark hair was now grey and thin, sticking out from under a worn-out hat. His face was tough and wrinkled from years of sun, wind and rain, showing he no longer cared about appearances. His eyes were sharp but wild, hinting at how his long time away from society had worn away any traces of refinement. He seemed strong but indifferent to the finer things in life as if he had given up on ever returning to the world he'd left behind.

From the first Eleanor and I could not help but feel a vague unease in his presence. Though he said little, there was a disquieting intensity about him, a sense that his eyes were ever watchful from behind the trees, tracking our movements as though we were interlopers on the land. His infrequent appearances and silent observations did little to ease our nerves, and after some time we spoke of our concerns to Madame Dufour.

She responded with a calmness born of long acquaintance with the peculiarities of her estranged husband. "Yes," she said with a wry smile, "Marcel is sometimes seen in the shadows, he has lived that way for many years and though his ways are strange you must not fear him. Think of him rather as a guardian. He watches over the estate in his own manner. There have been occasions in the past when poachers or vagrants with ill intentions have been driven away by his hand. He protects what is still, in his mind, his."

And so with this curious reassurance we accepted that Monsieur Dufour would be part of our lives here. A silent sentinel lurking in the woods, watching over us not as a threat but as a strange guardian of the land. The house and its grounds began to feel more like home with each passing day.

Even though Madame Dufour's words gave us some comfort, we still could not shake off the feeling of unease. In December the days had become much shorter and the new year of 1853 showed no perceivable difference in the lengthening of daylight hours. Winter seemed to fill every corner of our small house.

The cold brought a deep silence, and as it got dark each day, we began closing the shutters as soon as the light started to fade. The heavy wooden shutters made us feel safer as if they could protect us from the darkness outside, a darkness that felt like Monsieur Dufour was always watching us whether he really was or not.

Whenever my duties carried me farther afield, I made it a point to return home each evening even if it meant riding for two hours through the twilight or sometimes deep into the night. There was something about the familiarity of home, of Eleanor and Sophie waiting by the fire, that made the weariness of travel vanish the moment I stepped through the door. When the necessity arose for me to report back to Bordeaux, I would often bring Eleanor along if the weather was calm and the journey promised to be pleasant. Cap-Breton, a small but lively port, was but an hour's walk away and from there ships sailed regularly to Bordeaux. The journey, though reliant upon the whims of wind and tide, was generally swift, and anywhere from eleven to twenty hours away depending on the vessel and the mood of the sea.

On such occasions Sophie would stay behind, often in the company of Madame Dufour at her grand house. It was during one of these absences that Sophie confided in us upon our return, her voice tinged with the thrill of youthful adventure, that she had ventured to the edge of the forest she told us, and there hidden among the trees she had encountered Monsieur Dufour. He had beckoned her deeper into the woods where he revealed to her the secret places of the woods, the hidden nests of sleeping animals and pathways known only to those who live by the rhythms of nature. He had even shown her how to tickle trout in the millpond, his hands deft and patient as he demonstrated the art of quiet waiting. Sophie spoke with particular fascination of the tame rabbits he kept that he culled when the need arose, their soft fur a contrast to the rough life of the woodsman.

At first Eleanor and I were alarmed by this growing rapport between our daughter and the wild man of the woods. The image of our young Sophie being drawn into the forest alone with Monsieur Dufour stirred a deep unease within us, an unease we could not easily set aside. We approached Madame Dufour once again with our concerns, half expecting her to share in our worry, but she only smiled, her eyes hiding an expression that eluded us.

"Ah yes," she said, "Marcel has always had a way with children. Many from the village have visited him in the woods over the years. He delights in showing them the wonders of nature and they often leave with a small token, a pet rabbit perhaps or a rabbit's foot for luck. He is harmless, I assure you; if anything, he regrets never having children of his own and that I believe is the real reason he withdrew from society. It wounded him deeply not being able to have a family."

Her words were meant to be comforting and to some extent they were, but still Eleanor and I resolved to remain vigilant. We could not afford to rely entirely on the reassurances of a woman who, though kind-hearted, had long since made peace with her husband's eccentricities. The forest held its secrets, and while we had not been given any reason to doubt Monsieur Dufour's harmlessness, there was an undeniable strangeness to his ways that kept us on guard.

Eleanor for her part found a new joy in the freedom our life here afforded her. Unlike the stifling expectations she had known with Benoît at Vienne, here she was beholden to no one. We lived as equals much as I had once lived with Melinda, my first wife, during our brief marriage before her demise. The climate of the Landes, though more variable than the Rhône Valley, was gentler in winter. The cold, although it could sometimes be biting, was often broken by bursts of unexpected warmth. On sunny Sundays we would sit outside in a shaded spot basking in the rays of a low winter sun that seemed to hold the promise of spring even in the depths of January. But when the winds howled and the rain beat against the shutters, we would shut ourselves in, retreating to the comfort of our bedroom and secure in the knowledge that no one would disturb our peace.

Our love deepened with each passing day, the flame between us undimmed by the trials of daily life. We cherished the stolen moments of intimacy, the quiet glances that conveyed more than words ever could. Our passion was not the reckless fire of youth but a slow-burning flame, steady and warm, that gave us both a sense of belonging. In each other's arms we found not just pleasure but refuge, and as the old year of 1852 gave way to the new year of 1853 and then to February, I saw my work nearing completion. The railway construction had begun in earnest stretching out from Dax towards Bayonne and with it my duties at Bayonne were drawing to a close.

One late evening I returned home to find Eleanor in an unusually disquieting mood. Her voice when she spoke was tinged with an unfamiliar seriousness. She bade me sit, her expression unreadable in the dim light of the fire. For a moment I feared the worst but then she spoke the words that would change everything: she was with child. She had known for some time, she confessed, but had waited to tell me until she was certain.

For a moment I could not speak. Eleanor, ever watchful of my reaction, seemed tense, her eyes searching mine for any sign of disapproval. In England an unmarried woman with child would be a subject of scandal, often sent away to a workhouse or worse. Here in France, we knew not what the repercussions might be but none of that mattered to me. I smiled, unable to contain my joy, and before I could utter a single word Eleanor leapt into my arms, her face alight with relief and happiness. We kissed long and deeply, our way of sealing a wordless vow.

Later that evening Eleanor mentioned another curiosity. Someone had been adding firewood to the pile beside the house. She had not seen anyone do it and neither had Sophie, though the girl's smirk suggested she knew more than she let on. We both guessed it must have been Marcel Dufour quietly tending to us in his peculiar way.

In the nights that followed we occasionally heard shouts from the forest with Marcel Dufour's rough voice echoing through the trees. We knew he was keeping watch, driving off poachers or other scoundrels who might seek to trespass on the land. He may have been estranged from Madame Dufour, but he guarded her estate with the fierce loyalty of a man who, though forgotten by society, had never forgotten his own sense of duty.

Chapter 14

Upon the following Sabbath, the 13th February 1853, the heavens opened, unleashing a torrent of rain and the wind howled with savage force, driving in from the sea as though nature itself had conspired against my journey, for I was summoned back to Bordeaux to the Compagnie du Chemin de Fer du Midi, bearing the last of my surveyed plans and detailed notes later in the week. There could be no consideration of boarding a ship from Cap-Breton, for the tempest had driven all vessels into the safety of their harbours, seeking refuge from the fury of the ocean. My only recourse and the swiftest now available was to undertake the arduous journey on horseback. By maintaining a steady gallop and exchanging steeds at the post stations, I calculated the journey might span two days in each direction. A day would of necessity be consumed by the formalities of my meeting. Alas, the days were still brief and to press onward through the night in such conditions would be folly, for any hope of haste would be made impossible by the perilous roads.

Having bid a tender farewell to Eleanor and Sophie, I set forth into the storm's unrelenting fury, and as the hours stretched into days, the skies offered no mercy. The storm grew fiercer with no sign of a reprieve. I became restless, my thoughts consumed by the urgency to complete my business and return to the comforts of home. The journey had been long and hard for half of the distance. Thereafter, the storm, although severe, spared me the worst of its wrath. Among those present at the meeting was Monsieur Isaac Pereire who upon our assembly's conclusion, extended to me the offer of further employment. I expressed my interest though tempered it with the sentiment that I could not yet uproot my family, not so soon after we had settled in the marshlands of Orx between Dax and Bayonne. Monsieur Pereire being a man of understanding nodded thoughtfully. He remarked that the Emperor Napoleon III had grand designs for the département of Landes, a vast endeavour that would begin with a survey of the land and culminate in its drainage. I affirmed my willingness to serve, and he assured me that word would be sent in due course.

The return home proved to be again a gruelling ordeal, worse by far than my northward journey for the storm had grown in both ferocity and breadth, wreaking havoc on the land. Trees once proud and tall now lay broken across the sodden sandy trails, their limbs twisted and torn by the relentless winds. Those still standing had their branches stripped from them, sent hurtling through the air as dangerous projectiles. The marshlands had become a morass of flooded streams with bridges rendered impassable by the deluge. My heart was heavy with worry for Eleanor and Sophie for they might not yet have comprehended the sheer scale of the catchment area that fed into Lake Orx. Only the Boudigau River served to drain the flooded marshes and I feared that even the venerable old mill might be imperilled by such unprecedented weather.

What should have been a two-day ride home extended into four torturous days, and it was not until dusk on the fourth day that I finally approached the estate of Madame Dufour, a full eight days since my departure. Neither was it possible to send word to Eleanor, assuring her of my delayed return. The road was deserted save for the occasional eerie rumble of thunder and the crack of lightning illuminating the dismal sky. The rain, driven almost horizontally by the tempest, stung my face like icy needles as I pressed onward. Upon reaching the estate, the path was obstructed by fallen trees and I was forced to dismount, tethering my horse to a branch before proceeding on foot. The wind howled in my ears; the estate shrouded in an ominous gloom as I trudged towards our little abode. The sky, a dull slate grey, seemed to press down upon the land and the rain lashed at me in relentless sheets, blurring the world around me. The storm's fury had reduced visibility to a mere few yards ahead, but then something strange caught my eye.

With dread mounting in my chest, I cast my gaze towards our house. The front door swung open on its hinges, banging with each gust of wind, and the chimney emitted no smoke even though night was fast approaching. A queer sensation of unease settled over me. Where were Eleanor and Sophie? Perhaps, I reasoned, they had taken refuge with Madame Dufour in her grand house, fearing the floodwaters would overrun our modest home by the mill.

I hastened towards the house. I paid little heed to my surroundings as I entered, consumed with worry. My heart leapt into my throat as I caught sight by the fading daylight of a chair upturned and cast carelessly across the floor, but before I could take another step I felt a presence behind me. Someone was behind the door. There was no time to struggle, no time to think, only a swift descent into blackness.

The next sensation was that of an animal on the nape of my neck. The storm had abated and all was calm. As I attempted to move my head the creature made its escape – a rat, I thought to myself, as I opened my eyes and looked around. My vision was blurred, but with a feeling of shivering cold I saw my legs were still in water. Recollections were slow coming to me as I tried to understand my surroundings and how I had got there. It was then that I realised I had neither seen Eleanor nor Sophie, and with a strenuous effort I pulled myself out of the water, the millpond by the mill. The realisation hit me that someone had tried to kill me. Strength then surged through my body, I know not how, and I returned to our home. The door was open; I shouted but no one answered. I searched the bedrooms, and finding no one, I made my way to Madame Dufour's house.

Limping and with blurred vision I thought at first that my eyes had settled on a broken tree limb which was blocking my passage, tossed to the ground by the previous night's tempest, but as I drew closer a sickening realisation dawned on me.

Lying crumpled upon the sodden earth, half-covered in a waxed cloth overcoat, was the unmistakable outline of a body. I stopped in my tracks, the breath catching in my throat, and fear gripped my chest. I hurried forward, kneeling by the body, and with trembling hands I carefully pulled the coat away from the face.

What met my eyes was a scene more gruesome than I could have anticipated. The face once full of life was now a ghastly mask, half-obscured by blood that had streamed from a deep gash along the temple. The features were twisted in a final grimace of pain and a sickening red rivulet had snaked down the cheek. The eyes were closed but the stillness of his form left no doubt: it was Marcel Dufour and he was gone.

I recoiled for a moment, shaken by the horror before me, then leaned closer to examine him. The wound on his head was severe, the angle and depth of the injury suggesting that the bough of the oak tree lying a few feet away had struck him with force as it was ripped from the trunk by the storm as he had presumably passed beneath. I remained somewhat surprised as I looked upon the slain body on the ground that a woodsman could have been caught out in such a way. What could he have been doing out in the open in such weather? Perhaps, I thought, the house of Marguerite Dufour had suffered some damage, or

Marcel was fearful that it was a possibility and he was making his way there.

I rose to my feet, my eyes fixed on the body of poor Marcel. The violence of the storm had masked whatever had transpired here, and the truth of it, I feared, was buried beneath layers of mystery that the storm had only helped to conceal, for Marcel lay some feet away from the bough as though he had summoned a little energy to raise himself up, walk a few steps and then fall face down, sprawled on the ground with a definite finality, a position from which he could not rise. A creeping sense of unease settled over me. Perhaps this was not an accident and Marcel had been killed and placed by the tree just as I had been knocked unconscious and presumably thrown into the millpond to drown during the storm.

With my head filled with worry for Eleanor and Sophie, and my vision blurred, I stumbled towards Madame Dufour's house, falling upon steps some distance from the front door.

When next I awoke it was late afternoon, though I had little grasp of time or place. My vision was clouded and a sharp pain throbbed in my skull. Dim voices reached my ears as I attempted to stir, but a nurse clad in the uniform of her station laid a gentle hand upon my forehead, urging me to remain still. I tried to speak but my throat was dry, my words faint and unintelligible. A doctor standing nearby issued instructions I could barely discern, his voice drifting in and out of my conscious state.

In the confusion of my agitated mind my thoughts turned to Eleanor and in that moment, I saw her face, clear and radiant, standing at the foot of the bed. "Hartley," she whispered, her voice as soothing as a lullaby. "Do not trouble yourself with worry. I am here waiting for you." Her image stayed with me, framed by the strange distortion of my vision before darkness reclaimed me and I fell once more into a deep dreamless sleep.

It was not until the following morning that I awoke with any sense of clarity. Four figures stood at my bedside, their faces indistinct as I struggled to sit up. A sharp pain seared through my head and I winced. "Give him a little laudanum," the doctor commanded and I felt the nurse's gentle hands giving it to me and soon after I succumbed to the drug's soporific effect.

Sometime later as my senses gradually returned, I blinked into the dim light of the room, my eyes falling upon Marguerite Dufour who sat nearby and a stern-looking gendarme. They seemed to wait patiently yet expectantly as though I held the key to some riddle they sought to unravel. The gendarme broke the silence first, his voice echoing in my head.

"What do you recall since your return from Bordeaux, monsieur?" he asked.

Summoning what fragments of memory I could gather, I recounted the sequence of events: the journey through the storm, the harrowing obstacles along the road, the approach to my house and opening the door. I think I was attacked there for I awoke in the mill pond and with some difficulty returned to the house to look for Eleanor and Sophie before making my way to Mme Dufour's house. On the way I found Marcel Dufour who was dead a few feet from the bough of a large oak tree.

"That is all I remember," I said, my voice hoarse. "What of Eleanor? Where is she?"

Marguerite Dufour hesitated; her eyes cast down as though she bore the weight of a truth she dreaded to impart. At length, she spoke.

"She has left, monsieur," she said softly, her voice almost drowned by the rain that still tapped upon the window. "She departed of her own accord with her husband and Sophie. He came to fetch them."

A sharp denial burst from my lips, unbidden. "No, that cannot be. I saw her, not long ago, just here, in this very room."

Marguerite shook her head gently. "No, monsieur, you did not, she was not here."

Before I could protest further the doctor interjected, his voice calm though it did little to soothe my disquieted mind. "You suffered a grievous blow to the head. Such injuries can often produce vivid hallucinations. It is not uncommon."

"But…" I began, my thoughts whirling in confusion when Marguerite handed me an envelope.

"She left this for you," she said quietly.

I took it with trembling hands with a growing sense of dread. The letters swam before my eyes, my vision still clouded and my mind not yet fully clear. "I cannot read it," I murmured, holding the letter out. "Will you—?"

The gendarme stepped forward, taking the letter with the solemnity of an official act. He cleared his throat and began to read, and the words cut through the air like a blade:

"Hartley,
I have decided to return to Vienne.
My husband has come looking for me.
He forgives me for what I have done.
Sophie is happy to see her father again.
Do not attempt to follow me for I have no desire to rekindle what once was.
Return to England to your son who needs you more than I ever did.
I am sorry to envelope the news this way.
Eleanor"

A silence heavier than stone settled over the room as the gendarme folded the letter and handed it back to me. I stared at it, unseeing, as the meaning of those cruel words struck me with all the force of the storm that had passed. My world, once so precariously held together, crumbled in that moment. Eleanor, my dearest Eleanor, gone by her own hand and with her Sophie whom I had come to love as my own. My vision blurred not from the blow to my head but from the welling tears in my eyes.

I clung briefly to the hope that this was all some terrible dream. Surely Eleanor would never write such a cold brief note, it was not her way. She was thoughtful, deliberate, and this letter felt hasty, alien, as though dictated by some force beyond her control. I recoiled from the thought, yet it lingered like a ghost in my mind. Could this be true? Could she have truly left me so abruptly, so coldly, having announced only days before that she was expecting our child?

I forced myself to speak though my voice was hollow, the question emerging from the fog of my disordered thoughts. "When did Eleanor leave?"

Marguerite answered with care, her eyes direct and without sympathy. "Eleanor and Sophie departed the day after you left for Bordeaux. Her husband, Monsieur Benoît Fournier, arrived at my door seeking them. I called for Sophie who had been here in the house for the last two days. Upon seeing her father she ran to him with joy, crying out, 'Papa, Papa'. He lifted her into his arms and he told her they were going home. I believe Eleanor was already in the carriage by that time for I did not see her."

The words struck me anew; Eleanor had not even waited for me to return. She had left without a word, without even the courtesy of an explanation beyond the short letter I now clutched in my hand. My thoughts reeled, desperate for answers.

"And where was I found?" I repeated, seeking some grounding in the madness that swirled around me.

"After the storm subsided," Marguerite began, her voice laden with sorrow, "I went outside to survey the damage. That is when I found poor Marcel – he had been struck by a tree much like yourself, though his injuries were fatal. He had suffered a grievous blow to the head similar to your own. You were between where Marcel lay and the front of the house here but I could not move you myself so I hurried into Labenne to fetch the doctor and the gendarme."

Her words settled into me as I tried to make sense of the words. I had not been struck by a tree, I awoke in the mill pond, I insisted, as though thrown there by some malicious hand. My mind raced, piecing together fragments of memory, the feeling of having been attacked, the poachers we had heard days before I left, could it be connected? I was sure I had been assaulted and left for dead. How else could I have found myself on the edge of the mill pond? And what of Marcel? Had he suffered a similar fate or could it all be mere coincidence?

The gendarme, sensing my thoughts spoke once more. "We found aquatic vegetation on your person when you were found so it is probable that somehow you entered the water. There are no further questions, monsieur," he said with a finality that felt oppressive. "The death of Marcel Dufour will be recorded as accidental and as for you, rest now and recover your strength."

Marguerite, her voice gentle but firm, added, "You may stay here a few days longer, Mr Grisdale, until you are fully recovered."

Yet there was an unspoken meaning to her words. Though kind, they were formal and spoke of the desire for me to leave as soon as I was able. And why wouldn't she? In their eyes, I was the man who had disrupted a family, stolen another man's wife and caused turmoil in their peaceful lives. It didn't matter what had truly transpired, for in their minds, I was the one to blame. Benoît Fournier had come for his family and now that they were gone, I was an unwanted reminder of that upheaval.

But my mind was far from settling on guilt or shame. I was consumed by questions and questioning my reason. How had Benoît Fournier found us? How had he known where to come so precisely, just as I was away? Why had Eleanor left so suddenly? Her letter, its coldness, its brevity, it all felt wrong. I had spent enough time with Eleanor to know that she was not a woman who acted so rashly, nor would she abandon me with such little thought.

And then there was the matter of Marcel. His death, so similar to my own injury, filled me with unease. The night noises we had heard before, the distant cries in the woods, were they more than just poachers? Had he stumbled upon men more dangerous without realising it? I could not shake the sense that someone had intended to harm us. My head throbbed but it was not just from the physical pain of being attacked, it was also the mystery of these unanswered questions and the nagging feeling that something else may have happened.

"I need to sleep," I muttered, though the idea of sleep seemed impossible.

Marguerite nodded and rose from her seat signalling for the others to follow her. As they left the room, the doctor gave me a final look as though trying to assess the state of my mind as much as my body. When the door closed, I was left in silence.

I lay back on the bed, staring at the ceiling, trying to piece together the fragments of my thoughts. Had Eleanor really left of her own free will? Or had she been forced? Was Benoît's sudden appearance truly a coincidence or had he known where we were all along? And if so, how?

The more I pondered the more the letter in my hand began to feel like a lie. Something was terribly wrong, I needed answers but the very people who could provide them were now gone, leaving me with nothing but suspicions.

Chapter 15

Feeling increasingly unsettled by the prolonged stay at Marguerite Dufour's country house, I quickly took my leave and returned to the home I had shared with Eleanor. Yet as I crossed the threshold it became clear that the house was nothing but an empty shell, a hollow structure drained of life and warmth for its ambience was no more; it had departed with Eleanor and Sophie. In their absence the once-vibrant home stood desolate and stripped of its soul, reduced to mere walls and wooden beams. Their laughter and their presence had been the spirit that animated it; now, all was gone, and the silence of the rooms gripped me in a way that was impossible to ignore.

I stayed there for two days more, an eternity in which I tried to gather the shattered fragments of my thoughts. I was a man undone, struggling to comprehend the sudden and inexplicable end to the life I had begun to build with Eleanor. Surely, relationships do not wither away in such a manner. No, in the natural order of things only death, cold, irreversible death, separates souls with such finality. And yet here I was, left not by death's hand but by a swift and unanticipated desertion.

Eleanor had not been pretending; I was sure of it. The happiness she exuded during our time together, the joy that radiated from her in moments of shared intimacy, I had felt it deeply and it had felt true. She was no fragile or capricious woman easily swayed by passing whims. Rather she was a woman of substance rooted in the earth, practical both in mind and heart. Her words had always been straightforward, her actions clear, her intentions unwavering. In the few months I had known her she had given me no reason to doubt her sincerity – only a few days before, she told me she was with child, my child, and yet she had left me.

    I recalled the stories she had told me, of the forced marriage and degradation; I had witnessed myself the results of her brutal beating, the life she had endured with Benoît Fournier. She had confided in me that her marriage had been a sacrifice to protect her parents, immigrants from Italy who faced imprisonment or expulsion. It was not a union of love but one of grim necessity. Even so, when I met her in Vienne, I saw in her a woman who had, with quiet fortitude, accepted the cards life had dealt her. Perhaps in the end, the prospect of returning to a semblance of family unity, despite the past, was not a burden too heavy for her to bear. Perhaps she had decided for Sophie's sake that the sacrifice was worth making. And yet my heart rebelled against such a conclusion. The Eleanor I knew had found in our time together a spark of freedom and of joy that she had not known in her marriage. How could she have cast it aside so easily? The letter she had left behind so brief and cold was a far cry from the woman I had come to know and love. I was forced to confront the truth that she was gone, that whatever bond we had shared was severed. I had no choice but to summon the strength to face this new reality, painful though it was.

    I had already known loss, having buried my wife Melinda a little more than five years previously, a woman I had loved in a different way and yet the pain was no less acute. Memories of Eleanor clung to me like a heavy mist and I knew that to dwell on them would only deepen my sorrow. I resolved then to look forward, to leave this place behind me. But before I departed, I scoured the house, hoping against hope that some clue remained, some trace of her that might offer a different explanation for her sudden departure.

Eleanor had left behind many of her clothes as well as personal items she had cherished. Sophie's garments too were abandoned as though their departure had been hastily executed. It was easy to attribute this to the approaching storm and Benoît Fournier's hurried explanation to Madame Dufour. But another darker possibility gnawed at my mind. How had Benoît found us so quickly? Was it mere coincidence that he appeared just as I had left for Bordeaux? The noises we had heard in the nights before my departure, had they been more than the careless trespasses of poachers? Could they have been the sounds of men in Fournier's employ, watching and waiting for the moment to strike? Had Marcel Dufour witnessed something and been silenced for it?

I recalled the sensation of entering the house and then nothing until I found myself in the millpond with the storm abated. That was no figment of my imagination – the gendarme or the doctor had found aquatic plants upon me. Someone had been there, of that I was certain. The answer was clear: Benoît Fournier had surely not come alone, he had accomplices. It seemed likely that one of them had used my theodolite, which I found damaged, as a weapon to strike me down. The eyepiece was missing and despite my search in the house and about it, it was nowhere to be found. The blunt force of the instrument must have rendered me unconscious, after which they had cast me into the millpond, assuming surely that the storm would finish the work they had begun.

I gathered a few of my remaining possessions, including the broken theodolite, though it would need repair before I could return to my work. With a heavy heart I bade farewell to Madame Dufour, offering her my gratitude for her hospitality. Her response, though polite, carried the subtle undertone of a request for my swift departure. I understood, for I had no desire to prolong my stay in a place with such a sad memory where I felt a curse had been laid upon me.

Thus, on Friday 4th March 1853 I set out for Bordeaux, making my way northward with no haste and little purpose. Upon my arrival, I visited the offices of the Compagnie du Chemin de Fer de Midi, where I left a brief message for the Messieurs Pereire, informing them of my decision to return to England. There was nothing left for me in France, no work that could distract me from the emptiness that now filled my heart.

I might well have chosen to take the stagecoach back to England, returning with the swiftness of those cumbersome yet reliable conveyances, but instead, I resolved to journey on horseback, yearning for the solace of open skies and untamed paths. There were many moments along the road when my thoughts compelled me to turn my horse eastward with the maddening temptation to seek out Eleanor, to follow her delicate elusive shadow wherever it might lead. Yet what purpose would such a course of action serve? Should I pursue her and to what end would my journey draw me? She had made her decision plain, conveyed in a note of few words; it was both brief and cruel in its finality. She had returned to her husband for Sophie's sake, she had written. It was for the sake of that innocent child whose happiness she held dearer than her own. And if that be the case, what right had I to impose myself upon their lives anew? To arrive unbidden, a spectre from the past, would surely cast me into a deeper abyss than the one in which my soul already dwells. For am I not already a victim of that most merciless archer, Cupid, whose arrows pierce the heart with a force that no man can bear lightly? I, whose love, passionate and unyielding, has been kindled and then extinguished by the same cruel hand of fate that took Melinda from me. And what is love, if not a battle within the soul, an endless strife between desire and duty, between emotion and reason?

To pursue Eleanor, knowing she has returned to the embrace of another, would be to inflict upon myself the tortures of a love lost with no hope of resurrection.

And so I pressed northward away from the beckoning east, away from Eleanor, but my heart wavered, caught between the allure of impossible dreams and the cold reality that awaited me. The road wound through desolate landscapes, barren as the future that stretched before me, and with each passing mile, I grew more accustomed to the silence that enveloped me, for solitude was my only companion.

The journey though long and at times perilous offered a kind of grim respite. The solitude rather than oppressing me, seemed to relieve me of the need to mask my pain. I had no audience here but the wide sky and the unfeeling earth. The trivial chatter of strangers with their inconsequential tales and petty concerns no longer grated on my ear. Indeed, my own sorrows were more than sufficient, and I had neither the strength nor the will to engage in the woes of others.

The road stretched endlessly before me, as did the path of my life. Where it would lead, I could not say, for at first, I had no destination in mind other than escape from the memories that haunted me and from the love that could never be. Alone I rode onward towards the first port where a boat would take me home to England, my dark thoughts consuming my being, and eventually, in the fading light as the cold north wind whispered through the trees, came a strange sense of peace. A peace of resignation of a man who has to accept his fate. I would find my son and devote my life to his future.

Chapter 16

I had reached the final pages of Hartley Birkett's memoir. The endnote which was curiously placed at the beginning was dated 1871, yet Eleanor had returned to her husband in 1853, meaning a gap of nearly eighteen years remained unexplained. I noticed also the ink colour was slightly different, a browner shade of black, and the writing, whilst still sloping to the right in a beautiful script, looked a little larger. Perhaps, I thought, if it was written towards the end of his life, with failing eyesight his writing style would have evolved. I also thought about the missing time – had Hartley stopped writing after his affair had ended and he then returned to England? Had he completed this memoir just before his death? Or perhaps other volumes existed, left with other descendants waiting to be discovered.

My next step was to revisit the ancestral records, hoping to find traces of Hartley Birkett after 1853. This meant combing through the census records from 1861, 1871 and 1881, maybe even 1891 if he had lived that long. But once again, I found nothing. As I had speculated earlier, either he had deliberately erased himself from history, the digitised records may be incomplete, or he had never returned to England at all. The last option was improbable because his diary and theodolite were found in Alice Farnsworth's loft, but how long had they been there?

I searched through the invoices tucked away in the wooden box, remnants of everyday transactions, but they were disappointing. They merely documented sales of fruit, vegetables and eggs without names of buyers or sellers. Each document was a dead end, a reminder of the elusive nature of my ancestor and the bills could even have been put there by someone else at a later date. Investigating Hartley's descendants felt like an overwhelming and uncertain task given how far-flung and distant they might be. I resolved to take a DNA test through the ancestral research site, hoping to narrow down potential relatives. But that would take weeks if not longer to yield results with no guarantee that reaching out to anyone would necessarily produce a reply.

One option still remained: going to France and tracing my ancestor's footsteps. I wondered if there were any clues left to be found. But with the summer drawing to a close and my lecturing career resuming in September, I could now only go during the Christmas holidays. Ann of course had more family obligations over Christmas than I did, and I preferred to go alone anyway.

When I shared my plan with Ann the following month, she reproached me for not inviting her. Despite being swamped with her own family's Christmas plans, she offered me a half-hearted invitation to join them if I wanted, though I sensed she wasn't particularly bothered whether I accepted or declined. Reluctantly I also offered to book her a flight so she could join me in France, but she declined also, saying the dates I proposed didn't work for her.

So, I resigned myself to spending Christmas Day with Ann, her ageing parents and a sibling of hers in the UK, then fly out from Teesside airport on Boxing Day and transfer through Amsterdam. I preferred the smaller quieter airport of Teesside even if it cost a bit more. Manchester Airport was an experience I loathed for too many reasons to count.

I gave myself four days between Christmas and New Year to delve into Hartley Birkett's early life in France. I was eager to see if the hotel where he had once stayed was still standing. Perhaps it was fanciful, but I imagined myself wandering through the very rooms he had occupied. I also hoped to find equivalent French websites with census information and perhaps a library in Vienne where I might dig through old newspapers or archives. My French was passable though slow, so I decided to brush up over the next couple of months, taking the easy route, immersing myself in subtitled French films and YouTube videos instead of committing to night classes for an A-level I neither wanted nor needed. I probably had the equivalent knowledge already to get by in spoken French, lacking only French literature which I didn't require.

As the autumn evenings drew in, I found myself increasingly obsessed with online searches looking for Hartley, Eleanor and Benoît Fournier, though I uncovered little of value. Each hour spent delving into Hartley's life, Eleanor's choices and Benoît Fournier's shadowy presence heightened my conviction that visiting France was imperative. Ann on the other hand wasn't so thrilled. Whenever she stayed over, she would find me glued to the computer, poring over old documents. She began to accuse me of becoming obsessive and boring by always bringing up my research. Gradually her visits grew less frequent, with fewer overnight stays.

By the time Christmas arrived tension between us was deepening, especially when we spent the day with her family. Her sister, brother-in-law and parents who exchanged wary glances could also sense it. The absence of spoken words is often more telling than words spoken in disagreement. I had already packed my bags, ready to leave for Teesside airport the following morning. The early departure necessitated nearly a two-hour drive plus parking and check-in time. Consequently, it curtailed my alcohol consumption on Christmas Day to avoid driving over the legal alcohol limit on Boxing Day.

Early the next morning I felt invigorated as I stepped into the biting cold. It would be dark for another four hours and a sharp wind was accompanied by rain and sleet. I dreaded the possibility of snow across the Pennines on the A66, but the journey unfolded without incident. I parked at the airport and made my way through check-in with time to spare. The flight to Amsterdam was aboard a KLM Embraer that began its flight turbulently, climbing over the coastline of the North Sea, but it smoothed out once we had climbed above the clouds, then daylight broke just as we landed. It felt as though taxiing to the terminal took almost as long as the flight itself, such is the size of Amsterdam Schiphol airport.

I had a two-hour wait at the airport for the next flight to Lyon St Exupéry, or Satolas as I prefer to call it, the old name being much easier to pronounce. On the way to my departure gate I browsed through a few shops, resisting the allure of trinkets and tulip-themed souvenirs, from bulbs to 1970s-style clog wall hangings, mugs and painted wooden tulips. Souvenir shops didn't attract me. I'd much rather bring a pebble back off the beach from somewhere I had visited but a few tulip bulbs on the return flight might be worthwhile, or would that now be considered as smuggling post-Brexit?

Dressed casually in a blue and purple checked shirt, a brown leather waistcoat and dark jeans, my four-day stubble and messy hair completed the look. The businessman seated next to me didn't seem keen on conversation. He was absorbed in his laptop, fingers tapping away at a spreadsheet filled with figures preceding lots of zeros. "An accountant," I thought and almost immediately abandoned any thoughts of any small talk.

But feeling mischievous, I turned to him and asked, "Are you going to the concert at the Halle Tony Garnier tonight?"

After a long pause, during which he continued typing, he finally responded, "Who's playing?"

"Pendragon," I lied, assuming he'd never heard of the band.

To my surprise, he replied, "Really? I saw them in Morecambe, full weekend concert just before Covid struck. One of the best neo-prog groups around."

My plan had backfired and now I was stuck. Just as I was contemplating how to extricate myself from the conversation, he then added, "I'm just flying over for a meeting at the airport. Shame I can't make the concert."

The rest of the hour's flight turned into a lively discussion about bands we had seen, concerts we had attended and others we had missed but still wanted to see while they were still around including Mostly Autumn, Karnataka, Camel and Jethro Tull. He turned out to be great company, though I never did catch his name.

When we landed in Lyon, the flight had been smooth and on time. Thankfully, I had no checked-in hold luggage so I made it through passport control quickly and received my first post-Brexit passport stamp. A shuttle took me to the rental car park where I picked up a small Fiat 500, the cheapest there was but more than adequate for my four-day stay. Driving out of the hire car park, I said to myself, "Drive on the right, drive on the right," and a sense of optimistic expectation filled me. I headed towards the bypass and the A7 motorway to Vienne, sending Ann a quick message to let her know I'd arrived safely. Her delayed reply came the next day and made it clear just how much she didn't care.

Chapter 17

I arrived in Vienne late on a chilly Saturday afternoon with the remnants of the day's light fading across the Rhône. The drive from the airport had taken less than an hour and my first task was to find the hotel I had booked online. I had only booked two consecutive nights because I wanted to maintain flexibility in my movements and have the possibility of going to another hotel or Bed & Breakfast if I wasn't happy with the reservation I had made from home.

After checking in the next order of the day was food. I wandered along the main road that led from the Rhône to the railway station, looking at menus on the way in restaurant windows. I finally chose a modest establishment specialising in Lyonnaise cuisine. The name of the dish I ordered rolled off my tongue with a strange satisfaction: *Andouillette à la sauce moutarde et frites*, a local delicacy of tripe sausage in mustard sauce served with chips. The restaurant wasn't full, but the place was filled with gossip. I noticed that eating alone always has its peculiarities, the service is generally quicker and more efficient. Perhaps because a solitary diner is a person who, not having anyone to talk to opposite, doesn't hang around and passes most of their time on a mobile phone messaging or some other screen activity. My meal was as I expected, rich, satisfying and accompanied with a quarter-litre of red table wine. The crème brûlée that followed was an act of indulgence, with the burnt sugar cracking beneath the spoon, the smooth texture of the crème contrasting with the sharp pointed texture of the hard caramel covering. The whole experience was an exquisite taste for the senses that could hardly be prolonged for more than three or four minutes. Full and content, I returned to my hotel room in eager anticipation of the days ahead.

I had made a list of priorities, a set of small goals for my four-day stay. The library would be the first stop on Monday morning, consulting the census records and old newspapers that might hold clues to the past events I was looking for.

Sunday greeted me with clear skies and a fresh, biting chill. Breakfast was at eight with croissants, tartine and coffee. I threw my waterproof anorak into a small backpack along with the notes I had carefully brought from home, and set out to discover Vienne on foot. The streets were still, the only sound was the rhythmic toll of the cathedral bells calling the faithful to Mass; it was a reminder of the town's ancient traditions. I decided to follow the sound, walking towards the cathedral as Benoît, Eleanor and Sophie must have done over a century and a half ago.

Memories of my own childhood began to surface vividly. My grandmother, a strict Methodist, had always insisted I attend chapel whenever I stayed with my grandparents. I was too young to understand much of the sermons, but the hymns of the Harvest Festival, with its abundance of fruit and vegetables in front of the altar were a memorable and enjoyable experience. Later, my years in a Church of England secondary school had brought more of the same, a daily assembly with prayers. It was a forced ritual and its meaning continued to elude me. I never understood why the Catholic children at school were excused from attending. What was it that set them apart? Why could I not have been born a Catholic and remain in the playground? It wasn't until years later, after attending teachings by His Holiness the Fourteenth Dalai Lama and eventually taking refuge in Tibetan Buddhism, that I began to grasp a deeper understanding of spirituality.

Up until then Christianity had felt distant, an abstraction that failed to touch me. Now, having followed Buddhist teachings and practising meditation, I think I understood marginally more about Christian rituals and practices.

I approached the cathedral slowly, marvelling at its imposing structure. The stone walls rose above me and the sounds of organ music seemed to vibrate through its walls. It is still an awesome experience today but what must it have been like a few centuries ago before the technological era? As the sound filled that quarter of Vienne with peaceful energy, the last few worshippers were making their way up the steps, old men and women bent with age. Some leaned heavily on walking sticks, others were helped by those less frail, their slow ascent of the cathedral steps a silent act of faith. I stood on the pavement stones at the bottom, my eyes tracing the Gothic arches above, wondering how many people had walked up those steps each seeking something different, a moment of peace, forgiveness or hope. My own spiritual search was of a different nature, but I decided I would return to explore the interior later in the week if I had time.

I walked towards the temple of Augustus and Livia, evidence of the town's even more ancient Roman history. It was quiet as I opened Google Maps on my phone and walked towards the Place Jouvenet where I hoped to find the Hotel du Théâtre. The thought of discovering a living descendant of Sophie Fournier filled me with both excitement and apprehension. What if the family line had died out and even if I was to find a descendant, what would they know of their family history? Most people after all can only trace their lineage back two or three generations. Would I even find anything at all?

As I rounded the corner, my heart sank a little – there were no obvious signs of a hotel. I walked further, glancing up and down at the buildings for any trace. Then my eyes caught a faint inscription of peeling paint on a wall: Hôte… Thé… and there it was, I thought, evidence of the hotel's once existence. I stepped closer, studying the surrounding architecture and saw that what must have once been the hotel's grand entrance had now become a garage door. A few feet away to its side a wooden door led into what was now an apartment building, its façade stripped of the grandeur it had once known. I took a photo of a panel of eight modern push-button doorbells, noting the names next to them, some typically French, others Arab, one space left blank.

Just as I stepped back the door creaked open and an elderly man emerged with a small Jack Russell terrier on a lead which tugged impatiently in front of him. We both froze for a moment, surprised by the proximity of our encounter. The little dog barked persistently but with no real intent to bite. The man asked if I was looking for someone. I explained in my best French that I was researching an ancestor's diary and that the hotel name had been mentioned in it. His face softened with recognition of my English accent and he nodded, his voice dropping to a near whisper. "Ah, yes, that hotel, it must have been more than a century ago. I've lived here nearly seventy years and even before then, it was long gone."

He shared the story of his life, and his thought-provoking words stayed with me for a long time after I had walked away. His mother had brought him and his brother here to Vienne after his father's tragic death near Verdun, the result of a farming accident involving a tractor working in the field when an unexploded bomb from the First World War detonated as the tractor ran over it. His voice trembled slightly as he spoke. He knew little of the hotel's history though he'd heard said that it had once been owned by the town's mayor. I thanked him and walked away in the full knowledge that I had found where the hotel once existed but that it was long gone.

Walking back through the town to the river, I crossed the footbridge to St Colombe and walked along the riverbank upstream for a few metres where I found the Tour de Valois, still standing as an impressive, ruined stone tower. It was no longer surrounded by a walled garden but stands amidst tarmac and concrete, with a car park and pleached London plane trees on one side and local government offices on the other. I sat by the riverbank and brought out a photocopy of Hartley's diary. I re-read the passages of what amounted to his lovemaking to Eleanor, although it was described in a very romantic and discreet way. She, herself, having escaped the watchful eyes of her husband, Benoît Fournier. It then struck me that the old man I had seen that morning taking his dog for a walk referred to a past owner of the hotel being the maire of Vienne. Could it be then that Benoît Fournier, a local politician having returned to Vienne with Eleanor, had then become the maire? It seemed possible. I sat and contemplated, taking in the scene around me, imagining Hartley and Eleanor's passion in a walled garden only a few metres away from where I sat. What other scenes through nearly seven centuries had the walls of the Tour de Valois witnessed? If only we could read that history, the energy of which I am sure is still recorded in those stones, inaccessible today but perhaps one day in the future they will give up their secrets.

The afternoon was passing quickly so I decided to visit the Gallo-Roman Museum a few hundred metres away, before it closed. It was quite busy as I walked into the entrance hall. Two women and a man were occupied with talking to visitors and taking their entrance fees. I think there must have been a coach party for there were still at least a dozen people in front of me. Rather than wait behind the others as no one else was following me, I walked to the side, looking at a display board of what could be seen in the museum and other tourist attractions in the area.

Suddenly I felt a strange sensation, a feeling of being observed. I looked up and met the gaze of one of the receptionists. Her eyes were momentarily locked on mine, intense and probing, as though she could see straight through me. I looked away, surprised by the encounter, but when I glanced back, she was still watching me. If ever someone gave you the feeling that they were looking into you, observing something deep inside you, perhaps your soul, then it was at that moment.

The queue had dwindled and I stepped back into line. I was still behind two people remaining to be served when the same receptionist asked, "Can I help you, sir?" Her voice was soft and melodic, beckoning me forward with her hand. I stepped to the side and towards her at the reception desk. She smiled, a smile so warm and natural that it caught me off guard. Trying to compose myself, there was something about the way she looked at me that made my heart race. Her gaze was steady and searching. It stirred something deep inside me, something I couldn't place but that felt disturbingly familiar.

Feeling disorientated and momentarily lost within myself, I noticed that she was repeating the same question and then, "Would you also like an audio guide, sir?" I replied that I would. "In English, please." I looked the woman up and down as she had to avert her gaze to adjust the audio guide. She had shoulder-length hair, she wore a light-coloured blouse and jeans, was well proportioned from a man's point of view, aged somewhere between thirty-five and forty and stood at about one metre sixty.

As she handed me the audio guide, our fingers brushed and an electric shock shot through me, not a simple spark of static, but a jolt that sent the world spinning. For a brief disorienting moment I was transported, my mind flooded with an image so vivid it overwhelmed my senses: the same vision I had had standing outside the Devon chapel, her face, the woman beneath the floorboards of the ruined wooden building…

"Sir? Sir, are you alright?" I heard her voice coming to me from afar and I realised I had been standing there, dazed, for too long. Embarrassment made me blush and I stammered an apology, her concerned eyes not leaving mine. I felt weak and unsteady as though the ground beneath me wasn't quite solid. One of her colleagues brought over a chair and I sat, breathing deeply, trying to dispel the dizzying sensation. I wanted to blame it on fatigue, but I knew this was something else, something much stranger.

"I'm fine," I muttered, though the tightness in my body said otherwise. The receptionist, still watching me with that same unsettling intensity, insisted on refunding my entrance fee but I declined, feeling the need to escape rather than hang around any longer. I promised to return later in the week when I felt better. Her eyes followed me as I left, the double glass door sliding shut slowly behind me.

The walk back to my hotel was a blur. I replayed the moment over and over in my mind, the jolt, the vision, the woman's gaze. None of it made sense, yet it had all felt so real. By the time I reached my room my thoughts were a tangled knot of confusion, and a feeling of overwhelming exhaustion overcame me. Without bothering to undress, I collapsed onto the bed, and sank into a deep dreamless sleep that lasted through the night, the weight of the previous day's events pulling me under like a stone sinking in water.

Chapter 18

My visit to the library during the days between Christmas and New Year turned out to be a frustrating endeavour. Firstly, the holiday period resulted in limited opening hours and then to make matters worse, access to the census records was blocked due to a recent computer hack. No one seemed to know exactly when the system would be restored but it was hinted that it might take a few days.

However, I managed to uncover a bit of history related to the *"Hotel du Théâtre"* with the help of a local librarian. She seemed well-informed about the town›s history. "The hotel had been owned by Benoît Fournier who briefly acted as mayor," she told me. "Then it passed to Isabelle Fournier and eventually the property was sold and converted into flats in 1903." She suggested I search local newspaper archives for more information, offering me an online link and password to access six local newspapers. These included *"Le Courrier de l'Isère"*, which dated back to 1829, and "Le Journal de Vienne", which covered the town's happenings. There were also *"Le Patriote de l'Isère"*, *"Le Petit Dauphinois"*, *"Le Réveil du Dauphiné"* and *"Le Moniteur de l'Isère"*, all of which had various start dates in the 19th century. With these resources at my disposal, I felt more confident.

It didn't take long for me to learn that Benoît Fournier was never officially the mayor of Vienne. Instead, he stepped in for the then mayor Victor Faugier, who had fallen ill for a short time in 1853. Then I came across a paragraph that shocked me.

In the Journal de Vienne from 1853, I came across a brief mention in the births, deaths and marriages section:

"Benoît Fournier, conseiller municipale de Vienne a épousé le samedi 7 mai 1853 a la mairie de Vienne, Isabelle Dupont âgé de 23 ans, par le maire Victor Faugier, témoigné par son frère Jules Fournier de Condrieu. Aussi présent ... sa fille Sophie Fournier."

Translated this read: *Benoît Fournier, councillor of Vienne, married Isabelle Dupont, aged 23, on Saturday 7th May 1853, at Vienne town hall. The ceremony was officiated by Mayor Victor Faugier and witnessed by Benoît's brother, Jules Fournier, from Condrieu. Also present... his daughter Sophie Fournier.*

This suggested then that Eleanor, Benoît's first wife, must have passed away sometime after their return from the Landes and before his marriage to Isabelle, no more than three months later. Despite further digging into the archives with various keywords I couldn't unearth anything else that was relevant. All that turned up were reports of local political decisions in which Benoît Fournier was mentioned. The Fournier name also cropped up in relation to vineyards at Condrieu, a village situated twelve kilometres downstream from St. Colombe on the opposite bank of the Rhône.

As the library was closing, I decided I would return the following day hoping that the census material might finally be accessible. That evening and eager for a change of scene, I decided to explore a bit further afield and drove my little Fiat 500 hire car to Lyon. Given the holiday period I assumed the city would be relatively quiet as many people typically head off to the Alps to ski at this time of year.

Being a native of the countryside, I found Lyon busy, though the traffic wasn't too bad. There were no long lines of cars waiting to pass through the Fourvière tunnel and I had no trouble finding a parking spot in an underground car park at Place Bellecour. The evening was spent leisurely strolling through the narrow streets and "traboules" of the Quartier St. Jean, noticing the appealing aromas of French cuisine as I walked along. The scents of roasted meats, simmering stews and melted cheeses drifted from restaurant doorways, mingling with the sweetness of spiced desserts like bûche de Noël and crêpes Suzette. A cold winter breeze intensified these fragrances as warm air from open doorways met the air outside.

Inside cosy bistros families sat together, their conversations and laughter blending with the clatter of cutlery and the soft sizzle of dishes being prepared. Children, absorbed in their new Christmas toys, played quietly, a clever strategy by parents to ensure peaceful evening dinners that were likely to last two hours or more. The atmosphere was one of warmth and contentment with everyone enjoying the simple pleasures of good food and company during the festive season.

I selected a restaurant that wasn't too full, hoping to avoid a lengthy wait. Opting for a medium-rare steak with a side salad and gratin dauphinois, I settled in. Since I was in France, I decided to savour a local wine, choosing a single glass of a three-year-old Rhône Valley St. Joseph. The waitress, who was probably a university student, insisted on speaking English. It turned into a longer exchange than was necessary for had I been allowed to speak French we would have reached an understanding far quicker. For dessert I treated myself to a tarte tatin with a generous helping of cream.

As I was finishing, the waitress now more at ease, asked if I knew anyone who could participate in a language exchange. Her question confirmed my earlier guess that she was indeed a student. Regretfully I informed her that I didn't know anyone in her age group who would be willing to help out. When she brought me the bill I paid by credit card. The machine offered me the option to add a tip and I noticed the flicker of disappointment cross her face when I pressed "No". After the transaction, I discreetly handed her a five-euro note, smiling to myself as I thought, No electric jolts this time. Her expression softened and I explained, "I don't trust restaurant managers to distribute tips fairly. This way it goes directly to the person who deserves it." Whether she chose to keep it for herself or add it to a communal pot was up to her.

After leaving the restaurant I made the long climb up the seemingly endless steps to the Basilica. The funicular had already shut down for the evening but the effort was worth it. The view of Lyon at night was spectacular, with the dark ribbon of the river Saône winding below, marked only by the absence of light as it flowed south to merge with the Rhône near the 'space age', architectural Musée du Confluence. With its design in metal and glass having innumerable acute angles, it must have caused many a headache to the engineers and construction teams who built it.

I then walked back down the hill to retrieve the car and began the drive back to Vienne, content after spending a solitary but enjoyable evening amidst the lively streets of Lyon. As I cruised down the motorway, I found myself imagining my ancestor, Hartley Birkett, making a similar journey. He would have travelled by stagecoach, horseback or perhaps on a river steamer, taking several hours to return to Vienne. Unlike him, my trip lasted just thirty minutes once I'd left the outskirts of Lyon. The motorway, partially lit by street lamps and guided by the steady beams of my headlights, made the journey effortless.

As I drove, my thoughts wandered back to the events of the previous afternoon at the museum. Before returning to the library to continue my research I had already decided I would revisit the museum. There was something compelling me to see the receptionist again, the one I had encountered yesterday.

Later that evening I called Ann, noticing that she hadn't phoned me first. Our conversation was cordial though somewhat superficial and I sensed she regretted her attitude and moodiness on Christmas Day. I mentioned that I was looking forward to coming back home, which was only half true. She asked if my research had turned up anything interesting and I explained that I had found the location of the old hotel but that it was now converted into flats. I also told her that access to the census records was delayed due to a computer hack, but I was hopeful the issue would be resolved before my return. When I inquired about her activities she mentioned family visits over Christmas and attending the theatre. I suggested we spend New Year's Eve together, either quietly at my place or more festively at a pub, whatever she preferred.

The next morning the sky was overcast but dry as I set off. I crossed the footbridge to St. Colombe and walked towards the nearby road bridge leading to the museum at St. Romain-en-Gal a few hundred metres away, timing my arrival perfectly for the 10 am opening. Thankfully, there were few visitors and as I entered the main doors, I glanced around the room looking for the receptionist from Sunday, but she wasn't there. Disappointed but undeterred, I decided to tour the museum, hoping I might see her before I left.

At the entrance desk I was recognised by the staff member who had kindly offered me a chair on my previous visit. As I reached into my pocket to pay for admission, she smiled and said, "There's no charge, sir. You left on Sunday without collecting your refund." I was touched by her gesture and thanked her warmly. With a gratuitous entry I explored the museum including its outdoor area where Roman walls had been excavated. I was interested by the Roman history of the region and learned how the Rhône's banks once served as a bustling port with warehouses set back from the river.

Yet at the back of my mind, I couldn't shake off the feeling that I wanted to see the receptionist again. I couldn't explain why. Sure, I found her attractive, but it was more than that. I needed to see her face again to confirm if she resembled the girl from my previous vision at the Devon chapel or to understand why that memory had resurfaced so suddenly.

By midday, I had finished my tour and returned to the reception desk to ask about the woman who had helped me on Sunday. I explained that I wanted to thank her for assisting me when I had felt a bit faint. The staff member told me she had phoned in sick but was expected back on Thursday. I left feeling disappointed, yet it was more than disappointment: it was a deeper unnameable emotion that perplexed me. It wasn't as if I intended to ask her out on a date, tempting as that idea was.

I returned to the library in Vienne to continue my online research. On the way, I passed the Pyramid, believed to be the centre of a Roman stadium where chariots once raced. The contrast between the ancient and the modern was stark, nowhere more evident than in the library itself, a functional building. It was an architectural jumble of concrete beams crisscrossing at sharp angles, giving the unsettling impression that pulling just one beam would bring the whole structure tumbling down like a precarious game of Jenga.

I was fortunate to be greeted by the same librarian who had helped me the previous day. She apologised, confirming that the census records were still inaccessible and likely wouldn't be available until after the New Year. Resigned to my limited options, I returned to the newspaper archives. That afternoon, I uncovered three interesting facts.

The first was reported across several newspapers within a day of each other: *"Late in the evening on Wednesday, 15th June 1853, the saddled horse of Benoît Fournier was found without its rider on the Vienne side of the bridge connecting St. Colombe. There was no sign of the rider. The following day, the local gendarmerie found traces of blood on the parapet of the bridge and concluded that the horse, known for its skittish temperament, had probably been startled and thrown its rider. The rider likely hit the bridge, was knocked unconscious and unfortunately fell over the parapet. No body has been recovered from the Rhône. Mr. Fournier, a well-known councillor who stood in for Mayor Victor Faugier during his illness, was better known for his association with the family vineyards, the Domaine de Livie, at Condrieu. On the day of the accident, Mr. Fournier had been tending to family business at the vineyards and was returning to his residence at the Hotel du Théâtre in Vienne. Mr. Fournier is survived by his wife Isabelle and his daughter Sophie."*

If that revelation wasn't surprising enough, the second article added another twist: *"Isabelle Fournier gave birth to a son, named Benoît after his late father, on Monday 8th August 1853."*

Therefore, Isabelle must have become pregnant around November 1852, before Eleanor had eloped with Hartley. The couple had married in May of 1853, three months before their son was born and it appeared that Benoît Fournier had died in the month following his marriage to Isabelle Dupont. Benoît Fournier would never have seen his son, having fallen from his horse during the time of Isabelle's pregnancy.

The third was a brief announcement: *"Sophie Fournier married Édouard Dubois on Saturday, 7th April 1877."*

With that, my newspaper research had reached its conclusion. The next step was to determine how Eleanor had died. Although I lacked precise dates it must have been less than three months since her return from the Landes because Benoît Fournier had remarried in May 1853 and there was no mention of Eleanor in the newspapers. Without access to the census my time in Vienne was running out. I had two last options to explore: subscribe to a French ancestral research website or contact a local family history group if one existed.

I now knew Sophie's descendants may bear the surname Dubois which was unfortunately one of the most common names in France.

The following day, Wednesday, was my last full day in Vienne, with my return flight booked for Thursday afternoon.

Chapter 19

On Wednesday morning, I stayed in my hotel room. It was raining steadily and I decided to do some internet research as I had a good fast Wi-Fi connection. As I reread Hartley's journal, I noted that he had arrived in Vienne in February 1852, when Sophie Fournier was about ten years old. She married in 1877, making her around 25 at the time, quite late for that period I thought.

With access to a popular French genealogy website, I quickly located the names of Edouard Dubois and Sophie Fournier. Unfortunately, to access detailed family trees, I would need to pay for a subscription. I wondered if I could view information about living descendants without the tree owner's permission. After everything I had spent so far, a few more euros seemed trivial. I soon discovered there were three different family trees that cross-referenced each other with reliable sources. Following the direct line of descendants, I found seven possible names. Most of the families had moved away from the Vienne area but one appeared to be just up the road at Lyon and another still remained in Vienne. The Vienne-based individual was Jean-Marie Dubois (1940–2012). A female child was indicated on the family tree and presumably still living but her details were hidden.

My time was now limited so rather than also pursuing the Lyon family line I opted to focus on the local Dubois lineage. With Jean-Marie Dubois having lived locally, it made sense to start there.

Returning to the library, I sought out the helpful librarian and asked if the name Jean-Marie Dubois rang any bells. She paused then said she vaguely remembered something related to wine merchants. "As for children, I couldn't say. But you could inquire at the tourist office, they have a family history research group that meets there." I thanked her for all her assistance and headed out.

Another quick internet search confirmed that Dubois wine merchants had ceased trading with Jean-Marie Dubois's death in 2012, but no further details were available.

After lunch, I made my way to the *syndicat d'initiative*, essentially the Vienne tourist information office. It was another modern building located by the river, but in my eyes far more aesthetically pleasing than the library. In fact, I had walked past it several times without considering going in. Inside, it was quite busy, but my attention was immediately drawn to a large display of wines stacked up two storeys high. If I were going to find any trace of a family of wine merchants, this seemed like a good place to start.

At the reception desk, I was faced by a woman who, after a long delay without looking up from the counter, prompted me to speak first. Her demeanour suggested she wasn't having a good day. Her plain face was framed by heavy-rimmed glasses in a garish fuchsia, shaped like elongated cat's eyes and her hair was cut to a short back and sides. She stood tall and wiry, radiating impatience. I could tell from the outset that this was going to be difficult. I had a feeling that if it was a woman presenting herself to the reception and asking the question I was about to ask she would be better received than myself or any other man for that matter.

I began by explaining my research and the reason for my visit to Vienne. Glancing at her name tag, which read "Mme Suzanne Babineaux", I caught her noticing my gaze and suspected she thought I was eyeing her chest though I had merely been reading the name tag. I smiled, hoping to defuse any tension but it was clear from her expression that I wasn't making much headway.

I got as far as mentioning Jean-Marie Dubois, his death in 2012 and his possible connection to a wine merchant family with a daughter who might still live locally. I was hoping the family history group could help me trace her. Before Mme Babineaux could respond, I sensed the standard bureaucratic brush-off coming: "I'm afraid, Monsieur, we cannot give..."

But before she could finish, a young man, likely a student covering holiday shifts, stepped up from an office behind her. "You probably mean Tess Dubois," he said. "She works at the Gallo-Roman Museum. She's a friend of my mum's."

Mme Babineaux shot the young man a look that promised a reprimand as soon as I left. I thanked them both and made a quick exit.

As I walked out of the tourist office, my mind immediately returned to the woman I had seen at the Gallo-Roman Museum. Could it be the same person? The one who had looked at me so intently, whose touch had sent an electric jolt through me? It was possible though unlikely. There could be several women working there, from archaeologists to administrative staff or even receptionists on a rota.

By then, it was too late to return to St. Colombe, the museum would be closed. I decided to try again the next morning, my final half-day in Vienne.

The following morning, after breakfast, I refreshed my memory by reviewing Hartley Birkett's diary and the notes I had compiled since my arrival in Vienne. As I gathered my thoughts together, I began planning how to approach Tess Dubois if she turned out to be a direct descendant of Eleanor Fournier. Would she be aware of our shared 'family' history? Would she even care? It was entirely possible she had no interest or knowledge of the past that I was so intent on uncovering. Either way, I had to find out.

That night I couldn't sleep as my thoughts spun in circles. I kept replaying everything in my head, from reading Hartley's diary to all the research I'd done since coming to Vienne and that strange encounter with the receptionist at the Gallo-Roman Museum. And now, could she actually be a descendant of Eleanor Fournier, her fourth great-grandmother who had once been Hartley Birkett's lover and he, my third great-grandfather.

Ann's words echoed in my mind too. Was I becoming obsessed with finding someone I'd never met? Someone who might have no interest at all in the history I was so determined to uncover? After all, the people I was chasing had lived more than a century and a half ago.

The Thursday morning arrived and I was a bit groggy following a night of sleeplessness and unrest. I did, however, sleep well from 4 am to 9 am. Waking up made me realise I had been getting ahead of myself and overreacting during the night, but the little sleep I had managed to get had brought me back to my senses.

After breakfast, I packed my bag, settled my bill and headed for my car in the nearby car park. My destination was St. Colombe, where I found a spot in the museum's parking area further up the road. As I approached the sliding doors at the entrance, I noticed I was third in line in the queue. To my relief, I saw that the receptionist I was looking for was back at work.

As I moved forward in the queue of visitors, I let a family behind me go ahead in order to meet the same receptionist. A few moments later, she looked up, recognised me and greeted me with the same warm smile as our last encounter. I stepped forward and before I could speak, she asked, "Are you feeling better, sir?"

I assured her that I was then I returned the same question. She looked puzzled, unsure how I knew she hadn't been well, but she didn't press the matter.

"I'm sorry to be so direct," I began, "but are you Tess Dubois, daughter of Jean-Marie Dubois, who passed away in 2012?"

She nodded affirmatively, her expression curious, wondering where this was heading. I quickly explained that I had come to Vienne because of Hartley Birkett's diary, which detailed his involvement with her ancestor Eleanor Fournier, in 1852. I mentioned my flight back to England that afternoon and asked if we could speak privately for a few minutes.

Tess hesitated before replying, "I can't leave reception until midday and I need to be back by 2 pm." It seemed to be a hint that she may be available during her lunch break.

"Perhaps I could take you to lunch?" I suggested. "I'll drop you off before two o'clock and then I'll head to the airport."

Tess smiled and said, "Why not?" There was no hesitation and no hint of distrust. She agreed as easily as if we had known each other for years.

"I'll be in the white Fiat 500 at the end of the car park," I told her.

"Do you not want to visit the museum?" she asked.

I explained that I already had and that's how I knew she was off work.

"Oh, I see," she said with a slight smile.

I left the building feeling as though I was floating. A date, I thought to myself, though I knew it wasn't quite that; still, I was pleased with myself. I returned to my car, set the alarm on my phone and dozed off uncomfortably in the small space of the Fiat until ten minutes before noon.

At exactly twelve o'clock I saw Tess walking briskly along the car park's edge, glancing left and right as if she didn't want to be seen. The irony was that her hurried furtive manner probably made her more noticeable than if she'd just strolled casually. I stood beside my car and when she spotted me, she headed over, getting into the passenger seat.

I extended my hand. "Lynden Grisdale," I said. "Pleased to meet you."

She reached out but stopped herself. "Remember what happened last time?" she said, smiling. "You nearly passed out when I touched you and then I was off sick for three days." Instead of shaking hands she leaned forward and gave me a quick kiss on both cheeks. "That's a French greeting," she added with a grin.

"I saw a brasserie near the station," I said. "Is that alright with you?"

"Yes, that's fine," she replied enthusiastically, recognising it was one of the best restaurants in town.

The short drive took longer than expected due to five sets of traffic lights, parking outside the post office and a brief walk across the road to the restaurant. As we entered, I noticed Tess once again scanning the room, clearly trying to avoid being recognised. When the waiter approached, I asked for "a table for two". Tess chimed in, asking if we could sit at the table around the corner which was more secluded. "Of course," the waiter replied obligingly.

It was becoming apparent that Tess was wary about being seen in public with me. Perhaps, I thought, it was because she worked in a public-facing role and was known locally. Or maybe there were other reasons she didn't want to be spotted with an unknown man. I knew she was using her maiden name but that didn't reveal much about her personal life and now wasn't the time to ask.

We took our places at the table and as we each glanced at the menu, Tess looked up and asked, "Why have you been looking for me?"

I explained briefly that she was a direct descendant of Eleanor Fournier, the woman who had been involved romantically with my third great-grandfather, Hartley Birkett. I told her how Eleanor's loss seemed to have driven Hartley into isolation and how his diary chronicled their time together. "I have a photocopy of the diary in the car," I added. "I can leave it with you if you're interested."

"Yes, please," Tess replied eagerly.

The waiter returned to take our order, but we hadn't really made up our minds.

"Do you like shellfish?" I asked.

"I love it," she said, though she added, "But you don't have to..." It was the most expensive dish on the menu, costing over a hundred euros.

I asked the waiter if we had enough time for the seafood platter, "*l'assiette fruits de mer*", and leave at a quarter to two.

"Of course, Monsieur," he replied.

I opted for a light red wine to accompany the meal, even though white was the traditional pairing with shellfish. Tess smiled and agreed that she preferred red wine anyway. When the meal arrived, I poured Tess a glass and we both settled in for what promised to be a revealing conversation.

"Do you know anything about their affair from your family's history?" I asked Tess, then continued. "Apparently, Eleanor's husband, Benoît Fournier, was a local councillor in Vienne. He even stepped in as acting mayor when the actual mayor was ill so he would have been quite a prominent figure in town. He and his wife ran the 'Hotel du Théâtre' near the Roman amphitheatre. That's where my third great-grandfather, Hartley Birkett, stayed whilst working as a surveyor on the construction of the railway line that passes through the town and he became involved with Eleanor."

"Wow," Tess replied, her eyes widening. "You know more than I do. There was a story my grandmother told my mother and me when I was younger. It went back to my grandmother's grandparents. Yes, I knew the family once owned a hotel and I'd heard the Fournier family was involved in the wine business. That's actually how my father became a wine merchant," she added thoughtfully. "Then Benoît's wife ran off with an Englishman to England and never came back."

I was just about to correct Tess when the waiter arrived, bringing a spectacular display, upon a wire stand was placed a large platter of crab, oysters, mussels, langoustines, clams, prawns and winkles, all nestled on a pyramidal bed of ice. It came with handmade mayonnaise, brown wholemeal bread, butter and the necessary tools for cracking and prying open shells.

"Merci, Monsieur," I said, turning back to Tess, who was clearly drawn into the unfolding story.

"With respect, no," I gently corrected her, "according to Hartley's diary, they were living in the southwest of France, somewhere between Dax and Bayonne. He was attacked and left for dead and Eleanor, along with Sophie, your second great-grandmother, returned with Benoît."

"I don't think that's possible," Tess said, shaking her head. "From what I learned, Benoît had his marriage annulled after Eleanor abandoned him. He remarried but tragically, only a short time later, he was thrown from his horse into the Rhône River."

"I knew about that part," I said, nodding. "I found it in some old newspaper clippings here in Vienne."

At this point, my mind was racing to piece together a clearer picture. We both fell silent for a few moments, letting this version of the story sink in. Then I said, "I also have a copy of a handwritten note Eleanor left behind. I'd like to leave it for you, Tess. You can read it and form your own conclusions."

We finished our meal in what felt like no time at all, so engrossed were we in the conversation. We barely had enough time for a quick café gourmand, which was a strong espresso coffee served with several small pastries.

"Tess," I said, switching to the more informal 'tu' instead of the formal 'vous', "are you interested in going further with this? If so, I'll give you my email address and phone number."

"You bet!" she replied, sounding eager. She quickly rummaged through her handbag, pulling out a pen and scribbling her phone number and email address on a paper napkin. I did the same.

"But don't call me, please," Tess added with a smile. "Messages are fine though, I use WhatsApp."

The clock was ticking and I swiftly paid the bill. We walked briskly to the car and I drove Tess back to her workplace. As we approached, Tess asked, "Drive past it please and pull in further up the road." I did as she asked.

As she was about to get out of the car, I turned and leaned towards her. She smiled, clearly pleased with how things had gone. We exchanged kisses on both cheeks. "Goodbye Lynden," she said. I handed her the photocopied documents as she got out of the car. As I watched her walk back down the road, glancing left and right to check if anyone had seen her, I couldn't help but think of Hartley's descriptions of Eleanor. Their meetings had taken place less than five hundred yards from where we were, at the Tour de Valois.

It was two o'clock and for the past two hours I hadn't thought about anything other than Tess and our conversation about our intertwined ancestors. Suddenly, reality hit me. I had a flight to catch.

An hour and forty-five minutes later, I was passing through passport control for my flight back to Teesside via Amsterdam. As I waited at the boarding gate, my phone pinged. It was a message from Tess.

"Thank you for the lovely lunch. Have a good flight home. I promise to read everything you gave me. I'll be in touch soon. Bisous, Tess."

I quickly replied, "The pleasure was mine. Thank you for your company and for taking an interest. Speak soon. (emoji, kiss on cheek) Lynden."

As I settled into my seat for the flight, my thoughts kept returning to Tess. I'd enjoyed her company more than I could easily express. It felt natural, like we just clicked. There had been no awkward pauses or stilted conversations. I realised I was genuinely attracted to her. But was it mutual? I couldn't be certain. Maybe she was just naturally warm and convivial, qualities essential for her work.

I found myself wondering how old she was, perhaps thirty-five, maybe a little younger. One day, I'd ask her discreetly. I was forty-six but liked to think I looked younger. Though of course, everyone my age seemed older than me, at least to my eyes.

Then there was the matter of the conflicting stories about Eleanor Fournier. What Tess believed had happened didn't align with Hartley Birkett's diary. There had to be a simple explanation. I just hadn't figured it out yet.

Chapter 20

When I arrived home, it was past 10 pm and I noticed the downstairs lights were on. Ann had clearly let herself in. I unlocked the door and called out, "Hiya."

"Hi," she replied. "Did you have a good flight?"

"Yes, nice and smooth, everything on time," I said as she came over to give me a light kiss on the cheek.

"So, what do you want to do tonight?" I asked. "Go to the pub or stay in and see the New Year in?"

"Both," she said with a grin. "Let's grab a drink or two for an hour then come back here to welcome the New Year. After that you can tell me what you found out in France and who you found."

"Why do you say who?" I asked, raising an eyebrow.

She stepped closer, her eyes narrowing slightly. "Because when you came near me, I caught a very distinct scent of a woman's perfume on you."

I laughed softly. "Really? That's probably Tess's. Come on," I said, waving it off and probably blushing a little, "I'll tell you everything."

We couldn't talk much at the pub. It was too noisy and crowded with revellers who had already been there for hours. Still, we enjoyed a couple of drinks before deciding to head back. As we walked, my phone pinged with a WhatsApp message:

"Wishing you health and happiness for the New Year and good luck solving your 'our' (wink emoji) family's mystery. Bisous, Tess."

"Bisous" was her way of saying hugs or kisses. I stopped for a second, quickly sending back a similar greeting while realising that in France it was already the New Year.

Although nothing intimate had occurred between myself and Tess, Ann could sense as if by instinct that my attention had been drawn to another woman.

"Was that Tess?" she asked.

"Just New Year's best wishes," I replied, trying not to draw her attention to Tess.

"So, you exchanged phone numbers during the short time you were with her and now you're messaging each other?"

I fumbled with my keys under the dim light of the streetlamp, struggling to unlock the front door. "I'll explain where she fits in," I promised, finally getting the door open.

Once inside, I poured Ann a glass of chilled Clairette de Die 'Tradition', a sparkling white wine I always kept on hand. To me, it tasted better than Champagne and was certainly better than the overrated Prosecco. As for myself, I opted for a glass of Laphroaig whisky. The warm, peaty aroma filled the air as we settled in for what I knew would be a deeper conversation than either of us had planned.

We had about twenty minutes before midnight so I began to explain to Ann what had unfolded during my four-day absence.

"Do you want the television on in the background or the radio?" I asked, wanting to mark the exact moment when the New Year would arrive so we could raise a toast.

"BBC One," she said without hesitation.

I obliged, though nowadays I would have preferred something else.

"How are you going to find out more about Eleanor?" Ann asked.

"That's where I'm hoping Tess can help," I replied. "Once she reads through the photocopy of Hartley's diary I left her, she might be able to trace Eleanor's details through the French census. But that's only when they've resolved that computer hack at the public library."

The conversation drifted as we welcomed the New Year in together with a quiet toast. By half-past midnight we retired to bed.

As I sat on the edge of the bed undressing, tugging off my socks, Ann leaned over already under the covers. She reached out and touched the middle of my back, her fingers moving softly between my shoulder blades. A familiar tingle spread through me.

"How did you get that mark?" she asked, her fingertips grazing the triangular patch of slightly reddened skin.

"It's always been there," I said. "Since birth."

"Does it hurt or tickle?" she asked, her fingers lightly tracing the edges of the mark.

"No, it doesn't tickle but it's sensitive. If I scratch it, it stings a bit."

Without warning she reached up, placed her hands on both of my shoulders and gently pulled me back onto the bed. I laughed softly as we fell together into the covers. Strangely, the next morning when I awoke, I realised I was still wearing one sock.

Later, on New Year's Day, Ann returned home to her flat. For me it was back to the usual routine of preparing lectures for the upcoming term. It was hard to shake off the strange feeling that the brief trip to France had left behind. But life was rolling forward again as routinely as ever.

Two days later, I received another message from Tess. I had been wondering how long it would take before she got in touch and the fact that it hadn't even been a full week reassured me that she was motivated to help.

"Hi Lynden, I've read through all the photocopies you left me. It was a fantastic read! Our ancestors must have really loved each other but I agree, the ending is sad and strange. I'll go to the library on my day off to see if the census information is back online. Bisous, Tess."

I smiled. Tess's enthusiasm was contagious. I quickly typed back a reply.

"Thanks, Tess! You got through it quickly."

"Once I started, I couldn't stop. It was so interesting! I wasn't that interested in the early parts about the mining but when Hartley moved to France, especially when the railway construction started through Vienne and he stayed at the Hôtel du Théâtre, it got really interesting. It's about my ancestors. Benoît Fournier doesn't come across as a very nice man, does he? Tess."

"I agree. Not the friendliest character. Lynden."

A few minutes passed before her next message popped up.

"Do you think Hartley was trying to seduce Eleanor when he first moved to the Hôtel du Théâtre, now that he was a single man again? Emoji, wink, wink, Tess."

I paused for a moment, thinking it over before replying.

"From his diary, it doesn't seem that way to start with. He seemed to have a very professional attitude but what he wrote down and what was going through his mind at the time might have been two very different things. Lynden."

"True! Tess."

I set my phone down, leaning back in my chair. Tess had a knack for making the past feel alive, as though Hartley and Eleanor were more than just names on old, faded pages.

Now, the story felt closer to unfolding. The pieces were coming together slowly but I couldn't shake the feeling that there was more to be uncovered. Something that Hartley hadn't written in his diary. Something that might explain not only

Eleanor but the way this mystery had pulled us, Tess and I, two strangers, into its orbit.

I texted back to Tess. "Also, Eleanor was having a rough time with her husband, who was abusive, so she might have been looking for a way out."

"They definitely fell in love and Hartley was heartbroken. But according to what was passed down from my grandmother, Eleanor went with Hartley," she replied. "Got to go now. I'll contact you soon! Emoji, kiss on cheek, Tess."

I found myself feeling rather pleased with Tess's enthusiasm. Her quick responses and eagerness to dive deeper into the mystery were encouraging. I was now keenly awaiting her next message even if I wasn't quite sure what to expect.

The following day I hadn't planned on reaching out to Tess so soon, but something compelled me to check in with a quick message:

"Hi Tess, How are you…?"

Before I could even finish typing her reply came through:

"Don't send me any messages for a few days, please. I'll explain later. Tess."

I paused, staring at my screen. Although she hadn't mentioned it before I suspected she had a partner, someone who might be watching her interactions closely, perhaps viewing our communication as secretive even though it was innocent. The thought crossed my mind that our exchanges could easily be misinterpreted which made me slightly uneasy. Five days passed before I heard from her again.

"Hi, how are you? Tess."

"I'm okay, thanks. How are you?" I typed back quickly.

"Fine! I've been to the library. The hack has been fixed so I looked at the census details for the Hôtel du Théâtre. The records are taken every five years. I can confirm that from 1856 to 1901 Isabelle ran the hotel. The young Benoît was there also up to 1886 or shortly after, I don't know where he went after that. It seems the young Benoît had moved out sometime as an adult. Sophie Fournier appears to have left the hotel before the 1856 census, she had moved to a different address and she was studying to become a school mistress. I took photos of the monitor screen. I'll forward them to you. Bisous, Tess."

Her message ended with no explanation about her previous request not to send any messages. I thought about asking her but decided it could wait for another time.

I texted: "Tess, there's a three-year gap between 1853 and the 1856 census. Is it possible that Eleanor could have returned to Vienne with Sophie and Benoît? If she was being mistreated, she might have left and gone to live with relatives somewhere else allowing Benoît to get the marriage annulled before he remarried in May 1853."

"I suppose that's possible but would she have left Sophie behind? Tess."

I replied, "According to what you thought had happened she did that anyway when she left with Hartley for England. Maybe the story was made up by Benoît so that he could marry Isabelle who was already pregnant. As a local dignitary it would have been scandalous otherwise. And since Sophie adored her father, it would have been easier for her to stick to the same story."

"I can't believe Sophie, who lived until after 1903 and would have been over sixty years old by then, who had married and had become a school mistress, would have kept up a false story for so long, especially after her father's death. I really think she believed her mother had abandoned her and that she had eloped with her lover Hartley," Tess replied firmly.

I took a moment to consider her point then sent my reply:

"When I traced you, Tess, I found other descendants. If I send you the details of the other family trees I came across, could you check if Eleanor turned up anywhere else?"

"I'll have to do it on my day off but I'll look into it. T."

"Fair enough. Thanks. Speak soon! Emoji, kiss on cheek, Lynden."

As I hit send, I realised that last emoji might have been a little risky. There was a fine line we were walking and I wasn't sure how it would be received. But before I could dwell on it too long her reply popped up:

"Emoji, double kiss on cheek, T."

Well, that was… something. A small smile crept across my face as I wondered where this strange journey might take us next. It seemed that the search for Eleanor was not only uncovering old secrets but creating a new situation that I hadn't anticipated. What was clear was that Tess was now deeply involved in the mystery and that at least for now was enough to keep both of us intrigued.

We had begun texting almost daily by this point, sometimes about Eleanor, sometimes about other things as if the lines between solving the mystery and our personal lives were starting to blur. Then one evening Tess sent a message that intrigued me.

"I've gone through the family tree names you gave me," she wrote. "It was a tough search and there could be mistakes. They're scattered across France, many lost in wars. The Lyon family didn't turn up anything. T."

She followed up quickly with another thought:

"I have another theory," she texted. "Go back to Hartley's encounter with Madame Dufour after he was attacked and read what he wrote. Call me tomorrow at 7 pm, emoji kiss on cheek, Tess."

Curious, I found the passage in Hartley's diary she was referring to:

Marguerite answered with care, her eyes direct and without sympathy. "Eleanor and Sophie departed the day after you left for Bordeaux. Her husband, Monsieur Benoît Fournier, arrived at my door seeking them. I called for Sophie who had been here in the house for the last two days. Upon seeing her father she ran to him with joy, crying out, 'Papa, Papa'. He lifted her into his arms and he told her they were going home. I believe Eleanor was already in the carriage by that time for I did not see her."

I began to understand what Tess was getting at, but I wanted to hear her thoughts first.

The next evening at precisely 6 pm I typed in her number on WhatsApp video.

"Hi, Tess," I said as soon as she picked up, "I hope you meant 7 pm French time."

"Yes, I did. Why?" she replied with a small laugh.

"Because it's only 6 pm here. There's an hour difference between England and France."

"*Alors, j'ai eu de la chance,*" I thought I heard her mutter softly.

"Have you re-read the passage I was talking about, Lynden?" she asked, more seriously now.

"Yes," I answered.

"So, no one actually saw Eleanor," Tess continued. "Madame Dufour assumed she was in the carriage and we know that Sophie had been at the house for two days when Benoît arrived to collect her. It sounds very calculated and entirely possible that Benoît, after taking Sophie, told her that her mother had already left with Hartley. Remember, Sophie was barely eleven and adored her father. Why would she question him if he said her mother had left? She probably understood on some level that what her mother was doing by leaving with a lover was considered wrong by the standards of the time."

I paused for a moment before asking, "Do you think they were wrong, Tess?"

"No," she replied firmly. "For two reasons: one, they were in love; and two, Eleanor was being mistreated by her husband."

"Would you leave someone for love, Tess?"

"It almost happened once," she said, her voice softening but preferring not to go any further asked, "What about you?"

"Until I experience feelings that strong, I don't know," I admitted, to which she didn't reply for a few seconds, then finally spoke.

"You're leading me astray, Lynden…" she teased. "But do you realise what we could be looking at here?"

"You think Eleanor was murdered?" I asked, suddenly catching on.

"Look at the facts," Tess pressed. "There's no record of Eleanor in the censuses showing she returned to Vienne. Our family believed she eloped with Hartley to England, but his diary contradicts that. Hartley believed Eleanor went back to Vienne based on what Madame Dufour said, but remember, Madame Dufour didn't actually see Eleanor. It was a stormy night and Monsieur Dufour was found dead. The local gendarme chalked it up to a tree falling on him but even that may not have been the case. And then, don't forget, Hartley himself was knocked unconscious and left for dead in the mill pond. Plus, there were noises in the woods in the days before Hartley left for Bordeaux that were thought to have been poachers – they could have been Benoît Fournier's men spying out the lay of the land, waiting for the right moment to pounce and when they did Marcel Dufour got in the way and was murdered."

I sat up straighter. "You're right. This is starting to feel less like an elopement and more like a cover-up. We need to visit the Landes to see where they lived. I presume you want to find out what really happened?"

"Absolutely," she said with determination. "If we plan it well, I can make an excuse to come along with you."

"You need an excuse?" I asked, a bit surprised.

"Yes, I do. And it seems you might as well," she added with a playful tone.

"I'm not free until the Easter holidays then I'll have nearly two weeks off then," I replied, thinking ahead.

"I can take some annual leave around that time," she agreed.

A pause hung between us before she asked, "How old are you, Lynden?"

"Forty-six," I replied. "And you?"

"Thirty-eight," said Tess.

It seemed like our search for Eleanor was becoming more than just a quest for truth; it was now a thread that was drawing the two of us closer together.

Chapter 21

The Easter holidays came around at the latter end of their possible span, bringing some welcome warmth in April compared to March's persisting damp and cold. It was a weather forecast promising clearer skies and sunny days for our planned journey.

Tess and I had been messaging almost daily; our conversations filled us with anticipation as we thought through the next steps in unravelling the mystery of Eleanor Fournier and to a lesser degree Hartley Birkett. Tess had resolved that she wanted to accompany me to the Landes to pursue the mysteries of our joint ancestors together.

I planned to return to France by car. The route I envisioned would take me from Cumbria to Vienne where I hoped to pick up Tess. From there we would trace Hartley's path along the countryside roads running parallel to the railway line southward towards Avignon, then westward to Toulouse and Bordeaux and finally south again to Dax. I pictured this as a slow, deliberate journey, keeping clear of the motorways, savouring the landscape as we followed Hartley's trail. I shared my idea with Tess, telling her she'd need to prepare for five or six days away from home: two or three days in the Landes, a couple of days on the road and for me a few more for the entire round trip from Cumbria to the Lyon area.

The journey required careful planning, particularly regarding what I would tell Ann. While we weren't bound by any formal commitment, we were close friends who frequently shared the same bed and as we worked in the same college there was always a chance she might wish to join me over the holiday break. I couldn't quite envisage bringing both Tess and Ann on this journey through France; though Tess and I had only exchanged WhatsApp messages and shared a meal there was an undeniable feeling that something more intimate might occur between us. I could of course step back now before things deepened, but I didn't want to. I felt drawn to her with a sense of inevitability, as though surrendering to something beyond my control. And so, for once, I decided to follow my heart over caution whatever the consequences may hold.

Without lying to Ann, I carefully told her a half-truth, explaining I was driving down to Dax to research the second part of Hartley Birkett's life. My car was a sturdy Volvo estate but it was now past 260,000 miles and had been showing signs of wear. I'd arranged to trade it in for a recent Skoda Superb estate, and drive it to France instead. To save on expenses I mentioned I'd be sleeping in the car for a few nights. Knowing Ann's aversion to any form of rough sleeping, I was reasonably confident she would choose not to accompany me and indeed as expected she didn't press the issue.

As for Tess, she hadn't mentioned any particular family commitments, though I sensed the presence of someone in her life she was wary of us being seen together.

When the day came and I sent a text to Tess: "I'm on holiday now and setting off tomorrow morning. Any last-minute instructions? I'll arrive in Vienne around midday the day after tomorrow."

Her reply was swift: "Do you have the note written to Hartley, the one from Eleanor? Tess."

"Yes, why?" I responded, curious.

"Something struck me as odd about it. How did you come across it? Tess."

"It slipped out of one of the volumes of the diary," I replied. "Still in its envelope."

"Could you bring the original, just as you found it, with the envelope intact? It may be nothing but I'll explain it when you arrive. Tess."

"Where do I pick you up?" I asked.

Her final message was brief and teasing: "I'll tell you when you're nearby. Emoji three kisses on cheek, T."

And so, on that clear morning, I set off for the Dover Ferry. Easter holiday rates on the Channel Tunnel cost more than I was willing to pay, especially having forked out money for a newish car. Also, I figured the savings from the ferry would more than cover a few restaurant meals or a night or two in a modest hotel. Southward I drove, pressing on past Troyes until I pulled into a motorway *aire de repos*, a quiet roadside rest area where I could lay out my sleeping bag and stretch out in the back of the car. The stillness of early dawn was soon broken by the rumble of engines as the parked lorries began to start up. Waking with them, I slipped back onto the road, driving a hundred kilometres or so before stopping for a coffee and croissant and a quick shower at another motorway service station; that way I could arrive in Lyon feeling refreshed. My thoughts drifted to Tess, to where we'd spend our first night on the road. Somewhere between Valence and Montélimar seemed right, and I made a hotel reservation with the option to cancel just in case.

Further down the motorway, I sent a message to Tess. "Just passed Mâcon. Where should I pick you up?"

"I'll meet you at the dépose-minute by the TGV station at Lyon Saint-Exupéry Airport. Tess."

Picturing the train station within the airport, I typed back, "Are you sure, at the airport?"

"Yes, please," came her reply. "Message me five minutes before you get here and I'll come outside. We're getting a few heavy showers here. Emoji three kisses on cheek, Tess."

When I texted my arrival at "Satolas", Tess was already waiting at the end of the drop-off lane among taxis and cars, patiently watching for me. I pulled up, shifted into park and climbed out to put her bag into the boot. We exchanged a brief, warm peck on the cheek. She moved instinctively towards the driver's door and smiling I raised the car keys for her. Realising her error, she laughed, quick to circle back to the passenger side. "The steering wheel is on the wrong side," she teased, settling into the car.

Once inside, we closed our doors in unison and I leaned over, brushing her elbow lightly as I drew her towards me. Our lips met in a gentle, lingering kiss. A few moments passed before the blare of a horn startled us; either the driver behind us was a voyeur, impatient, or they simply needed more space. Tess and I broke apart, sharing a quick laugh and I slipped the car into drive, easing out of the drop-off lane.

As we left behind the sleek, metallic structure of the TGV station, Tess reached across to take my hand and I glanced over, catching her gaze in between watching the road. We drove in silence for a few moments, both of us letting the depth of what had just unfolded settle around us, each pondering the path this moment could lead us down.

After a moment, I spoke. "Tess, why here? Why not just meet in Vienne?"

Her reply was short and direct. "I told my partner I was heading out with some college friends for a week's hiking in the Alps. Here at least I could leave my car where it wouldn't be noticed."

"I'll cover the parking cost," I offered.

"That's alright," she said with a smile.

"We'll see," I replied.

I sensed now wasn't the time to probe further into her private life. She would share what she felt ready to in her own time, and I could wait.

Our itinerary was already loosely sketched out and she'd agreed to my idea of taking the slower route south. I wanted to see firsthand the rugged terrain that Hartley Birkett had once travelled, to get a sense of the land as it would have been in his day. This scenic road was long, however, winding through towns and villages on the west side of the Rhône, each one slowing us with frequent stops at red traffic lights. Tess didn't complain but when I suggested we went back onto the motorway because of the slow progress on the old road, she smiled and leaned over to plant a quick kiss on my cheek

"This isn't just for me, Tess," I murmured. "Let me know if you're getting tired of this."

She met my gaze with a steady look. "I'm alright," she answered calmly.

Once we were back on the motorway it took only another thirty minutes to reach our hotel, tucked on the western bank of the Rhône in a small village called Baix in the département of Ardèche. The village lay nestled between the steep Ardèche hills and the winding Rhône canal, with road, rail and the river itself crowded together in a narrow corridor of stone, metal and water. The compact layout gave Baix a quaint charm, its narrow streets crammed between houses that clung closely together, occasionally joined by ancient stone arches.

We located the hotel and with both Tess's overnight bag and my own in hand, I rang the bell at reception. Tess stepped back a bit as I spoke to the receptionist. "I have two rooms reserved under the name Grisdale," I said, handing over my card. The receptionist nodded and handed me two keys with weighty brass fobs and gestured us towards the staircase. I turned to Tess, only to find her staring at me, a glint of surprise and something like amusement in her eyes.

"Are you alright?" I asked.

"Are we spending the next week in separate rooms?" she replied, barely masking her disbelief.

I felt my face blush. "Tess, this is our first time travelling together. I didn't want to assume…"

She cut me short with a grin that bloomed into a laugh. "Quite the English gentleman, aren't you?"

Still blushing, I took hold of our bags and followed her up the narrow staircase. Tess, holding the keys, walked ahead and once we reached the door of the first room, she opened it and stepped aside. An awkward pause fell as we stood in the doorway, both waiting for the other to speak. She looked at me expectantly, perhaps waiting for me to say something like, "Whose room will this be?" Instead, I set the bags down, closed the door behind us and took her gently by the shoulders, pulling her into a kiss that was long and deep.

As we sank onto the bed Tess let out a surprised squeal, laughing against my lips until her voice turned to a soft sigh. She'd bitten her tongue in our tumble but neither of us seemed to mind. By morning, the maid would find one room immaculate and untouched.

That evening we dined at a Moroccan restaurant a five-minute walk away. I chose a royal couscous with three different meats while Tess ordered a rich, aromatic tagine. The meal was accompanied by a red wine from Meknès and we finished with sweet Moroccan pastries and mint tea, looking at each other over the candlelit table. The evening grew darker outside and when we finally walked back to our hotel, twilight was gone, the street lights casting long shadows, and small pools of light from shopfronts lit our way.

Back in our hotel room, I glanced towards the bathroom. "Who's taking the first shower?"

"Go ahead," Tess replied, her smile warm.

After a few minutes, I emerged from a mist of steam, the persisting scent of cedarwood soap on my skin. The room was dimly lit, casting a soft glow that made Tess's figure at the window look almost ethereal. She stood gazing out, her outline softened by the glow of the village lights filtering through the curtains. My skin was still warm from the shower and for a moment, I simply watched her, transfixed by the quiet grace of her posture.

Sensing my gaze, Tess turned slowly, her eyes wandering over me in a deliberate way. Without a word, she moved towards me, her fingers lightly grazing the back of a chair as if to steady herself. As she neared, she lifted her hand, her cool fingertips brushing my shoulder in a gentle touch that sent a shiver down my spine. I leaned in closer, feeling the slight tremble in her breath and she let her hand slide down to the edge of my towel, her fingers brushing my hip.

We stood there, enveloped in a moment suspended between us, the double-glazed windows isolating us from the faint sound of talking on the street below. We were close enough to feel the warmth of each other's breath, yet we remained still, caught in a fragile equilibrium. Then with a smile she slipped past me, my hand resting on her waist just briefly as she passed.

As she reached the bathroom door, she paused, glancing over her shoulder. "What's that mark on the back of your shoulder?" Tess asked, curiosity flickering in her eyes.

"I don't know," I replied, glancing away. "It's just a skin discolouration. A birthmark."

Tess looked at me, her lips parted as if words were about to escape but she thought better of it. Her mouth closed and with a quiet turn she vanished into the bathroom. The door closed gently and then the sound of water filled the space between us. I sat on the edge of the bed feeling the cool sheets beneath my fingers. Outside life moved on indifferent to us, but in the quiet of our hotel room a sense of anticipation gave an inkling at what was yet to come.

The bathroom door opened with a soft click and warm, misty air wafted into the room. Tess emerged, wrapped in a hotel robe, her damp hair curling lightly into gentle waves. I straightened as she moved towards me, her bare feet padding softly across the wooden floor, each step making only the faintest sound. She seemed more relaxed now as she caught my gaze for a fleeting second, then looked away, tucking a damp strand of hair behind her ear.

She stopped at the foot of the bed, fingers toying absently with the tie of her robe. The fabric slipped just enough to reveal her naked body beneath. I reached for her, capturing her wrist, and she remained still as I drew her closer and she came to me in slow deliberate steps, like a shallow wave flowing quietly towards the shore. She placed her hands on my shoulders, unsure at first but becoming more confident as she leaned in. The fresh scent of soap and warm skin filled the space between us and an unspoken feeling passed between us both, delicate yet impossible to ignore.

The robe slipped from her shoulders in a smooth fluid motion to the floor. I guided her down beside me, the cool sheets gathering around us as she settled into the crook of my arm, her fingertips tracing slow circles across my chest, a wordless conversation in the slide of skin against skin and the soft pressure of her body as she pressed closer against mine. We lay there for a long time, letting the silence stretch between us as if neither of us wanted to break the spell that held us in that hushed suspended moment.

The feeling afterwards was one of elation. We had both been to a place of eternity and we were returning back slowly to this world. We could not tell how much time had elapsed. I felt no sense of guilt at that moment. I am sure neither did Tess. We lay in each other's arms; no words were spoken because no words needed to be spoken as we drifted quietly to sleep for a few hours.

I woke sometime in the middle of the night; it was calm outside until fighting cats squealed like the sound of a baby crying.

Feeling thirsty, I moved to reclaim my arm from beneath Tess, who stirred and curled away. Undisturbed, I slipped out of bed and went to the bathroom for a glass of water. When I returned Tess was, I thought, in a deep sleep, and I eased carefully back into bed behind her, moulding my body against hers and feeling her warmth against me. As I placed my arm over her, she murmured drowsily, "Don't even think of it."

The morning light and the stir of Tess lying next to me brought me back into this world from a night of sound sleep and forgotten dreams.

After breakfast in the small hotel restaurant, we returned to our room to go over our plans for the day.

"Did you bring the note Eleanor wrote?" Tess asked.

I reached into my bag and took out the letter, carefully protected within its original envelope, which I'd placed inside a larger stiff-backed envelope. "It's fragile," I said, handing it to her.

"I'll be careful," she replied, as she gently pulled the letter from its envelope and began to read.

The letter read:

Hartley,
I have decided to return to Vienne. My husband has come looking for me.
He forgives me for what I have done. Sophie is so happy to see her father again.

Do not attempt to follow me for I have no desire to rekindle what once was.
Return to England to your son who needs you more than I ever did.
I am sorry to envelope the news this way.
Eleanor

After a moment Tess looked up, frowning slightly.

"It's probably just my English which isn't good enough but why did Eleanor write, 'I am sorry to envelope the news this way'?"

"I think it's just the way they expressed things back then," I replied. "You wouldn't phrase it like that today. I think she meant I'm sorry to deliver the news like this."

Tess tilted her head thoughtfully. "But an envelope is also what contains the letter," she said.

"Yes," I replied, nodding.

Tess held up the envelope to the light, her eyes narrowing as she examined it.

"I think there's faint writing on the inside," she said suddenly.

"What, you're joking."

"People used invisible ink, often something acidic like vinegar or lemon juice when lemons became freely available. Sometimes raw milk was used although it could leave a slight glossy sheen."

I looked at her, surprised. "How do you know all that?"

She gave a small smile. "I work in a museum, remember? I'm just on reception but I pick up a lot from the archaeologists and curators."

I was impressed. "And how would we reveal it if there is something there?"

"Heat," she replied. "The trick is to heat it gradually or you could burn the paper before revealing anything. You could send it for expert examination but that might be expensive and take a long time."

"Let's try it here," I said, feeling a thrill of excitement. "Do we need a cigarette lighter?"

"Oh, goodness, no! That would burn it for sure, it's old dry paper," she said. "We could try holding it over a lightbulb with one of us filming in case the writing fades quickly."

"It's your envelope," she added, "so you should hold it."

"But Eleanor was your ancestor, Tess."

She smiled but there was a hint of nervousness.

"Alright, I'll do itm but I won't take any blame if it goes wrong."

"Fair enough."

We moved the bedside lamp to the middle of the room and positioned ourselves around it. Tess carefully unfolded the envelope, her movements delicate. The light cast a warm glow over the thin paper.

"Which side should be up?" I asked.

"I'm not sure," she murmured, "let's start by heating it from below."

The light wasn't quite enough to reveal anything clearly, though faint marks began to emerge. Tess reached for her bag.

"I have a hair straightener here or we could try the hotel iron, it has a low setting."

"Let's go with the straightener if it doesn't get too hot," I said.

She pressed the paper gently between the heated plates then pulled it away after a few seconds. And there, as if rising from the depths of the past, brown coloured ink began to appear, faded but unmistakable. We stared; our breaths held. Tess sank onto the bed, tears slipping silently down her cheeks as I sat beside her, speechless.

"Take a photo," she whispered, her voice almost inaudible. "In case it fades."

We gazed at the words together:

My husband has come with two men to take Sophie.
M......................
I am certain he intends to kill me once I finish this letter,
and to kill you upon your return.
If there is a heaven we shall meet there.
If another life awaits us, I'll find you again.
All my love,
Eleanor.

A sudden knock shattered the stillness; the housekeeper, checking if we'd left. I went to the door.

"We'll be here for another hour," I said softly and she moved on.

Tess lay pale and still and I knew she needed a moment to gather her senses. My mind buzzed with what we'd uncovered, with Eleanor's desperate warning and the tragedy of Hartley, my ancestor, who would never have known the truth behind Eleanor's disappearance.

I let Tess rest and sitting quietly in an armchair, my own thoughts were in turmoil. At last, she sat up, her eyes red and her face stricken. I too felt the burden of the revelation, the ache for Hartley who must have lived his life in sorrow, never knowing why Eleanor had vanished and the message he was meant to receive was with him always but forever hidden until now.

"There's a missing line though," I added.

"I'm afraid there is no way it can be revealed. Remember Eleanor was in such a stressful situation anticipating that she was going to be killed and the writing is over a century and a half old," replied Tess.

"You know what we have to do next?" Tess said softly, her voice steady despite her tears.

"Yes. We go to Landes and find where they lived," I replied.

Chapter 22

We gathered our bags and made our way to the car. Tess was deep in contemplation as was I.

"I think we should skip the country roads, Tess. If you agree, let's head directly to Dax," I suggested.

"Yes," she replied, her voice tinged with a sombre tone.

We set off, merging onto the motorway with at least a six-hour drive ahead of us.

"What's on your mind?" I inquired as we settled into the flow of traffic. The motorway was busy; the Easter holidays combined with sunny weather seemed to have brought the whole of Europe out and they were travelling south down the Rhône valley.

As we passed Montélimar, the distinct charm of Provence surrounded us. Tall, slender cypress trees lined the road like sentinels, their vertical forms offering shelter to the small fields that lay in between, an asset to farmers when the fierce mistral winds swept through. The landscape, dominated by bare limestone outcrops and resilient evergreen oaks, spoke of a rugged beauty. We took the junction westward at Orange heading towards Nîmes, Montpellier and Narbonne. The trees here, mostly evergreen oaks, were modest in stature. Some areas were blackened by fire; the frequency of fires probably explained why the trees never reached maturity.

"I feel the need to talk but you might think I'm crazy," Tess confessed, breaking the contemplative silence.

"I promise I won't," I reassured her.

She grasped my left hand, resting on the armrest.

"The day you visited the museum," she began, "why were you staring at me in particular?"

"I didn't think I was, I thought you were the one looking at me."

"What we both perceived was the energy flowing between us," Tess added, "when we crossed glances it just seemed as though the time was much longer."

"Like we slowed down time," I ventured.

"Exactly. With everything that has transpired since our meeting at the museum, do you think it's mere coincidence or are we bound by destiny?" Tess pondered.

"I don't know. I haven't thought about it in that way. You mean it's our karma?"

"Possibly," Tess replied, her tone thoughtful. "Do you believe in karma?"

"Are we speaking from a Buddhist perspective or a Hindu one?"

"What's the difference?" Tess asked, curiosity piqued.

I explained, "In Hinduism, karma is seen as more fixed. Your past actions strongly shape your future and you are bound by those consequences. In Buddhism, karma is more flexible. It focuses on your actions in the present and encourages you to make conscious choices that may change your future path and move towards enlightenment."

"So, karma isn't set in stone; it can be changed?" she asked, seeking clarity.

"Perhaps, but it's not that straightforward. I'll explain. Imagine you're walking along a road, let's call it the road of life. When you reach a junction, you have the option to go left or right. If you consistently choose left at every junction, by the time you arrive at the hundredth junction you still have the freedom to choose, but which way will you turn?"

"Left," Tess replied confidently.

"Exactly, because your past decisions have conditioned you," I added. "Now what if you alternate your choices? At the first junction you go right, then left, then right again and so forth, until you reach the hundredth junction where you chose left. At the next junction, what will you likely choose, even with the freedom to decide?"

"Right," she guessed.

"Precisely. We operate under the illusion of free choice, yet our decisions often follow established patterns," I explained.

"Hold on a moment," she interrupted, "what if the choices are random? Left, left, right, left, right, right, right and so on?"

"Three possibilities," I responded. "Either the number of roads is insufficient for a pattern to emerge, or a pattern exists but it eludes our perception, or perhaps it's something beyond the human mind that has been shaped by past experiences and is unable to choose based on its prior encounters."

"If it's not the human mind, then what is it?" Tess pressed.

"I don't know," I admitted with a chuckle. "I just thought it up."

We both laughed, the tension easing as the landscape of Provence rolled by.

"But our minds are conditioned from the moment of birth, perhaps even from conception," I remarked thoughtfully. "It's akin to what happens with animals, like Pavlov's dogs."

"I've heard the name. What does it mean?" Tess inquired.

"Ivan Pavlov, a Russian physiologist, discovered conditioning in psychology. Initially studying digestion, he noticed dogs salivated not just at food but also at their feeders. He experimented with pairing a bell with food, leading dogs to salivate at the bell alone. His work became the foundation of behavioural psychology."

"Fascinating," Tess said, absorbing the information.

I sensed I might have ventured too deeply into a dry subject but before I could second-guess myself, Tess chimed in again, obviously following her line of thought.

"There are energies I sense that other people often dismiss as nonsense."

"Like chakras?" I ventured.

"Yes, but I haven't received any formal training," she clarified. "I can't actually see or hear these energies; rather, it's a subtle awareness that develops in their presence. Occasionally, I can feel them through touch. Since Christmas, when we first met, if I've been thinking about you, then almost like clockwork I receive a message from you moments later. It feels like my thoughts align perfectly with the instant you're reaching out to me."

"I experience the same with you," I confessed. "In fact, I've come to wonder if I might just be thinking about you too often and that could explain it."

We both shared a laugh and as Tess turned her head towards me, I returned her gaze for a fleeting moment. The roads were congested, demanding my full attention and I could only manage a brief glance. Yet even that fleeting connection ignited a warmth within me, a melting feeling and I exhaled, feeling a relaxing sensation ripple through me. It dawned on me that Tess was starting to have a serious effect on me.

"What happened to you at the museum, when our hands briefly touched?" she asked, her tone suddenly serious.

I felt embarrassed and Tess could detect my embarrassment. She added, "After last night in the hotel bedroom I think we can afford to be open with each other."

The brief flashback in my mind of our bodies entwined and a glance towards Tess convinced me firstly to drive a bit slower and seek the slow lane rather than stay in the faster motorway middle lane.

"Do you really want to know?" I asked. "Well, you're the one who is now going to think I'm crazy."

"Don't be so certain," she replied, her eyes sparkling with curiosity.

"I think it was a form of dizziness that overcame me. It came through a jolt I felt completely traversing my body. I felt transported to a place of timelessness and in that moment, a vivid recollection resurfaced, a vision I had not long ago. In fact, it started about the time I picked up Hartley Birkett's diaries. I saw a dead woman lying beneath a dilapidated shed, her..."

Tess cut me off.

"You don't have to say the rest," she said. "I saw it too..."

"What?" I exclaimed; my surprise evident.

I switched on my indicator to pull into an *aire de repos*, with a restaurant just three hundred metres ahead. I slowed down, scanning for an open parking spot. None were available so I pulled into a space designated for lorries and cars pulling caravans.

After a pause, Tess continued.

"In that contact between us I saw what you saw. Our energies were united for a brief moment. We became a single entity. It drained me completely and it was why I had to take three days off work. I had touched you with the fingers of my left hand. It's more sensitive than my right hand although I am right-handed. You left, perhaps you didn't see me, but I tried to follow you out of the building a few moments later but you had vanished."

"When I left, you must have thought you would never see me again," I said, reflecting on the intensity of the moment.

"I didn't doubt that you would come back," said Tess. "It had to be. The energy between us had established a connection, an invisible link."

"I'm perhaps a bit more pragmatic," I said, "but I agree what is happening between us is stranger than a random encounter."

"Let's take a break and grab something to eat. I'll treat you," Tess offered.

I smiled, responding, "Well, yes for the break and no for the offer of paying."

We took our time selecting a self-service meal, watching the steady flow of people around us. Families bustled about, children moaning for sweets displayed temptingly at the tills while parents queued to pay for their fuel. The restroom facilities were remarkably clean, a testament to the maintenance of this busy stop.

Just under an hour later, we resumed our journey, the road ahead still stretching long before us.

"While you drive," Tess suggested, "I'll look for a hotel. How far do you think we can get?"

"Let's aim to reach the other side of Toulouse. With this heavy traffic, it's a long drive. I propose Auch, if you are in agreement. Do you want to take a turn at the wheel, Tess?"

"No, thank you," she replied, amusingly. "With the steering wheel on the wrong side and my unfamiliarity with driving an automatic I'd rather leave it to you. What kind of hotel do you prefer?"

"Clean," I stated matter-of-factly. "Two or three stars would suffice, nothing too modern. I'd like air conditioning that can be turned off, windows that actually open and ideally no noisy street nearby."

"Is that all, sir?" she teased.

"And free parking that's visible from our hotel room," I added with a grin.

"One or two bedrooms?" Tess inquired playfully, prompting laughter as we exchanged glances. She leaned over and kissed me on the cheek. If only I had turned my head in time, it might have landed on my lips but I missed the moment.

Given the criteria I had laid out, the hotel Tess found was surprisingly reasonable. It overlooked the Gers, the river that lent its name to the county and from our window, I could see the car parked below. On the way, we had stopped at a *traiteur* to buy some food for our room; neither of us wanting to eat a large meal that evening. The day's driving had taken its toll on our stamina. A good night's sleep was in order.

After showers, we lay side by side, discussing nothing in particular. Night was drawing in and then my phone rang. It was Ann. Tess, sensing the personal nature of the call, began to rise from the bed but I reached out, grasping her hand in a silent request for her to stay. My responses to Ann were short and likely raised suspicions. A pang of guilt washed over me.

"Yes, nearly there," I said. "The weather's quite good." I winced inwardly. "Yes, there was a lot of traffic." ... "No, I'll let you know if we find anything. Bye, speak soon."

"You said 'we', not 'I'," Tess pointed out, her eyebrows raised.

"Oh, shit, I did, didn't I?"

"Do you think she picked up on your slip of the tongue?"

In the excitement of the moment, I was candid. "I don't know and honestly, it's all the same to me," I replied playfully, leaning over to kiss Tess fully on the lips.

Tess pulled back, a frown on her face.

"That's not a very nice thing to say."

"I spoke without thinking. It doesn't mean I don't care. It's just that it's possible to have different relationships with different people for different reasons," I explained, hoping to bridge the gap between us. "Don't you agree?"

"Let's just get some rest," Tess replied, clearly not wishing to delve deeper into the subject.

I lay back and thought of what I had just said. Perhaps I was a little harsh, but I was also hoping that Tess would open up a bit more about her views and her own circumstances.

In the morning, we were eager to set off early. We decided to book a hotel in Dax and do some geographical research on the area before continuing our journey.

Then, setting off from Auch, we noticed how much the landscape had changed in this area, characterised by gentle, undulating, cultivated ploughed fields, dotted with low-roofed stone-walled farms and scattered copses of deciduous woods.

"By the way, Tess," I began, "what did you mean yesterday about your left hand when you mentioned our hands touching at the museum?"

She turned to show me her open left palm.

"You haven't noticed?"

"No," I replied, trying to keep my focus on the winding road while stealing glances at her hand. "What is it?"

"It's a birthmark," she revealed, a hint of pride in her voice.

I noticed a small, square area on her palm, slightly darker than the surrounding skin.

"It's where I feel more receptive to energies coming and going from my body. I experience a warming and tightening sensation there, though it doesn't happen very often. I've never been able to correlate it with specific events. As a child, it was just a mark, but after puberty I started sensing the ebb and flow of energy. My mother took me to a doctor once who dismissed it as psychological, saying it would pass. Of course, it never did. I kept it to myself after that and hardly ever talked about it. I was afraid school friends would think I was weird if I mentioned it.

"When you came to the museum and we touched hands, it was the strongest sensation I have ever felt. Just look at the effect it had on you, and it drained me completely."

"Why isn't it happening now?" I asked, intrigued.

"I don't know," Tess replied thoughtfully. "But I feel we're being drawn together. I wouldn't have gone away with you like this normally and you're feeling a sense of remorse regarding Ann, aren't you?"

"Mmmm," I muttered, considering her words but avoiding a direct answer. "So, who is Tess Dubois?"

"What do you want to know?" she asked, tilting her head slightly.

"Your background," I prompted.

"As a child, I lived in a village just outside Vienne. I attended college there and worked locally as a secretary or receptionist for various companies before landing my job at the museum five years ago. I've been married, had two children and then divorced. Now, I've been living with my current partner, Alexandre, for seven years."

Tess continued, feeling the need to contextualise our situation.

"I want you to understand, Lynden, that this is the first time I've done anything like this, coming away with you for a week. I've not had other relationships."

"So, are we in a relationship?" I asked, my curiosity getting the better of me.

Tess regarded me with a quizzical look, tilting her head slightly.

"Aren't we?"

I paused, considering her question as I reached for her left hand with my free hand while steering with the other.

"I guess we are in a way," I replied cautiously, "but I'm not planning to radically change my lifestyle."

"Neither am I," Tess stated, her tone resolute.

As we left the Gers region behind, heading west towards Mont-de-Marsan in the Landes, the landscape evolved. Maritime pines became the more dominant trees, the land flattening and low farmhouses with shallow roofs nestled deeper within the forest.

"So, is your relationship with Alexandre working well?" I inquired, sensing a need for deeper understanding.

"Like every other couple who's been together for a few years, routine sets in. Sex is a procedure you go through to maintain a certain stability in a couple. From a woman's perspective, it becomes an obligation because men are more demanding which means the pleasure is not always there. We each have our own set of friends and activities. If we do anything together it's very often a reluctant engagement by one or the other of us but we oblige."

"Is that better than living alone?" I asked, genuinely curious.

"I think so," she answered thoughtfully. "It allows us to share a nice house that neither of us could afford on our own and then there are the children and family who, after witnessing me go through a divorce, would get very upset if I separated again."

"And what about you?" Tess pressed.

"I mostly agree with what you say. I care for Ann but I can't shake the feeling that there's someone out there who would be the right match for me, someone with whom routine wouldn't set in and we would be attentive to each other's needs with genuine love."

"That sounds a bit utopian," she remarked.

"Until it happens, I'll just stay as I am," I replied. "I think Hartley and Eleanor found that kind of love, don't you?"

"It's possible they simply hadn't been together long enough for routine to develop and their secret meetings added to the excitement, even if neither of them wanted to be discovered," Tess speculated.

"So, you think that's all it was, newly found love and the thrill of clandestine encounters?" I queried.

"Actually, no," she replied, her voice dropping slightly. "I believe whatever happened between them was eternal. Just look at the message Eleanor left for Hartley."

We continued our journey, finally arriving in Dax, and crossed the river Adour. I thought of Hartley's own journey across that same river, the bridge we crossed having been built back in the 1850s. The château d'Ax no longer stood, replaced by a hotel on one side and the remnants of old ramparts set back on the other.

Our satnav guided us around the town to our hotel at the Place de Salines.

Chapter 23

We arrived in Dax far too early to check into our hotel so I suggested we find a bar nearby and take some time to reorient ourselves before tomorrow's excursion. Having researched the town's points of interest online, we decided to make our way to the *Fontaine Chaude*, located at the end of one of the town's large squares. Unfortunately, the once-grand space had now been reduced to little more than a nondescript car park.

We approached the fountain, eager to touch the hot water that still flowed from the mouths of three lion heads cast in copper-stained bronze, sculptures that, though reminiscent of Roman design, were probably of relatively recent origin. Stepping down into the basin we quickly discovered that it was impossible to keep our hands under the hot water. The heat was intense and as steam rose from the stream of water, it became clear that our hands would be burnt if we left them there. We could only pass our hands quickly through water from one side to the other. The water gushed away into a drainage channel, leaving little behind but the scent of sulphurous minerals and the persisting haze of steam.

Across from the fountain, we found a bar with a perfect view of the arches that framed the hot spring. I couldn't help but think it was such a waste, this remarkable water, which is still the pride of Dax and here it just flowed away into the Adour River. Still, I reminded myself that the town must have much more, for Dax was well known throughout France for its thermal baths and related medical treatments. The weather was warm enough to sit outside so I ordered a tea for myself and a hot chocolate for Tess. We pulled out the photocopied pages of Hartley's diary and began leafing through them, stopping when we reached Hartley and Eleanor's arrival in Dax.

"By late afternoon we crossed the river Adour on a bridge of unique design and the imposing Château d'Ax came into view, a fortress that once housed the powerful Dukes of Aquitaine and boasted a history reaching back to Richard the Lionheart. Massive walls surrounded and protected the town of Dax. We had been directed to lodgings near the Fontaine Chaude, a natural hot spring renowned for its hot mineral waters, and Sophie, with her persistent youthful energy despite the day's journey, eagerly led the way to the bubbling basin. Though the water could scald one if it was held there for too long the sight of it, gushing forth from the earth through brass lion heads, fascinated her."

I looked up from the page, glancing around at the stone buildings that surrounded the square. The fountain, though aged, seemed unchanged from the description given by Hartley when he had stayed here with Eleanor and Sophie.

"Tess, can you imagine? It was in one of these buildings that Hartley, Eleanor and Sophie rented their rooms."

"Yes," she replied, a faraway look in her eyes, "we're getting closer."

After a moment of quiet, she asked, "If you're a Buddhist, do you meditate?"

"Sometimes," I replied, "though not as often as I would like to."

"Would you show me how?" she asked.

"Sure," I said, "I can show you later, at the hotel."

I pulled out my iPad and opened Google Maps.

"Look, Tess," I said, zooming in on a nearby location, "this is where we need to go. The Marais d'Orx. And here," I pointed at the map, "is the outlet of the Boudigau River, which drains it."

An hour passed quickly as we wandered back through the narrow streets, taking in the sights and browsing the shop windows. Tess stopped in front of the shoe and clothing stores, muttering under her breath, "Everything looks so expensive here." I, on the other hand, stopped more infrequently, drawn instead to the outdoor gear shops, gadgets, cameras and the occasional piece of technology. At one point, I popped into a hardware store and bought a couple of candles and from a tobacconist's a box of matches.

We were given a hotel room overlooking the Place de Salines and as soon as we entered, we placed our bags on the floor. Tess, being attentive to detail, began to carefully arrange her clothes in the cupboard provided. I, on the other hand, never bothered with such things in hotels. I was always a little fearful of leaving something behind, especially the charging cables for my phone, those small essential objects that seemed to disappear when you most needed them, all the more so when a European plug adapter was attached.

"Are you going to show me how to meditate, then?" Tess asked, turning towards me.

"Sure," I replied. "Do you want to try it now?"

"Yes," she said.

"Alright, first you need to be comfortable. Ideally, cross-legged on the floor. Here, sit on this cushion."

Tess sank down into the soft fabric, her posture tentative.

"Maybe orient yourself away from the window," I suggested, "to avoid visual distractions. Things like birds flying past or perching on the iron railing of the balcony."

Tess nodded and shifted slightly, following my instructions.

"The cushion is a bit too soft," I observed. "Let me adjust it." I gave her another cushion, placing it under her buttocks. "Bend forward a little, and I'll tuck it beneath your backside." I adjusted her posture carefully. "That's better. Now your knees are almost touching the floor and your bum is raised, forming a triangle with your knees. You should be feeling comfortable."

She nodded she was and I continued, "Now, bring your thumb and index finger together and place the palms of your hands gently on your knees. Perfect."

Tess had followed my instructions to the letter.

"Now, let's finish adjusting your posture," I said. "Think about each part of your body and work your way upwards. Your legs are crossed comfortably; your arms should feel relaxed with your hands on your knees. Now, here's the important part: focus on your spine. Think about your vertebrae, one by one, and work up your back to your neck."

To help her concentrate, I lightly traced my hand along her back.

"Your back needs to be perfectly straight," I continued, "with your neck and head in alignment." Gently, I cupped her head in my hands, adjusting it slightly so she could feel the right position. "When it's right, you'll know."

"Am I supposed to shut my eyes and stop thinking?" she asked, her voice quiet.

"It's probably best to close your eyes at first to avoid distractions," I suggested, "but if you prefer not to, that's fine. And I'll light the candle, so you have that as an option too. As for your thoughts..." I paused, allowing her time to settle. "You can't not think."

"What do you mean?" she asked, curious.

"Well," I began, "oh ... you've already moved from your original position. Now, think about your body again, your limbs, your back, work your way up to your head, keeping your spine straight." I observed Tess for a moment, noting how she had regained the right posture, then I said, "Try not to think of an elephant."

"I can't!" Tess exclaimed. "You've made me think of elephants!"

"Exactly," I said with a small smile. "You see, you can't not think. It's just part of the way the mind works. I'll explain what to do in a few moments."

I lit the candle and placed it in a drinking glass on the small coffee table, about two metres in front of Tess. The soft flicker of the flame cast a gentle light across the room.

"Now," I said, settling beside her, "I'll guide you. Close your eyes and focus your mind on your breathing. Don't force it, just observe it. As you inhale, think, I'm breathing in and as you exhale, think, I'm breathing out." I watched her chest rise and fall, then continued, guiding her through a few more breaths. "Keep going. Don't worry about your thoughts; just bring your attention back to your breath."

I stayed by her side for a while, observing her movements, then gently stepped back. I left her to it, trusting she would find her rhythm.

After about a minute, I asked softly, "What are you thinking about?"

"I'm sorry," Tess said, sounding slightly apologetic. "My mind wandered."

"That's exactly what happens," I said calmly. "It's perfectly normal. What you have to do when your mind wanders is to simply bring it back to your breathing. Inhale, exhale. Inhale, exhale. Just keep it simple. Breathe in, breathe out."

I paused, allowing Tess to focus, then waited for her response. After a moment, she sighed.

"This is harder than I thought," she said, a slight laugh in her voice. "I'm now thinking about what we're going to eat later."

I smiled quietly. "That's progress. You've already recognised that your mind wandered to food and by realising it was just a thought, you're now in a position to bring your focus back to your breathing. The more you practise this, the more control you'll gain over your mind and your emotions. You'll learn not to let them control you."

"What do you mean by 'my emotions controlling me'?" Tess asked.

I paused, considering how best to explain. "Right, let me start with something simple. Take that framed print on the wall, for example. There are only three ways of perceiving what you feel about it: you might like it, you might not like it, or you might be indifferent to it. The same goes for a person. You might be drawn to someone because you like them, repulsed because you don't like them, or be indifferent to them. But why? It's not because the print or the person possesses those characteristics. It's because of the conditioned interpretation of your senses. What you see, what you hear or even what you smell is processed by your brain and then your mind projects an opinion. Someone's clothes may make you think they look smart, scruffy or it's a fashion out of date etc. A tattoo on an arm or face could be interpreted differently as being either artistic or intimidating. It's not just what we see, our senses are constantly gathering data, and we form opinions based on that information. We like someone, dislike them or don't care at all. But here's the catch: in forming those opinions, we project our own thoughts onto the other person and believe that those characteristics come from them and not us, but no… Someone else might form the complete opposite opinion to yourself because their life experiences and conditioning are different to mine or yours. People's judgements may be class-based or culture-based. So, it's not the person who is 'smart' or 'scruffy', it's us, projecting our own beliefs onto them."

I glanced at Tess to make sure she was following. She nodded so I continued.

"Think about how the media works these days. They often take a position of judgment about a person rather than differentiating the person from what they say. They communicate that judgment to the wider public and this creates confusion. There's a blur between the subject and the object. For example, someone may be labelled racist or homophobic not because of who they are but because of something they said, which someone else interpreted as racist or homophobic. There's a difference. But people confuse the subject, the person, with the object, their words or actions. When that happens, they become intolerant of other perspectives. They can't separate the person from the spoken words. It becomes less about the opinion and more about attacking the individual. For example, shortening a term describing someone's ethnic origin from four syllables to two might now be interpreted as offensive or racist. While the person using it decades ago may not have intended harm, the meaning has evolved and the abbreviated form is now widely considered unacceptable."

Tess's eyes narrowed thoughtfully.

"So how can meditation help with this?"

I paused then offered a suggestion.

"Do you want to move around a bit? If you're feeling uncomfortable, it's always good to stand up, stretch your legs, walk around the room a couple of times and then return to your seated position. It'll help reset your body."

"I'll do that," Tess said, rising from her position with a small stretch.

As she got up and walked a few paces, I kept my eyes on her, ensuring she would be comfortable when she returned. She settled back into position and I adjusted her shoulders gently to help her find balance again.

"Okay," I said, "let's continue. The same way you work to control your wandering mind by bringing it back to your breathing, meditation helps us recognise that our emotions are just thoughts. Nothing more. It helps us avoid becoming attached to them. Let me give you an example: think about someone on the street who is an alcoholic or a drug addict. It all began with a single thought, the idea to have a drink or take a pill that made them feel good. But that thought repeated itself again and again and the person becomes trapped. At first, it was just a fleeting idea but over time, that thought led to an addiction. The same goes for road rage. If someone makes an error when driving, it can trigger an intense reaction in another person. The second person then decides to act on it, getting angry and even violent. What's happening is that they've made a quick judgment based on a thought and because they can't let it go, they've cultivated a negative thought to a point that they have lost control of their emotions. It harms them in the process, though they may not realise it."

Tess looked at me with interest, so I pressed on.

"The way around this is to recognise when an emotion like anger, jealousy or frustration starts to rise within you, to realise that it's only a thought. Imagine it like a small cloud in a clear blue sky. At first, it's just one cloud. But if you persist with those thoughts, then more clouds form and the sky darkens; your thoughts become a storm of anger or jealousy. Eventually though, as time goes by and your mind turns to other things, those clouds start to clear and the sky returns to being blue. All our emotions work this way. When you can identify that an emotion is just the conclusion of your thinking process, you can become an observer of it instead of getting caught up in it. That is key."

I paused for a moment to let the idea sink in before continuing.

"Another important part of meditation is the concept of impermanence. Everything around us is in a state of constant change, always shifting from one year to the next, from one second to another. Of course, we know this intellectually but Buddhism teaches us that because we resist change and try to cling to the things we want to hold onto, we create our own frustration and suffering. Take the loss of a loved one, for example: it may be a broken love affair or a death. It's painful but we want to cling to those moments that made us feel good. We want to preserve them, but they couldn't last forever. We know that but it's when we resist it that we suffer. This is particularly hard for young people, children being bullied at school or teenagers obsessed with what others say about them on social media. They can't see it at the time but years later, when they look back, those things won't matter. It's just a distant memory. But living in the moment, it feels real and overwhelming for them."

Tess absorbed my words quietly. After a long pause, she looked up, her expression thoughtful.

"I think I'm starting to understand," she said. "It's all about letting go."

"Exactly," I said with a small smile. "Letting go is the heart of it."

I continued, "We can use the candle as a support in our meditation. A flickering flame is forever changing before our eyes. It is a symbol of impermanence and interdependence. The flame cannot exist independently of the candle, but like us it is destined to become extinguished."

I stopped talking and left Tess in the silence of her meditation. A minute later I saw her head drop forwards. She then awoke with a start.

"Was I that boring?" I asked with a note of humour in my voice.

"No, I just felt relaxed and nodded off."

It happens to me sometimes, particularly if I meditate for half an hour or more.

"I think we should stop there for today," I said. "Your next lesson is tantric sex."

"What's that?" said Tess.

"I know what it is and how it's supposed to work but I've never found the right partner to experience it with."

"And you think I am?" enquired Tess.

"Perhaps," I said with a gleam in my eye, "but not yet."

The late afternoon and early evening had drifted by in a pleasant, leisurely haze. It was time once more to consider dinner.

"What do you fancy eating tonight, Tess?" I asked.

"I don't mind," she replied casually. "There's a cafeteria across the square. It's cheap, quick and easy."

"What about Indian, Thai or Chinese?" I ventured.

"Not Indian. It's too spicy," she said with a small grimace.

"Alright, let's look for a Thai or Chinese place then."

We didn't have to wander far before we stumbled upon a cosy-looking Thai restaurant. Stepping inside, I asked if they had a table for two.

"Have you reserved?" came the predictable response from a short middle-aged woman who I guessed was the proprietor rather than just an employee.

"No," I replied simply.

"Then follow me," she said, leading us to a table by the window. I could already sense what was coming. Tess never liked sitting by the window, even in a town where she knew no one.

"Could we sit over there?" Tess asked, pointing to a different table.

"It's reserved for seven-thirty," the woman informed us.

"We'll be gone by then," Tess and I said in unison, exchanging a smile with the lady.

The proprietor didn't seem bothered; it was more of a customary routine than a genuine issue.

"Let's start with an aperitif," I suggested. "The house cocktail looks interesting."

The younger Thai waitress who took our order asked, "With or without alcohol?"

I glanced at Tess.

"With," she said decisively.

"And the same for me," I added.

Our drinks arrived quickly accompanied by prawn crackers and the waitress lit a small candle on our table. A few moments later, she returned to ask if we were ready to order.

"Just a few more minutes, please," I said.

"We can meditate with the candles in the meantime," Tess teased.

I chuckled and added, "On weekend retreats I used to attend, there was a lama who told us that even a minute or two of mindful breathing at red traffic lights could be beneficial, but he did warn us not to fall asleep."

"Seriously?"

"Yes, really," I nodded. "At another retreat, a Tibetan lama with a great sense of humour was taking questions. A woman sitting cross-legged at the front asked if we had lived before. Without cracking a smile, he replied, 'Yes, you were all hens in a chicken coop and I was a cock.' She looked utterly flummoxed until the rest of us burst out laughing."

"I'd love to go on a weekend retreat with you," Tess said.

"With pleasure. Shall we have another cocktail and order dinner?"

"Alright," she agreed with a grin. "But I'll be pompette," she warned, using the French word for tipsy.

That was something I wanted to see.

We decided to start with Nems and Thai salad, followed by duck with black mushrooms for Tess and chicken with noodles for me. A bottle of local red wine, *Vin de Tursan*, was our choice of drink and we finished off with banana fritters and jasmine tea.

"What do you think we'll find tomorrow?" Tess asked as the meal wound down.

"Probably nothing," I admitted. "The whole area has seen a lot of development since the railway went through. Labenne, the nearest village, is now a town. There's Labenne-Océan with houses built near the sea and the motorway has cut right through the Landes Forest nearby. I think we should just head to the Marais d'Orx nature reserve to get a feel for the place. Maybe you'll pick up on some kind of energy. If so, we can follow the outlet river all the way to the ocean if necessary, though it's quite a trek. It flows north to the port of Capbreton."

"I can't just summon those energies on demand and I don't even know why they happen," Tess said with a slight shrug.

"Fair enough," I replied. "Just follow your instincts and let me know if you sense anything."

"I think we should start at the local library tomorrow morning and try to locate the house of Mme Dufour. That should put us in the right area."

We paid the bill and as we stood up to leave, Tess grabbed my arm for balance.

"Are you alright, Tess? Is it the energy field talking to you?" I joked.

"No," she laughed. "It's the cocktail and red wine. I'm pompette."

We made our way back to the hotel without incident. The moment we entered the room, Tess flopped backwards onto the bed, arms splayed out.

"I'll be fine in a minute," she murmured.

"I'm going to take a shower. Do you want the bathroom first?" I asked.

"I'm fine, you go ahead," she replied, her eyes already half-closed.

I had been under a stream of warm water for about five minutes when Tess opened the bathroom door and walked in. Looking through steam and droplets of water slowly falling down the perspective door, I saw she was ready to join me. I opened the door and she came and stood beside me.

"Are you ready to share the water, Lynden? I'm cold."

The shower cubicle was small and cosy.

"Sure," I said. "Do you want me to lather you over?"

As I poured shower gel into my hands, Tess turned towards me. Looking upwards, she pressed against me and clasped her arms around the back of my head and kissed me. It was an urgent, long-lasting French kiss. I held Tess close to me, water cascading over our heads, one arm holding her back, the other hand placed on her buttocks, pulling her closer against me. My body was predictably starting to react. Tess had unclasped her hands and was tracing slow circles over my shoulder blades when, without warning, I felt a jolt of static electricity surge through me. It wasn't just a tingle; it was like being struck by a current from another time. My vision blurred and I was suddenly pulled into a trance-like state. I was no longer myself but was seeing through the eyes of Hartley on that fateful, stormy night in 1853.

I felt the cold, damp air of the forest pressing in, the heavy silence broken only by the distant rumble of thunder. I was moving through the underbrush, Hartley's pulse hammering in my ears, his dread rising with every step. I rushed to our house, only to find it abandoned, the door hanging open, banging in the wind, the rooms eerily silent. And then, nothing, a black void.

Cold water brought me back to the present with a shock. I gasped, disoriented, as the icy stream drenched us both. Tess, too, seemed to have been caught in whatever had just happened. She stood frozen, her eyes wide and unseeing, as if she were still elsewhere. I quickly turned off the shower, wondering if one of us had accidentally knocked the lever to cold. Tess stepped out first, shivering violently, and reached for a towel, her breath coming in shallow, ragged bursts.

"What the hell was that?" she managed to say, wrapping herself tightly with a towel, trying to warm herself up.

I tried the shower again, turning the dial to test it. There was no hot water left. It was as if the heat had been siphoned away by some unseen force.

"We've run out of hot water," I said, though the mundane explanation felt hollow, insufficient after what had just transpired.

Still half-stunned, we headed straight to the bed, slipping beneath the covers, our bodies pressed together in search of warmth. The cold of the shower caused us both to shiver, but there was something more, a haunting sense of the otherworldly.

"What happened, Tess?" I asked, my voice barely a whisper.

She lay on her back, staring up at the ceiling as though searching for an answer in the shadows.

"I don't know," she breathed. "I felt it too, like I was seeing through your eyes or someone else's. It was like being dragged into another person's memory, but I couldn't tell if it was yours or... someone long dead."

I swallowed hard, replaying the vision in my mind.

"It was Hartley," I said finally. "I saw what he saw that night in the forest. I felt his fear, finding the house empty."

Tess turned to look at me, her eyes focusing on me as though coming out of a daze.

"You saw that too? I thought it was just me or that I was somehow picking it up from you."

"I don't think it was just you," I said, shaking my head slowly. "It felt like we were both there, together. As if we'd crossed into something that wasn't ours to see."

A shiver ran down her spine and she pulled the blanket tighter around her shoulders.

"I've never experienced anything like that before. It was so vivid. Almost... physical."

"I know," I said softly, brushing a damp strand of hair away from her face. "It was real. Too real."

We lay there in silence, the room eerily quiet except for our breathing. The sensation of the cold water, the vision, the fear, it all felt too connected to be a coincidence.

"I think we've disturbed something," she said finally, her voice hushed, almost reverent. "Something tied to that place. Maybe tomorrow when we go there, we'll find out what it is."

I nodded, though an unease crept into me.

"Maybe. But whatever it is, it's not just the past. It's here with us now."

Tess took a deep, shaky breath and curled up closer against me. I wrapped my arm around her, pulling her in as the chill of the vision slowly ebbed away, replaced by the steady warmth of our bodies.

"We should sleep," she murmured. "But be ready. Tomorrow might bring more than we bargained for."

"I'm ready," I said, though I wasn't entirely sure if I believed the words I was saying. With the memory of that stormy night still clinging to the edges of my mind, sleep felt a long way off.

With her teeth chattering, Tess said, "I remember getting into the shower. I remember warm water dripping over our heads and kissing you and I held my hands behind your head. I touched… oh my God."

"What, Tess, what?" I asked, somewhat alarmed by her startled tone of voice.

"Go through it second by second," she said.

"I just got that jolt again like back at the museum. We were in a close embrace when it happened and I found myself standing in Hartley's shoes and feeling panicked when I went to a small wooden house. The next thing I remember, we were standing under a cold shower. It brought me round."

"Turn over on your stomach, Lynden."

I did as Tess asked.

"Shut your eyes so that you don't see me."

Again, I did as Tess requested.

"This sounds as though it's going to be exciting," I replied, as I felt a hand hit the back of my head.

"Ow," I said.

"Shhh," said Tess. "Be serious for a moment. What am I doing?"

I lay still and then, "I can feel it," I said.

"Feel what?"

"You're passing your hand over my shoulder blade and it's getting warmer. Wow, it's very hot now. How are you doing that, Tess?" I asked.

"I'm not actually touching you. It's your birthmark on your shoulder blade and my birthmark on my hand. Our energies are connecting through them, that's what's happening. On both occasions, at the museum and here, when it happened, you are connecting with your ancestor Hartley," replied Tess.

"Something else has happened, Tess. When did we leave the restaurant?"

"About 7:15, I think. It was reserved from 7:30 and we came straight back here."

"And what time is it now?"

"Nearly nine-thirty," replied Tess, looking at the bedside table clock. "It's probably wrong. Oh my God, my watch says the same time and it's dark outside. What does your watch say?"

"Nine-thirty. What happened? There's over an hour missing," I said. "That's why we are cold. We used up all the hotel's hot water stood under the shower. It's like time slowed down for us."

Tess lay still, her breath shallow, her body still damp from the cold shower. The room felt too quiet, too still. Her voice broke through the calm, faintly trembling.

"Lynden... What are you saying? You think we somehow... lost an hour?"

I stared at the ceiling, trying to make sense of what had just happened. The sharp, disorienting jolt I had felt when we kissed in the shower still echoed in my body. And now it was clear: time had shifted. We both felt it. The cold, the confusion, it wasn't just the water. Something else had happened. Something that had to do with Hartley and Eleanor that night.

"I don't know exactly," I said, sitting up slowly, trying to shake off the eerie feeling that enveloped us. "But this isn't normal. The way the energy shifted between us, it's like we're stepping into something... otherworldly. I felt Hartley's panic, his rush through the forest. And then... suddenly it was like I was caught in his memory, reliving it through him."

Tess sat up too, her eyes wide, her face pale.

"When I touched your shoulder, I felt it too. But I didn't understand what it was. It wasn't just the warmth or the energy. It was like I was pulling something out of you, or you were pulling something from me..."

"Exactly," I said, feeling my heart rate pick up. "And then there was the missing hour. We were under that shower for less than five minutes, or so we thought, and we both lost track of time. You didn't even realise until we saw our watches and looked outside. It was almost nine-thirty and everything was dark. The water had gone cold; we were both shivering... we didn't feel time pass. It didn't make sense."

Tess was silent for a moment, clearly processing what I had said. I could feel her focus shift as she thought it over.

"I don't understand," she said quietly, her voice edged with disbelief. "How could this happen? Why now?"

I took a deep breath, trying to steady myself.

"I don't know. But it's connected to the place. The house where Hartley and Eleanor had moved to. The energies in this area are tied to something much bigger than us. It's as if we're... channelling those memories. Maybe it's the same reason we both felt the pull when we were at the museum. But we're close now. We're nearing where everything happened. There's something that links us to this... history, this trauma."

Tess's eyes darkened, her lips trembling.

"And what if we can't control it?"

I didn't have an answer for that, but I could feel it too, the unsettling certainty that whatever was happening was becoming more intense. The closer we got to the house in the Landes Forest, to the heart of the story, the more we seemed to be slipping into something deeper. Something far beyond what we had anticipated.

"There's only one way to find out," I said, my voice low. "We need to go to the Marais d'Orx tomorrow, to the nature reserve. We'll follow the outlet river, see if we can feel more of it, the energy, the pull. But we'll have to stay grounded. We have to keep our wits about us."

Tess nodded slowly, her eyes distant. She looked out of the window as if she could see something more, something beyond the ordinary world.

"I don't know what's happening," she said, her voice barely a whisper. "But I think it's something that we can't escape, Lynden. Whatever this is, whatever we're tapping into, it's already here. And I don't think it's letting go."

I exhaled slowly, the impact of her words sinking in. She was right. There was no running from it now. This wasn't just about exploring the past. This was about the past reaching for us.

I sat there for a moment, processing everything. Then, turning to Tess, I said, "We'll go to the library tomorrow and we'll look for the house. If we find it, we'll see what happens. But I have a feeling that things will only escalate from here."

Tess nodded again, her gaze softening as she met my eyes. She seemed calmer now, as if she had made peace with something, perhaps with the realisation that we were already in too deep to turn back.

"I'll go along with it," she said, a quiet determination in her voice. "But I want you to promise me something."

"What?"

"Promise me we won't get lost in this," she said, her tone both pleading and resolute. "Promise me that, no matter what happens, we won't let it take us. We have to stay connected to reality."

I took her hand, squeezing it firmly.

"I promise, Tess. We'll face it together. But we can't ignore what's happening. We need to understand it, even if it drags us in further."

Tess's grip tightened on my hand as if she needed the reassurance.

"Okay. Together," she whispered, her voice steady now.

We both lay back down, tiredness taking hold of us and tomorrow would be a new day. The answers might be out there waiting for us, but one thing was certain, there was no going back from this.

And as I drifted off to sleep, I couldn't help but wonder: What had we just touched? What force was pulling us towards it?

Chapter 24

The following morning, I noticed that I had received a short-recorded message on my mobile from Swann and Cartwright solicitors: "Could you please contact us at your earliest convenience."

I phoned back, telling the secretary who answered the phone that I would be back in the country in a few days if it could wait and I'd contact them again then.

Tess and I then headed to the municipal archives of Dax, housed at the Hôtel de Ville, to consult historical maps of the area. We hoped to uncover traces of old water mills or country houses around Labenne and the Marais d'Orx. However, the maps we were shown either lacked the level of detail we needed or didn't seem to document anything of interest. We were certain something relevant could be found eventually, but with the limited time available to us we decided not to dive into details such as land ownership records or voter lists that might hold more clues.

Tess, ever practical, had an idea.

"Why not check the census records for the Dufour family near the Marais d'Orx? We might find a more specific location or details about their occupation, like if any of them worked as millers," she suggested.

"Great idea," I agreed. "And while we're at it, we should look up any newspaper articles from around 1852–1853. Marcel Dufour's death must have made the local news."

When we asked the archivist, we were directed to the local library where we could access more relevant records.

The library was only a short walk away, just two minutes from the Hôtel de Ville. Inside, we quickly asked for computer access to the online genealogy databases. Tess, with her nimble fingers and quick reflexes on the keyboard, took charge. She sifted through the 1851 census for Labenne and after a bit of searching found two Dufour families listed in the area.

Looking closer, we discovered that Marguerite Dufour was living at *La Maison de la Pinède* while Marcel Dufour was at *L'abris du Pinède*, both located in the Quartier du Moulin in Labenne.

Next, we enquired about the local newspapers from the period and were given the names *Le Courrier des Landes* and *Le Petit Journal des Landes*. Both had been digitised, which sped up our search. In *Le Courrier des Landes*, we found two articles detailing the tragic death of Marcel Dufour during a violent storm on Friday, February 18th, 1853. This was the crucial date that Hartley's diary had failed to mention. Unfortunately, the location details were just as vague as the information we'd found in the genealogical records.

The article read:

Tragic Accident in the Commune of Labenne – Extract, 26th February 1853
On the night of Friday, February 18th, 1853, a storm of unparalleled ferocity, the likes of which has not been seen in living memory, struck this region. It was during this dreadful tempest that the lifeless body of Mr. Marcel Dufour was discovered, lying at the base of a mighty oak. Mr. Dufour, the estranged husband of Dame Marguerite Dufour, who inherited vast estates from her late father, Mr. Nicolas Poullin, is believed to have continued residing at La Maison de la Pinède, situated in the Quartier du Moulin of the commune of Labenne.

It is reported that despite their separation, Mr. Dufour, ever vigilant in his care for his wife's properties, ventured out into the night to inspect the damage wrought by the storm upon the surrounding grounds. Alas, it was at this moment that a large branch, torn free by the furious gusts, fell upon him, inflicting a mortal wound to the head. According to initial testimonies, the depth of the injury claimed the unfortunate man's life instantly, sparing him by divine mercy any further suffering.

The local gendarmerie, called to the scene to verify the incident, gathered evidence and provided their findings to the coroner the following day. The coroner could only record a verdict of accidental death, a conclusion readily accepted by the community which remains deeply saddened by this tragedy occurring under such calamitous circumstances.

Thus passes a life, reminding all of the fragility of our earthly existence before the unyielding forces of nature.

By the time we finished at the library it was already late morning. Despite our early start at the Hôtel de Ville our research had taken longer than we'd anticipated. We decided to head out of Dax, taking the back road that ran alongside the Adour River before joining the long straight stretch of road that would lead us towards our destination.

Tess glanced over at me and asked, "Are you happy with a sandwich or a quiche Lorraine for lunch?"

"Sure, as long as there's dessert," I replied. "I'll stop at the next village."

A few miles later, we pulled into a small boulangerie in St. Geours-de-Maremne. Tess hopped out of the car to grab our lunch while I stayed behind, parked on the roadside, engine running. I gazed absentmindedly at the old fortified church across the road, the bell tower rising against the morning sky, while Tess made her way into the bakery. An ordinary church in a small village that would have been the centre of life of the community, I thought; births, deaths and marriage ceremonies all conducted by a succession of local priests for hundreds of years, a building that would record the local population ascending and descending its steps, witnessing happiness and tragedies in the course of human existence. Tess's return brought me back to the present.

"I got ham and cheese sandwiches, water and a raspberry dessert with two spoons," said Tess, holding up the bag triumphantly.

"Let's park outside the village to eat," I suggested, feeling the need for a quiet spot.

"Oh, and the woman at the boulangerie warned me about a speed camera on the road to St. Vincent de Tyrosse. She could tell I wasn't a local," Tess added with a smile.

"That was kind of her," I replied, amused by her quick rapport with strangers.

Just beyond the village we spotted a narrow track leading off towards what seemed like an abandoned farm. I turned off the busy main road and parked under some pine trees, eager to escape the traffic, and we settled down to eat our sandwiches in peace. As we unwrapped our food, Tess nodded towards the building opposite.

"See that factory over there? It's probably the best-known manufacturer of foie gras in France."

"Really? I loved the foie gras," I said, savouring the thought of eating it again.

We finished our sandwiches and shared the *framboisier* raspberry dessert, a sweet, raspberry and cream-filled delight. Afterwards, we continued along the road.

"There's the speed camera," Tess pointed out.

I made sure to keep my speed under 50 mph though I was unsure whether the limit was 50 or 56 mph. I had noticed crossing France that different counties have different speed regulations and crossing from one into another rarely comes with a clear speed limit road sign. Yet every corner seems to have a reminder of a maximum speed limit to go around it, part of the charm, the frustration and the unpredictability of driving in France, I thought.

As we drove through St. Vincent de Tyrosse, it was a place I recognised by name, known for producing several international French rugby players. Now we were only minutes away from our destination.

"Let's take a detour around the Marais d'Orx first. Then we can park and start our walk from there," I suggested.

Tess glanced at Google Maps on her phone. "No point," she said. "The road takes a wide detour; it doesn't actually go around the lake edge and marsh. We'd be better off heading straight to where the river Boudigau flows out. There's a sand or gravel quarry nearby." She dropped a pin on the online map and I followed the route.

"Let's stop by the post office first," I said suddenly.

"What? Why?"

"If we ask at the post office they might know where the Quartier du Moulin is. It could save us a long walk to the coast."

"Ha ha, good thinking," Tess laughed. "I'll go in. They might be more helpful if they don't hear your accent."

Cheeky, I thought, but she had a point. We pulled into a car park opposite. While she was inside, I zoomed in on Google Maps, studying the satellite view, trying to piece together where this mysterious area might be. About fifteen minutes later, Tess returned.

"There was a bit of a wait," she said, slightly out of breath. "The young woman at the counter didn't know anything so she called over one of the older postmen. He had just come back from his round. He said there isn't a Quartier du Moulin in the commune and the only Dufour family he knows moved into town six months ago. He suggested that if a Quartier du Moulin ever existed, it would have been near water and the only river here is the Boudigau."

"That much we already figured out," I said.

"He also recommended checking in the next commune, Ondres. Apparently, the boundary between the two communes isn't clear, especially in the forest."

We continued to the spot Tess had marked earlier. The pin led us to a small clearing near the underpass of the A63 motorway where the noise of cars and lorries rumbled overhead.

Stepping out of the car, we looked for a path that led to the Marais d'Orx. We found a narrow trail heading east but it cut across cultivated land. Tall vegetation along the riverbanks limited our view of the water. The walk to the canal originally built to drain the lake and marshes took us about half an hour, and it was another half-hour back.

As we walked, we held hands, enjoying the simple comfort of each other's presence. Upon our return we passed the car and continued further towards Labenne, passing under the motorway again and skirting the edge of town. We crossed the main road to Bayonne, searching for a safe spot to get over the railway line. Despite our efforts the river remained almost invisible, obscured by a thick growth of willows, alders and tangled underbrush. Beyond the railway, the vast expanse of Maritime pine forest seemed to stretch forever.

I felt my optimism draining away with each step. Sensing my change in mood, Tess squeezed my hand and said, "Lynden, if we want to keep going, we're going to need a boat."

"Where are we going to find a boat? Besides, the river's shallow. A boat might not even help and if we hit fallen trees, we'll be stuck."

She looked at me with a determined glint in her eyes. "We have to try. It's the only way we'll make any real progress from here."

I sighed but her resolve was contagious. "Alright then, let's find a boat."

"We could rent an inflatable canoe or maybe even buy one if they aren't too pricey. They sell them at those shops by the beaches," suggested Tess, a hint of excitement in her voice.

"I can't really picture us paddling down this tiny river in a kids' canoe," I replied, chuckling.

"Don't laugh at the idea, Lynden," Tess shot back with a playful glare. "They make inflatable canoes big enough for two adults. And if you're not keen on going into a beach shop we can stop by the outdoor store at St. Paul-lès-Dax on our way back to the hotel. I already looked it up," she added, sealing her suggestion with a kiss that left me with no room to refuse.

We had already spent most of the day driving in circles, asking questions and getting next to nowhere. The dense vegetation along the river made it impossible to explore on foot – it was clear a canoe would be our best option.

"You can take the canoe back to England with you, Lynden. I can't really show up at home with a canoe, having said I was hiking in the Alpes with friends for a few days," Tess said with an ironic smile.

Her words gave me a sinking feeling in my stomach. It was a stark reminder that our time together was limited, that soon we'd have to part ways, and the feeling in my heart was that I didn't want us to be separated. Despite everything I had told her that clinging to thoughts or emotions leads to unhappiness, I found myself struggling with exactly that. It's easy to say, I thought, but much harder to live by.

On the drive back to the hotel we made a detour to an outdoor activities shop where we bought a two-seat olive-coloured canoe, life jackets, paddles and a foot pump. The gear took up a fair proportion of the boot space. On impulse I added waterproofs and wellington boots. It wasn't warm enough for swimwear if we ended up out of the sun. I dreaded the moment we'd launch the canoe, imagining the spectacle of us tipping over and becoming a source of amusement for any onlookers.

We returned to the hotel and stopped at the bar for a beer before eating in their restaurant for dinner. After a day of sandwiches, I wanted something hot but not too heavy. I opted for the soup of the day followed by a braised flatfish. Unfortunately, there was no foie gras on the menu. Tess chose goat cheese on toast with salad for a starter, then salmon served with green beans. We refused coffee and settled for herbal teas to finish off the meal. I asked for the bill to be added to our room.

Before leaving the table, Tess reached across and held my hand. It was one of those moments when silence said everything. We had done everything we could to solve the mystery of Eleanor Fournier. I had spent nearly five hundred euros on a canoe and its accessories without any guarantee of concluding a successful outcome. But we had narrowed down our search area and with the thick vegetation along the river there was still hope of discovering the abandoned house or mill.

"Let's go upstairs," I said softly.

Tess led the way, thanking the restaurant staff as we left. When we reached our room, she turned to me with a smile.

"I'm going to take a shower," she announced.

"Fancy some meditation afterwards? I'll meditate with you," I offered; my tone was casual, I had a plan in mind.

"Sure," Tess agreed, oblivious to my intentions.

"I'll take a shower too, the hot water will relax my muscles; but after you, so we don't have a repeat of last night."

While Tess was in the bathroom I prepared the room. I closed the window shutters, dimmed the lights and set the two bedside lamps on the floor. I arranged the cushions so we could sit facing each other, then lit a small candle, placing it in a glass between us.

By the time I finished setting up Tess had emerged from the bathroom, wearing a hotel flannel bathrobe.

"I'll let you get comfortable whilst I take my shower, Tess." As she took up her cross-legged position I bent down and gave her a firm kiss on the lips before stepping away.

Needless to say, I didn't waste time in the shower. It was a brisk five-minute affair plus another minute to brush my teeth. I also put on a hotel-supplied flannel bathrobe and gathered my shirt, jeans, underwear and socks, and ushered them into the corner of the bedroom near my bag.

I then took up my position opposite Tess, the flickering candle between us.

"Lynden, you're only wearing a bathrobe," she pointed out, grinning.

"Yes, I know, but it's a long one, but anyway so are you and it's shorter," I said with a wink.

"I hadn't noticed…" Tess teased still smiling but in the full knowledge that her bathrobe didn't entirely cover all her thigh.

"Close your eyes and focus on your breathing, Tess," I murmured.

We sat opposite each other in silence, the dim light of the flickering candle between us casting shadows on the floor. The room was still except for the gentle rhythm of our breathing. I guided Tess through the meditation, my voice soft and steady. As I spoke, I found myself staring at the flame; its dance was almost hypnotic.

After a few moments I felt relaxed in the warmth and intimacy of our shared silence. My awareness of the world outside seemed to dissolve, leaving only the space between us and the invisible energy of our connection.

Tess remained motionless as if lost in a trance, her newfound practice absorbing her completely. It was the simplicity of it all, the closeness, the quiet intimacy, that stirred something deep inside me. Every detail seemed to intensify from the way the candlelight lit up her skin to the subtle rise and fall of her chest as she inhaled and exhaled. It wasn't just an emotional response, it was physical too, as my thoughts drifted from the philosophy of impermanence to a more visceral desire.

Almost as if sensing the change, Tess slowly opened one eye then the other, her gaze locking onto mine. It was as if the atmosphere had shifted completely and the delicate balance of the moment was suddenly infused with something more alive. Her laughter was a reminder of how easily even the most profound moments can slip into light-heartedness, how they unravel into the ordinary yet beautiful reality of human emotion. I found myself laughing too, realising that the space we had created wasn't just about the calmness of meditation, it was about the shared joy and the happiness that enveloped us.

I leaned forward, moving the candle aside and pinched the wick between my finger and thumb. A thin wisp of smoke curled and twisted into the air. Tess stood up, facing me, and moved towards me as I sat in my cross-legged meditation position. Her inner thigh brushed against my face and the faintest detection of her odour briefly coincided with my intake of breath. The effect was immediate. Pheromones, I said to myself as she slowly repositioned herself to sit on my lap, her legs becoming entwined behind my back as our bodies became joined slowly and carefully in the most intimate of ways.

In a low soothing voice I whispered, "Let's be still, don't rush, don't move. Let our bodies find their own harmony. This is Yab-Yum, the mystical union of wisdom and compassion.

Our union will transcend the illusion of duality or Maya, the false separation between subject and object. Feel the energy rise between us and retain it for as long as we can."

I fell silent, our eyes locked, so close that our noses almost touched. We did not kiss; instead, we gazed deeply into each other's eyes. Time seemed to dissolve. Minutes passed, though we had no sense of it, lost in a timeless space beyond ordinary perception. Then, I felt Tess's arms tighten around me, a silent signal. She made no sound and I, too, quietly gave the gift of the seed of life. Tess then said softly and from a dreamlike state, "We are Eleanor and Hartley."

As the sensation of cramp began creeping into our limbs, the need to move broke the spell. We gently disentangled ourselves, exchanging a long-lasting kiss before separating.

"Was that tantric sex then?" Tess asked, her tone practical, now far removed from the moment that had passed.

"Well, it was a first attempt at what I think it's meant to be," I replied with a smile. "Like I said before, I've never had a partner with whom I feel such a strong spiritual link."

I hesitated, then added, "But what did you mean when you said, 'We are Eleanor and Hartley'?"

"Did I really say that?" Tess asked, a trace of doubt in her voice.

"Yes, you did."

She paused, searching her own memory. "At the most intimate moment, I felt that we were them," came her reply.

Chapter 25

That night Tess and I were cuddled close together as if the world beyond us had ceased to exist. Wrapped in each other's arms, we were tangled up in a love that was undeniable and we knew that our inevitable parting was getting nearer with every passing hour. My life was pulling me back to Cumbria, while Tess's commitments tied her to Vienne. She had a partner but it was a subject she evaded, just as I did when it came to mentioning Ann. It was an implicit no-go area between us. The past and the future didn't matter, all that counted was the present, our precious moments together.

In the morning over breakfast, we checked the satellite images on Google Maps, searching for the perfect spot to park the car and launch our river adventure. After some debate we decided that the best access point would be a service road near observatory five on the marsh. The only drawback was a weir between the main road and the railway line, a minor obstacle we thought. Starting lower down the river could mean missing the outlet part of the river from the marsh entirely so this seemed our best choice.

The weather forecast was for hot sunny weather with the risk of thunderstorms later in the day. It felt like a metaphor for us: intense and bright now with an unpredictable storm lurking somewhere on the horizon.

We stopped by the same boulangerie as the day before, hurriedly grabbing fresh sandwiches. By half past ten we had the inflatable canoe ready to launch and our anticipation grew as we pushed off into the river. Tess took her place at the front and it took a few paddle strokes before we found the correct rhythm. More than once, we veered towards the riverbank, laughing as our strokes went out of sync, too strong on one side then too strong on the other.

"Tess, there's really no need for you to paddle if you don't want to," I called out with a grin. "But keep an eye out for submerged branches; I'd rather not get stuck."

The river was narrow, just two to four metres across and quite shallow, no more than a metre deep on the outside bends. I assumed it would deepen somewhere further downstream where it became tidal, but I hadn't checked the tides; perhaps it was an oversight.

"How are we going to get back, Lynden?" Tess asked, turning her head. "Can we really paddle all the way upstream back to the car?"

Her question caught me off guard; I hadn't thought that far ahead. "It should be fine," I replied, trying to sound confident. "But if it's too much we can leave the canoe somewhere, grab a taxi and come back for it with the car."

The riverbed was sandy and we soon found that progress was slower than I'd hoped. More than once, I had to jump out to lighten our load and pull the canoe, while Tess sat, looking both amused and a little guilty. The overhanging branches of willow trees added to the challenge, forcing us to duck down low and let the gentle current sweep us beneath them.

It took us about twenty minutes before we glided under the main road then steered towards the right bank. The weir was ahead, a small drop but enough to risk tearing a hole in our inflatable vessel.

"I'd rather we carry the canoe around the weir, Tess," I said, a little breathless. "It's not worth the risk — even if it's not a big drop we could put a hole in the canoe or capsize."

"I couldn't agree more, Lynden," she replied, relief softening her voice. "I'm not ready to end my days here."

We hauled the canoe up the bank, circumventing the weir without much trouble and set off once more. I had estimated that we wouldn't need to travel more than five miles from the Orx marsh. But as the trees thickened around us and the river wound deeper into the forest, a nagging worry crept into my mind: what if there was no phone signal further into the forest?

"Tess, is your phone fully charged?" I asked, trying to sound not particularly concerned.

She turned to me, eyebrows raised, the corners of her lips curving into a playful smile. "Are you getting nervous, Lynden?"

"Not nervous," I persuaded myself to say, "Just… thinking ahead."

We shared a look that was both conspiratorial and tender, a glance that spoke of more than just the day's adventure. It was as if we both knew that, like the river, our time together was winding towards an end and neither of us wanted it to happen nor to admit how soon it might come.

"It was full this morning. Now it's at eighty-five percent. Why?" Tess asked, her brow furrowed as she checked her phone.

"Could you do me a favour?" I said. "Pull up Google Maps, switch to satellite view and take screenshots of the river Boudigau, covering the stretch all the way to Labenne Océan and then email them to me, please."

"You still haven't said why," she repeated, a note of curiosity tinged with frustration.

"It's just a precaution," I explained. "If we lose the phone signal in the forest, it's better to have images on both our phones. There aren't many paths here but the forest is divided into parcels and the pine trees vary in height so it should help us navigate if we lose the phone signal."

Tess gave me a sceptical look. "We're hardly going to get lost on a small river between two villages only a few kilometres apart, are we, Lynden?" Her voice trailed off, tinged with a trace of doubt.

"I'm from Cumbria, Tess," I said, with a knowing smile. "You might not understand now but I'll take you up on the fells on a misty day sometime. Then you'll get it. It doesn't take much to become disoriented. And don't forget, I was a boy scout, be prepared and all that," I added with a wink, hoping to reassure her.

Moments later, her email came through. I quickly downloaded the screenshots and switched my phone off to conserve the battery.

"What exactly are we searching for out here, Lynden? Stone ruins?" she asked, leaning back in her seat.

"It's possible but I doubt it. I don't think we will find many stones or rocks here, but keep an eye out for square outlines, maybe house foundations or a heap of old timber. Also look for a small canal branching off into a pond next to the river," I replied.

Another thirty minutes downstream and we were in the heart of the forest. The landscape was mostly flat with remnants of old sand dunes forming undulations with long gentle slopes. The flat valley floor was waterlogged. Now we were surrounded by clusters of willows and alders, their leaves casting playful shadows on the water, Tess had gone quiet. I leaned forward to see if she'd dozed off in the front of the canoe, but before I could ask, a distant rumble of thunder rolled across the sky.

"Did you hear that, Tess?" I called out. "I think we might be in for a soaking before the day's over."

The river here was crystal clear; we could see the sandy bottom rippling beneath us. The large arching fronds of royal ferns brushed against the sides of the canoe. Sunlight streamed through the canopy, creating a dappled pattern on the surface.

Bright blue damselflies darted back and forth, sparkling like tiny jewels as they hovered above the water.

I was about to comment on the beauty of the spot when Tess suddenly gasped.

"Look, Lynden!" she cried, pointing towards the trees over there. "There's an old woman behind the willows, she's waving us over, maybe she needs help."

I turned just in time to catch a fleeting glimpse of her, an elderly figure partially hidden by the foliage. Yet as the ripples spread from our canoe's path she seemed to vanish behind the trees. It wasn't possible to stop right there but about another thirty metres further downstream we managed to pull onto a sandy bank.

We both clambered out and I dragged the canoe up onto dry land. "Let's go see what she wants," I said, feeling a surge of curiosity mixed with concern. Together we headed back to where Tess had seen her. But the woman had moved deeper into the forest, stepping away from the riverbank.

"Bonjour!" I called out, scanning the undergrowth. But there was no response, only the whisper of leaves stirred by a faint breeze. We pushed on a little further, our feet crunching over pine needles. When we reached the spot where she had last been there was no one in sight.

"She must have kept walking straight on," I muttered, glancing around. "But where could she have gone?"

About a hundred metres from where we left the canoe, the ground sloped gently upwards. There, half-hidden beneath a thick veil of ivy and brambles, stood the ruins of what once must have been a large house. The remaining walls were at the most only a metre high, built of squarely worked stone blocks and mortar. The sight took me by surprise. Then I remembered reading somewhere that the Adour River had flowed north through this area a few hundred years ago before being diverted towards Bayonne in the late sixteenth century. If it had been navigable back then, they could have transported stone from inland quarries or even from the Pyrenees as there were no stone outcrops to be found in this part of Landes that could have been quarried.

Another rumble of thunder rolled in from the south-west, louder this time and a slight breeze rustled the treetops, bringing with it the smell of rain.

"Tess," I said, turning to her, "if you hadn't seen that old woman waving us over, we would never have found this place."

Tess had gone pale, her face drained of colour as she stared at me.

"Lynden... don't you get it?"

"Get what?" I asked, confused.

"That woman who guided us here, she was a ghost," Tess said, her voice barely above a whisper.

I laughed, though it sounded hollow even to my own ears. "Just because she didn't want to stick around doesn't mean she was a ghost, Tess. I saw her as clear as the light of day."

She shook her head slowly, her eyes wide with a fear I couldn't quite dismiss. "You didn't see her properly, Lynden; there was something... different about her. Something not of this world."

Tess's words sent a shiver down my spine despite the warmth of the afternoon. I glanced back at the ruin with the ivy twisting like skeletal fingers around the old stones. For the first time the air felt colder and the shadows seemed darker.

"Well, ghost or not," I said, trying to sound light-hearted, "she led us to something interesting, didn't she?"

But even as I spoke, I couldn't shake the feeling that we had stumbled into a place where the past wasn't quite ready to let go.

"Lynden, what about what Hartley saw when the steamer docked at Vienne, the old woman dressed in black?" she muttered, her voice filled with an eerie certainty. "We're here,

Lynden. This is where we were guided to, just as you explained to me before. It's our karma." Her eyes held a depth I hadn't seen before as though she could glimpse something far beyond our world.

I wrapped my arms around her waist, pulling her close. The kiss we shared felt different, charged with a strange electricity as if our souls were momentarily connected by invisible threads of fate. It wasn't just a kiss; it was confirmation that we were exactly where we were supposed to be. For a brief moment everything felt perfectly aligned as though we were being guided by something ancient and powerful.

The wind picked up, now twisting through the trees with an almost howling sound. Thunder rolled ominously above us, the sky darkening as the storm closed in.

"Look, Tess," I said, pointing towards a patch of disturbed ground about fifty metres away where the remnants of what must have been a small house once stood. We moved closer but all that remained were broken roof tiles scattered around and some rusted iron fragments, the relics of someone's life long gone. It was as if the forest itself had purposefully tried to hide the past.

Suddenly, Tess's demeanour changed; her gaze turned distant; her expression glassy.

In a voice barely above a whisper, she said, "We lived here, Hartley. Please, find me."

Alarmed, I gripped her shoulders, giving her a gentle shake. "Tess, are you alright?" I asked, searching her eyes for recognition. She blinked slowly, like someone waking from a deep sleep.

"Sorry, what did you say?" she asked, momentarily herself again.

Then as if a veil had been drawn over her, she slipped back into that dazed otherworldly state. The atmosphere around us felt electrically charged as though the very ground was exhaling its memories. A jagged flash of lightning split the sky, striking the earth only metres away and the ensuing thunderclap was deafening, as if the past itself was announcing its presence to us as on the night of 18th February 1853.

With a hollow, chilling voice Tess looked directly at me, her eyes hollow and empty. "Find me, Hartley," she insisted, her arm lifting to point towards a shadowed area shrouded in thick bushes. I took her hand, feeling the cold sweat on her palm and we moved together towards the spot she had indicated about thirty metres away. It was as if we were being pulled along by an invisible presence.

A wave of nausea hit me, a sickening feeling of déjà vu. The ground beneath our feet was soft and moss-covered, almost sponge-like as though we were being transported through time to a distant past. The wind died down and sunlight filtered through the treetops, casting an almost golden glow. Ahead, a row of dark brown stones marked the edge of what had once been a mill pond now long filled with sediment. It was eerily quiet, the only sound the faint trickle of water. My grip on Tess's hand tightened; she walked beside me, her body rigid, her eyes unblinking as if in a trance. It felt like we were moving through a dream, I was reliving exactly the same visions I had experienced outside the chapel near Alice Farnsworth's cottage in Devon.

The landscape around us shifted, blurring the line between past and present. For a brief moment, I was no longer in the forest of today but transported to a long-lost world. The grand house of Marguerite Dufour towered behind us; its stone walls bathed in sunlight. I could see the smaller wooden house where Hartley, Eleanor and little Sophie had once lived. Ahead of us a small wooden framed mill stood, like a silent witness to the passing years.

Reality flickered back and we found ourselves at the edge of a low stone wall. The stones, stained a deep rust colour, were made from the local *'Alios des Landes'*, an iron pan that forms naturally just below the surface of the sandy soil. I edged further forward and found myself crossing a wooden beam floor in an advanced state of decay, and the ground beneath me squeaked with the sound of rotting timber. Below, I could see the hollow where a horizontal water wheel once turned, a space now filled with darkness.

    I knelt down, my hands trembling and I began to pull away the decayed wood, feeling the history of the place seep into my skin. Then I saw it, a flash of white against the gloom. A shiver ran down my spine as I uncovered a piece of cloth, still intact, followed by the unmistakable curve of a human skull. I paused, almost unable to breathe. The sunlight pierced through the canopy, casting a spotlight on the skeletal remains, illuminating the bones of a person who had been buried here for more than a century and a half. I knew immediately that it was the woman from my trance-like visions and today she had a name, Eleanor Fournier.

    Behind me Tess watched in silence, but I could sense a shift in her presence. As I leaned forward to look closer, something caught my eye: it was a bright metallic object clenched in the bone knuckles of Eleanor's left hand. I automatically leaned forward to see what it was, then carefully I reached down. At that stage I don't know if it was because of my high emotional state working on my imagination but I swore I saw the bones of the hand open to release the content. It was the eyepiece of a theodolite. Taking it, I rose slowly, turning to face Tess but it wasn't Tess standing before me anymore. It was Eleanor, her features softened by the pale sunlight, her dress was that of another era. She took my hands in hers as we clutched the eyepiece between us.

    "I love you, Hartley," she whispered, her voice full of longing.

    We kissed, a kiss that bridged time itself. The rain began to fall, soft at first then heavier, drenching us as we stood there but we didn't care. It was as though we were suspended in that moment, surrounded by the spirits of the past.

We were fully absorbed in the scene of a day in February 1853, the big house rose above us, we were in a clearing of the forest, spectral figures moving in the periphery of my vision, Marguerite Dufour at the door, Marcel Dufour slipping between the trees, little Sophie cuddling a rabbit, her giggles like the chime of a distant bell. Smoke curled lazily from the chimney of our small wooden house, the mill stood empty but not silent as water gushed along the race, cascading through the lower rooms.

Then another reality reluctantly returned as gradually the vivid scene faded; Eleanor and I wanted that moment to last for ever, the feeling of love and of union. It felt like part of me had been torn away, a connection severed too soon, the forest around us reclaiming its present form. I looked at Tess, who now appeared fully herself again but there was a sadness in her eyes, a few tears rolling down her cheeks for she too had felt the wrenching return of present-day reality return too soon. We stood silently for a few minutes, not speaking, with our minds trying to hold on to the experience we had just been through.

It had even occurred to me that just by holding hands and holding the relic eyepiece of a theodolite that perhaps we had allowed our bodies to become possessed by the spirits of Hartley and Eleanor. Tess was to give me another explanation later.

"We need to give Eleanor a proper burial," Tess said as emotion choked her voice. "But not here. Back in Vienne, where she belongs."

To which I answered softly, "And we will have to go to the Gendarmerie."

Tess nodded, her fingers already swiping at her phone. "I'll drop a pin on Google Maps. There's a faint signal," she said, her voice steady but distant.

We retraced our steps back to the canoe, finding the river swollen and its level risen. I pushed us off into the current, giving us a swifter ride.

"The ride to Labenne Ocean won't take long," I said distantly but each word felt as though I was reciting someone else's farewell.

Chapter 26

As we neared Labenne Océan, we pulled the canoe up onto the bank of the Boudigau and hid it beneath the overhanging trees. Then we set off on foot towards the centre of town. The twenty-minute walk passed in silence, both of us absorbed in our own thoughts of the events that had just unfolded. At some point, Tess slipped her hand into mine, but we didn't speak.

A man walking his dog pointed us towards the nearest gendarmerie which, as it turned out, was in Capbreton. Rather than spend another hour in the canoe, we flagged down a taxi, deciding to recover it later.

The gendarmerie was anything but welcoming: high fences, barred windows and a bell at the metal grid door. We rang it, waited and after about twenty seconds the door buzzed open. Inside we were met by a young volunteer gendarme at the reception desk whose name we discovered was Martin. After filling in a form giving our names, we explained that we'd discovered a skeleton in the woods, and he scurried off in search of his superior, the Brigadier-Chef.

Within minutes we were invited to sit opposite the Brigadier Chef's desk while Martin was thanked by his superior, a polite way of dismissing him to return to the reception desk.

"I understand from my colleague that you've discovered a skeleton in the nearby woods," came the Brigadier Chef's first question.

Tess took the lead, her tone calm and measured. "Yes, we were exploring the forest searching for the remnants of ruined buildings and we found the skeleton beneath the floorboards of an old mill."

The Brigadier Chef leaned forward slightly, his gaze sharpening. "Why were you looking for these ruins and where exactly are they located?"

Tess answered without hesitation. "We believe our ancestors once lived there, the buildings are near the river Boudigau."

His attention shifted to me, his eyes scanning the paper on his desk. "And you, Monsieur Grisdale, what is your connection to this?"

I cleared my throat, choosing my words carefully. "My ancestor was also involved. It was through genealogical research that I eventually connected with Tess Dubois here who decided to accompany me on this journey."

He considered my response then asked, "What makes you so certain the skeleton is old and not more recent?" His gaze glanced back and forth between us as if weighing up our credibility.

This time I spoke up. "For two reasons. Firstly, the body was found beneath floorboards in a ruined water mill that has clearly remained undisturbed for over one hundred and fifty years. Secondly, I have a copy of an old diary in the car. It contains information that contradicts the official account of what supposedly happened to Tess's ancestor based on her grandmother's recollections."

The Brigadier Chef nodded, slowly absorbing it all. "I see. But now you have disturbed the site, a potential crime scene, if as you say the remains are human and beneath floorboards. Can you pinpoint its exact location?"

"We had to reach it by canoe," Tess explained.

I added, "We marked the location on Google Maps."

After a pause, Brigadier Chef Antoine Blanchard said, "If you could provide the diary and the coordinates of the mill, that would be helpful. We'll need to involve the brigade de recherche for a forensic examination of the remains. In the meantime, please let me know where you're staying and remain there for the next few days in case we need to contact you. Is there anything else I should be aware of?"

Tess leaned forward slightly, her voice touched with emotion. "I'd like the remains to be repatriated to Vienne for burial please. Also, how long do you expect us to stay at the hotel? We both need to return to work soon, Lynden has to go back to England and frankly our funds are running low."

The Brigadier Chef's reply was abrupt, without emotion and apparent understanding. "That will depend on the brigade de recherche."

After signing witness statements, we left the office. I retrieved the diary from the car, marking the relevant pages. When I asked if he would like us to translate the text, his response again was brief – it must somehow go with the job: "We have people who can translate." While I didn't doubt this, I had hoped to accelerate the process.

Back at the hotel our emotions were shaken, there being a mixture of satisfaction at having found Eleanor's remains and also sorrow for the tragic end she had met over a century and a half ago.

"You don't think there's any doubt it was Eleanor's husband who killed her?" Tess asked as we settled into the room.

"Or one of his associates," I replied, the legacy of our joint family history looming over us.

"What do you think about taking the canoe out again tomorrow, Tess, and seeing what's happening at the site? They never said we couldn't move around, only that we had to provide an address where we're staying."

Tess's expression turned sceptical.

"I think that would be pushing it, Lynden. I'm sure we can find another way to pass the time."

Catching the hint, I nodded. "You're right. Actually, I need to prepare lectures for the new term." I leaned over and kissed her before we both flopped down onto the bed, the conversation temporarily forgotten.

"Well, that was an hour well spent," I said afterward, stretching lazily. "What should we do next?"

Tess responded with a playful swat across the top of my head and we both laughed.

Three days later, Tess's phone buzzed with a call from Brigadier Chef Antoine Blanchard. She answered and his dull, low-toned voice spoke.

"Bonjour, Mademoiselle Dubois. The forensic team has recovered the skeletal remains and transferred them to the morgue for further examination. Beneath the skull, they discovered a piece of jewellery, a ruby necklace. While we're awaiting the full forensic report, it's already clear this was no ordinary burial site and we can confirm that the remains are very old.

"That said, you and Mr Grisdale are free to leave your hotel and resume your plans. The copy of your diary has been sent for translation, which we hope will help corroborate your witness statements. I will contact you once we have more information. Congratulations to both of you on uncovering not just the remains but also a long-forgotten history of those buildings in our area. It seems they had been entirely lost to local memory."

After hanging up, Tess relayed the news and we began packing for our departure. It was going to be a long journey back to Saint-Exupéry Airport, where Tess's car was waiting.

The drive proved challenging as extensive roadworks on the motorway recommended us to divert northward through

Landes to Bordeaux before cutting across the country via Brive, Clermont-Ferrand and Tarare on the A89. As we left Dax the sky darkened and torrential rain battered the car, only easing up some hundred kilometres east of Bordeaux.

The mood during the drive was subdued. We had achieved much more than we thought we could achieve, we had found Tess's long-lost ancestor, Hartley's lover, Eleanor Fournier, but the tragic impact of our joint family histories remained with us.

"Tess," I said as we passed yet another endless stretch of drenched highway, "those feelings and visions we had in the forest, do you think they were real? They seem to have faded for me."

"They were real, Lynden," Tess replied softly, gazing out at the rain-soaked landscape. "I can still feel them, though the clarity is fading. Everyday distractions have a way of pulling us back into the present. I think the meditation exercises helped us clear our minds, which made us more open to the experience. Also, we were more receptive to the earth energy being there."

The last point I let pass.

"What happens now, Tess?"

She turned to me, her expression having a look of concern.

"What do you mean?"

"I mean, about us," I clarified.

She paused, as if choosing her words carefully.

"Whatever happens and wherever life takes us, together or apart, we are both Hartley and Eleanor and we are also Lynden and Tess. Who else could we possibly be?"

Her words struck a deep chord in me, resonating with a spiritual finality. I found myself reflecting on how Tess seemed to embody an almost Buddhist wisdom, more so than I ever had despite my own inclinations towards that philosophy.

One thought, however, remained in my mind unanswered.

"You know, Tess, the old woman you saw in the forest... and that comment you made about Hartley seeing someone on the quays in Vienne, I agree it feels as though there has to be a connection. Maybe she's tied to your family lineage perhaps before Hartley arrived in Vienne. It might be worth looking into if you're interested."

"It does feel like more than a coincidence. She might hold the key to another piece of this jigsaw. Yes, Lynden, I think I'll pursue it."

The rain continued to fall as we pressed on, the motorway winding ahead of us in large curves. We still had a mystery to untangle.

"Tess, what would you have done if you were in Hartley's place, thinking Eleanor had returned to her husband?" I asked, my voice reflective.

After a pause, she replied with quiet certainty.

"After what we felt when we relived their experiences? He wouldn't have accepted it. He would have sought answers, one way or another."

I nodded, her conviction matching my own.

"That's what I think too. We still have more work to do before we can bring their story to a close."

The rain had now passed, and the sun was shining through clouds. Another fifty kilometres and no cloud was to be seen as our journey neared its end. Traffic updates on the radio warned of blockades by French farmers disrupting main roads and motorways around Lyon. Thankfully, Tess knew the area well and suggested a detour along minor roads.

We hadn't had a chance to eat so we stopped at a boulangerie and looked for somewhere quiet to eat in peace.

I spotted a small lake north of Givors, west of the river Rhône, which appeared interesting and isolated. However, heading towards it we discovered it was a quarry and closed to the public. Driving on a small lane at the back of the quarry we arrived at an area of rocks, prickly shrubs and trees.

"Let's climb up there," I pointed out to Tess. I took her hand and led her through the prickly undergrowth. We found an area of flat weathered rocks where no vegetation grew, which retained the sun's warmth. There we sat and ate our sandwiches. Feeling full, we discarded our outer garments and laid back on them, using them to cushion us. We both closed our eyes, enjoying the last hour of being together. The sun poured over us, warm and gentle, wrapping us in a golden embrace as if it too wanted to delay our ultimate separation. Tess's head rested lightly on my stomach; her hair soft against my shirt. I could feel her breathing, rising and falling in harmony with mine. My fingers wandered absentmindedly across her arm, tracing the gentle curve of her shoulder as I appreciated the softness of her skin. The world beyond the trees felt distant and insignificant. There were only us, cradled by the rounded rocks and the sound of rustling leaves.

Tess stirred her body, shifting ever so slightly, and then she tilted her face towards me and our eyes met. She smiled, that subtle cheerful smile of hers that always made my heart miss a beat.

Without a word she stretched upward, her lips finding mine. The kiss was soft and slow, drawing us back into a familiar embrace. Her hand slid to the side of my face; her touch as delicate as the soft breeze moving through the scented hawthorn blossoms above us.

I held her closer, my hand resting on her lower back. The scent of flowers surrounded us and as my fingertips caressed the curve of her waist, I felt that this moment might dissolve if I didn't hold onto it gently enough.

The sunlight shone through the trees, creating dappled patterns that danced across our faces, and we kissed again, unable to resist the pull of each other. Each touch, each breath between us, felt like spring itself, new, alive and achingly beautiful. The rocks beneath us were warm, the air alive with the buzz of nature, and for those precious moments nothing else existed but Tess and me, alone in the wild, lost in each other.

In that secluded glade, we entered a state of profound emotional connection that was both physical and deeply spiritual. The world outside had receded to nothing as we fused with the rhythms of nature, unshackling ourselves from the chains of everyday life. For those brief luminous moments we felt untethered by time, fully aware now of the lives we had shared in the past and the ones still to come. Our love was eternal, of that we both believed.

Later, as we prepared to leave, Tess glanced back at the clearing with a wistful smile.

"We'll call this place Le Rocher," she said softly.

I nodded, knowing that this place would always remain sacred to us, etched into our hearts and memories, a sanctuary of love whenever we recalled the echoes of this day and this perfect pause in time.

But the day's enchantment was soon overshadowed by the practicalities of parting. At the Saint-Exupéry airport car park, our time together came to an end, for now.

"How are you going to explain getting back home later than planned? Doesn't Alexandre ever call to check in on you?" I asked in a neutral tone, but my curiosity was genuine.

Tess's expression shifted, guarded.

"I'll think of something," she replied, offering no further details. Perhaps she didn't want to stir my emotions by speaking of another man in her life, as surely it would have done.

We shared a brief, bittersweet kiss before going our separate ways.

The long drive home gave me plenty of time to reflect on the events of the last few days. With each passing mile, I felt as though I was slowly waking from a vivid dream, the intensity of our shared experiences fading like mist in the morning sun.

 By the following day I was back home and the day after that, I returned to work and life resumed its familiar rhythm, but the memories of those eventful days would stay with me, with an underlying realisation that Eleanor Fournier must have been murdered by her husband.

Chapter 27

Routine reasserted itself quickly after my return to work, delayed by three days. Initially the college principal and fellow lecturers who had covered for me during my absence greeted me with disapproval. This scepticism soon gave way to curiosity when I shared an account of discovering a skeleton in the woods. I explained that the local gendarmerie had requested my presence until forensics could confirm the remains were historical. Most enquiries about the identity of the deceased were deflected with ambiguous remarks: "I hope the gendarmerie will contact me with more information", or "It wasn't clear from the remains whether it was a man or a woman nor if the death was natural or otherwise".

Ann had maintained a noticeable distance from me since my return. Rather than let the unease deepen between us I invited her out for a meal at the pub.

Questions swirled in my mind but it was Ann who broke the silence as I lifted a pint of hand-pulled beer to my lips. She had opted for a glass of cider then gazing directly at me, she spoke.

"So," she began, with her characteristic bluntness, though her tone betrayed nothing of her inner thoughts, "are you and Tess together now after your little holiday?"

I hesitated, attempting to sidestep her probing. "We met up to do some joint genealogical research," I offered, my tone deliberately neutral.

"And you slept together," she shot back without hesitation. "Lynden, don't take me for an idiot. I know you probably better than you know yourself. I hope you were sensible and used precautions." The statement, more interrogative than declarative, rolled seamlessly into another: "Is Tess single?"

Relieved to latch onto her final question I replied, "No, I don't think so. But she avoided talking about any partner or close friend she might have."

Ann's sharp tone cut through again. "And did you talk about me?"

"Of course not," I retorted, my voice tinged with irritation.

The exchange was veering in a direction I hadn't anticipated and I sought to steer it elsewhere, but Ann continued. "So, where does that leave us, do you want your keys back?"

Her persistence cornered me. Thoughts raced through my head. How much truth could I reveal? How could I begin to explain the spiritual energy Tess and I had felt, the inexplicable conviction that was growing in both of us that we had lived as Hartley and Eleanor in a past life? This shared belief had led us to the skeletal remains of Eleanor herself. Ann would dismiss it as madness or, worse, accuse Tess of manipulating me.

I chose my words carefully. "Tess and I are deeply interested in the intertwined history of our ancestors. We've almost pieced the puzzle together."

Ann's response was sardonic. "Oh, I see. So, you're reenacting your ancestors' love affair and since the puzzle isn't complete, you'll be going back to her, won't you?"

Her intuition unnerved me and I found myself without a response. Mercifully, one of the bar staff arrived to take our order, providing a brief reprieve.

Once the waiter left, Ann resumed. "From now on we remain colleagues and friends only with a small 'f'. And what's good for the goose is good for the gander," she concluded.

The rest of the meal unfolded amicably enough. Ann even seemed genuinely intrigued by how Tess and I had stumbled upon Eleanor's long-hidden remains, recounting how we had pursued a mysterious old woman who vanished as suddenly as she had appeared.

"It's just coincidence," Ann scoffed. "Don't tell me you now believe it was a ghost."

"What about Hartley's diary entry?" I countered. "When he arrived in Vienne, he wrote about an old woman on the quayside pointing him towards the hotel."

"But he didn't say she was a ghost, did he?" Ann teased, her tone mocking me.

We finished our meal with desserts and Ann seemed to accept, albeit begrudgingly, that if new discoveries emerged, I would return to France and to Tess.

I walked Ann back to her flat in the courteous manner I had been brought up with since my youth. She knew me well enough to understand that it wasn't an attempt to stay the night. As I said goodnight, I gave her a peck on the cheek and left. As she hadn't returned my house keys it led me to believe that we had some sort of relationship remaining once she had quietened down.

The next day I contacted the solicitors, Swann and Cartwright. Mr Swann's secretary answered the call and I offered a brief apology for the delay, explaining vaguely that I had been preoccupied with urgent matters involving a death abroad. That explanation seemed to satisfy her and she offered her condolences, assuming the loss was personal and recent.

"I'll put you through to Mr Swann," she said, and the line clicked over.

"Mr Grisdale, good day, sir. Thank you for getting back to me," began Mr Swann, his voice carrying the polished precision of a seasoned solicitor. "You'll recall the day we met for the reading of Alice Farnsworth's will with Jane and Mary Mason.

Well, they discovered a letter and a diary they thought might be of interest to you. They dropped them off at my office for safekeeping. They didn't mention wanting them returned but it might be worth discussing that with them directly. Do you plan to drop by my office anytime soon?"

I replied, "It would be helpful, Mr Swann, if your secretary could forward the items to me via secure delivery. I'm happy to cover the cost – it should be less expensive than the petrol or train fare for a round trip from Cumbria to Devon."

"Certainly, sir. I'll make the arrangements and enclose a note with the documents with the Masons' phone numbers," he said, concluding the matter with his characteristic efficiency.

After thanking Mr Swann I ended the call and decided it was time to phone Tess. She picked up on the first ring.

"Lynden! What a coincidence," she said in a melodic tone. "I was just about to call you. How are things since you've been back?"

"I'm doing alright, thanks," I replied. "Though my relationship with Ann is a little strained at the moment. She seems to think she's figured us out, she even suggested we're trying to relive Hartley and Eleanor's lives."

Tess's tone shifted, edged with concern. "What did you say to make her think that?"

"Nothing really, she's just perceptive like you," I said trying to explain.

Tess's laughter rippled through the line easing the conversation. "Anything new?" she asked, her mood buoyant again.

"I just spoke with the solicitor," I began. "One of the two women who inherited from Alice Farnsworth's estate found a letter and a diary in the display case they took. Of course, it might have nothing to do with Hartley and Eleanor but they're sending it to me via secure delivery. It should arrive in the next day or two. How about you?"

Tess launched into her own update, her voice animated. "I've been following up on Sophie Fournier's story. Remember the newspaper article mentioning that Benoît Fournier remarried? I thought the best lead would be through Isabelle Dupont or Fournier as she became after Benoît's death. Her son, also named Benoît, carried on the line. Well, the Fournier family is still local and I tracked down a descendant. As luck would have it, he's a member of the genealogy association here in Vienne. I met him, his name is Jacques-Marie Fournier. He's very keen on obtaining a copy of Hartley's diary, especially after I told him about Eleanor's remains. I said I'd ask you. He doesn't know you already gave me a copy."

Before I could respond Tess suddenly interrupted herself.

"Oops, I have another call, it's the gendarmerie!"

She hung up abruptly, leaving me in suspense. A few minutes later she called back, her voice subdued, trembling with emotion.

"Lynden," she began, "Brigadier Chef Antoine Blanchard just called. They've confirmed the skeletal remains belong to a young woman who died violently, struck on the skull. The finger bones of her left hand were missing; likely taken by animals they thought. Weren't those the finger bones you saw move that gave up the theodolite eyepiece?"

I didn't have time to affirm before she continued, her words spilling out.

"They also believe she was pregnant. Apparently, it's rare for a foetus without any solid bones to leave traces but sediment must have washed over her remains at just the right moment. A soft fossil-like impression of the baby was left in the mud. They took photos but the imprint itself was lost when the skeleton was removed."

"That's incredible," I murmured, awed by the revelation. "But also, tragic."

Tess's voice faltered as she delivered more news.

"Lynden, that's not all. They found other bones nearby."

"What?" I exclaimed. "You're joking!"

"No," she said gravely. "The remains of two young children were discovered, each beneath a large slab of stone. They were placed under what would have been the mill pond. The gendarmerie thinks that they date from the same period but there's no information about who they might have been. Traces of their identities seem to have vanished. Do you remember what Hartley wrote about Marcel, that he and Eleanor thought he was… peculiar?"

"You're jumping to conclusions, Tess," I cautioned. "There was a miller at one point too. I agree it doesn't seem accidental if large slabs were deliberately placed over them, but we can't be sure; perhaps there was a small graveyard there before the mill was built, linked to the large house, that could explain it also, especially if more remains are found."

"The gendarme asked if we had any other records from that time," Tess added. "I told him no but promised to share anything new."

"Bloody hell," I muttered. "What about Eleanor's remains? When will they be released for burial?"

"They're waiting on authorisation," Tess explained. "It could take another month or two."

"When the time comes and you've planned the burial, I'd like to be there with you," I said earnestly.

To my surprise Tess replied softly, "I love you", adding "I've never said that to anyone before, even with my exes."

"Tess," I said, trying to lighten her mood, "you didn't finish your story about meeting Jacques-Marie Fournier." As I said those words I thought, was she referring to her ex-husband and perhaps Alexandre also; whatever – her confession of love was another one of those Cupid's arrows moments.

"Ah, yes," she said, regaining focus. "Jacques-Marie showed me a letter written by Sophie Fournier, m. Dubois the day of her wedding. It was addressed to 'the benefactor who saved me'. After Benoît Fournier Senior's death on the Rhône bridge a trust was established to provide Sophie with an education. It removed her from Isabelle's influence, her stepmother, who was running the hotel by then. Sophie became a teacher at the local girls' school. Jacques-Marie suspects someone from the local political class might have been the anonymous benefactor."

"Did Jacques-Marie have any idea who was behind the trust?" I asked.

"No," she admitted. "He wondered the same thing. He promised to give me a copy of Sophie's letter. When I get it, I'll scan and send you a translation."

Our conversation ended shortly after and as we said our goodbyes I confessed, "I love you too."

Two days later the package from Swann and Cartwright arrived. Inside, it contained the third diary of Hartley Birkett and an unopened letter, its brittle envelope bearing a two-and-a-half-pence Queen Victoria blue stamp. The address read:

Sophie Fournier, Maîtresse de l'Ecole des Filles, Vienne, France.

It had never been sent and no one had broken the seal.

Chapter 28

As I opened the pages of Hartley's third diary, I immediately noticed its condition was similar to the previous two volumes, meaning it would also require scanning and preparation before it could be read with ease and without damaging the original.

The letter, however, was in far worse shape. Its deterioration was likely due to the lack of a protective hardcover, unlike the inner pages of the two-volume diary. Though I was tempted to delve straight into the letter, I hesitated. It required expert intervention to salvage it without aggravating the damage.

I contacted a company specialising in the restoration and preservation of historical documents. Their reputation for handling delicate materials was impeccable, but the cost they quoted, several hundred pounds per page, made me pause. It would be a gamble. What if the letter contained nothing of significance to Tess or me? Or what if it was decipherable without an expensive restoration? The company secretary over the phone assured me that the full amount would not be charged if no specialist treatment was needed, giving me some reassurance; but because at forty-six years old I had become increasingly wary of verbal assurances, I requested a written estimate.

Based across the Pennines in Durham, the company boasted glowing references for its work with ancient texts including manuscripts from the bishops of the county dating back centuries. During our conversation the secretary proposed an interesting option:

"Why not bring it over yourself? We can book you an appointment to observe part of the process with our chief restoration officer."

Encouraged by this attitude, I made a counter proposition: "How about I authorise its restoration up to £150; if it costs more then please provide a written estimate, and I'll send it by special delivery in firm protected packaging."

My proposition was accepted and I would pick it up in a few weeks when the work was done.

Now with time on my hands I turned my attention to the third part of the diary. My first job was to inspect its back pages and compare the tears there with the damaged, misplaced page from the front of the first diary. To my satisfaction the tears matched precisely, giving me a solution to another piece of the puzzle.

I sent Tess a quick message, updating her on the letter's restoration process and informing her that I was working through the last of Hartley Birkett's third diary.

"Will you send them to me, please, when you're finished?" she replied, punctuating her request with an affectionate emoji kiss on cheeks.

"Sure, no problem. I miss you," I responded, signing off with two emojis kiss on lips.

I was determined to read the third diary once again without interruptions, choosing a Friday evening to begin, and allowing myself the luxury of a full weekend to read it if necessary.

So, the following Friday evening, having completed the scan, I set out on an almost ritualistic routine. Sunk into my armchair I placed a glass of Armagnac, my chosen indulgence for the evening, on the small table beside me. The rich amber drink glowed as the table lamp cast its light upon it, and I took my first sip and started reading.

My thoughts, as I made my way homeward across northern France turned to Samuel, my son, so tender in age, who had been orphaned of his mother and by my absence of five long years deprived of a father. The weight of despair constant in my mind began to change, shifting to a resolute determination to return to him and ensure his well-being. With each passing day this resolve quickened my pace, urging me to hasten my return and I decided upon the crossing from Saint-Malo to Southampton.

In my urgency I sold my horse at a price far below its worth, knowing that negotiation required time I could ill afford. Yet the loss troubled me little; the years spent labouring in France had seen my earnings accumulate, split prudently between the banks of England and France. Moreover, my investments in railway ventures, both in shares earned through partnerships and those purchased independently, promised considerable returns. I prided myself on my shrewd judgement, having chosen lines that served burgeoning local industries and appeared destined to yield substantial dividends compared to their construction costs, of which I knew well.

It was on the evening of 23rd March 1853 that I arrived at Lowe Manor. A hansom cab had carried me directly to its imposing front door. As the house loomed before me a mix of emotions stirred within me, not quite the warmth of homecoming nor the excitement of reunion, but a complicated blend of familiarity, sorrow and nostalgia. Memories of happier days with my beloved Melinda, who was so cruelly torn from this world only minutes after giving birth to Samuel, mingled with the ever-present ache of her loss.

After paying the cabman I approached the door but before I could knock, Jane came rushing out, her apron fluttering as she called out my name with evident relief.

She was breathless and flustered, proclaiming her joy at seeing me again, but she was the bearer of grievous news.

A chill ran through me and my heart sank, I felt I was exhaling my last breath with my mind ticking over, what's happened to Samuel. Jane, seeing the look of concern on my face, assured me that it was not Samuel but poor Mr Lowe. He was struck down by apoplexy just ten days past, the doctor was with him now but he was paralysed down one side and could not speak.

A wave of relief mixed with fresh anxiety overcame me and I told Jane that I would see him once the doctor had finished his work. I also asked, with as much composure as I could muster, where Samuel was.

Jane told me that he had been sent to the finest school in Exeter upon the insistence of George Lowe as he wished to prepare Samuel to become a gentleman.

I said that I thought that Samuel was a little young for such an undertaking, to which Jane did not comment.

Some twenty minutes later I observed the doctor departing from the sickroom. He was a tall, gaunt figure, his heavy brow and prominent features lending him an austere countenance. He carried a black bag in one hand and a top hat in the other; once perched atop his head it must have rendered him near seven feet tall. His wavy black hair fell to his ears, completing the sombre aspect of a man who might as easily have been mistaken for a mortician as a physician.

Introducing myself as George's son-in-law and nearest relative, I sought a brief audience. I recognised the doctor from years past and reminded him of it, he having arrived too late to attend to Melinda during her tragic passing.

In a low, solemn voice the doctor emphasised how unfortunate it was to meet again under such sad circumstances. He explained that Mr Lowe had suffered a violent apoplexy, that in such cases further attacks were probable and that George Lowe's time on this earth may be limited. He was prescribed leeches to reduce cranial pressure, laudanum to ensure tranquillity and meadowsweet tincture to be administered in water four times daily to thin the blood. Cold compresses to the head and warm ones to the feet would aid in redirecting the blood flow. Beyond this, explained the doctor, his fate lay in the hands of the Almighty.

I politely expressed my gratitude for his care and took my leave, with the sentiment turning over in my mind that if he had arrived sooner, perhaps he could have saved Melinda. I then entered George Lowe's chamber.

Walking into the large bedroom was an experience in itself – it was a vision of Renaissance opulence. Its walls bore exquisite frescos framed by ornate plaster mouldings and against the back wall stood a magnificent four-poster bed. George lay within, his eyes closed, the toll of his condition evident in every line of his face. A nurse sat beside him, vigilant and unobtrusive. As I approached, he stirred, his eyelids fluttering open. He attempted to speak but managed only guttural sounds, the paralysis cruelly robbing him of coherent speech. With his good hand he gestured for the nurse to assist him into a sitting position, to fetch pen and paper and then leave us to our privacy.

Seating myself near his bed I told George that it grieved me to see him like this, and I prayed that he finds strength to recover his health in the days ahead.

George shook his head slowly, his expression resigned. He dragged his hand across his throat to signal his belief that his fate was sealed. Raising his thumb and two fingers he conveyed that his time, be it days, weeks or months, was drawing to its close.

Over the next half-hour we communicated through laboriously written notes, George writing large script on the sheets of paper as I firmly held a board beneath them. He informed me that he had sent Samuel to school, believing it the finest opportunity for the boy to secure his future. I replied aloud that I knew that from Jane, for his hearing remained sharp.

George wrote that he had bequeathed his business to his grandson, requesting that I oversaw the company until Samuel was of age. If I did not want to accept this role, trustees would be appointed.

I replied firmly that I would prefer the company be run by those who best knew its workings.

George's next note outlined his will: the estate left to Samuel, small bequests to friends and money set aside for Jane, his nanny-cum-housekeeper, to care for Samuel upon his return. He insisted that he must not inherit a large sum until he is twenty-one and proves himself capable of managing the business. To me, he offered the old cottage on the estate and requested that I tend to the maintenance of the old chapel where Melinda lay, for he wished to rest beside her.

George then asked about my life the past five years.

I recounted all in detail, sparing nothing, including my attack in the forest of Landes, which had left me slightly lame and a scar stretching from my head to the left shoulder blade. George placed his hand upon mine; it was a gesture of sympathy that needed no words. His final note urged me to return to France and seek Eleanor, suggesting I bring her and her daughter to England if they so desired.

George's strength began to wane as the laudanum took hold. I left him to his rest and walked across the estate to the chapel. Standing before Melinda's gravestone, a wave of guilt swept over me as I thought of Eleanor. Yet I told myself that Melinda, in her love, would have wished for Samuel to have the best education and for me to find some semblance of happiness.

Five years had passed, and, in that span, I felt as though I had lived another lifetime, it seeming both so long ago and yet only a brief chapter in the span of a man's life. Time is so strange a concept; we mark its passing with ever greater precision for it needs to keep up with the ever-faster ways that we travel. Local time no longer suffices; "railway time" introduced Greenwich Mean Time and the electric telegraph running alongside the railways ensured the accuracy of time at all the stations along the line. As I placed flowers upon the headstone, my thoughts turned to Melinda, her smiling face still vivid in my mind, yet interwoven with the haunting image of her as she might now be, for below me in the chill of the earth lay but a skeleton. Melinda, once so lovely, her fair features now lost to time and decay. Naught remained of her beauty and yet in that memory a part of her would still live for so long as I draw breath. I picked a few flowers from around me and placed them against the headstone, my simple offering of remembrance before departing as tears swelled up in my eyes.

I went to the cottage George Lowe had wished to bequeath me. It was modest yet charming, a humble dwelling that suited my inclinations. Surrounded by a parcel of land, it held the promise of self-sufficiency, a life where a few chickens might roam freely, rabbits could be raised and vegetables grown to sustain me. The simplicity of it appealed to my weary soul, offering the prospect of tranquillity amidst the chaos that had recently consumed my life.

The following morning, I paid a brief visit to George. During the night he had suffered another attack of apoplexy. The doctor, summoned once more, gave a grave pronouncement: the time had come to send for the holy man to administer the last rites. George Lowe slipped away from this world at three minutes past nine in the morning of Thursday 24th March 1853. I could do no other than to ask myself by what providence had George Lowe remained alive for over ten days only to die the day after my arrival from France.

Ever the practical man, George had foreseen his demise long before illness seized him. His trustees, as arranged, assumed control of his business the very next day. True to his word, the unused yet meticulously maintained cottage on the edge of the estate was handed over to me along with the private chapel. This, I learned, was not merely for its upkeep, as George had implied, but entirely in my care. Alongside it came a sufficient sum for repairs and the maintenance of the burial grounds, projected to serve for half a century or longer. Jane, the loyal housekeeper and Samuel's steadfast nanny, retained her position in the household. She was to live in the manor as long as she desired, at least until Samuel reached adulthood and made alternate arrangements for her should he decide to take over the estate.

George's funeral was held five days after his passing. The service drew numerous associates from his business circles, all of whom spoke highly of his character and generosity, before he was finally laid to rest beside his daughter Melinda in the grounds of the family chapel.

I retreated to the cottage, intending to remain there for the following month. During that time, I wrote to the boarding school in Exeter where Samuel resided, arranging to visit him within the next two days, thereby excluding the opportunity for the school to decline my request. When I arrived, I found my son, a mere five years of age, polite and well mannered, his behaviour reflecting the decorum drilled into him by the schoolmasters. Yet beneath this veneer of refinement lay an unsettling absence of emotion. Even when informed of his grandfather's death, his youthful face betrayed no grief. I departed the school within the hour, deeply troubled by this disconnection. It was not the reaction I expected from my child. Perhaps the absence of both parents had left scars too deep for outward display, and upon returning to Lowe Manor I resolved to discuss this matter with Jane at the earliest opportunity.

The twice three-hour journey on horseback between Lowe Manor and Exeter afforded ample time for reflection. My thoughts inevitably returned to Eleanor. Her decision to rejoin her husband haunted me, though I tried to convince myself her letter was written under duress. It was not an ordinary course of events, particularly given her discovery that she was with child. A month had now passed since I had left Landes and the urgency to return and offer her a chance to come to England with Sophie weighed heavily upon me. Surely, Benoît Fournier would not dare to pursue her a second time if she sought refuge on English soil.

That evening, I unfolded her letter once more, reading it by the dim light of the fire.

"Hartley,
I have decided to return to Vienne.
My husband has come looking for me.
He forgives me for what I have done.
Sophie is happy to see her father again.
Do not attempt to follow me for I have no desire to rekindle what once was.
Return to England to your son who needs you more than I ever did.
I am sorry to envelope the news this way.
Eleanor"

Something felt amiss. Her words lacked the natural flow of sincerity, as though it was carefully crafted to mask another truth. My resolve became determined; I would return to France and bring Eleanor home to England. I would then withdraw Samuel from the school and at last, we should live as a family. In but a few months he would have a brother or sister to welcome into the world. Yet I felt, with increasing urgency, that time could not be lost. Eleanor must make the journey before it became too great a burden to bear and Sophie must decide, painful though the choice may be, whether she would stay beside her father or return with us to Devonshire, England.

Preparations for the journey began in earnest. My work permit had not yet expired, sparing me the inconvenience of renewing it and I set off again for France on 8th June 1853. Travel was now far swifter than it had been in years past, thanks to the expanding railway networks. From Calais, the Chemin de Fer du Nord would deliver me to Paris. From there, a cab would carry me across the city to connect with the Paris-Lyon-Marseille line, taking me as far as Chalon-sur-Saône. A diligence would then convey me to Lyon. Returning to Vienne during daylight hours, however, would require discretion. I resolved to adopt a new appearance: a beard and spectacles, I thought, would suffice to render me unrecognisable. Any gendarme inspecting my papers might merely think me a traveller too busy to shave.

I calculated that I would need a week in Vienne to contact Eleanor, out of the reach of her husband Benoît. I hoped to locate her either at her aunt's home in Saint-Colombe or elsewhere in the town. Lodging posed another challenge. Staying in a regular hotel would necessitate presenting my identification papers, which I wished to avoid. Coaching inns, though offering greater anonymity, required careful planning. Frequenting establishments too near one another on consecutive nights might arouse suspicion.

The journey took three days, during which my thoughts alternated between Eleanor and professional admiration for the railway's engineering marvels. I marvelled at the ingenuity of the tunnels, cuttings and bridges that enabled such swift travel across the land.

Upon arriving in Lyon, I sought lodgings in the bustling quarter of Saint-Jean, the old city nestled along the Saône River. Its narrow streets lined with passageways called traboules concealed the comings and goings of their inhabitants, making it an ideal place to remain inconspicuous. Signs for lodgings were plentiful, many offered by private households. I secured a clean and quiet room in the home of a widow who asked no questions, neither did she require paperwork. An evening meal was included in the price, and over supper, the kind lady recommended her nephew's stables for the hire of a horse.

The next morning, I visited the stables on the city's outskirts. After inspecting the animals, I settled on a horse named Étoile, a modest creature, a little worn but well suited to my unassuming guise. At six francs a day excluding feed, the price was reasonable and his unremarkable appearance would draw no undue attention. Thus equipped, I prepared to take the next step to find Eleanor.

I set off at a leisurely pace, taking care not to draw attention to myself. I chose to lodge at an inn in Seyssuel, a small village just north of Vienne. The establishment was run by two brothers who showed no interest in prying into my affairs. I informed them that I intended to stay for three nights and might return late in the evenings as I had local business to attend to.

The room I was given was modest but clean, with freshly laundered linens and basic washing facilities. A water pump stood in the courtyard, allowing me to fetch extra water should the two buckets in my room prove insufficient. The absence of a woman's influence in the inn's upkeep was evident. There was a certain ruggedness to the place but perhaps this was for the best. A woman's curiosity might have led to awkward questions I was not prepared to answer.

The next morning at seven o'clock, I found my horse Étoile already saddled by one of the brothers. Grateful for the courtesy, I mounted and made my way towards the town. My altered appearance, a scruffy beard, old spectacles and patched breeches, was enough to ensure I passed unnoticed. My worn attire, deliberately chosen, suggested a man of limited means, deterring street vendors and others seeking to offer their services.

I dismounted near the ancient theatre and walked beside Étoile, keeping my face partially obscured by the horse's head as we passed the Hôtel du Théâtre. There was no sign of Benoît Fournier on this occasion and the establishment appeared quiet. Hoping the area might grow livelier later in the day, I led Étoile up into the hills above the town. There, amidst the roadside grass, I allowed my horse to graze while I lay back to rest.

By mid-afternoon, I ventured back into Vienne, this time passing the Hôtel du Théâtre once more. As I approached, I saw Sophie struggling to carry a visitor's bag into the building. My heart raced at the thought of seeing Eleanor but as Sophie glanced briefly in my direction, she showed no sign of recognition. A moment later, a young woman descended from the front steps, her demeanour sharp and commanding. She appeared to be scolding Sophie, who immediately hurried inside, clearly intimidated. I halted briefly, hoping for a glimpse of Eleanor but there was no sign of her. Unwilling to attract attention by loitering, I returned to the inn, resolving to intercept Eleanor at the market the following morning.

Feeling emboldened, I left Étoile tied up the next day and walked among the market stalls, searching for a familiar face. I approached a merchant I had seen serve Eleanor in the past. Feigning casual interest, I enquired about his business and whether he still supplied the Hôtel du Théâtre.

He replied negatively and asked to know why I should be interested, to which I replied that I had once stayed there and recalled fond memories, in particular the good food that was prepared by the owner's wife, though I couldn't recall her name.

The merchant's expression softened as he laughed, explaining that would have been the first Madame Fournier and that she had run off with an Englishman working in the town. He recounted how it caused quite a scandal, 'putting our local politician's nose out of joint', that also he didn't waste any time and found himself another wife soon enough. The market stall merchant thought that she had been his mistress all along. I was also told that she's the one running the place now, she was bossy and none too kind to the little girl, referring to Sophie. What sort of mother abandons her child, he asked, not expecting an answer but adding that he worked on the railway, the rumour being that the tunnel near the station was his work. Little did the merchant realise that it was I he was referring to.

    His words struck me like a blow. Could Benoît have harmed Eleanor, as she had feared? My mind reeled at the implications.

    Mounting Étoile once more, I felt the need for further confirmation. If this tale were true, the entire town would surely know of it and a local bar seemed the best place to hear the gossip and gather further information. As I rode towards the Roman amphitheatre, I noticed Étoile limping. Dismounting to inspect him, I discovered he had thrown a shoe. A young boy pointed me towards a blacksmith on the road leading to the south of town.

    The acrid smell of coal and burnt hoof filled the air long before I reached the forge. Three horses were tied outside and the blacksmith, a burly man with soot-streaked arms, was filing the hoof of another horse. Without looking up, he spoke brusquely, giving me his price of two francs per shoe and that it couldn't be done for another hour.

    I told him I only required a replacement for the one shoe that's missing, to which he replied if one's gone, the others will follow soon enough and it's best to have all four done at once. Then, glancing up and assessing my appearance, he relented that he would just do the one shoe.

    Leaving Étoile in his care, I walked to a nearby bar and ordered a glass of red wine, as it seemed to be the drink of choice amongst the men sat around tables in the bar. Taking a seat near a group of three men, I nodded in greeting.

One local man, not recognising me as a regular to the establishment, then asked if I was passing through the town.

I told him that my horse had cast a shoe but that I had stayed in town for a few days last year at the Hôtel du Théâtre.

An older man with shoulder-length white hair who sat at the same table then asked if I had gone back there this year, to which I replied that no, I hadn't.

He then recounted that the place has gone downhill since his wife ran off with that Englishman, who had an accent like mine. Pausing, he waited for me to comment, before adding that Fournier got the marriage annulled quickly enough but his poor daughter is worked like a slave by the new wife. Referring to Benoît Fournier, he said that the man spends more time drunk at his vineyards than looking after the hotel and that he wouldn't vote for him again.

The others nodded in agreement, adding their own grumbles about the politician's neglect of his business and his moral failings.

After exchanging some small talk for nearly an hour and buying them a glass of red wine each, I thanked them for their company and returned to the forge to collect Étoile. My mind was left disturbed by what I had heard. If the stories were true, Eleanor's fate remained uncertain, but I was now more determined than ever to uncover the truth.

Chapter 29

The day waned with unseemly haste and my thoughts turned with increasing determination to intercept Benoît Fournier to discover the fate of Eleanor. It appeared a grim possibility that he had been the architect of his wife's demise since their return to Vienne. The conclusion haunted me with its sinister certainty, and I resolved that answers must be gained from the man himself.

A meeting was to be sought in a place of solitude, where no prying eyes could bear witness nor inquisitive ears overhear the exchange. The narrow streets of St. Colombe and Vienne, with their bustling throngs and close-pressed houses, offered no such sanctuary. Moreover, as several roads converged upon St. Colombe from the south and south-west, I could ill afford the gamble of choosing incorrectly. My only viable recourse was the bridge spanning the Rhône, a natural bottleneck.

My plan formed with clarity based upon the habits of Benoît Fournier, habits that had been forthcoming from the encounters I had made the last two days. From the Vienne side, under cover of dusk, I would tether Étoile to a stake and lie in wait by the bridge. Should Benoît Fournier approach astride his steed, I would intercept him amidst the shadowed crossing.

As the hours stretched and the night deepened, the bridge grew ever quieter, the earlier bustle dwindling to occasional passersby. Twice I mistook lone riders swaying precariously under the influence of drink for my quarry. The air grew colder as the wind whispered down the valley, the moon offering fleeting illumination between passing clouds that plunged the world into impenetrable blackness. By midnight only the faintest glimmers of candlelight remained in the distant windows. I crouched by one of the bridge's sturdy stone pillars, the chill biting through my cape and into my very bones. To combat the creeping numbness, I stood and paced, letting movement restore warmth to my fingers and toes.

It was then that I discerned the sound of hoofbeats, a measured deliberate rhythm echoing upon the bridge's ancient stones. Emerging from the shadows a dark silhouette took shape. The faint gleam of a brass ornament upon the horse's harness caught the intermittent moonlight, betraying its slow advance. My heart quickened.

Drawing my cape about my face, I stepped forward and called out, "Monsieur Fournier." My voice carried across the stillness, and the rider halted.

"Step into the light," came his reply, terse and commanding.

The moon emerged from behind a shroud of clouds, illuminating the scene in monochrome shades of grey. I closed the distance between us, gripping his horse's bridle firmly as it shied at my sudden presence. My tone tolerated no ambiguity as I demanded, "Where is Eleanor Fournier?"

He answered with a practised nonchalance, "She is gone, who are you to ask such questions?"

Pressing forward I let my voice sharpen. "Gone where? She left a note; she wrote that she had returned to Vienne with you. Where is she now?"

The man stiffened, his composure fraying at the edges. "She ran away to England with her lover," he retorted.

"No, Monsieur Fournier," I said with mounting intensity. "Her note spoke of nothing but her return to Vienne, with you. Do not insult me with falsehoods, what have you done with her?"

At this his face darkened. "Who are you," he demanded, his voice rising, "to hurl accusations at me? You spread falsehoods like a vagrant."

Ignoring his bluster, I pressed further, my voice unyielding. "Do you deny travelling to the Département of Landes? Do you deny being accompanied by another? That very man attacked me and left me for dead. Do you deny that Marcel Dufour was murdered? And yet you returned with Sophie."

At this, Fournier's bravado faltered. His voice dropped, grudgingly yielding the truth. "Yes, I went to Landes. I searched for Eleanor and Sophie. There was a storm that night, a wretched tempest, and Sophie was found at the home of Marguerite Dufour. Eleanor, however, was gone. She had gone already."

"Gone?" I scoffed. "Do you truly believe Eleanor would abandon Sophie? The very idea is preposterous. I know your lies, Benoît Fournier. Tell me now, where did you kill her?"

At these words Fournier's anger exploded. With a sudden vicious movement, he lashed out at me with his riding whip, the leather hissing through the air and missing my face by a mere inch. But I held firm, gripping the bridle and steadying the panicked horse.

"You cannot silence the truth," I said, my voice unwavering despite the sting of his malice. "You will answer for Eleanor, and for your crime."

With that Benoît Fournier, his rage unbridled, lashed out once more with his whip. This time the cruel leather struck the side of my face and in his frenzy grazed the face of his horse as well. Staggering from the force of the blow, I fell to the ground just as his horse, rearing in panic, dislodged him from the saddle. His hands now bereft of control over the reins, flailed as he tumbled backwards. I watched horrified, as his head struck the stone wall of the bridge with a sickening crack, the momentum sending his body over the parapet and into the silent fast current below.

The horse, wild-eyed with fear, bolted forward, its hooves pounding dangerously close to where I lay. One hoof struck my abdomen with a force that knocked the air from my lungs. Gasping I clutched at my side, paralysed for a moment by the searing pain. In mere seconds the beast had thundered across the bridge and disappeared into the dark streets leading towards Vienne.

Struggling for breath, I rose unsteadily, my ribs protesting with each movement. Staggering to the parapet I peered over its edge. The Rhône's dark waters swirled, betraying no sign of the man who had just been carried into its depths. The moonlight danced on the surface, revealing nothing but the river's relentless flow towards its delta south of Arles. As I leaned against the stone, I noticed a warm wetness on my fingers. Bringing them to my face, I saw the faint gleam of liquid in the moon's glow. Blood. Whether it was mine or Benoît Fournier's, I could not yet determine.

It was evident that Fournier would have been unconscious before the river claimed him. The force of his head striking the parapet had surely cracked his skull, sealing his fate before the unforgiving waters could do so. Yet, this was no time to loiter for the scene of this calamity could easily be misconstrued, and I, the lover of Eleanor Fournier, would be the natural suspect in any inquiry into Fournier's demise.

I stumbled away from the bridge, each step a battle against the throbbing in my side. Reaching Étoile I untied her from the stake and mounting her with difficulty, I rode silently back to the inn at Seyssuel. Upon my arrival I sought the privacy of my chamber and washed myself in the dim light, ensuring that no trace of blood remained on my person. Yet though my hands were clean, my thoughts were heavy with the burden of the night's events. Sleep eluded me as I replayed the brief yet damning conversation with Benoît Fournier.

He had admitted to returning Sophie to Vienne but had steadfastly refused to confess to any harm done to Eleanor. Still, his lies were evident in every evasive word he spoke. The gendarme called to the house of Marguerite Dufour in Labenne had found no trace of Eleanor, which meant she must lie elsewhere. The question that tormented me was whether Sophie had seen her mother before being whisked away to Vienne. Marguerite Dufour's words echoed in my mind: Sophie had been instructed to go straight to the waiting carriage. Now, with painful clarity, I doubted that Eleanor had ever joined her there, the sequence of events was becoming clear to me: Benoît Fournier with another man had staked out our house and either seen me leave or knew of my departure; he or his accomplice had killed Eleanor. He then must have gone to Mme Dufour to take Sophie, returning to Vienne immediately. Sophie would have been told that her mother had run away to England with me. The accomplice would then have stayed behind for a few days and upon my return, struck me the blow that rendered me unconscious, disposing of me in the mill pond. It also seemed possible that Marcel Dufour had witnessed the last part of the procedure, perhaps intervening himself and been killed by the assailant. Placing his body by the broken bough of a mighty oak would serve as a cover for his crime before leaving the area.

As dawn broke, I washed once more and a glance in the mirror showed little more than a faint scratch on my face, an injury that time would swiftly mend. Yet the ache in my chest, both physical and emotional, was another matter entirely.

My thoughts turned to Sophie. Barely eleven years old, she was now bereft of both parents. Though I longed to go to her to offer what comfort and support I could, I hesitated. As a witness to her father's death and given the circumstances of our encounter, my presence might invite suspicion and ill will. It was a cruel dilemma and I resolved that the news of her father's demise was best delivered by another.

I left the inn and rode towards the outskirts of Lyon, the gentle sway of the saddle allowing my thoughts to drift. The weight of losing Eleanor pressed heavily upon me. With Fournier gone any hope of uncovering her fate now seemed extinguished. The void left in my soul was profound, but amidst the sorrow a single resolve crystallised: I would honour Eleanor's memory by dedicating myself to Sophie. Though she was not my child she had become dear to me in the brief time we had shared. Her courage and industrious spirit deserved a future far better than the one her father had bequeathed her through her stepmother.

Upon reaching Lyon, I stabled Étoile and returned to the inn where I had stayed before. There, I penned a letter to Monsieur Paulin Talabot, requesting urgently if it be possible, the favour of his time. His response arrived by evening, graciously inviting me to meet him the following day at his office.

When the appointed hour came, I was collected by one of Monsieur Talabot's carriages and conveyed to their newly established offices. I was greeted warmly by both Talabot and his assistant, Jacques Moreau. As I stepped into the oak-panelled room, my eyes were drawn to the large inscription above: *La Compagnie des chemins de fer de Paris à Lyon et à la Méditerranée*. Observing my interest, Talabot explained that this would become the company's official name once La Compagnie du chemin de fer de *Lyon à la Méditerranée* and *La Compagnie du chemin de fer de Paris à Lyon* were hopefully merged in the near future.

Our conversation turned to the events on the bridge and the turbulent months that had preceded them. Though Talabot's initial tone carried a hint of reproach regarding my association with Eleanor, his demeanour softened as I recounted the suffering she had endured at Fournier's hands. Compassion replaced judgement and both men listened intently as I outlined my intentions.

I expressed my desire to honour Eleanor by ensuring Sophie's future. Talabot, moved by my resolve, offered me a position working on tributary lines north of Lyon. While grateful, I explained that my theodolite required repair and that I needed time in England to settle my affairs before considering a return to France. Talabot, ever generous, offered to have my baggage sent to England via their company's travel boxes, sparing me the burden of carrying it. This kindness I accepted with heartfelt thanks, and as I departed, I felt a glimmer of hope amidst the shadow of loss.

Chapter 30

I placed the diary down, having reached the penultimate page. The final written entry was the torn page we had discovered tucked into the front of the first volume. Beyond it, the remaining pages were blank to the back cover.

It felt like the right moment to update Tess and find out if she had managed to secure a copy of Sophie's letter from Jacques-Marie Fournier. I sent her a quick message on WhatsApp.

"Hi Tess, how are you? Can you call me when it's convenient?"

To my surprise, Tess called back almost immediately.

"Hi, Lynden," she greeted warmly.

"How are you?" I asked.

"I'm well, thanks. And you?"

"I'm great, actually. I just finished reading the third volume of Hartley's diary. It's much shorter than the other two and the torn page we found in the first volume matches the tear marks on the final page of this one. I'll email you a copy. As for the letter, I'm still waiting for news from the restorer. How about you? Any news?"

"Yes I do," Tess replied. "I managed to get a copy of Sophie's letter from Jacques-Marie Fournier. I'll send it to you by email. Oh, and just so you know, you can call me anytime. I'm on my own."

Her words caught me off guard but a smile crept onto my face as I responded, "Thanks".

Did it mean Tess and Alexandre had argued, had he left her and was it temporary or permanent, what were Tess's intentions now? I didn't push for further explanations, knowing this wasn't the right time. Instead, I told her how much I missed her and how I couldn't wait to see her again during the forthcoming school holidays.

"Same here," Tess assured me. Then, after a pause, she added, "The undertakers contacted me about Eleanor's burial. I know you'll want to be there so I'll try to schedule it for that time. If it's too far off, I'll arrange it for a Saturday so you can fly over Friday evening. Can you give me an idea of your dates?"

"Of course, I'll confirm as soon as I can," I promised. Then I hesitated before asking the question that had been going through my mind. "Tess, what are your thoughts on Hartley and Eleanor and what happened to us in the forest near her remains? I think of it all the time. The visions we shared… it felt like stepping into a dream or perhaps even another reality. But we both experienced the same thing. What happened?"

"It was real, Lynden," Tess replied firmly. "Look at where we are now. The feelings we have for each other, the energy that surged through us when our hands first touched at the museum and later during our most intimate moments, it's undeniable. I've never felt a connection like this with anyone else. You can believe it: we are Eleanor and Hartley returned. It's our reality."

Tess paused briefly; her voice thoughtful as she continued. "I also think that Eleanor's murder left an energy imprint at the old mill. That imprint was released when we were there, meant only for us to experience. That's why we had those visions. I've even wondered if we could uncover more details through hypnosis by reliving Eleanor's final moments."

"Wouldn't that be dangerous? Especially for you?" I asked, concern in my voice.

"Perhaps," Tess admitted, "but it's worth considering."

"I'll call you as soon as I've read Sophie's letter," I promised.
"It's in French, I assume?"

"Yes," Tess confirmed, "but I've translated it for you. I'll send both versions just in case the translation isn't perfect."

We said our goodbyes and I added, "Let me know your thoughts after you've read Hartley's final diary entry."

"I will. Goodbye, my love," Tess replied.

Her parting words struck a deep chord within me. Tess wasn't one to use such phrases lightly and hearing them filled me with warmth.

Moments later, her email arrived. I opened it eagerly and began reading Sophie's letter.

Vienne, France
Saturday 7th April 1877

Dearest Benefactor,
As the first cry of the cuckoo announces its arrival in Vienne, I find myself calling out to you, though I know not where you may reside nor whether these words will ever reach the kind heart to whom they are intended. Yet, it is my greatest hope that they might find their way to you, for they carry my deepest gratitude and a longing that has remained unspoken far too long.
It is on the day of a most joyous occasion, the beginning of my life as the wife of Edouard Dubois, that I feel compelled to reflect upon the path that has brought me to this moment. A path I know that would have been lost in darkness were it not for your unseen hand.
I remember with sharp clarity the cruelty and despair that clouded my early years.
My mother's disappearance amidst the storm near the Marais d'Orx still haunts my dreams, though I have not seen her face since 1853. Then the loss of my dear father, so suddenly and

cruelly as he crossed the bridge from Saint-Colombe, left me orphaned, the last anchor to my life.

The harshness of Isabelle, my father's second wife, in the unforgiving shadows of the Hôtel du Théâtre seemed to seal my fate. I feared I would never escape those long dreary days of servitude where each moment stripped a little more of my spirit.

Then, as if by providence, your benevolence swept into my life. You, who remain a mystery to me, extended a kindness that I can scarcely comprehend even now. It was through your generosity that I was lifted from despair and given the means to study, to learn and to rise above the treachery that once engulfed me. It was your provision that transformed a lost girl into the schoolmistress of Vienne, respected and fulfilled, with a future bright enough to banish the shadows of my past.

I am forever indebted to you, yet I am burdened by the ache of never knowing you. Who are you, dearest benefactor? What moved your heart to rescue an orphan such as I? There are nights when I dream of your face, imagining the kind eyes and steady hands that reached across the void to save me. I yearn for but a moment to offer you my thanks in person, to hold your hand in mine and assure you that your kindness has borne fruit far beyond what you might have imagined.

Though I am today married, my heart cannot rest entirely without expressing this to you. It is because of you that I have found Edouard, a man of honour and tenderness, who loves me and I, he. It is because of you that I stand here, unshackled from the chains of my past, ready to build a new life of love and purpose.

I write this letter in the hope that somehow, someday, it may reach you. Though I have never seen your face, you are as dear to me as family, as essential to my life as those I have lost. If you should ever reveal yourself, you would find in me not only a grateful heart but also an unwavering friend.

May God bless you abundantly for the mercy you have shown me. You have given me not only the gift of education but also the gift of life itself and I am forever in your debt.
Yours in eternal gratitude,
Sophie Fournier

As I closed my computer screen, I felt deeply moved by the poignant emotions expressed in the letter. Though I lacked definitive proof, I was convinced that Hartley Birkett had been the one to provide for Sophie Fournier. The letter, found among her possessions at the end of her life, had clearly been cherished year after year. Signed as Sophie Fournier rather than Sophie Dubois, her married name, it was full of meaning, a deliberate choice that must have held deep personal meaning for her as she left her young tragic life behind to step into that of a contented woman looking to future happiness.

The following day, Tess called me via a WhatsApp video. It was a joy to see her smiling face in place of a succession of text messages. I placed the phone on loudspeaker and held it in front of me, the next best thing to being together in person.

"I've read the final part of Hartley's diary," Tess began. "It fits in with some of the historical details I found in the local library. But, Lynden, don't you think something feels... odd?"

I was intrigued. "What do you mean, Tess?"

She leaned closer to the phone's camera. "Hartley wrote down his conversation with Benoît on the bridge word for word, right?"

"Yes, I suppose so," I replied cautiously.

"Well, when Benoît was cornered, he admitted he went to Landes to search for Eleanor and Sophie, but he didn't confess to killing Eleanor."

"That's true," I conceded. "But it makes sense; admitting to tracking them down, even with the intent of bringing them back to Vienne is one thing, but confessing to murder is another. Don't forget, Eleanor was terrified of him; she said so. She feared he would kill her or even both of them."

Tess nodded but pressed on. "Still, if Benoît didn't find Eleanor, it's also reasonable to assume he thought she had already fled with Hartley."

"Possibly," I agreed. "But as Hartley wrote, Benoît was probably lying. He also claimed Eleanor wouldn't have left without Sophie."

"Unless," Tess interjected, her voice dropping, "Eleanor had already been killed before Benoît arrived, perhaps during the storm that night."

I felt a chill at her suggestion. "But by whom?"

Tess's expression grew more serious. "Remember when the gendarmes in the Landes called? They said they'd discovered two skeletons they believed to be of children."

"Yes," I said slowly, "we discussed it before."

"So," Tess continued, "what are the chances of there being two killers operating in the same small area of forest?"

I considered her words. "You're right, it's highly unlikely. That suggests either Benoît killed Eleanor and someone else, whoever got in the way, or that the other remains aren't those of two children but small adults."

Tess nodded thoughtfully. "If the river was high and the mill pond overflowing, it wouldn't have been an ideal time to dispose of a body, even with rocks to weigh it down. And don't forget, there was only one other man known to be in the area, Marcel Dufour."

"I suppose we'll never know for certain, and as I said before it could have been the place of legitimate burials for the Dufour family who owned the large house or anyone who lived there before then," I said with a sigh.

Our conversations and speculations continued over the next few days, each theory raising as many questions as it answered.

Then, unexpectedly, I received an email from the company in Durham. The restoration of the letter was complete and they wanted to know when I could collect it.

With my weekdays consumed by work, I asked if they had staff available on Saturday mornings. They confirmed that I could pick it up then, though no restorer would be on site to discuss it. The cost would be £130 and it fell within the amount I had budgeted. The reasonable price suggested the letter was either brief or required minimal restoration. I paid the invoice over the phone, ensuring all that remained was to collect it in person and taking my passport or driving licence for identification with me.

The following Saturday morning, I drove to Durham, a city I'd always loved for its charm and small size. I never missed an opportunity to visit its cathedral and the tomb of Saint Cuthbert, though I couldn't quite explain the attraction they held for me. Perhaps it was the name of St Cuthbert itself, which seemed to be everywhere in the north of England, church names, corpse roads and street names.

To ensure I arrived before midday, I took the faster A66 to Scotch Corner and continued north on the A1. On the return journey, I planned to take the slower route across the Pennine moors, enjoying the rugged beauty of the heather-clad landscape.

At the reception desk, a young woman greeted me warmly. "You must be Lynden Grisdale," she said as I entered.

"That's right," I replied, handing her my driving licence for verification.

She returned shortly with an envelope. After thanking her I left and took it back to my car. Sitting in the driver's seat, I carefully opened it. Inside, I found the restored letter, accompanied by a typed transcription for ease of reading and a memory stick containing images of the original, its restored state and the transcription.

Eagerly, I began to read the typed copy.

Thursday, 10th July 1879

Dearest Sophie,
I write to you now, though my hand trembles with this confession, uncertain if you will still see me with understanding once you know the truth. I have carried these words within me for many years and though I resolved never to speak them, I now find my resolve breaking with each passing day. It is time you know what I have withheld, not for lack of love but for fear of what my presence might mean to you.
It was I who established the trust that secured your education, your care and your escape from the cruel confines of the Hôtel du Théâtre. It was I who could not bear to see you, a child so undeserving of sorrow, burdened with your stepmother's coldness and disdain. I have followed you from afar, unwilling to risk casting my shadow over your life yet unable to turn away.
You deserve to know why I have done this and why I have remained silent. Your mother, Eleanor, was the light of my life and although married to your father we found love that neither of us had experienced before. When I learned of her disappearance, it was as though the earth itself had swallowed part of me.
Not long after, I came to Vienne, wanting to know how and where she disappeared, for she had not accompanied me to England, such was the rumour that was widely spread locally.
I met your father, Benoît Fournier, and by chance, though fate, cruel as it may be, soon played its hand. I was present the night his horse reared on the bridge from Saint-Colombe. I saw the moment unfold, powerless to stop it, as the beast threw him into the Rhône. It was an accident, Sophie, a tragic misfortune for which I have borne guilt far beyond what the truth demands. But

to have stayed would have been to risk suspicion, disrupting the fragile balance of your world.

I have loved you as I would my own daughter, Sophie, though I have not the right to call you such. For the brief time I knew you as a child, your strength and spirit reminded me of your mother Eleanor and I knew I could not abandon you to a life of suffering. Through the associates of Monsieur Talabot of the P.L.M., I established the trust to ensure you had what I could not give you myself: safety, education and the chance to rise above the misfortunes that had befallen you. For the first decade I vowed to remain anonymous, believing that secrecy was the only way to protect you from the whispers of scandal that might follow me.

You must know that every action I have taken, every decision I made to stay distant was rooted in love, not only for you but for your mother. I could think of no greater way to honour her memory than to ensure the happiness and future of her only child. Eleanor loved you more than life itself, Sophie, and I hope you can believe that I loved her just as deeply.

I do not ask for forgiveness, though I pray you may find it in your heart. I only ask that you understand the choices I made, the reasons for my silence and the depth of the love that guided me. If you can accept this truth, then perhaps I may one day earn the privilege of knowing you not as a shadow but as a friend, one who holds you in the highest regard.

With all the love and hope that I can offer,

Hartley Birkett

As I sat in my car tears formed in my eyes. This was the letter written by Hartley, a letter he must have believed he had sent, only for it to fall behind a piece of furniture and remain hidden for over a century and a half. The weight of its words and the lost opportunity for it to reach Sophie filled me with sadness.

Overwhelmed, I called Tess on a video chat. The moment she answered her expression shifted, sensing the despair in my tone and the sorrow etched on my face.

"What's happened, are you alright?" she asked, her voice sounding concerned.

I assured her that nothing was wrong, at least not in the immediate sense, but I explained how deeply the contents of the letter had affected me. "It's the letter Hartley wrote to Sophie," I said. "He never sent it. It stayed hidden all these years. He must have thought he had sent it. It's just… so heartbreaking."

Tess listened intently as I read the letter aloud to her. When I finished, I thought I caught the glimmer of a tear in her eye also.

"Oh my God," she whispered, her voice trembling. "It's so tragic. And yet, look at what Hartley did, how he honoured Eleanor's memory by protecting Sophie, even when he couldn't be with her."

For a moment, we sat in silence, the emotions of the letter and its long-buried truths binding us together in shared sorrow.

Breaking the quiet, Tess said softly, "Lynden, I've managed to arrange Eleanor's funeral during the dates you're available. Will you be staying longer?"

The hope in her voice was unmistakable.

"You can count on it," I replied firmly, my answer leaving no room for doubt.

Chapter 31

I arrived at Lyon-Saint Exupéry Airport on the first day of the college break, landing mid-morning. Tess was waiting for me at arrivals, watching the progression of passengers passing through the automatic doors of the arrivals hall. I was one of the last passengers of the flight to get through customs and baggage collection, bringing with me a larger hold bag as I would be staying for over a week. This would be the first time Tess had invited me to stay over at her house.

Searching along the line of waiting people at arrivals, our eyes met in a gap over the heads of two small children playing near the barrier. That moment of recognition, our smiles and the brightness in our eyes would have betrayed to any onlooker that we were more than just friends. Yet mindful of ourselves, we greeted each other with restraint, exchanging customary pecks on either cheek.

We walked towards the short-term car park hand in hand. I carried a small rucksack on my back and a hold-all in my free hand. Once in Tess's compact Peugeot car, we both reached towards each other and kissed passionately on the lips. I felt Tess's eagerness as she put her hand at the back of my head, prolonging the moment for longer. As we disengaged, we both had that glint in our eyes confirming that time and distance had done nothing to diminish our feelings for each other since we last met.

Tess started the car and we drove towards her home, which I was to discover was a modern two-bedroom bungalow with a small garden in a housing estate on the north-eastern outskirts of Vienne. Arriving and parking on her driveway, I felt that we were transported into a secretive world full of large leafy plants growing along the property's boundary. They enclosed the space, giving protection from the view of any curious neighbours. The garden had a peaceful tropical feel with bamboos, a Lagerstroemia tree and different coloured Canna varieties. A small bed of white arums grew between red flowering floribunda roses in front of a terrace that led through the patio doors into the living room. The cosiness was made even more apparent by the lack of a lawn, which would have opened the space had the garden been bigger.

Inside, the house was bright and minimal. White walls reflected the natural light and the furnishings were modern. There was little decoration but everything felt balanced, as though Tess had put care into every detail without overcomplicating the space.

She led me to her bedroom, where I placed my bags on the floor. As I turned, she stepped closer and we embraced again, this time without hesitation. My hands rested firmly on her back, pulling her towards me. As we tumbled onto the bed her hand found the remote control and with a quick glance she lowered the electric shutters partway, dimming the room. Enough daylight filtered through for us to see one another as we let the world outside fade. The next hour or two passed in a blur of intimacy that we had both missed, followed by a late afternoon nap.

When we awoke and feeling hungry, we decided to go out for an early evening meal, driving back into Vienne. The first thing I noticed as we walked looking at restaurant menus was that Tess was more at ease, no longer glancing around her to see if anyone was looking our way. I concluded that she must have distanced herself from Alexandre or he from her, which now gave her a sense of freedom and happiness as we walked hand in hand.

We settled on a homely bistro with a starter of a few oysters. Tess then chose Coquilles St Jacques on a bed of lentils whilst I chose steak tartare with a pot of Côte de Rhône wine. We finished with a shared Vacherin dessert; its cream and crisp meringue was a treat, albeit too high in sugar content.

Our discussion turned to the burial of Eleanor's remains, scheduled to take place in three days' time at the Pipet Cemetery. Tess had wanted my confirmation of the arrangements, having decided to lay Eleanor to rest in an old family vault. The ceremony would be private, with only the two of us present plus Jacques-Marie Fournier, should he wish to attend. We had briefly considered cremation, hoping to reunite Eleanor's ashes with Hartley's remains, but his final resting place still remained a mystery. It left me wondering if further investigation might reveal something, perhaps at Lowe Manor Chapel when I next returned to Devon.

Over the next two days Tess and I made the most of each other's company with a mutual feeling that we were becoming ever more inseparable. The subject needed to be discussed seriously, but there was still time before my return home. We also looked back at the brief time we had known each other and the mystical events that had surrounded us. We both felt that if we could relive the experience of the visions we had in the Landes Forest, they might give us an insight into how Eleanor met her death. Tess's sensitivity with energy and chakras had brought her into contact with like-minded people locally and it was through one of these contacts that she had found a hypnotist who specialised in past life regression who would take each of us in turn. The séances would be recorded, but those were plans for after the funeral. For now, our focus was on the solemn task ahead, a simple but meaningful farewell for Eleanor.

On the day of the funeral, Tess and I went straight to the cemetery where the family crypt had already been opened.

The air carried a faint scent of stagnant air and earth. We stood together hand in hand, silent for most of the time. When we spoke, our voices were hushed as a respectful moment of reverence.

The hearse arrived quietly and two men emerged to unload the coffin. It was simple and unadorned, made of plain pine. Its modest weight was a moving reminder of the little that remained of Eleanor. They carried it to the crypt and placed it gently on two trestles in front of the open vault.

Tess had arranged for a priest to attend, believing it fitting to honour Eleanor's faith. From Hartley's diary, we knew that church services had been a meaningful part of her life, and Tess wanted the ceremony to reflect that.

"Why are you looking up at the sky, Lynden?"

I replied softly, "I'm looking for a rainbow," which made us both chuckle under our breaths, but it didn't happen; neither were there any signs of thunderclouds.

As the priest prepared to say his prayers, Jacques-Marie Fournier arrived. His expression was appropriately sombre for the occasion. Tess introduced us briefly and we used the few moments before the simple ceremony began to share a condensed version of the events that had led to this day.

Before the priest began to say his prayers, Jacques-Marie Fournier and I each placed an envelope on top of the coffin, part of an arrangement that had been made previously. Tess had arranged for the ruby necklace to lie with Eleanor in her repose.

When the prayers began, Tess's grip on my hand tightened. I glanced at her and saw that her face was pale, her body trembling slightly. The sensation seemed to pass into me, leaving me lightheaded and disoriented. The priest's voice seemed to fade, the air around us thickening as time and our breathing seemed to slow. Tess nudged me gently, urging me to look ahead.

Above the crypt, a weathered stone angel stood with its head bowed and arms folded. It had lichen-covered stone wings but as I stared at it, the angel began to change, its worn features growing clearer and more defined. Slowly, it glowed with an unearthly white light, its entire form becoming radiant. The angel lifted its head and feathers seemed to move on the underside of the wings as it extended its arms outward, as though inviting us to come closer.

Behind it, a figure emerged, the old woman we had seen in the forest of Landes near the Marais d'Orx. And we now knew it was also unmistakably the same woman Hartley had described seeing when his river steamer had docked on the Rhône more than a century and a half ago. She stood silently; her dark eyes fixed on us. There was no malice in her presence. Before fading she pointed down to the old Roman town of Vienne, her form becoming a translucent dark shadow before dissipating into nothingness.

I turned to Tess and lightly pulled her hand, drawing her attention to the town below as the old woman had indicated. Vienne stretched out before us but it was not the modern town we knew. Smoke rose from chimneys and cobbled streets bustled with activity. Horses' hooves echoed faintly and children's laughter floated up to us as they played in the streets. Near the Place Jouvenet, the Hôtel du Théâtre stood prominently, its façade transporting us to a time long past.

As though illuminated by an unseen spotlight, a woman appeared, hanging laundry to dry. Beside her in close proximity stood a man. Simultaneously, they turned their heads towards us, their faces momentarily clear before they turned back to each other and shared a tender kiss.

The priest's voice grew louder, pulling us back to the present. The ethereal vision faded, leaving us standing once more in the quiet cemetery. The undertakers carefully placed the coffin into the crypt, the two envelopes that Jacques-Marie and I had placed on top of the coffin still resting there. The vault was sealed and with that, the ceremony came to an end.

Tess thanked the priest and Jacques-Marie Fournier for their presence. We hung around a few minutes more, gazing at the crypt that now held the remains of Eleanor Fournier in the company of her family. We then walked back into town, as usual hand in hand but silent, each lost in our thoughts. Eventually, I broke the silence.

"I need a drink," I said.

"So do I," Tess replied, her voice tinged with both exhaustion and relief.

"It was a lovely long-awaited farewell for Eleanor," I said to Tess.

That evening, we sat together and recounted what had happened at the cemetery. It quickly became clear that we had experienced the exact same visions.

"It was a lovely gesture, giving up that letter," Tess said softly.

"I think Eleanor would have loved Hartley all the more for what he did for Sophie," I replied.

"And Jacques-Marie? Why did he decide to give up his letter?"

"I told him about our plans," Tess said, "and he felt it was the right way to honour Eleanor's memory."

"Did you see into the courtyard of the Hôtel du Théâtre, by the washing line?" I asked.

"It was Hartley and Eleanor," replied Tess, adding, "Did you feel how we connected to them?"

"Yes, I felt a tingle go through me as they looked up. Was it the same for you?"

"I felt the same. I'm sure they must have seen something. Why else would they have looked up at us? We are Hartley and Eleanor. They are Lynden and Tess. We are one and the same, joined across time," said Tess thoughtfully and softly.

"If that's the case then perhaps we are connected further back to other ancestors in the same way. After all, we share their genes. Perhaps we have become sensitive to genetic memory," I added.

Thinking aloud, Tess then said, "And what of the future? When people see mysterious orbs of light that appear, that remain unexplained, perhaps they are beings or spirits looking back in time at us."

That was a deep reflection from Tess to which I felt there was nothing I could add.

Chapter 32

Gustave Leroy had compiled an extensive archive of verified past-life regression cases, the most compelling being that of Elise Perrin from Montpellier who had been featured in a television documentary three years previously. Between the ages of four and seven, Elise repeatedly mumbled a peculiar phrase to her parents: "Breng me naar huis, naar mijn mama en papa," which no one was able to understand. At first, her words were dismissed by her parents as childish gibberish until it was discovered they were Dutch words. She was in fact pleading to be taken home to her parents, her "mama and papa".

Her fixation on leaving her current home grew so intense that social services were eventually involved to rule out the possibility of child brutality or other forms of abuse. Despite various medical consultations and prescribed treatments, doctors could offer no explanation or relief to her parents. Finally, a psychiatrist recommended past-life regression therapy and Gustave Leroy was brought in to take Elise back in time through hypnosis.

Under Gustave's careful guidance, Elise was hypnotised and taken back to a former life. Speaking in a blend of Dutch and French, she recounted vivid memories of being Emma Janssen, a young girl from the Netherlands. Elise described being in a car with her parents on the way to the seaside when a big lorry hurt her as they were going to the seaside. She also described details of the house where she lived and the toys she played with in remarkable detail, facts her current family could not have known.

With the assistance of a television research team, Gustave traced Emma Janssen's story to a tragic motorway accident near Nîmes twelve years earlier. The Dutch Janssen family had been travelling to the Mediterranean coast when their car was caught in a fatal pile-up. Emma's parents had survived, but were left to mourn the loss of their daughter.

The documentary's producers arranged a meeting between Elise, her parents and the Janssens at their home near Apeldoorn. Upon entering the home, Elise ran to her previous-life parents hugging them. She then led the crew to a bedroom where she pointed out toys and accurately described the contents of a closed drawer. The Janssens, overcome with emotion and in tears, confirmed her claims, revealing they had kept Emma's room untouched as a memorial.

From that day forward, the two families stayed in close contact and Elise spent every school holiday visiting the Janssens, sleeping in Emma's old room. The case, widely documented elsewhere after the TV documentary had aired, left no doubt that past-life regression could turn up convincing results, though many people considered it to be a hoax or a series of coincidences, even though newspaper articles from the time had reported the tragic motorway accident.

Tess and I arrived at Gustave's house from where he ran his practice. He welcomed us with a warm smile and invited us into his kitchen for a cup of tea. We explained in the fullest detail all the events that had led up to this day, including the visions and the old lady who disappeared. Gustave listened intently, nodding thoughtfully as we spoke. He seemed confident that he could guide us into the past if we were open to the process. Resistance, he explained, often stemmed from subconscious blocks rather than a conscious unwillingness.

Gustave insisted on working with us individually to prevent any mutual influence. Tess volunteered me to go first, reassuring me with a smile as she waited in the small sitting room.

The consultancy room was compact, roughly the size of a modern bedroom, but well equipped with soundproofed walls and a therapy couch occupied the centre of the space. An upright chair stood beside it while a large screen hung on one wall. A small table held recording equipment. The window had been blacked out and various lighting arrangements adorned the room.

Following Gustave's instructions, I lay on the couch as he explained the process and asked if I had any questions or concerns. He began by guiding me through a series of relaxation techniques, encouraging me to focus on my breathing and release tension from every part of my body. Being used to meditation techniques this part held no difficulty, but as he introduced deeper hypnotic suggestions, I blocked, preventing further progress. Despite his efforts I could not progress into the trance-like state he required.

When we concluded, Gustave politely requested that I refrain from sharing any details with Tess as it might influence her session. We switched places and I went to the waiting room, giving Tess an encouraging wink as she went in. It was nearly an hour before Tess returned, whereas for me it had been only twenty-five minutes. Gustave invited us at the end of our séances to summarise our experiences, saying that I was not able to enter the hypnotic state. As I looked at Tess she was visibly shaken and tired but could not recollect anything she had said whilst in a hypnotic state. What Gustave had to tell us left us shocked and surprised.

Gustave handed us a memory stick containing a recording of Tess's session, suggesting we listen to it together. Thanking Gustave, we then returned to Tess's home to listen to the recording – although exhausted by the experience, Tess wanted to listen to what she was able to recall under hypnosis straight away.

The first ten minutes of the recording mirrored my own experience: relaxation techniques and initial instructions. Then, Gustave's voice took on a firmer tone.

"I want you to go back to the forest of Landes," he instructed. "You're in a canoe, drifting down the river. You see a woman calling to you from the shore. What did you do next?"

Tess's voice, faint and distant, responded: "Pull over, Lynden. There's a woman in the forest waving to us. I think she needs our help."

"You both got out of the canoe," Gustave continued. "The woman led you to an area of ruins. Describe what you saw."

"The wind is getting stronger, the clouds blowing over the forest are dark, there's less light in the forest now, there's the rumble of thunder, Lynden has seen a patch of disturbed ground and is walking towards it, it was where our small house stood," Tess recounted.

Gustave's tone softened. "Tess, at that moment, you became Eleanor. The house is no longer a ruin, it stands before you. Look around and tell me what you see and feel."

The recording paused for a moment and we exchanged a glance, our anticipation growing.

"There's a terrible storm," Tess recounted, her voice trembling. "Someone is outside the house, banging on the door. He's shouting, 'It's me, Marcel, I've brought you some dry wood for the fire.'

"I opened the door to Marcel. He asked where Sophie was and I told him she was at the big house working for Madame Dufour. Then he said two men had been asking for me and Sophie in the village, one claiming to be my husband."

Tess's tone grew sharper, more agitated. "Then Marcel rushed at me, grabbing me."

Gustave's voice remained calm, soothing. "You're remembering events from a long time ago, Eleanor. There's no danger now. What is happening?"

"He's telling me to take paper and quill to write a letter. Then he drags me by the hair, ties me to the chair and forces me to write what he says. A jug of milk spills and the table is sticky and wet. I'm tied to the chair and the table. Marcel leaves, he's gone to Marguerite's house but he comes back quickly. I've finished the letter and I've written a message on the envelope."

Her breathing quickened. "He unties me and tries to kiss me. It's horrible. I'm struggling trying to get away, but his arms are too strong. I reach out and scratch his face and he gets angry, so angry. He grabs Hartley's theodolite and swings it at me. I try to block it with my hand but I'm falling… I'm falling to the ground."

Gustave's voice softened further. "Now, Eleanor, don't be frightened, nothing can hurt you anymore. You can see your body on the ground. You are above it, looking down."

Tess's voice became quieter, almost serene. "Yes, I'm above my body now. Marcel is lying on top of me. I see a white light, I'm in a tunnel and I'm moving towards the light. It's beautiful, full of love. I don't want to go back to my body."

"Before you go into the tunnel," Gustave said gently, "look around as Eleanor. You're at peace now. What's happening outside the house?"

"I see Marcel carrying my body to the mill," she said softly.

"What else is happening, Eleanor? You are outside of time, the minutes and the days are all the same," asked Gustave.

"Marcel is in our house waiting for Hartley. When Hartley arrives, Marcel swings at him with the theodolite and takes his body to the mill pond. Marcel walks towards Marguerite's house, looking for Sophie, but a tree falls on him before he gets there."

Gustave's voice shifted slightly. "Now you are no longer Eleanor, you are Tess again. You're leaving the forest and falling into a deep dreamless sleep. When I count to three, you will awaken, refreshed and unaware of what you've said."

When the recording finished, Tess and I sat in silence, processing what we had just heard. Tess burst into tears and I felt shaken to the core. I put my arm around her, letting her take her time.

Eventually, Tess broke the silence. "Did I hear that right? It was Marcel who killed Eleanor, not Benoît?"

"It seems so," I said, gathering my thoughts. "Let's go over the events as they happened."

I continued, "First, Hartley left for Bordeaux to report to his superiors. A storm delayed his return by a few days. Meanwhile, Benoît Fournier had come looking for Eleanor and Sophie. Perhaps it was the coincidence or the threat that made Marcel act. He decided to kill Eleanor."

"Why did he ask where Sophie was?" Tess asked.

"Maybe to ensure she was out of the way, or worse, because she was his intended target," I said grimly. "Remember what the gendarme said near Labenne? They found two children's skeletons and Marcel had a habit of luring children to his forest hideout to 'play with rabbits'."

Tess shuddered. "So, Marcel left Eleanor tied to the table but went to check on something at Marguerite's. That gave Eleanor just enough time to write the message on the envelope. She must have used the spilled milk as ink because she couldn't move freely anywhere else. Then, when Marcel returned…"

I finished the thought. "He probably raped her. Whether she was unconscious, dying or already dead, we'll never know. But he hid her body under the mill's floorboards before Hartley came back."

"How could he have done all that so quickly?" Tess asked. "Hartley arrived home, saw the door open and then Marcel knocked him out."

"We don't know exactly how much time passed between the events," I said. "Under hypnosis, you weren't tied to the passage of time. It could have been hours or even a day or two. All we know is that Marcel was ready and waiting for Hartley when he returned. He used the theodolite to try and kill him just as he had tried with Eleanor."

Tess nodded, piecing it together. "And then he went to Marguerite's house, but a falling tree killed him before he got there."

"It seems that way, yes," I replied. "And before you ask why Benoît didn't see Marcel's body lying on the ground, we can't be certain where the path between the two houses and the mill lay."

"I wasn't going to ask that," Tess said quietly. "I've already figured that part out."

"Sorry," I said, giving her an apologetic smile.

Tess continued, "I'm asking myself what did Marguerite know about her estranged husband's behaviour. Did she suspect him? Was she protecting Sophie or was she complicit, supplying girls like her to Marcel?"

Her words sent a chill through me. "We may never know," I admitted. "And perhaps it's better that way."

Tess sighed. "Marguerite must have lied to Benoît about Eleanor leaving with Hartley, because Marcel must have given Marguerite the letter before the bough of the tree killed him. I think she was complicit, Sophie had been working at *La Maison de la Pinède* for two days. At least Benoît got there in time to save Sophie. And I'm relieved to think my ancestor wasn't a murderer, even if he was cruel to his wife."

"I agree," I said. "And poor Hartley spent the rest of his life mourning Eleanor. First, he thought she had gone back to her husband and then later, he believed Benoît had killed her."

"For his lifetime, yes," Tess said softly. "But not for eternity, Lynden. We are also Hartley and Eleanor; I feel it in my soul."

She looked at me with such conviction that I found myself nodding.

"You've convinced me, Tess. So, what happens next between us?"

She gave me a sly smile and a kiss.

"Let's go to bed. I'm tired," I said.

Tess looked at me straight in the eye, without saying a word, prompting me to continue.

"I didn't mean it like that," I said, though I couldn't help smiling back.

"Oh, I know what you meant," she teased.

Chapter 33

I had another four full days in France before having to return to the UK. It was quality time to spend with Tess and reflect on where our journey might lead us next. The way all the events had unrolled from receiving news of an unexpected inheritance to discovering that my third great grandfather's lover had been murdered felt surreal. Then falling in love with Tess who through past life regressions was able to go back in time and solve the murder, was unbelievable. I always had difficulty in accepting reincarnation as a reality, but now I firmly believed I was Hartley in a past life and Tess was Eleanor. Somewhere inside me I had a gut feeling that I have come back in this life to learn lessons that remain unfinished.

Hartley in a past life had found love with Eleanor of the deepest and most profound nature. Eleanor had reciprocated, leaving behind an unhappy marriage to Benoît as proof of her feelings. But their love came at a cost. Benoît and Eleanor both met tragic ends and Sophie, their daughter, was left to bear the consequences.

In the torn-out page from Hartley's diary, placed at the front of the first journal, he had written:

If there be any purpose to this account, let it be a caution, perhaps, to those who come after, a reminder of the hazards that beset those who seek to shape their own fate.

Hartley was a Quaker and I couldn't help but wonder if his faith's values paralleled the karmic understanding in Buddhism. Were these two philosophies merely different faces of the same truth?

Losing Eleanor plummeted Hartley into melancholy, what we'd call deep depression today. Knowing her death was imminent and believing Benoît would be her killer, Eleanor had written her final thoughts in a secret message, convinced that one day she would find her lover Hartley again.

It seemed impossible yet here we are today, Tess and I standing face to face with the knowledge of what had happened in our past lives and now deciding how to move forward.

Perhaps it is a mercy that the memories and traumas of past lives faded away. Imagine carrying the weight of every decision, every experience and every loss. We'd be crushed by the sheer enormity of it all. Sleep enables the body to refresh itself and start anew each day. Death does the same, wiping the slate clean between lives, with only the slimmest of vague memories passing from one life to the next to those who are sensitive enough to perceive them.

Hand in hand we took a walk along the quays of the river Rhône in Vienne, where modern-day river cruises dock and where Hartley had first disembarked in February 1852. We crossed the busy main road and found the peace and quiet of the 'jardin de ville'. I marvelled at the Roman road, partly excavated with worn rut marks where the metal rims of carts had worn away stone two thousand years ago. We sat on a bench and I asked Tess how she saw her future.

Her reply was, "I want our love to remain forever, as strong as it is today, but to do that will be very difficult. I don't want the ordinary banal events of our lives to detract or to dilute what we have now."

"In what way?" I asked.

Tess replied, "You know what happens. People fall in love and start to have sex together or start having sex and then believe that they have fallen in love because they cannot distinguish one from the other. They live together, enjoy each other's company and then the routines of life take over, like who's doing the shopping this week and do you want to come to the theatre with me… no, I'd rather watch a football match on television. After a few years they are no longer on the same parallel rails of life but have diverged and are heading off in different directions, each with their own interests and their compatibility is lost. The love they once cherished fades, but many couples still stay together because they are trapped by economic necessity, the need to raise children or they want to avoid the negative social stigma of divorce. Some couples will stay together even after a loving relationship is finished because it is a less painful choice than separation. As the saying goes, 'familiarity breeds contempt', meaning you can lose respect or become careless in your relationship when you know a person very well, which in turn leads to unhappiness, arguments or even violence in extreme cases. Is that not wasting the remaining time we have before us in this life?"

"So, what do you think is the solution?" I asked.

Instead of answering, Tess turned the question back to me. "What do you want?"

"I've often heard it said that true love means giving someone the freedom to live their own life without possessiveness," I began thoughtfully. "But the desire to be with that person as much as possible, the need for closeness is somewhat contradictory with that ideal. It can slip into possessiveness, even jealousy. So, for me it has to start somewhere in between to show committal because too much freedom… can start to feel like indifference."

"And in practical terms?" asked Tess.

"I work in England and you work here in France. We must continue to work in ways that our souls remain woven together no matter how far apart we may be physically, and cultivate our relationship in ways that defy the monotony of modern life.

We live in an age of endless distractions, but we can use the technology to create 'shared virtual adventures'. In addition to daily video calls, once or twice a week we could explore online art galleries, cook the same meal over video calls, meditate together or watch films simultaneously, talking to each other as though we were side by side. When we each have holidays, we prioritise visiting each other, go for walks, eat out at restaurants and create surprises that we think the other will enjoy. We can build up the frequency of these events to a point when we decide if we move in together. What do you think, Tess?"

Tess smiled. "I like the idea but what about your relationship with Ann?"

I looked Tess in the eyes. "I won't hide from her what's happening. She feels it anyway and she deserves honesty."

I continued, "We are bound by something greater. Our karma and our love must be an anchor for each other to nurture a sense of purpose that we feel as one. We now have the opportunity to break the cycle of rebirth, as we have done since 1853, searching for each other."

Then, reaching into my pocket I pulled out a small box lined with velvet. Opening it I presented Tess with a one and a half carat, flawless diamond, on a delicate white gold necklace saying that in view of our ancestors' history I thought a necklace was more appropriate than a ring.

Tess said, after a passionate kiss of acceptance, "Now we are engaged."

As we raised our heads from the park bench, we looked towards the worn pavement stones of the exposed Roman road. There appeared the old lady dressed in black, our guardian angel, looking straight back at us. She then raised her hands to her face in a position of prayer. We waved to her as she glided to the edge of the stone slabs before dissolving into thin air.

THE END